Raka of the Last Neanderthal Clan

THE LAST NEANDERTHAL CLAN

2nd Edition

CHARLIE BORING

The Last Neanderthal Clan: Raka of the Last Neanderthal Clan

Publication Date: June 2022

ISBN: 978-1-63892-739-6

Printed in United States of America This book is printed on acid-free paper.

DEDICATION

T he writing of The Last Neanderthal Clan began in the author's mind when he was a child who read novels about pre-historic man. When the author's daughter, Lisa Lareau, was young, the author would invent stories about prehistoric men, women, and children and tell them to her for her entertainment. Lisa loved those stories and always asked for another. Lisa grew into an intelligent, professional, young woman and joined the author in the writing of this book. Tragedy struck Lisa and her unborn twin girls and she was taken by the Spirit-in-the-Fire. This book is dedicated to Lisa and other young mothers that do not get the chance to grow old with their mates.

TABLE OF CONTENTS

FOREWORD

T he setting for this book is in the late Pleistocene epoch. The Pleistocene epoch has been dated by modern scientists from about 2.6 million to 12,000 years before present times. During this period there were repeated ice-ages and mini-ice ages, all of which affected ecosystems all over the world. Glaciers advanced and receded over time and with each recession of the ice cover, life advanced northward in the northern hemisphere. This author does not claim to be a scientist, but for the purpose of this book, the author has attempted to create a story that is true to known science, except where such truthfulness might detract from the story being told.

The modern continents were essentially at their present positions during the Pleistocene period. They may have drifted a hundred meters or so in one direction or another; but they were, for all intents and purposes, in the positions that we find them in today. The setting for this book is Western Europe, initially north of the Alpine Mountain Range in what is now Germany and Austria.

During a Pleistocene ice-age the maximum glacial coverage of the Earth's surface by ice is normally estimated at about 30%, which would have covered all of northern Europe and most of central Europe and resulted in a zone of permafrost that stretched southward from the edge of the ice sheet a few hundred miles. The mean annual temperature at the edge of the ice has been estimated to have been about 20 °F and, at the edge of the permafrost, to be about 32 °F.

The ice sheet that covered Northern Europe and the Alpine ice sheet which covered the Alpine Mountain Range were the primary natural forces considered in this book.

Through time, during an ice age, as the ice cover progressed southward, these two ice sheets would become one continuous ice sheet and then separate, as the ice age receded and warmer conditions enveloped the earth.

Severe climatic changes during the various ice ages had major impacts on animals and plants living in the affected areas. With each ice-age, large areas of Europe were almost totally void of plants and animals. Trees, grasses and other plants were the first to disappear to the south. The lack of plant food supply forced the retreat of plant-eating animal populations toward the south in front of the advancing glaciers. With the disappearance of the plant eaters, the meat-eaters also moved south. In essence, the drastic climatic changes reduced living space and curtailed food supply.

Major extinctions of large mammals, including mammoths, mastodons, saber-toothed cats, Irish elk, cave bears, and short-faced bears, began late in the Pleistocene. The humanoid species known as Neanderthals also became extinct during this period.

At the end of the last major ice age, trees, grasses and other plants were able to grow further north. These plants spread northward through root migration and through seeds that were spread by wind, water, birds and other animals. Cold-blooded animals, smaller mammals like wood mice, migratory birds, and swifter animals like whitetail and bush deer often were the first to replace the large animals and swiftly migrated north.

The beginning and the end of an ice-age were not clearly defined. The end of an ice age was a gradual change; denoted by some years marked by complete ice cover for the entire year in a particular area followed by a slightly warmer year, during which the ice cover might disappear in that area for a short duration. As time passed the ice cover would disappear for a longer period of time. The eventual result was a warmer climate over time and the flourishing of plant life.

Prehistoric man occupied a significant niche in this ecosystem. During the Pleistocene epoch, prehistoric men were primarily composed of both the human race as we know it today, called Cro-Magnons and another human species known as Neanderthals, who became extinct before our time. Possibly as many as 350,000 years ago, as the ice covers receded, Neanderthals spread northward from Africa. They sparsely populated northern and southern Europe, living as nomadic hunters. Their passage to northern Europe most probably occurred through the middle-east. Their entry into northern Europe came from the east, since the Alpine ice sheet would have probably, at least initially, hindered their movement through the Alps.

Cro-Magnon humans followed Neanderthal migration, perhaps 35,000 to 43,000 years ago, also spreading northward from Africa; first occupying southern Europe and then migrating around the eastern edge of the Alps to northern Europe and Asia. As Cro-Magnon groups entered Europe, they came into contact with Neanderthals. Cro-Magnons were better able to survive encounters between the two groups than Neanderthals; since Cro-Magnons were equipped with a brain which could conceptualize better than a Neanderthal's brain.

An important difference between Neanderthal and Cro-Magnon species is suspected by many scientists. Neanderthals lived a life of early maturity and early death, compared to the Cro-Magnon. A Neanderthal adolescent may have matured as early as twelve years of age, while a Cro-Magnon adolescent matured at about fifteen years of age. The typical Neanderthal, who died a natural death, would have lived to be in his/her early forties at the oldest, while a Cro-Magnon may have lived into the fifty-year range.

Cro-Magnon clans steadily encroached on the hunting grounds that had previously been to sole province of Neanderthals. This competition for resources led to continuing battles between the two species, where Darwin's theory of "Survival of the Fittest" came into play. The two species interacted in war and possibly trade and undoubtedly mated; producing humans that possessed some of the genetic traits of both species.

Early communications between men included a large amount of body language, gestures, etc. and, as time passed, these gestures were supplemented with sounds, including words, to communicate. Widely dispersed clans developed different languages including gestures; but each language had many common gestures allowing different clans to communicate with each other through universally understood gestures to some degree. Many words and gestures used by the clans of this book have been provided to the reader in the *Glossary of Terms* at the end of the book.

As indicated earlier, the setting for this novel is in Western Europe at a time when the climate is warming at the end of a mini-ice-age that had separated the environment north of the Alpine Mountain range from the area south of the mountain range. At the time of this book, there have been many generations that have learned to exist north of the Alps, but the Alpine glacier has prevented any movement directly from north of the Alps to the far warmer south. Neanderthal people have become extinct south of the Alpine Mountain Range, but Neanderthal clans still existed north of the Alps.

Neanderthals were more prevalent in the southern area north of the mountains, since Cro-Magnon clans had slowly and methodically occupied space previously used by only the Neanderthals and had driven the Neanderthal clans

4

southward toward the Alps. The Neanderthals are referred to in this story as the southern clans. Neanderthal clans could be classified into two groups, the first group is those clans that were cannibalistic, attacking, killing and eating both other Neanderthal and Cro- Magnon people. The second group is those clans that were not cannibals and existed primarily by hunting large animals. Additionally, Neanderthal clans can be separated into those clans that followed the migration of the reindeer herds and those whose hunting grounds were limited to the areas nearer to the Alpine Mountain range.

While the Neanderthal species was short and muscular and had dark black hair, the Cro-Magnon clans north of the Alps could either be very tall people or a people of a more normal height. Those Cro-Magnon who lived further north were a very tall people with a lighter complexion and hair varying from brown to almost blond. All Cro-Magnons were a people taller than the Neanderthals, but the Cro-Magnons north of the Alps in what is now known as Austria, and the Cro-Magnons south of the Alps were shorter than their northern Cro-Magnon competitors and had black hair and a darker complexion.

The Cro-Magnon species, which made its home in northern Europe during these times, is referred to in this book as the northern clans. As with the Neanderthals, these clans could be classified into two groups, those clans that were cannibalistic, which killed and ate Neanderthal people, and those clans that were not cannibals and existed by hunting large and small animals and gathering edible plants. Additionally, northern clans could be separated into those clans that followed the migration of the reindeer herds and those whose hunting grounds were in more defined areas of northern Europe. Since the Cro-Magnon species was in direct competition with Neanderthals for hunting areas and available resources, it is easy to imagine the continuous struggle between the two species for resources; primarily animals that these humans needed to hunt, kill and eat in order to survive.

The diet of Neanderthals was composed of about 85% meat. It is possible that the Neanderthals became primarily meat-eaters in order to survive in the very cold environment that they encountered during an ice age. The Neanderthal species was short and very muscular and capable of enormous feats of strength, such as jamming a thrusting spear deeply into the body of a large animal, such as a wooly mammoth. In the competition for resources with the Cro-Magnon, Neanderthals suffered the disadvantage of not being able to run as swiftly as the Cro-Magnon. The ability to travel fast and far would allow hunters to arrive at a hunting site before their competition or would allow a group to out distance another attacking group, when outnumbered. Speed offered an obvious advantage for hunters and warriors.

The diet of Cro-Magnon species, on the other hand, was composed of about 50% meat. The remainder of their diet was made up of a wide assortment of plants and plant products, including leaves, seeds, nuts, fruits and roots. Perhaps this ability to exist on a broader range of food stuff combined with the ability to travel further and faster than the Neanderthals helped the Cro-Magnon species to out-compete the Neanderthal species in the struggle for survival.

It is interesting to imagine that humans, in order to survive, were required to live in small groups; but that these small groups had to be large enough to allow effective group hunting of large animals and to support an effective collective defense against meat-eaters and other human groups. If the group was too large, then the food supply in a particular area may be too small to support the group. If the group was too small, the types of hunting that could be successfully practiced were limited and the advantage of a collective defense was lost.

During these times men, women and children lived in family groups called "clans." Members of the clan shared food supplies, developed social organizations and participated in the hunts and collective defense to defeat meat-eaters and hostile clans, alike. Within a clan there could be a number of different ways that nature might cause the clan to organize. A clan organization might develop along family lines or in accordance with some political hierarchy. Mating between family members was common among many clans, but, as science now tells us, often resulted in inferior genetic traits; therefore, as time progressed, clans that developed traditions that supported mating with other clans and discouraged mating among family members were more successful than those clans whose traditions supported mating between relatives.

As this book begins, the experience of most clans has taught them that individuals and very small groups had very little chance of survival in this harsh environment. Therefore, clans tended to stay together and new clans only came into existence when necessity forced a group to break away from the mother clan. A situation that might force the birth of a new clan could be that the mother clan became too large such that available resources in a particular area were not great enough to support such a large clan. Another possibility is that discontent might develop and an aspiring leader might lead a portion of the clan to another hunting area and form a new clan. A new clan might also be formed when members of the mother clan were banished from the clan for some perceived infraction of clan traditions.

The clans were very superstitious and attributed any misfortunate event to individual failure to follow accepted customs or traditions of the clan. An individual, who brought misfortune to the clan, might be banished from the clan by the other clan members, as a way of protecting the clan. Typically, banishment like this resulted in the individual's eventual death and of course, failure to reproduce likeminded offspring.

During this time, it is easy to imagine that some clans of both species might gradually try to push the envelope and venture into unknown areas or try new methods of hunting or fighting, which, when you stop to think about it, has been the engine for man's advancement since the beginning of time.

CHAPTER 1

ENCOUNTER WITH A SOUTHERN CLAN

I t was a briskly cold morning with layers of fog filling the low-lying valleys and waterlogged lowlands. To the north were the foothills of a vast mountain range, which extended further than the eye could see. Clouds obscured the mountains to the north, as they rose above the tops of the preceding foothills, but if the clouds were to lift, one could see that they were still covered in snow and ice. A large bird of prey, probably a cousin of the great modern brown eagle, flew along the river, which cascaded down from the melting glaciers in the mountains and exited from the mountain range between two snow-covered hills, which protected the southern approach to the mountain range.

As the bird flew above the river, his unbelievably keen eyesight could make out the breath-taking details of the landscape from the mountains to the north, the foothills in front of them to their south, above the valley through which the river carried its rich bounty of fertile soil to dump the valley flood plains and eventually into the sea far to the west.

The bird's keen eyes probably noted forests of massive evergreens, the floor of which were covered with numerous varieties of plants, where the bird often found small animals which composed much of its diet. The bird's wingspan was almost six feet, so he was large enough to be able to hunt creatures as large as a small deer, a small mountain goat or a small wild boar. On this day, he saw no interesting movement in the forest; so, with a small change in the angle of his enormous wings, he changed his flight path to follow the surging river, which was filled up to its highest natural banks as a result of melting glacier ice from the mountains.

As the river exited the foothills, its width was nearly one hundred meters across. Fog and water spray hung low over the river, as it splashed its way from between the two foothills, creating froth-laden swirls of blue-green water. Even with his keen eyesight, the bird probably could not see potential prey in the water below the fog. As the river continued its course through the valley toward the sea, it widened even more and the mixture of water spray and fog slowly dissipated revealing occasional views of the river surface to the bird. The bird glided in that direction, high above the river apparently intent on detecting what the river water might be hiding. The giant bird saw a mother Irish elk with a newly born fawn and momentarily considered trying for the fawn; but in the end decided to continue searching the river.

The river surface was intermittently broken by images of rolling logs, complete trees and even an occasional animal carcass, dumped there by the recent flooding. The bird continued to follow the course of the river and, if he had been interested, he would have noted an unexpected group of craggily shaped cliffs to the north of the river. The bird ignored these cliffs for he had learned that these cliffs contained less potential prey than the mountains and the valley through which the river made its way. The bird had on occasion been able to kill a small ibex (mountain goat) in these cliffs; but such opportunities were rare. A change in the bird's flight showed that the bird's attention was suddenly drawn to the river surface where he saw a sparkle of light reflect off of a moving body. The bird probably knew this image and, without hesitation, he fell into a steep dive toward the river. As he silently dropped toward what proved to be a two-foot-long fish, he changed the angle of his wings, allowing him to enter the water feet first. His talons sank deep into the back of what looked like a sturgeon and his wings began the labor of pulling the fish out of the water. The bird slowly gained height and speed as he flew toward the forest carrying his captured meal. The meal would be shared with his two eaglets and his female. The eagle was one of the species, as was the timber wolf, that would stay with his mate for life.

All of this had been observed by the young man, known as Raka, as he crouched against a large rock more than half way up on the cliffs north of the river. This man did not resemble the other human inhabitants of this area south of the mountains. His hair was a dirty blond and his eyes were blue; whereas, the other men who roamed this area had black hair and brown eyes. His face was not as broad as the others and his beard was sparser and colored a light brown. He stood a little over six feet two inches tall, compared to others who seldom exceeded five feet and nine inches. His arms and legs were strong with elongated muscles, developed this way from long runs and throwing of his various weapons. The others in the area were more muscular, capable of great feats of strength, including the delivery of a killing blow to a mammoth with a large thrusting spear. If one examined this man in comparison to other few humans in the valley and surrounding hills, two conclusions would be unavoidable. First, this man was not a close relative of the other humans in this area and second, he had not lived the same type of life; therefore, his body had developed differently, creating a lean, angular appearance, as opposed to an appearance of great strength.

Crouched within an arm's length of the young man was a sight not previously seen in this land. A large gray, almost black, timber wolf with yellow eyes had also observed the flight of the giant bird. His eyes followed the man's eyes and observed what Raka observed. Raka called the animal a "kopsut," which meant wolf in his language. He had given the animal a name to which he responded. The animal's name was "Kop."

Raka closely watched the bird that he knew as a "kawl." It first searched for prey far above the river and finally, when the bird swooped down for the attack on the unsuspecting fish. The man thought that he understood what the bird was probably thinking and feeling, for he had often experienced the same thoughts and emotions during his hunts and struggle to survive. He had often observed eagles (kawls) and knew them to be the most majestic of birds, which were devoted to their mates and eaglets. He admired their freedom to move about and see new things and most of all he admired their devotion to their mate. His mother had instilled within him a dedication to the clan and a loyalty to one chosen mate.

It was cold and damp in the very early spring of the year; so, the man was clothed in a soft leather upper garment made from deerskin and a thicker, courser set of what looked like hairy trousers, possibly made from wolf skin. He also wore a large robe made from bearskin, which covered his head and torso and hung below waist. His feet were encased in a leather wrap, tied around his calves with lengths of a leather cord. The man had stuffed dried grass into the leather to provide insulation. There was a piece of leather about two inches wide around his waist which served not only to secure the upper garment to his body and retain his body heat, but also to be used as a utility belt of sorts. The belt had a crude ax dangling from it. The ax was made with a sharpened piece of flint rock for the head. The head had been secured between the split ends of a piece of wood about two feet long by thin strips of leather tied above and below the ax head. Next to the ax, a strange split-ended club was hanging. This split-ended club was used to throw flat rocks with remarkable accuracy and speed. A leather pouch was also attached to the belt. The pouch held the tools that he needed to survive in this hostile environment.

Raka used the pouch to carry a piece of flint rock used for

cutting, a piece of flint used for scraping, three spearheads made of flint rock, and a couple of spearheads made from deer antlers. Also, there was a piece of ivory which he used for making holes in leather and chipping the flint rock into the shape he needed. There was also a piece of flint that would someday be shaped into spearheads, or another tool. But now, it was used as a striker to start a fire. Another item in the pouch, which was essential for fire making, was a piece of iron-pyrite. The pouch also held a dry bird's nest, which he used as kindling for starting a fire and a ball of sinew; which he used as lace, when needed. Finally, he had five smooth, round rocks and a piece of deer skin fastened on two sides to two-foot-long lengths of deerskin cut about three centimeters wide. This assembly was his slingshot, possibly the only one in existence in this part of the world. Lastly, the pouch held a ball of moss soaked in what he believed was magic plant juice that the man kept to treat minor injuries.

The moss had been gathered in the forest. The young man's mother had taught him the types of plants to use to treat open wounds and also how to use the last item in his pouch, a slender curved piece of bone. The young man used the curved piece of bone to close a wound to stop the bleeding.

A backpack had also been fashioned over the upper outer lining of the bearskin robe. This pack held another blouse, a deer skin robe, dried grass and his remaining food supply. His remaining food consisted of dried slivers of deer meat, some sea salt, and a partially eaten carcass of a mountain hare, three roots, which were similar to turnips and five large mushrooms.

He would need to dedicate some time to hunting soon. The weight of these items rested comfortably against his upper back and shoulders, allowing him to move easily under the burden.

Slung across his back, the man had a leather sheath

containing a piece of wood about three feet long and two inches thick with a groove cut down one side, which was open on one end and blocked on the other. The men of this area would not recognize this item. Raka used it as a spear thrower, giving him an added distance to a thrown spear. The sheath also contained five spears made from cedar wood, which were about five feet long and tipped with a sharp, flint spearhead. Next to the sheath, the man carried the stomach of a deer, which he used to carry water.

Starting a fire was not a skill that every man in this area possessed. Many of the clans in the vicinity kept a hot coal that was used to start a fire. Some of the clans still started fires using friction caused from rubbing sticks together. Raka knew their fire-making methods because he had watched them from hiding. When he wanted to observe these people, he chose a hiding place downwind with the sun behind his back. He always used his best camouflage to blend into the surroundings. These people seemed to think that fire possessed magical powers. They often conducted rituals in its honor. He believed that they only allowed respected members of their clan to carry the hot coal and produce fire. Raka called the clan member, trusted with the burning coal, the "Fire Keeper." When the Clan that he was watching had prepared to move, the Fire Keeper had placed hot embers in a container that appeared to be made from a gourd and covered it with ashes. He then placed the gourd in a pouch that he wore slung around his neck.

Raka had learned his fire-making skill from his mother's clan. Fire was made by striking the flint rock against the iron-pyrite and causing a spark to be thrown into the dry bird's nest or another appropriate kindling.

Raka believed that the clan that he was currently following suspected his presence. They may have smelled or heard him; but, most likely, they had discovered a sign of his passing, when they checked their back trail. Raka had observed that the men in the clan had become more watchful and kept their spears close at hand.

The spears that this clan used were about six to seven feet long and about three inches thick. They were obviously used for thrusting and not for throwing. The tips of the spears were made from sharpened deer antlers. Raka intended to watch this clan during a hunt to see what techniques they used. He believed that they probably stalked their game, driving the animals into an ambush conducted by hidden clansmen; but he wasn't sure. He had been following the clan for three days; but they were moving their camp and the only game that they had killed were mountain hares and a deer fawn, which they had surprised during their march.

The clan was approaching the cliffs from which Raka had been watching the kawl. They were not in his range of vision unless he stood and looked through a gap between two rock outcroppings. The kopsut had positioned himself on the top of a boulder where he had an unobstructed view of the valley. Raka stood and moved his head slightly above the cliff rim and looked at the clan, as they moved away from the river toward the cliffs. The clan was a small group, only composed of fifteen adult members. He remembered the number as three hands. They were strung out in a line-of-march about fifty meters long. A very large man with a heavy black beard was in the lead. He wore a large robe made from a cave bear hide and carried a thrusting spear larger than the spears of the other men in the clan. The way that he deftly handled the large spear showed his enormous strength. He was probably the clan leader, thought Raka.

He was followed by another man, younger in appearance and not as large, but with very similar characteristics. Raka thought that this was possibly the leader's younger brother; or maybe, he was his son.

There were five other men in the group, one bringing up

the rear and the other four dispersed among the other clan members. The remaining eight adult members of the clan were composed of six mature females, one young female and one young male. The young female and male appeared to be about eleven to thirteen years old. Six children, including two infants and four children of various ages, accompanied the young female and the other females. Raka was interested in the young female. She had an appealing appearance with dark raven-black hair, dark eyes, and an olive complexion. In the few days that Raka had been watching this clan, only one man, who was possibly the oldest of the clansmen, had approached this young female. Like the rest of the clan, she wore deerskin garments covered with a bearskin robe. Raka had had no contact with a female for about a year. He could feel the physical desire rise within him, as he gazed upon the young female.

This clan did not appear to be a prosperous clan. Many of the members appeared to be weak and dejected. Although Raka had no way of knowing this fact, the clan's success at hunting during the fall had been poor. The winter had been passed hungry and they had left the shelter of their winter cave early this year to try to find meat. Although there was still a chance of more snow and more cold weather, spring plants were starting to appear in places where the snow had melted.

Their winter camp had been made in a large cave above the river at the foot of the mountains. They had not been able to properly prepare for the winter. They had chosen their winter home later in the fall than usual, due to injuries that some of the men had sustained. Large game had been scarce in the area and winter had closed in early, cutting the time that they had to prepare.

The women had saved the group from starvation by obtaining and drying a large quantity of fish, a large number of mountain hares and various types of roots, greens, nuts and berries. During the coldest part of the winter, the men and women of the clan had limited success in spearing fish in the river. The available food had just been enough to keep them alive; but the entire clan had been hungry throughout the entire winter.

The massive leader of the clan had lost much of his bulk during the winter; but other members of the clan had suffered more, since the leader always ate before other clan members. He continued to lead the clan toward the cliffs, where Raka was hiding. As he reached the foot of the cliffs about three hundred meters east of Raka's position, he motioned for the small procession to stop. The men of the clan gathered around him and a discussion ensued. The leader pointed further east at the face of the cliffs. All of the men looked toward where he was pointing.

Although Raka could not see the area on the face of the cliff toward which the leader was pointing, he recalled that there was a small cave about mid-way up the side of the cliff. In fact, Raka had climbed the face of the cliff to check it out and had discovered a series of ledges, which led to the cave, making it very easy to defend, even when heavily outnumbered. Raka had considered using the cave for himself, if this clan were to settle in the area for at least a short period of time.

The leader of the clan motioned to a small wiry clansman to go check the cave out. The clansman slowly moved forward, not anxious to face the unknown that the cave might hold. He looked at the other clansmen to see if someone would come with him; but was disappointed to see that no one volunteered. Arriving at the foot of the cliff face, he slowly climbed up a steep slope about ten feet high, where he could reach a five- foot-wide ledge that gradually ran from left to right up the face of the cliff. After climbing about thirty feet on the ledge, the clansman was able to gain access to another ledge about three feet wide, which ascended from right to left to an additional height of thirty feet on the cliff face. This ledge ended abruptly, but the clansman was able to crawl onto another ledge, also about three feet wide, which led him directly to the cave mouth.

The clansman cautiously looked into the cave mouth. At first, he could not see anything; but as his eyes adjusted to the darkness of the cave, he could see that the small opening on the cliff face, which was only about four feet wide and five feet high, expanded into a large grotto, easily large enough for the small clan. He smelled the air in the cave and listened for any sounds coming from the cave. The air was stale; but he did not smell any dangers. The only sound he heard was the sound of trickling water coming from the back of the cave. He picked up a rock off of the ledge in front of the cave entrance and tossed it into the grotto. He held his spear at ready in case the rock alerted a dangerous animal. He heard a rustling from the rear of the cave. Peering closely, he could make out a small pool of water that was fed by water trickling down the back wall of the cave. He walked closer to see if the water was drinkable and it appeared that it was, as he tasted it with his hand. To the right of the pool of water he was startled to see a snake, which glistened from the light filtering through the cave entrance. His first thought was "danger!" But his immediate second thought was "food!"

He stepped further toward the snake and advanced on it slowly with his spear at ready to be used as a club. The snake coiled ready to strike. The man quickly used his spear to pin down the snake's head. With one hand he secured a firm hold behind the snake's head, effectively preventing the snake from biting, or escaping.

He walked to the edge of the ledge outside of the cave entrance and triumphantly held the five-feet-long snake above his head, yelling, "HAWWW" and motioning, as if to say that he was the clan's bravest hunter by hitting his chest with his free hand. He tossed the live snake toward the women on the ground below the cave. He knew that they would kill the snake and prepare it for a meal.

As the snake landed among the small group of women, it immediately coiled and struck at the thing closest to it. The closest thing to it was the young woman's right leg. The snake sank its fangs into the girl's calf and recoiled to strike again.

But before the snake could strike a second time, the other women were on top of it, killing it with blows to the head and body using the walking sticks, or clubs that they all carried.

Raka and the kopsut watched this occurrence from their hiding place at the top of the cliff. When the snake bit the young woman, Raka jumped, wanting to leap to her defense. The kopsut sprang to his feet; since he recognized that Raka sensed danger. Raka controlled his urge to leap to the young woman's defense and hoped that the clan knew how to stop the snake's death message. Raka had learned the treatment for snakebite from his mother. His mother had been taught many magical things by his father, whom Raka had never known.

It had been his father who had told his mother that his clan had once tamed the spirit of a young kopsut who accompanied the clan on their hunts.

This clan leader's woman was also very muscular and beautiful in a rough way. It was obvious that she was the leader of the women. She picked up the dead snake and tossed it to another woman. With grunts and gestures, she ordered the other woman to clean the snake for the meal. Then she turned to look at the young woman who had been bitten by the snake.

Her dark eyes held no sympathy for the young woman. Her face instead held a look of disdain and triumph. The young woman and the leader's woman had a history between them, which had caused the leader's woman to hate her. The young woman's mother had been a favorite of the clansmen. She had given birth to the girl; but no one in the clan knew who the father was. Many, including the leader's woman, believed that the father had been the leader of the clan. The clan's leader had shown favoritism toward the girl's mother before she became with child and only the anger of the leader's woman had prevented their mating in public.

When the girl was only three, her mother died after being gored by a wounded deer. The leader's woman had advised the leader that the baby was a curse to the clan and should be left to die on her own. The leader was not convinced and had awarded the baby to an old woman, who had no children to mother.

The old woman was happy to have a child and protected her from the hatred of the leader's woman. But during the last fall hunt, two clansmen and the old woman had been injured by the attack of a wounded cave bear. The two men recovered, but the old woman had died of a severe infection. Her body had been too weakened by age to defeat the infection. So, the girl, now a young woman, had been left alone through the winter.

The leader's woman had maintained a daily diatribe directed toward the leader and the other members of the clan, blaming the bear's attack and the resultant winter hunger on the curse, which she insisted was carried by the young woman. She played on the fear of the clan for the unknown, saying why else would the clan suffer so. She insisted that it was obvious that the old woman had been punished by the spirits-in-the- fire for caring for the girl and that the clan was being punished for the same reason.

The wiry clansman, who had captured the snake, returned to the group near the girl, as the leader's woman stood before the clan. Looking at the leader, she said that the snakebite was proof of the girl's curse. She insisted that the clan had to leave the girl and get away from the curse, or more of them would die. She said that the girl would die anyway and that if the leader continued to protect the cursed girl, the spirits-in-the- fire might make him their next victim. No one rose to the girl's defense; they had been through too much suffering since the fall and did not have the energy to take any more.

The young woman was frightened and tried to plead for help from the other members of the clan. The leader's woman deftly hit her on the side of her head with her walking stick, knocking her unconscious. With the young woman unconscious, the leader's woman became more solicitous, asking the leader to consider moving the clan away from this place that had been spoiled by the young woman's curse?

Although the leader was not completely convinced by his woman's argument, he knew that if he did not do something, any bad thing that happened to the clan would be blamed upon him and his decision to keep the young woman with the clan. He suspected that she would probably die from the serpent's death bite anyway. Without further hesitation, the clan leader ordered the clan members to move east away from the cliffs, leaving the young woman unconscious and alone in an unforgiving world.

The leader led the clan away from the cliffs back toward the river; but moved more eastward. The other members of the clan fell into their familiar places in the order-of-march, as they moved away. First, they moved at a walk and then increased their pace to a slow trot, quickly putting more distance between the clan and the cursed young woman.

As the clan moved away from the cliffs, Raka could see that they were abandoning the young woman. He started moving along the top of the cliffs to a location above where the young woman lay unconscious. He saw that he could climb down to a ledge above the cave entrance and drop onto the ledge in front of the entrance. He did so without further hesitation. He removed his bulky robe and pack and placed them in front of the cave; but kept his water bladder and his spears.

Then he climbed down the ledges that the wiry clansman had previously ascended, until he was beside the young woman. She looked pale. The kopsut had leaped to the ledge in front of the cave and now followed Raka down.

Raka thought, "The wound on the side of her head should not be serious." He had seen worse head wounds from which people had quickly recovered. There was a moderate amount of blood on the head wound and already a large bump had swelled up to about two inches high. He looked at the snakebite. It was located in the thick calf muscle above the Achilles tendon of her right leg and looked as if it was starting to turn an angry red. He knew that he needed to bleed the snake's death message from the wound. The kopsut saw that Raka treated the female like a member of his pack and approached her, smelling and licking her wounds.

Quickly Raka took a sharp spearhead from his pouch and made a ragged cut across the two fang- punctures in her leg. The leg started to bleed; but not fast enough, he thought. He messaged the area around the cut causing additional, faster bleeding. Finally, he was satisfied that he had bled her as much as possible. He took the ball of moss from his pouch and tore off a piece and placed it over the snakebite. He tied it in place with a strip of sinew from his pouch. Next, he poured a small amount of water onto the moss. The moss began to release a brown liquid that coated the snake bite. The old woman had told him that the water would release the healing magic from the moss. "Well," Raka told the kopsut, "that is all I can do for the snakebite."

He turned his attention to the head wound. The bleeding had slowed, but the cut was gaping open about ½-inch wide. Raka took the slender piece of bone from his pouch and began to make holes in the skin on each side of the wound. He used this instrument to sew the wound closed using sinew from his pouch. It took five stitches to close the wound. Slowly the bleeding stopped. He tied another piece of the medicated moss over the head-wound. Finally, he poured water over the wound washing away much of the blood.

The young woman had still not awakened. He easily lifted her and placed her on his right shoulder. He carried her up the cliff's face until, after some hard work, they were in front of the cave. He lowered her to the ground and took his robe and pack into the cave. A quick look around did not reveal any signs of danger. The kopsut waited on the ground below.

He carried the young woman into the cave and placed her on the robe. As he laid her down, she began to groan.

He looked at her closely. She was beautiful with long black hair, now matted with blood. Although young, it was obvious that she was a grown woman, as attested to by her small breasts and wide hips. He looked under the deerskin wrap that she wore over her waist. She had a full mat of hair covering her womanhood.

As he placed her waist wrap back in its place, he looked and she was staring at him, trying to understand where she was. She jumped back away from him and off of the robe toward the cave wall farthest away, yelling, "YAWWW." Her teeth were bared, as if she was going to emit a snarl.

"This "YAWWW" seems to be a common expression in this clan," thought Raka.

She drew her hands up in front of her and bared her teeth even more, ready to defend herself from this frightening strange being. Then she paled and began to retch and vomited onto the cave floor.

With gestures, the man tried to calm her. He motioned toward her snake-bit leg; which she could see had a wrapping around it.

She looked confused and then became frightened, as she remembered what had happened. Suddenly she became ill again and vomited against the cave wall. He offered her a drink of water from his water bladder. She accepted it, tentatively, and took a long drink. She looked feverish and, as if to confirm his suspicion, she began to tremble. He motioned for her to lie on the robe and she did so immediately. Almost instantly, she fell into a feverish sleep.

Raka placed the water bladder and a spear next to the woman and left the cave. They would need firewood and, if possible, some fresh meat, if she was going to live. He had seen many animal tracks in the valley, as he had stalked the clan. He knew most of the tracks. He had seen the tracks of a small group of red-deer, as they had moved east. Two saber-toothed cats, followed by at least four giant spotted hyenas, were stalking the red-deer. He also saw older signs of horse and a small group of wooly mammoths. None of these signs looked promising for a one-day hunt by a lone man. When he had followed the clan through the river bed a day earlier, he had seen the cloven-foot sign of wild pigs, which he knew could be killed by a lone man.

He climbed down the ledges until he reached the ground that sloped toward the river. His first task was to build a fire in the cave. A fire would be needed, not only to defend against the cold, but also to help protect them from meat-eaters. Among the clans that Raka knew, fire was considered to contain protective spirits, which, when properly encouraged, could be used to protect the fire-makers. When the spirits-in-the-fire were angry, they could also destroy. He gathered a large amount of wood and took it to the cave. He arranged rocks for a fire, one larger rock in each of the four directions, north, south, east and west. This was the manner that his mother had taught him which showed respect to the spirits-in-the-fire. Then, using his flint striker and iron pyrite, along with a piece of the dry bird's nest, he started a slow burning fire.

He descended again to the bottom of the cliffs. Careful not to go east in the direction that the clan had traveled, he turned west-northwest and headed for the river followed by the kopsut. It was cold without the robe and he decided to travel at a slow run, as he did most of the time when not stalking prey.

He reached the river in about ½-hour. As he neared the river, he discovered the first fresh cloven tracks and slowed to a crouching walk and readied his spear thrower by loading a spear and holding it in a throwing position. The kopsut smelled the tracks and looked at the man to see what he would do. When they were almost in sight of the river water, Raka heard a splashing noise emanating from below the bank of the river. Crouching low, he slowing moved toward the noise below the river bank. The kopsut followed his lead.

The sound seemed to be an animal splashing in shallow water. The wind was coming from the north; so, he was downwind of the animal, if it was an animal. He could smell it; but could not quite decide what it was. Carefully, he raised himself from his crouched position until he could see what was making the noise. The animal saw him at the same time that he saw it. The animal bolted, running to the east along the bank of the river in the shallow water trying to reach the shelter of the forest about a hundred yards east on the south bank. Quickly he ran after the animal; as did the kopsut, until he saw it clearly before it was able to reach the edge of the woods. In one swift motion the spear was launched toward the animal, flying at incredible speed. The flint tipped spear buried itself behind the wild animal's right shoulder just before the kopsut grabbed the animal's throat in a vicious grip. The animal dropped immediately, struggled for a minute and then died.

The animal was a wild pig (or "ponk" in the language of the Step Clan), a distant cousin of modern-day wild boars. Raka had never killed ponk before; but he recognized their sign and knew of their succulent meat. In any case he knew that this was meat and, by all appearances, it would make many good meals. The animal was as large as a medium-size deer. Quickly, he took his cutting flint from his pouch and began slaughtering the animal. It looked healthy and he first opened the abdomen and removed the liver. He rinsed it in the river water and ate half of it raw. He pitched the other innards to the kopsut, who ate them ravenously. He cut the animal into quarters; knowing that if he was going to try to use the entire animal, he would have to make four trips to carry the carcass to the cave. He dragged the quartered carcass to the edge of the river bank and weighed them down with rocks until they were covered with water, all except one quarter section. If he worked hard, he should be able to retrieve the other pieces before other meat-eaters were able to get them, he thought.

He shouldered the remaining quarter of the carcass that he had not put in the river and started trotting toward the cliffs and the cave, which now contained the woman. As he neared the cave, he picked up several more dead pieces of wood that he would need to keep a fire burning. He was sweating profusely from the run and the burden that he was carrying. He relished the feeling; it made him feel strong and alive! He carried his load up to the cave and dumped it on the cave floor.

The girl was still asleep, moaning and groaning, trapped in a feverish dream. Her leg with the snakebite was swollen to a point that the covering skin was stretched tight. Raka removed the moss cover and looked at the wound. The wound around the snakebite was now a fiery red color, swollen into a two-inch bulge from under the bandage around the site of the bite. He replaced the moss cover and took the water bladder and poured a small amount of water on the moss cover and into her dry, cracked lips. She hungrily drank the water without waking. He poured a little water on her forehead and on the moss cover of the head wound.

Next, he built up the fire using some of the wood that he had carried into the cave. Then he went to the bottom of the cliffs and gathered more wood and carried it to the cave. Quickly he departed at a trot for his second trip to retrieve more of the animal carcass. Again, the kopsut followed him. He made two such trips; until upon his return to the site of the dead boar for the last time, he discovered that what appeared by the sign to be a large cat had stolen the last quarter of the carcass. On the final trip back to the cave, he carefully watched the kopsut. He knew that the kopsut would sense the big cat before he did. He knew that the cat would follow the smell of the carcass to the cave, when he was hungry again. He would have to be vigilant and not allow the cat to surprise him. The fire would probably be enough to prevent the cat from entering the cave, if he kept the fire large enough. The kopsut seldom entered the area near the fire when he made camp, sleeping instead just outside of the range of the fire light.

After the three quarters of the animal were in the cave and Raka had carried a week's supply of wood into the cave, he started preparing the meat. He placed flat rocks on each side of the fire about two feet high. Before leaving the cave the last time, he had soaked sharpened sticks in the water in the shallow depression at the back of the cave. He now took the sharpened sticks and skewed them through two large pieces of shoulder meat and balanced them just above the fire on the flat rocks, so that they would cook slowly. The fire was burning with little smoke since the wood had been dead for a long time and was very dry. The smoke that the fire did cause was white and dissipated quickly before it rose above the tops of the cliffs. Raka's primary concern was that the woman's clan might notice the fire, which could cause them to return to the cave. He placed much of the wood next to the fire, so that it would completely dry before he burned it.

He checked on the woman again. She was still unconscious; but didn't seem to be any worse. Her eyes were moving behind her eyelids and she occasionally moaned. She still looked feverish. He gave her another drink of water, which she drank without awakening, and poured some more water on her forehead and both wounds.

He looked at the cave roof and closely examining the cracks and small crevices. He decided that he could suspend some of the meat over the fire and allow it to slowly dry. This would delay the rotting process a few days. His mother had taught him the skills of meat preservation, which she had learned from his father. At the bottom of the cliff, he had seen several pieces of cedar about the size of a thrusting spear. He decided that these might work as meat skewers.

He went to the cave entrance and carefully examined the surrounding area. He realized that if the big cat were to try to surprise him near the cave, it would probably do so by jumping on him from above the cave entrance. He smelled the air outside the cave and took a long look at the rocks above the cave entrance. He did not see anything that looked threatening; so, he climbed down the ledges to the base of the cliffs and found the two pieces of cedar that he had previously seen. The kopsut had disappeared; but Raka knew that he would return. The kopsut lived an independent life; but accompanied Raka and joined him in his hunts.

He carried the two ten-foot-long pieces of wood to the cave and checked the length. He verified that he could wedge them in the crevices of the roof above the fire. He sharpened one end of one pole with his flint ax and skewered all of the remaining meat with the pole. It was difficult; but he was able to lift the meat-laden pole and wedge it in the cracks of the roof, so that the meat hung above the fire. Then he wedged the other piece of cedar next to the first. This piece would be used to suspend thin pieces of meat over the fire allowing them to dry more quickly. He would have rather smoked and dried the meat using reed baskets, as his mother had taught him; but he had none.

A shoulder roast that was cooking over the fire looked like it was ready to eat. He bit the roast and cut off a piece with his flint cutting tool and stuffed it in his mouth, getting grease on his beard. It was a very succulent meat and he made a mental note to try to get more ponk meat. He thought about putting some of the sea salt on it; but decided not to waste it. Salt was very difficult to find and was a much-cherished commodity, which made valuable trading material with clans that were approachable.

After he had eaten his fill, he went the pool of water at the rear of the cave and drank by placing his mouth on the water surface and drawing the water in noiselessly. Then he went to check on the woman again. She still slept; but her breathing was no longer as loud as it had been before. He gave her another drink of water, which she drank unconsciously as before. He thought he could fix her something that she could eat without awakening. He looked around the cave. He had seen a rock toward the back of the cave which had a depression in the middle of it where water had splashed for ages. He retrieved the rock, which was about a foot across and six inches thick with a two-inch depression in the middle of it. He placed the rock directly onto the hot coals, which he had raked to the surrounding edge of the fire. He raked additional hot coals around the rock to heat it more quickly.

He cut a piece of thick, fat meat off of the pieces hanging above the fire and placed it in the depression. He poured water from his water bladder filling the depression and covering the meat. Raka believed that the meat should cook in the water and that he could get the woman to drink the broth. He remembered that the old woman of the River Clan had done this for him, when he had been wounded. He had a little time before dark. He needed to replenish the water in the water bladder.

He went to the rear of the cave and replenished the water in his water bladder. The water trickled down the back wall collecting in a pool, which was about two feet deep. As more water ran into the pool and the pool overfilled, the excess ran out toward the right side of the back wall, disappearing through a crack between the right wall and floor.

Raka went to the front of the cave. It was starting to grow dark. He could hear the sounds of the prowling meat-eaters and the night birds of prey. The meat-eaters would undoubtedly smell the trail that he had left carrying the meat to the cave. He didn't want the fire to be seen during the night; so, he made a pile of rocks on the side of the fire closest to the cave entrance, effectively blocking a direct view of the flames from the cave entrance. He built up the fire at the entrance and checked on the broth that he was making for the woman. It was thick and smelled delicious.

He had saved the pig's stomach to use as a small bladder to carry water. He had washed it in the river, tied one end with sinew. On the other end, he had fashioned a sinew noose which could be opened and closed and had placed it above the fire to dry. He retrieved the bladder and tilting the hollowed rock with a stick poured much of the meat broth into the bladder. He couldn't help but spill much of it; but was able to get about a cup of the broth into the bladder. He let it cool for a few minutes.

He went to the woman. She was still unconscious and muttering. He raised her head and poured some of the liquid into her mouth. She drank it hungrily without opening her eyes until the bladder was more than half empty. She returned to a fitful sleep; her breath even and restful. Her bite wound appeared no worse than before. Her leg was now swollen all the way up to her hip and the moss cover had absorbed a large amount of drainage from the wound. He replaced the moss with a new piece and poured water over it. Her head wound had not changed.

Raka had once seen a child who had been bitten by a snake. The child had been very sick for a few days; but had recovered completely. The old woman's cure for snake bite might help this woman recover more quickly, he thought.

Raka took the piece of meat that had cooked in the water, skewered it on a forked stick and hung it over the fire. He made sure the fire was high, checked the dark beyond the reach of the firelight and retreated to the other side of the fire, where he lay down with a throwing spear by his side. He knew that he would need to fashion a thrusting spear that he could use in close encounters, such as the cave entrance. It would not be very comfortable sleeping without his robe, which the woman was currently using. He considered crawling into the robe with her to share her warmth; but decided against it.

He was a light sleeper and slept only an hour or two at a time. Any noise awakened him and he grabbed the spear and checked the dark outside of the cave entrance. The night animals were prowling at the foot of the cliffs, undoubtedly attracted by the scent of the boar carcass. Occasionally, he thought he saw eyes flickering in the firelight on the ledge in front of the cave entrance; but when he went toward them with the spear, they disappeared down the ledge. Each time that he awakened, he replenished the wood on the fire. The spirits-in- the-fire were protecting him and the female this night.

As he drifted off to sleep, he remembered his childhood in a land far on the north side of the river and the vast mountain range.

CHAPTER 2

THE STEP CLAN

The Step Clan was a large and very successful clan that lived as nomads, roaming the plains north of the great mountain range from early spring until late autumn. The clan lived in nomadic camps during these warmer months and spent the colder months camped in a cave in the foothills leading up into the vast mountain range.

The plains north of the mountain range were covered with forests primarily of evergreen trees, although there were deciduous trees in the lower elevations. After the retreat of the most recent glacial period the first trees to return to the plains north of the great mountain range were the evergreen trees. Most of these trees were conifers; some producing cones that contained edible nuts that men and animals found nutritious and tasty. Deciduous trees and bushes had returned to the plains north of the mountains more slowly after the retreat of the glaciers. Many of these trees, however, produced either fruit or nuts, which were also a good source of food for the clan. But the Step Clan was primarily a meat-eating clan and resorted to eating plants and plant products only sparingly. The digestive system of these clan members was not adapted to processing plant products as well as it could have been. Clan members often experienced abdominal discomfort from a failure to completely digest plants, after eating some plants and plant products.

The Step Clan had learned not only to exist in this changing environment, but to excel to a limited degree in the competition for limited resources on which to survive. The Step Clan culture over the years had adapted to a warming environment in which there were more lakes and fuller running rivers. Trees and other plants were expanding their presence geometrically, while animals which fed on the plants experienced a surge in their population levels, as well.

The Step Clan culture had developed such that the men had become hunters of the many animals that attributed their existence to the expanding flora (primarily grasses) north of the mountains. In the forests, the Step Clan hunted bush-antlered and red deer (conk) and the Irish elk (spo). In the grassier plains, the Step Clan hunted wild horses, the occasional wooly mammoth, seasonal rain-deer and the very scarce wooly rhinoceros.

Often, there were other, smaller game animals available, such as wild boar in the areas where water was plentiful. The average clansman spent his days participating in a hunt, preparing for a hunt, or making weapons. The type of hunt was dependent upon the time of year and the location that the clan chose for its nomadic journeys. All hunts had some common characteristics. Hunts were conducted as a group. The Step Clan was a large clan by local standards; therefore, they had sufficient numbers such that they could separate into more than one hunting group. In fact, for such a large clan, it was necessary to separate into more than one hunting party in order to feed the entire clan.

When not living in a cave dwelling, the Step Clan fashioned tents made from tree limbs covered with animal skins for their shelter. When the clan moved its camp, they did not carry these limbs; but cut new ones near their new camp site. They did transport the animal skins that they used to cover the shelters; thus, it was more convenient for family groups to share a shelter. Transport during travel was performed by the use of back packs and two-man poles on which to attach the packs; therefore, only a limited amount of goods could be carried.

The Step Clan employed several hunting techniques no matter what type of hunt they were conducting. These techniques included the ambush. There were two types of ambushes conducted by the Step Clan. One was a hidden-ambush in which the hunters hid along a game trail and waited for their prey to pass by, resulting in a simultaneous attack by all members of the hunting party using thrusting spears. Recently, the Step Clan had added a new weapon to its arsenal, the spear-thrower.

Another type of ambush conducted by the Step Clan was the drive-ambush, in which the hunting party separated into two groups. The first group drove the prey toward the second group, which ambushed the prey, as it passed by their hiding places.

In planning an ambush, the Step Clan considered the direction of the wind and the direction of the sun. The wind had to be blowing from the prey toward the ambush site and the sun should preferably be in the prey's eyes, as they looked at the ambush site. Additionally, the hunters had to select an ambush site that allowed concealment and surprise. In a drive- ambush it was also important that the prey's direction of retreat be toward the ambush site; therefore, the Step Clan members were students of animal behavior and had learned to predict how their prey would react.

The Step Clan also employed a hunting technique called "fire-hunting." Fire hunting was typically the use of fire to drive prey toward an ambush, or a location from which there was little chance to escape.

While the clansmen were hunting, the Step Clan culture had developed such that the clan women searched for small game. Small game included such animals as the mountain hair and birds, which they killed with rocks or large sticks that they carried for that purpose and for self-defense. The women also had become adept fishermen and food "gatherers." They searched for edible plants, fruits and nuts; but these food stuffs did not make up a large portion of their diet. The women of the Step Clan possessed a vast amount of knowledge concerning edible and useful plants in the area north of the great mountain range.

While the clan men and women were participation in their hunting and gathering activities, the meat-eaters were conducting ambushes of their own. The meat-eaters hunted the same game that the clansmen hunted and also hunted the clan's men, women, and children. The Step Clan had also studied the ways of these meat-eaters. They had learned how to defend against the cave bear, the giant cheetah, the saber-toothed cat, the timber wolf and the short-faced spotted hyena.

When in the camp, the clan used fire to keep the meat-eaters away. It was their belief that the fire contained spirits, which would protect them from the meat-eaters, if these spirits were not angry. If the spirits-in-the-fire were angry, it was a bad omen. If they were not angry, it was a good omen. When on the move, they used look-outs in all directions and positioned men with spears at strategic positions in the order of march to leap to the defense of the clan, if attacked. The Step Clan considered it a good omen indeed, if they were able to kill a meat-eater.

The evenings for the Step Clan were a time in which the men sat around the fire and repaired weapons and other tools, while the women made or repaired useful items, such as robes, covers for tents or reed baskets. The Step Clan's primary weapon had always been the thrusting spear until recently; when they had added a smaller spear and a spear-thrower. The spear thrower and small spear allowed clansmen to kill game from a longer distance away. They used other rock, or bone tools for cutting, drilling and scraping.

Typically, the women were beasts of burden, leaving the men's hands free to defend against an attack.

To carry their burdens of food, tools, hides and babies, the clan women used a back pack frame made of wood, which attached to their backs with strips of hide. A deer hide was used for a pack to carry their goods. They also used two-man poles from which they could sling packs, carcasses, and hides.

Evening also might be devoted to the telling of a Clan "legend." Legends were used to pass on knowledge learned from their ancestors and often taught the clan members a lesson that would aid them in their struggle to survive.

Competition for resources was intense, not only between the meat-eaters and the clan; but also, between the Step Clan and other clans that they occasionally encountered. The areas through which the Clan roamed were sparsely inhabited; but recent years had seen an increase in the number of clans hunting in these areas. For many years the southern clans, like the Step Clan, had been relatively numerous in the area north of the great mountain range. But as time passed, many of these clans had disappeared, falling to attacks from other southern clans and the tall, fierce northern clans. To make the Step Clan successful in this competition, the Step Clan had become a fast-moving organization. When they travelled, they did so at a fast walk or trot; whereas most clans only ran in fear, or during a hunt.

This ability to move quickly had often allowed the Step Clan to escape a threatening encounter with another clan, or to arrive at a promising hunting location before the competition. Any member of the Step Clan was capable of maintaining a slow run for hours.

The Step Clan culture did not encourage peaceful encounters with other clans. They considered other clans to be a bad omen and, when sign of another clan was found, the

Step Clan took action to avoid the other clan. To date, this avoidance of other clans had contributed to the Step Clan's success. The Step Clan seldom lost members to battles with other clans and the areas in which they hunted were routinely not overhunted.

Such a tradition also had its disadvantages, which would affect the survival of the clan over time. The first disadvantage was the resultant inbreeding, due to the non-availability of mates from other clans. Regressive, unwanted genes would become more prevalent in the clan and characteristics would develop, which would adversely affect the survival of the clan. A second disadvantage was the reduction of potential knowledge and riches that could be gained through trade and exchange of ideas with other clans.

Into this environment babies were born; but many unknown dangers existed, which were exasperated by the limited contact with other clans. The Step Clan gene-pool was not expanding; but narrowing, resulting in members with unsuccessful characteristics, such as more susceptibility to diseases and hereditary deformations and illnesses. Undesired characteristics became more prevalent, as recessive genes defined new off-spring characteristics. The increased inbreeding within the Step Clan could spell the clan's doom over time.

CHAPTER 3

THE BIRTH OF RAKA

A s Raka dreamed, his mind returned to his earliest memories, far, far back into the recesses of his mind. Many of his memories of those times were not so much memories as feelings, impressions and instincts.

He recognized that there was pain, accompanied by low groans, suppressed by someone with him. He seemed to hear a low cry, which was quickly silenced by low warnings from the person with him. He had impressions of the dark with flashes of light and pain and finally, he knew that all of his memories contained the images of his mother, warning him to be silent, hiding him in the animal skins, feeding him and nuzzling him.

Those early memories were all that he knew of the beginning of his life. To him they were impressions that most of all connected him to his mother and sustained him, when his life became almost unbearable. From those memories, he developed his sense of caution and his desire to be alone away from the dangers associated with other humans.

He was born into the "Step Clan," which was a large, successful clan that roamed the hills and plains north of the great mountain range. In the warmer months they lived in nomadic camps and spent the colder months camped in a cave in the foothills leading up into the vast mountain range.

The Step Clan had experienced a long, successful reign over the small area in which they lived, primarily due to the fact that they faced little competition from other clans in the area; but also due to the fact that the Step Clan had had a long line of very able leaders. The last of these able leaders had been called "Kruf," a clan word used to describe a "hunter," when used with a spear-thrusting gesture.

Kruf had led the clan for a generation of successful years. During his time as leader, the clan had improved their hunting and fishing techniques. Before Kruf, fishing had only been done by the men of the clan primarily using spears and resulting in limited success. The clan preferred red meat; but fish were a good supplement to their diet. Kruf had allowed the clan women to use a new method for fishing, which had been the idea of his woman. The fishing technique allowed women to use sinew, similar to the sinew they used to connect animal hides together for robes, threaded through a hole in a curved fish bone. Kruf's woman had taken the curved bone that clan women used for sewing and attached it to the sinew line. She had noticed that the fish in the rivers often ate insects floating on the water. She impaled one of these insects on the sharp end of the curved bone and threw it in the water. When the fish took the insect in its mouth, she yanked the fish out of the water and onto the bank where it flopped around until other women grabbed it. This fishing procedure was referred to as "kropin" in the clan language. "Krop" meant fish in the Step Clan language, when used with a hand gesture of a swimming fish. Kropin had come to mean "fish getting," when used with a yanking gesture. Kropin had allowed the Step Clan to add to their winter supplies at a greater rate than other clans in the area. This made the Step Clan stronger.

Kruf had died from pneumonia that he contracted during a particularly cold winter and that ravished his body due to old age. During his advanced years he had no longer led the men during hunts. He had allowed his son Krufen to lead the hunting parties.

Kruf had been the Step Clan's strongest spear thrower, in

a land where most southern clans depended on the thrusting spear. Kruf had observed northern clans, as they threw their spears at reindeer, and realized that an important limitation on how far a man could throw a spear was the ability to grip the spear and release it at the right moment. Kruf spent his last year sitting around the fire and experiencing insights that some might call visions. During one such vision, he had come up with the idea of the "spear-thrower." He had enlisted the help two clansmen, a strong, young spear thrower and an old man who was the clan's best carver of bone and wood. He had the wood carver produce a three-foot-long piece of cedar, which was two inches thick, into a cylinder with a groove cut into one side with one end of the groove open and the other closed. Kruf had insisted that he had seen this instrument in a vision; but in actual fact, he had obtained the idea from observing a northern clan.

He demonstrated to the young spear thrower how the equipment should be used and watched as the young man developed the ability to throw a spear a much longer distance than any man had ever been able to achieve before that time. Once the spear thrower was introduced by Kruf, all of the clansmen wanted to have one and the old wood carver worked diligently producing spear throwers. Before a month had passed most of the clansmen had become experts at using the spear thrower. The spear thrower increased the distance that a thrown spear could travel by one third and increased the speed of the spear and, thus the penetration power, by a similar percentage. The spear-thrower made the clan one of the most successful southern clans in the area just north of the great mountain range. They used the spear thrower to attack the only other two southern clans that operated in their hunting area, resulting in the eventual disappearance of those clans.

During his years as an infant, Raka had only known his mother. Other members of the clan were distant sounds and momentary glimpses. His mother's low growl warned him

41

that those sounds and glimpses represented danger and he remained hidden in the skins in which he was wrapped. At night when they were alone, she would take him out of the skins and cuddle him. During those times, he could see the fire and the sleeping figures of the clan surrounding it.

He learned to recognize the leader of the clan by his loud, over-bearing voice. He knew that the leader represented the greatest danger, due to his mother's low growl and shiver as the leader approached. When the leader was near, Raka always remained silent and still. The other members of the clan referred to the leader as "Krufen," a word which meant "great hunter" in the clan language, when used with a spear-thrusting gesture.

The other women in the clan wanted to see the infant; but Raka's mother refused, growling and hastily taking her baby away. The clan women resented her attitude; but accepted it as the unexplained protective actions of a new mother. Many of the women ridiculed her, when she was not present and she became an unpopular member of the clan.

Although most clan babies were not given a name until they exhibited some trait later in life, his mother called him "Raka," the word the clan often used to describe the giant Cheetahs, when used with a swift left to right gesture across the front of the body. Rakas swiftly ran down their prey on these plains north of the mountains. Raka's father had been like a giant cheetah, able to run down prey faster than other men. He would later come to know that his mother's name was "Kardi," which meant "lost" in the clan language, when used with a gesture away from the body. As a young girl Kardi had been prone to wander away from camp and had been given the name as a result.

Life was difficult for the young mother and her new baby. She had no man; so, she had to share the fire of her father. Her mother was dead, killed by an unknown animal during a river crossing. Her father had taken another woman, who now had a child of her own. So, the group around her father's fire was led by her father, a wiry man with coal-black hair and dark eyes. Her father was called "Kroli," which meant "stalker" in the clan language, when used with an open hand gesture in front of the body motioning down toward the ground. Kroli was a patient man, not prone to the bullying nature that defined many of the men of this clan. He was the oldest man in the clan, almost 40 years of age, as compared to the leader, who was about 30 years old.

Another member of the group around this fire was her father's new wife, who was about 18 years old, only two years older than Raka's mother. Her name was "Gruma," a word meaning "gatherer," when used with a picking gesture. She was not remarkable for her beauty; but she was devoted to Kardi's father. She had broad, strong features and dark hair and she was a hard worker. She did not understand the young mother's reluctance to allow her to see her baby; but she accepted it, following Kroli's lead of allowing Raka's mother to do as she pleased.

Kroli's new wife also had a one-year-old child that shared the fire. The child had not been given a name and was a typical member of the clan with raven black hair, very dark eyes and olive-colored skin. Like most clan babies, he seldom cried and was kept in soft animal-skin wraps until he was about a year and a half old. Most clan infants were not named until they were young children and exhibited some trait, which the clan could attribute to an animal spirit, which lived within the body.

Another member of the group around Kroli's fire was Kardi's older brother, "Milka." Milka had received his name, when he had jumped to the defense of his sister when she had returned from being lost.

When Kardi was found after being lost, she had the smell

43

of another clan on her and this was considered a bad omen to the clan. When the clan leader had started to beat her, Milka was present and had taken the blows intended for her. This brave act persuaded the leader to forgive her and he changed her brother's name to Milka, which meant "Bear" in Step Clan language, when used with a gesture of both arms raised in front of the body.

Milka's woman and four-year old child were also members of the group around Kroli's fire. She was called Garki, a word which meant rabbit in the Step Clan language, when used with a gesture of both index fingers pointed upward in front of the face. Her child had not been named yet.

Many clan infants did not live to be older than two years. Many of them died of childhood diseases, such as rubella, whooping cough, dysentery and pneumonia before they were two years old. After they were removed from the animal skins, they had to be protected from predatory animals and other dangers.

Normally, the clan women assisted each other in protecting the children; since there was a great deal of work to be done searching for herbs, roots, and other plants and gathering and preparing food, etc. Some of the women were selected by the leader's wife to gather fish. The leader's wife normally selected one or two women to perform the duty of taking care of the children. Kardi and Gruma had been selected to care for the children, since both were nursing infants and could nurse another child in an emergency. Since Kardi would not leave her baby alone with other clan women, she was a good selection for this task.

Kardi was careful to keep her baby with her while caring for the clan's children, while Gruma was a ball of energy herding the toddlers who moved around the camp and area near the camp. Gruma normally left her child with Kardi along with four other infants and gave her attention to the eight clan toddlers. She was assisted by two young females that were about nine years old.

Raka was dreaming of these early days, when his mother kept him with the other infants. Raka was perhaps two years old and had not been allowed out of the animal skins, while the other infants were months younger when they were allowed out of the skins. He enjoyed these times because, when there were no other adults near, he could see and hear the other babies. The sounds, sights and smells were exciting. When any of the other adults returned, his mother would warn him to be quiet and close the flap of the skins in which he was wrapped.

Clan women wrapped their infants in soft animal skin, usually mountain hare or deer. When the clan was on the move, the skins were attached to a rack made of wood, which was carried on the woman's back or some women slung their babies in front of them across their breasts and wrapped inside their robe in cold weather.

Now the clan was living in their winter cave, even though late spring had arrived. The clan women's days were filled with carrying for the children, fishing, gathering roots and green spring plants, preparing meat for cooking, preparing the meals and repairing robes. Another task that women performed was the carrying of the game that the clansmen killed. Typically, women might accompany the men on a hunt; slaughter the killed animal and carry much of the meat back to the camp.

The winter had been passed eating food obtained in the fall and the fish and mountain hairs that were caught during the winter. Occasionally, the men went on long winter hunts high in the mountains and killed reindeer, or ibex, distant relative of mountain goats. But these ibex hunts could be very risky due to the weather and the risk of falls.

On this day the store of red meat was very low; so, the men needed to go on more hunts. The reindeer had migrated north and the women encouraged them to bring back meat, since the clan member's digestive systems could not support a large amount of plant material.

When the hunting parties were not in the camp, Kardi was more comfortable, allowing Raka to watch from his animal-skin haven. It was a nice day, when the only adults in the camp were Kardi and Gruma. Gruma had taken the toddlers out of the cave to the river to bath; so, Kardi had allowed Raka to crawl out of his haven and around the cave. She noticed that he was becoming strong and trying to stand and walk. It was at that moment that she realized that she was going to have to find a way that he could roam freely among other members of the clan.

The sun shining through the cave entrance showed a thin, pale boy with brown to blond hair. Kardi needed to find a way to disguise the fact that Galik was not Raka's father and that in all likelihood, judging from his appearance; he had been fathered by someone not like anyone in the Step Clan. Kardi's greatest fear was that Raka would be discovered to be different and she would be cast out of the clan with her baby or possibly even killed.

CHAPTER 4

A STEP CLAN MAMMOTH HUNT

I t was late spring and the weather on this day was sunny and cold with only a few clouds in the sky. The Step Clan had remained in their winter cave, since there was an abundance of fish to be had from the river. The cave was comfortable and the dangers in the area were known and therefore, not feared. Krumen intended to stay near the river, as long as the women were catching fish and finding an abundance of edible spring plants to gather. But the clan was becoming hungry for the taste of fresh red meat.

Each day, the clan men had to venture further away from the cave in search of game. As spring was coming to an end, the rivers were swollen with flood water, which hindered the movement of many larger animals, resulting in opportunities for the clan to trap and kill an animal that could feed them all for days. As fortune would have it, the clan's luck helped them to find and kill a hairy mammoth near the mountains.

The clan's hunger for red meat had caused Krumen to split up the hunters into two hunting parties in the hope that at least one party would be successful in their hunt. One party was led by Golik, Krumen's favorite hunter. Golik's party had headed east of the cave in search of conk; while the other party led by Krumen headed west of the cave, hoping to find reindeer that had not started their northern migration.

Kroli was in Krumen's party, as they approached a plateau which overlooked the river. Kroli was the clan's best tracker and was about 150 yards in front of the remainder of the party, when he discovered mammoth tracks leading toward the river. He smelled the air and could faintly make out the rank mammoth odor. The smell of a mammoth was distinctive and pungent, similar in strength to that of a ponk (boar). The wind was blowing from the south; so, the mammoth scent was carried toward the clansmen, as opposed to the opposite. He motioned for the group to stop by holding crossed arms above his head and silently retraced his steps until he was next to Krumen.

Without speaking, he made a gesture with his arm like the truck of a mammoth. Everyone understood. He motioned that they should proceed forward quietly to a rise overlooking the plateau to get a better look. The group of hunters followed Kroli in stalking crouches, so as not to be visible above the ridge- line. As the group arrived at the edge of the rise, they slowly peeked over the top. They discovered that three mammoths were feeding on spring grass near a rocky ledge overlooking the flood-gorged river. Over the years, the river and glacial ice had gouged a deep cut into the rocky surface, creating a steep drop from the top of the plateau, where the mammoths now grazed.

The group withdrew a short distance and through gestures discussed how to attack the mammoths. Krumen decided to use a fire hunt. In a Step Clan fire hunt, fire was used to startle the giant animals and get them running toward a trap, an ambush, or, as in this case, the ledge above the river. The clan had used this hunting method before, on the rare occasion that they were able to hunt the hairy beasts, and knew that a mammoth's initial reaction to the scent of fire was to flee away from the fire at a dead run. Although the bright green spring grass covered the plateau, it was much shorter than the large amount of dry, tall grass that had been left dead from the winter cold. The plateau was covered with this tall, dead grass up to where the mammoths were grazing. The three mammoths were grazing slowly toward the river and had not yet noticed the hunting party. Krumen ordered the clansmen to spread out about three hundred yards across the edge of the plateau and upon his raised hand to quickly set fires across this wide area.

Each man did as he was told and moved to a position on the edge of the plateau that allowed the hunting party to set a wall of fire across the only retreat direction available to the mammoths. Each man prepared a pile of dried grass and used slivers of grease-wood and striking flints and iron pyrite to start a fire, as Krumen raised his arm. The fire was fanned by the wind from the south, pushing a wide wall of flames toward the three mammoths in a matter of moments.

The mammoths quickly noticed the danger of fire, with which the older female was very familiar. The leader of the group was a large female and she immediately laid her large ears back against her neck and trumpeted an alarm to the other two mammoths. The other two mammoths were a younger adult female and a smaller adult male. They began to run away from the fire toward the ledge above the river. The hunting party maintained its spread across the plateau and approached the mammoths from behind the flames. As the mammoths neared the ledge the men charged through breaks in the flames with their thrusting spears raised, yelling as loud as they could. The young male mammoth panicked and careened over the ledge, dying as he landed on the rocks below. The other two mammoths turned and charged the clansmen.

The clansmen turned and fled toward the flames, intending to use the fire as protection and allow the remaining two mammoths to escape, if they could get through the flames. Krumen's sixteen-year-old son, Epto, was in the path of the large lead female mammoth. The mammoth fixed her eyes on the young clansman and charged him. Epto recognized the danger and sprinted toward the flames, intending to dart through a break in the fire and use the fire to protect himself from the enraged mammoth.

As he darted through a break in the flames, smoke filled his eyes and he did not see a bolder lying in his path. He tripped over it and was quickly trampled by the massive mammoth. Epto was dead immediately, his head and upper torso crushed by the mammoth.

Epto had been given his name by his father Krumen, when he had been selected as keeper of the fire. The keeper of the fire was a ceremonial position in the Step Clan, since the clan had not been required to carry fire with them for two generations. Their skill at fire-making using flint rock and iron pyrite sparks had been learned from a clan of the far north. Epto was a word in the Step Clan language which meant fire-keeper, when used with a two-handed cupping gesture. The word for fire in the Step Clan language was Ept, when used with a gesture of waiving the fingers of one hand pointed upwards. One hand meant small fire and two hands meant large fire.

Krumen had seen the death of his son. Epto had been a well-liked member of the clan. All of the men thought that this was a bad omen to lose such a favorite member of the clan. Killing the mammoth was a good omen; but losing Epto cancelled the good fortune. Krumen decided that he would have Epto buried near the place of death. He ordered the other clansmen to make their way down the ledge to the rocks near the river to where the mammoth lay dead, while he, Krumen, buried his son.

Krumen knew that dressing and carrying the mammoth back to the cave would be a lot of work. They had to work swiftly, keeping guard against the predators that would begin to arrive. Krumen thought that he could already smell giant spotted hyenas nearby. He gestured to a younger member of the clan, Brom, and to Kroli to return to the cave and get the help of some of the women. They immediately set off at a trot toward the cave, which was located to the east. The other men descended to the bottom of the ledge and began to dress the mammoth.

Krumen chose a deep crevice and placed Epto's body into it and covered it with rocks to protect him from predators. Then he joined the other clansmen dressing the mammoth. The clansmen were silent, even fearful. The loss of Epto was a bad omen for the clan; they all believed.

The Step Clan typically travelled at a trot, when not carrying a burden. Most of the clans did not travel in this manner, being more careful and deliberate in their movements. Many generations before, a leader of the Step Clan had used this technique to out distance rival clans. It had helped make the Step Clan successful; so, the practice had continued until Krumen became leader. Krumen did not believe that fast traveling gained the clan any advantage. On the contrary, he believed that it exposed the clan to more danger and therefore, had stopped requiring it. Some of the older clansmen, such as Kroli, continued the practice on their own initiative, when circumstances allowed it.

Brom had been given his name during a mammoth hunt. On an occasion when Brom had been the first to spot a mammoth herd, he was given the name Brom, which meant mammoth in clan language, when used with an arm gesture like the trunk of a mammoth. Brom was much younger than

Kroli and joined him in his slow trot back to the cave. He even admonished Kroli for the slow pace of the "old man." Kroli accepted the admonishment with no sign of resentment, allowing the arrogance of youth to prevail.

They arrived at the cave in the early afternoon without incident. There were several women there and Kroli made the mammoth gesture with his arm and said, "Brom," as he used the spear throwing gesture to indicate they had hunted it. He motioned that five of the women should accompany Brom back to the mammoth site. The women were excited at the prospect of late season brom to eat. The five women that were selected quickly left with Brom to go the site where the brom had been killed.

Kroli chose to remain at the cave since the return of the hunting parties might be late and the remaining clan women and children at the cave should not be without men after dark. Golik's hunting party had also not yet returned to the cave.

Kroli's wife Gruma had met Kroli, as he had entered the camp. He nuzzled her neck and asked about Kardi. Gruma pointed to the cave, as if he should have known where she would be. Kroli turned and walked toward the cave.

As he entered the cave, he saw that Kardi was sitting with the infants. She held one infant that he had never seen. He realized that it was her baby, Raka. Raka had sooty black hair, but he was thinner and paler than the other clan children. Kroli went to Kardi and motioned for the boy. Kardi shook her head no and took the baby to the rear of the cave. Kroli thought, "Young mothers are difficult." He turned on his heels and left the cave.

Earlier that morning, after the hunting parties had departed and the women had left the camp for other purposes, Kardi had mixed black ashes from the fire with water, making a dark emulsion, which she had applied to Raka's hair. The mixture had colored his hair black, but had a strange sooty appearance. She hoped that it would help Raka pass as a member of the clan. Time would tell after the return of the hunters.

CHAPTER 5

A STEP CLAN RED DEER HUNT

After Krumen had decided to separate the clan into two hunting parties, Golik and his group of six hunters had proceeded east along the river, where he knew the forest contained many conks. Golik had taken the hunters that Krumen had not chosen to go with his hunting party. Golik's hunting party consisted of Golik, Minar (meaning mountain hare), Kops (meaning hyena), Mok (meaning cave), Golo (meaning large cat), Kobo (meaning swimmer) and Conk (meaning red deer).

Golik was not a democratic leader. He was a domineering and bullying type of man, who brooked no disagreement, nor accepted any advice. Immediately after departing from the cave, he took Minar, a younger clansman of whom he was not particularly fond, off to the side and gave him instructions. He ordered him to proceed to about one hundred yards in front of the party and about one hundred yards to the right toward the mountains and to watch for recent signs of game animals. He sent Conk to the left front of the party, closer to the river for the same purpose, but not as far away. Both were instructed that when they discovered fresh tracks to return to the group. The group travelled for more than half a day in this manner without discovering any fresh sign of large animals. They had hunted this area many times before and it appeared that game animals were becoming scarcer, as the days passed.

As the sun was at its highest, Golik heard a scream off to his right. The group ran in that direction with their spears raised and arrived to see a saber-toothed cat standing over the Minar's body.

The cat was standing in front of Minar's body and it growled piercingly indicating an intention to defend its kill. The clansmen formed a semi-circle around the cat and advanced toward it with their thrusting spears at ready.

Conk, who was the clansman sent out to scout to the left, had also heard the scream and now joined the group, which was already advancing toward the cat. Conk was the only member of this group that had become a master of the art of spear throwing, using a spear thrower. He loaded a spear into his spear thrower and advanced on the cat from the right end of the semi-circle. Conk hissed that the other clansmen should stop their advance. The semi-circle halted and awaited his next move. He advanced two more steps and in one swift motion launched the spear toward the cat. His spear hit the cat in its left side; the spear buried itself deeply into the cat's chest cavity. The large cat leapt into the air and turned to fight the spear, which had caused it so much pain. As the cat landed, it writhed in pain for a couple of moments before collapsing into a heap on top of Minar's body. When the clansmen rushed to check on Minar, they found that he was already dead from a broken neck.

Conk had been awarded his name when he had been the first clan hunter to kill a red deer with a spear using a spear thrower. Conk was the name used by the clan to indicate a red deer, when used in conjunction with a gesture of four fingers on each hand on the side of the speaker's head.

Golik ordered the clansmen to start dressing the cat; the skin would be a valuable possession. They would cut the cat into four pieces and carry all of it, including the entrails, back to the cave, where the females would prepare it for eating and preserving.

Golik now was faced with the problem of what to do with the Minar's body. The Step Clan usually buried their dead under rocks in a burial cave; but this tradition was not a hard and fast clan rule. In situations like this, it would be acceptable to bury the man close to the death site and cover the body with rocks. Minar had no woman, siblings, or parents; so, mourning would be limited to his more distant relatives in the clan. Golik and one other clansman attended to the burial task, as Conk supervised the dressing of his kill. Golik had decided that he would claim the skin for himself, unless Krumen took it from him. The leader always got his pick of the bounty from a hunt.

Golik had placed the man's body into a shallow crevice and covered it with large rocks that should keep the predators, such as hyenas, away. Golik thought that Krumen would punish him for losing a man since it had been Golik's idea to send Minar far out front of the other hunters; so, he intended to tell Krumen that it had been Minar's idea to be so far away from the hunting party.

When the men finished dressing the cat, it was approaching darkness. It was far too dangerous to travel during the night, unless absolutely necessary; so, the little hunting party gathered wood; built a fire and prepared to spend the night. They cooked some of the cat meat to eat and curled up in their robes near the fire and slept. All clansmen were light sleepers; so, any noise would awaken them. They kept the fire high to keep predators away.

A group of giant spotted hyenas tried to approach the fire after midnight to get at the cat meat, or attack the sleeping humans; but their fear of the fire kept them at a distance just outside of the fire's light. Later, a pack of large black timber wolves also prowled near the sleeping humans. They circled the camp site looking for a safe way to get the cat meat, or attack a human; but eventually departed for fear of the hyenas, which they could smell. Additionally, they had an understanding that there was no easy prey to be had at the camp site.

Tomorrow at sunrise Golik intended to continue his hunt for conk; but he would move closer to the mountains and hunt back in the direction of the Step Clan cave. Ultimately, he knew that he would lead his hunting party triumphantly back to the cave with, or without a conk; since they had killed the saber-toothed cat. Before Golik drifted off to sleep his thoughts concluded that Krumen had been wrong to stay in the cave for such a late date into the spring. Available hunting was too far away from the clan and separation of the clan into two hunting groups was ultimately too dangerous. He convinced himself the Krumen had caused Minar's death by splitting the group up to hunt so far away from the cave. He wondered how the other clansmen felt. He would find out. He, Golik, was the clan's best leader and, if the clan wanted, they could make him leader instead of Krumen. But Golik was afraid of Krumen and he knew that he had to be very careful in discussing this situation with the other clansmen.

Krumen was not very smart; but he was shrewd and conniving. He would recognize any effort to turn the clan against him. In the end, Golik knew that he would have to fight Krumen, if he wanted to replace him as leader. He also realized that fighting Krumen was not something that he wanted to do. Krumen was the strongest man that Golik had ever known and a fight with him was akin to suicide.

The Step Clan leadership had been stable for many years. The succession of power had passed routinely down to the next man most able to lead the clan. This new leader was typically chosen by the old leader; but had to at least be tolerated by the other male clansmen. This stability occurred due to good decisions made by able leaders and no substantive challenges to the authority of those leaders. When things were going well for the clan, there was no reason to question the leadership. However, this had been a very tough winter in which the men of the clan did not feel very secure. When the clansmen did not feel secure, their women reflected that sentiment. The clan had always left the cave to nomadically follow the game migrations beginning no later than early April, but usually in the middle of March. This year it was already early May and Krumen continued to keep the clan in the cave and had not announced when they would leave. Many clansmen were beginning to question this decision and attributed any and all unfortunate occurrences to that decision. Thus, rumblings of discontent with Krumen's leadership were starting, giving an opening to Golik's quest to become leader.

Golik woke the members of his hunting party with a swift kick to each of them just as dawn started to break. The clansmen quickly ate the remainder of the cat meat that they had cooked the night before, drank water from the river and gathered their weapons and equipment to continue the hunt. Four of the men were now burdened with the cat meat and hide. That left two men with their hands free to use their hunting spears without the delay that would be caused by dropping the cat meat and grabbing the spear.

Golik motioned to the group that he and Conk would advance about two hundred yards in front of the group, so that they might see a conk before the conk noticed the hunting party. Conk trotted ahead of Golik until he was at least three hundred yards in front of the clansmen. Then he slowed to a walk and began searching for animal sign at the edge of the forest toward the foothills. Golik grunted his displeasure at Conk's impudence to move ahead of him without his approval; but Conk acted as if he did not hear the grunt.

It was only about an hour before Conk saw fresh sign of a large conk. Conk smelled the lingering odor near the tracks and realized that the conk was a female. Female conk meat was more tender than adult males. The tracks indicated that the conk had come from the forest sometime during the night to browse on the bushes and trees at the edge of the forest. There were also fresh tracks indicating that she had returned to the forest. The returning tracks were free of morning dew, indicating that the conk had made them less than two hours earlier.

Conk looked in the direction of Golik and saw that he was still about three hundred yards behind him. Golik saw that Conk had stopped and was studying the ground. He gestured to Conk to keep moving; but Conk made the gesture of a conk and pointed toward the forest. Golik covered the distance between then quickly and joined Conk in studying the tracks.

The two men agreed that the conk had returned to the forest to bed down for the day. Both men knew that conk tended to find a small grove of trees in which they could sleep during the major part of the day and return to feed in the late evening and night. The wind was from the northwest; so, the two men agreed that they would need to approach the conk's hiding place from the southeast, or to lay an ambush on the animal trail that led southeast and send a hunter from the northwest to spook the animal in that direction.

Golik decided on the latter. For this hunt he would need the other hunters and he glanced in their direction and saw that they were just coming into sight. He gestured for the men to hurry and they jogged up to the two clansmen.

Golik explained his plan. Mok would remain with the cat meat; while Conk circled to the northwest to approach the conks hiding place from that direction. Golik and the other three hunters would lay an ambush along the animal trail and wait for Conk to herd the animal toward their hiding place. As the four hunters hid themselves beside the animal trail, Conk circled toward the northwest. For this type of hunt, it was unnecessary to know the exact location of the conk, since the clansman tasked to drive the conk would approach the general area making noise which would cause the animal to move away from him along the animal trail. If the conk chose to abandon the animal trail, the hunters would hear it and adjust their ambush.

Conk heard the animal as it moved from a small stand of trees near a stream. As predicted, the red deer trotted southeast on the animal trail, which it had probably used many times before. As the animal navigated a turn in the trail to the north, the four hunters simultaneously threw their spears, striking the animal killing blows from both sides. The red deer leaped and ran a few bounds before it fell on its side and kicked for only a few minutes, as its lifeblood flowed out of its body and onto the forest floor.

The hunters surrounded the kill and struck additional blows to the animal with their thrusting spears. Golik stopped the excessive slaughter and sent three men back for Mok and the cat meat, as the other hunters began to butcher the conk. Golik and Conk drank the spewing blood as it squirted out of the red deer's body. The Step Clan routinely drank the blood of their kills while it was still warm.

It was about two hours before the red deer was ready for transport. The hunters would now be heavily burdened by both the cat and the red deer meat; but it would be a happy burden. The successful hunt would help remove the disappointment of the death of Minar.

Using thrusting spears as two-man carrying poles, the men were able to carry all of the meat and they started their journey back to the cave with Golik leading the way.

CHAPTER 6

THE MAN FROM THE NORD CLAN

Meanwhile, in the midst of a clan on the decline and the growing discontent of the clan, Kardi had to raise her child. Raka could no longer be hidden away from the other clan members in the animal wrappings. He was becoming too mature and too large. Kardi often dwelled upon the reason that she believed she had to keep Raka hidden from the rest of the clan.

It went back to the time when she was but a young woman, not much more that a girl. She had not yet been given to a man. The Step Clan tradition required that the clan leader decide when she was ready to be given to a man and to choose the man to whom she would be given.

The Step Clan traditions concerning mating were akin to the characteristics of the wolf. Wolves mated for life and were normally monogamous. Men and women of the Step Clan were expected to mate for life and were normally monogamous. Exceptions to monogamy occasionally occurred when a clansman died leaving a wife without a mate. A kinsman might assume another female at his fire for the good of the clan.

Many other southern clans did not practice monogamy; thus, patterning their traditions after the red deer, or Irish elk. Cannibalistic tribes were never monogamous and often did not recognize a family structure. Northern tribes that were not cannibals were more often than not monogamous and mated for life.

Krumen had been watching Kardi closely and listening to the counsel of his woman. His woman was called Kropin, since she controlled the clan's fishing enterprise. Kropin counseled Krumen that Kardi was not ready for a man; but that when she was ready, he should give her to Minar.

On that fateful day when Kardi had become separated from the clan, she was still a virgin. Her mother had just been killed by an unidentified animal and Kardi was given the task of helping to care for the clan toddlers. Mardi was one of the clan women who normally worked at the fishing task. Mardi had been given her name due to a silver streak in her hair, which had developed due to a childhood head injury. The name meant lightning in the Step Clan language.

Mardi had been ordered by Kropin to go to the river and fish; however, it was raining and she did not want to perform this task. She sought out Kardi and after administering a cuffing on her head and her ears, she told Kardi to go to the river to fish and not to return until she had at least five fish. Mardi said that she would watch the toddlers in Kardi's place.

Kardi was afraid of the woman and had no mother to protect her; so, she set off to do as she was told. It was in the early fall and raining much of the time. She first caught several insects to use on the bone hooks and then sat down on the bank and threw the line into the water. She did this for over an hour with no luck. She decided to move to a different spot further down the river. She continued to move down river looking for a spot where the fish would bite; but had no luck.

As the day began to approach night, she realized that she had wandered too far down river and became concerned about being alone and started to run back up the river toward the clan camp. All of a sudden, there was a man, the like of which she had never seen before, standing in the trail blocking her path. He was not the same kind of man as the

64

clansmen that she knew. He was very tall with very light hair and a lighter complexion. He examined her body closely; his eyes settling on her well-developed hips.

His look sent shivers up her spine, which she did not understand. She became afraid and as she started to yell for help, he quickly stepped toward her and knocked her unconscious with a sharp blow to the chin.

Kardi did not know it; but the man easily picked her up and placed her across his shoulders. He crossed the river at a point where it was no deeper than his chest and started trotting through the woods toward the hills north of the river. The man saw the approaching rain clouds and angled his trot northwest toward one of the closest hills, which he knew to be filled with caves and grottos. After he had been traveling for about a half hour, the rain started and came down very hard. Within minutes after the rain started, the man changed the direction of his travel to the northeast, angling toward a smaller hill further away and more distant from the river that he had crossed.

As they travelled toward the small hill, Kardi began to awaken and realized her plight. She started to struggle and the man stopped and placed her on the ground in front of him. He gestured that she should not make sounds and she should follow him. With gestures he made her understand that he would use his spear on her, if she did not do as he instructed. He entered a stream and motioned for her to do the same. They travelled east along the stream bed until they were directly south of the smaller hill, which was his ultimate destination. By the time that they had arrived at this point, the water in the stream had risen to chest level. He exited the stream bed and Kardi followed, examining the man, as he swiftly walked in front of her.

The man wore only a short robe which ended midway down his thighs. The robe was held closed by a belt of deer skin around his waist. Kardi saw that attached to the belt were two pouches and a flint cutting stone with a wooden handle.

Across his back, the man carried a pouch containing a spear- thrower and five thin spears about three feet long. There was a hollow feeling in the pit of Kardi's stomach which she had never experience before.

For some reason she did not fear the man. He gestured for her to follow him and she did so with little consternation. He started to trot as the Step Clan often did and as she trotted after him. The man grunted his approval that she could maintain his pace.

Their path continued to the north through heavily a wooded valley toward the smaller hill which was to the northeast of the Step Clan camp. Kardi could see that they were headed toward some low cliffs near a second, but smaller river. The Step Clan had once hunted this area, but not in a long time. Kardi remembered the women getting fish from this small river.

As the two runners arrived at the base of the cliffs, the man stopped and rolled a large boulder to the right behind a clump of bushes. The boulder had hidden an opening to a small grotto which was about twelve yards deep and six yards wide. The opening was only about three feet wide and three feet tall. As they entered the grotto and Kardi's eyes adjusted to the poor light, she saw that there was a small pool of water at the back of the grotto. The man had a pre-prepared fire circle near the right grotto wall. Kardi saw that any smoke from the fire would exit the grotto through a crack along the top of that wall.

Kardi could not know it; but the man had chosen this grotto because ultimately, the smoke would exit the cliffs at the top and be dispersed by a large grove of pine trees and brush on top of the cliff that surrounded the crack's exit. This would make it difficult for anyone to pin-point the location of their fire, should they smell the smoke. The man started a small fire in the fire circle using very dry wood which he took from a large pile he had placed in the cave. Kardi noticed that he used the same method that the Step Clan used to start fires. The man returned to the grotto entrance and rolled the stone back in front of the grotto, effectively closing the grotto entrance to any escape Kardi might contemplate, assuming that she was not strong enough to move the large rock. Kardi was deceptively strong; but she was unsure if she could move the rock.

The man motioned for her to sit by the fire and she complied immediately. He withdrew six fish from one of his pouches and pitched them to her. It was obvious that he wanted her to prepare them for a meal. Kardi reached into her pouch and withdrew a piece of flint that she used for cutting.

Deftly, she cleaned and scaled the fish. She soaked two twigs in the water at the back of the grotto for about five minutes; then skewered three fish on each twig. From her pouch she removed a few sprigs of a plant that smelled like sage and stuffed the sprigs inside of the fish. The fire had burned down to a low flame and hot coals. Kardi placed the twigs across the surface of the circular fire pit balancing each end of the twigs on rocks that had been placed there for that purpose.

As the man waited for the fish to cook, he motioned for Kardi to come to him. She nervously approached him, her face and eyes tilted toward the ground. This was the typical demeanor of a Step Clan woman summoned to a man. Upon arrival in front of the man, she kneeled and placed her head only inches above the ground in front of him, as she had seen other clan women do many times.

The man looked annoyed and used words she did not

understand, while motioning for her to stand up. He stood in front of her and showed through his gestures that she should stand tall and proud. He motioned to the spot where she had been kneeling and used a dismissal gesture to indicate that she should not kneel.

He then motioned for her to sit and said the word, "kof." Kof was obviously his word for sit. Kardi sat down in front of him.

The man motioned toward himself, touching his chest and saying the word, "Carni." And then he touched her chest with his index finger. She understood that the man's name was Carni; so, she responded by touching her chest and saying "Kardi." The man smiled; he had known her name since he had heard other women call her name, as he had spied upon the clan. He was enjoying being able to communicate with her.

Kardi moved back to the fire and turned the fish to prevent burning on the side nearest to the fire. Again, the man smiled. Kardi did not know why; but when he smiled, she felt very warm inside and smiled back at him.

Kardi wanted to communicate with the man. Slowly, she pointed to herself and used gestures to indicate all around her and held up many fingers while saying the name of her clan, "Step."

The man understood and using the same gestures said, "Nord."

Kardi wanted to know what his name, Carni, meant so she said her name, "Kardi," while gesturing away from the body.

The man looked puzzled. Kardi pointed to her chest again and repeated her name with the lost gesture. The man's face lit up and he understood. Kardi then pointed to Carni and said his name with a gesture of palms up.

Carni said, "Carni!" and made a growl like a bear. So, Kardi thought, carni must be their word for cave bear.

Kardi asked, "Carni hada?" While making a gesture with two fingers pointing downward? Hada was the Step Clan word for woman.

Apparently, this was a universal sign for Carni understood. He smiled and made the dismissing gesture and continued with a gesture outward sweeping his arm around and said, "Wontu."

Kardi thought he meant that he was a wanderer, or traveler.

Carni's eyes turned inward as he remembered his selection as a wontu.

It was impossible for Kardi to understand why Carni was a wanderer. In the Nord Clan certain men were selected as "Clan Guides," referred to in the Nord Clan language as wontu. The senior guide served the clan as a sort of medicine man and was referred to as "wonto." There was only one guide allowed to remain in the clan at one time. He was the "Wonto."

About every ten years, the clan chose four young men to become guides and sent them out alone to explore the world in all four directions and bring back magic and knowledge that the clan could use. One guide was sent in each direction, north, south, east and west. It was an honor to be chosen; however, it was a very dangerous undertaking. The wontus must wander the world in their assigned direction for at least one year before returning in order to be considered successful. If a wontu returned before the one-year period was complete, he was cast out of the clan, or given the life of a hunter's helper, which was normally the roll of an inexperienced young man. When a wontu returned after the one-year period, he placed the knowledge that he had gained during his travels before the clan and, if deemed acceptable, he could be chosen as the new Wonto. The old Wonto would become the Clan leader's counselor, if still alive. If the wontu was not chosen as the new Wonto, he would be sent out for an additional one year of exploration, normally in a direction from which a wontu had not returned.

Becoming a wontu was so dangerous that many men did not return to the clan. The current Wonto had been the only wontu to return twenty years earlier. He had returned with tales that astounded to Nord Clan. He had brought knowledge from the east, which included the use of the spear thrower and tales of having seen men who ran with wolves and who captured and held wild animals for use in carrying their supplies.

Ten years earlier none of the four wontu that were sent out had returned to the clan from their travels. This was considered a bad omen for the clan. The leader of the Nord Clan had declared that if a wontu did not return from this current group that would be sent out, the clan might cease to exist. All members of the Nord Clan had offered themselves as a sacrifice to help this crop of wontu. It became the most important event in the recent Nord Clan history that the wontu sent out this time be successful.

When Carni was chosen as a wontu, he was ecstatic. There was no higher honor given to any man in the clan. This was his chance to save the Nord Clan. The leader of the clan was usually selected by the old leader; but all leaders were obliged to follow the guidance of the Wonto. The current Wonto was old and a new Wonto was needed quickly. Without a Wonto, the Nord Clan believed that they would suffer unbearable calamities.

After his selection had been announced, along with the other three wontu, in a midnight ceremony, Carni was prepared for his departure in accordance with the Wonto's instruction. He cleansed his body in a sweat lodge and cold bath. Women applied oils to his skin to ward off evil. He would travel light, wearing a deerskin tunic, wolf-hide trousers and a short bear-skin robe. He would carry spears for throwing, a spear-thrower, a thrusting spear, cutting flints and fire-making equipment.

The four selected wontu spent thirty days and nights with the Wonto receiving training in what to expect during their journeys, how to confront problems and the type of information the clan would be interested in obtaining. The clan was interested in new weapons, new food sources, new techniques, other clans' customs and characteristics and descriptions of the lands through which they passed. But just as important, each wontu was instructed that he should mate with a female in the clans of the lands through which he passed in order to spread the seed of the Nord Clan in all directions, thus purifying the blood of foreign clans throughout the known world. The Wonto indicated that the mating was to be only that and nothing more. The wontu must not take a mate; but must only spread the Nord Clan seed to other clans. The Nord Clan considered the blood of many other clans to be inferior and females from these clans were only maintained as slaves.

The Wonto dispatched Carni to the south. The land to the south was more unknown to the Nord Clan than lands to the north, east and west. No wontu had ever returned from his travels to the southern lands. To the south, the land was fertile, as it rose toward the mountains. The giant mountain range could not be seen from Nord Clan lands; but was a part of the verbal history that the Nord Clan elders passed on to their young. There were many large rivers to cross and many clans that would not welcome a strange human from the north. The Wonto warned Carni of the southern clans, who were little better than animals in the Nord Clan's eyes. He also told him that many of the clans to the south were probably cannibals.

On the morning following the final day of their training, with the entire clan watching, the wontu took off at a run in all four directions. Carni ran for about an hour before slowing to a trot and continuing to travel until about two hours before dark. He then stopped to seek shelter, to make camp and to plan the initial phase of his journey.

He found shelter in a small grove of trees slightly offset from the forest. A stream passed through the grove and Carni selected a tree-blow-down for his camp site, where he could be approached from only one side. Two trees had been blown down on top of one another forming a virtual cavern of limbs. Carni sniffed the air from the tree-cavern and smelled the pungent odor of a "ponk," or wild pig. Ponk could be very dangerous and were known to have killed and even eaten members of the Nord Clan. He decided to enter the ponk lair with his thrusting spear at ready. This would be his first test as a wontu. Would this be a good omen for his travels?

As he crouched and stepped into the lair, he heard a loud snort and the sounds of the ponk charging. He could see little in the darkness of the lair. He controlled his desire to flee and crouched low onto one knee. With the thrusting spear in front of him with the point just below waist level, he jammed the butt of the spear into the ground. He saw the ponk as it saw him and he braced to receive the attack. The ponk lowered its head and charged Carni, tusks prepared to rip into the intruder with a toss of its head. The point of the thrusting spear buried itself deeply into the ponk's chest, the ponk being unable to halt its momentum. A terrific snort and squeal followed before the ponk fell on its side, thrashing about. Carni drew a throwing spear and drove the spear into the ponk's body, just behind its left front leg. The ponk's struggle slowed and then stopped, as it died.

He could see that the ponk was about to produce a litter

and knew that these piglets would make a good meal. The ponk weighed about 150 pounds; so, Carni pulled the animal from the tree-cavern entrance to the small stream running through the grove of trees. Before dressing the ponk, he built large fire near the body to help keep away other predators. He took his cutting flints from his pouch and deftly dressed the ponk, setting aside the unborn piglets for separate attention. He decided to prepare some of the meat for travel and prepare the piglets to eat this evening and tomorrow. He would leave the remainder as an offer of friendship to the scavengers and other meat-eaters.

Carni was torn from his memory by Kardi's voice. With gestures that were becoming routine, Kardi tried to ask why Carni had taken her from her clan. What did he intend for her?

Carni immediately understood the essence of her query. His knowledge of universal gestures was insufficient to explain that he was a strong spear hunter, brave and a wontu. That he had been stalking the Step Clan since they had started their travels toward the mountains in the early summer and that he had chosen her as the best female in the clan. He needed to use her to accomplish one of his primary tasks as a wontu, to spread the Nord Clan seed to the southern clans before his ultimate return to the Nord Clan. So, since he could not explain himself clearly, he simply gestured to her that he intended that they would mate.

CHAPTER 7

THE MATING

W hen Carni informed her that he and she would mate, Kardi was somewhat surprised; but for some reason, she was not fearful. She had seen men and women mating many times in the Step Clan and knew that it was her destiny. When she had seen others in the Step Clan mate, they both seemed to enjoy it. For some time now, when she had seen two people mating, she had become excited and anxious at the same time. The Step Clan tradition required an observer to avert their eyes, when mating occurred in their presence.

Now that the time for her first mating had arrived, she excitedly looked forward to it, even though the man was not of the Step Clan. When she looked at Carni, she felt weak and excited at the same time. She cast her eyes toward the ground, as she had seen other Step Clan women do; but then she remembered that Carni had expressed anger at that reaction and she quickly looked up and directly into his eyes. A shiver ran down her spine.

Carni smiled at her and slowly rose; stirred the fire and added wood, before reaching for her arm and pulling her to her feet. Standing in front of the fire, he examined her entire body starting with her hair. Kardi shivered under his gaze. Kardi's hair was long and thick with a shiny black hue. His fingers ran through her hair and grasped handfuls, as he pulled her closer to him. He played with her hair, running it through his fingers and slowly massaging her head with his right hand, as his left hand stroked her breasts.

Kardi was of normal height for a Step Clan woman, reaching about 5 feet, 2 inches at full maturity, which for southern clan women was about fourteen years old. Step Clan women typically were awarded to a man by the time they were fourteen. Although she was ready to receive a man and she felt the normal female urges of a young and vibrant woman, Step Clan custom had prevented her from experiencing a mating until the Clan leader declared that she was ready.

Carni was a very tall man, a little over six feet two inches in height. Members of the Nord Clan were a class of people referred to as "The Tall Ones" by other clans. Typically, the Nord Clan men were at least six inches taller that their Step Clan adversaries. Kardi looked at Carni in awe as he picked her up with his hands beneath her shoulders. She seemed to be no heavier that a stick of wood to Carni. He carried her to his sleeping mat in the left rear of the grotto.

The sleeping area was a mat of pine boughs covered by a conk skin. Before laying her down on the mat, Carni lifted her to his face and looked deeply into her eyes. Kardi felt as if his eyes reached down through her body to her womanhood; her excitement mounted, almost beyond containment. Her hands reached for his face and stroked is fine reddish beard. His beard was not dark and course like the Step Clan men and it felt smooth to her touch and she grabbed handfuls of it in her hands. He drew her further to his face and touched his mouth to hers; his tongue lancing into her mouth with the surprise of a frontal attack. Step Clan couples did not kiss and Kardi's excitement became frenzied. The closest that Step Clan couples came to exchanging a kiss was to nuzzle each other with their noses.

As Carni and Kardi held the kiss, it became stronger, feeding her excitement like dry wood to a fire. Clan women wore no garments under the robe of deer hide. As they kissed, he held her to him with his left hand, Carni deftly reached her womanhood with his right hand, his fingers entering her forcefully. Kardi felt a sharp pain and at the same time an uncontrollable desire. Her legs clamped onto his hand, as he lifted her and laid her down on the pine bough mat.

Kardi was no longer in control of her actions; she was completely submissive to his will. He ripped off her robe, as his eyes devoured her body. Then slowly he lowered himself onto her; his mouth seizing hers in another fiery kiss before his manhood entered her body, forcing its way to its limits, as she violently began to undulate. His strokes increased in their tempo developing a rhythm that matched hers as his breathing became steady, as if he were locked in a steady run.

As the speed of the two lovers' gyrations increased, they experienced a simultaneous climax, Kardi screaming and collapsing beneath him. Both partners lay on the pine bough mat, breathing deeply and enjoying the aftermath of a very satisfying experience.

Carni stroked her hair and nuzzled her ear. "This is a fine woman," thought Carni. "If she were Nord Clan, I could keep her," his thoughts continued.

Eventually, Carni rolled off of Kardi and reached for her robe; covering her, as he held her close to him. Kardi was bewildered at the depth of her feelings and she clung to him, as that both fell asleep. The only sound in the cave was the crackle of the fire.

Carni dreamed about his experiences before he had stolen Kardi from the Step Clan.

CHAPTER 8

CARNI THE WONTU

(Carni dreams.)

Carni dreamed about the year that he had spent as a wontu. The Wonto had told him of the dangers of becoming too attached to the women who were destined to become vessels for the Nord Clan seed. He had explained that if he were to bring a southern clan woman back to the Nord Clan, the woman would be sacrificed in order to prevent bad fortune from falling on the clan. The Wonto had insisted that the success of his journey as a wontu depended upon the woman returning to her clan with the seed of the Nord Clan in her. The Wonto had shared the Nord Clan's strategy concerning other clans with each of the wontu.

The Nord Clan, as with other clans, had recently experienced some very lean years during which the reindeer herds had become smaller and other game had become extremely difficult to find. The weather had been extraordinarily cold and the snow heavy. The Nord Clan had been forced to compete with other clans for the few reindeer that were available to satisfy the hunger that the entire clan experienced. Many of the young and the very old died. The southern clans had been their greatest source of competition, since their diet consisted primarily of meat and the only prey available was the reindeer. The Nord Clan, as with the other northern clans, had begun a period in which they attacked the southern clans at every opportunity in order to take these clans reindeer kills and also to reduce the amount of competition for this precious resource.

The Wonto had also convinced the Nord Clan leader that the southern clans were inferior to the Nord Clan and that the Nord Clan should plant its seed in the southern clan women in order to spread the Nord Clan descendants all over the land.

During his first night alone in the tree-blow-down lair, Carni had prepared the piglets for eating by digging a shallow pit near his fire, lining it with hot coals and a layer of rocks and placing the piglets on the rocks before covering them with a layer of wet, green grass and another layer of rocks. He then covered the rocks with hot coals from the fire. He added more hot coals after a few minutes.

He had also taken a hindquarter and the loin from the ponk. He hung these pieces of ponk over the fire to allow them to slowly cook throughout the night. He took the thrusting spear that he had used to kill the ponk and cleaned the flint point, checking to ensure that it had maintained its edge. He saw that one edge must have struck a bone and was no longer sharp. He took out the bone tool that he used to break off chips of flint to make it sharp and resurfaced the spearhead. He then opened the pit where the piglets had been cooking and recovered one with a sharp stick. They were completely cooked to the point that they melted in his mouth. He ate two of the five piglets and placed the other three on a flat rock near the fire. He knew that they would dry some and he would eat those tomorrow. Before he went to sleep, he made sure that the fire had enough wood on it for a couple of hours. Habitually, he slept at two-hour intervals, awakening and checking the area for danger and replenishing the wood on the fire. He slept in the lair with the fire at the entrance to the lair, his thrusting spear in his right hand. During the night he heard the sounds of meat-eaters. He also could smell them. These particular meat-eaters were the spotted hyenas that would steal your meat or kill and eat you with equal ease.

Several times they tried to find a way into the lair on the side away from the fire, but there was no other entrance and they soon departed in search of easier prey.

When he awakened just at dawn, he checked the fire and added more wood. The piglets had hardened on the hot flat rock near the fire and the hindquarter and loin of the ponk were cooked through and should last a few days before spoiling. He took one of the piglets and ate it. He placed the other two piglets and the hindquarter and loin in a deerskin that he intended to use as a pack and tied the deerskin around them. He cut six flexible pine boughs into three-foot lengths and fashioned them into a frame to hold his pack of ponk meat. He tied the pack to the frame and hefted to his back to see if he could carry it comfortably. It seemed okay; he was ready to continue his journey as a wontu. He headed south toward the great mountain range that he had heard so much about from the Wonto; but had never seen.

He knew that a man alone in this inhospitable environment would likely face many dangers that would consume most men. The Wonto had told him that his survival would depend upon him being constantly alert and ready to battle, as well as depending upon his ability to out-think his adversaries. So, as he travelled, he carried his thrusting spear at the ready position.

He did not travel at a trot, as he was normally prone to do, since the smell of meat was with him and would probably attract meat-eaters. He was more careful in his travels now; he was alone and would have to face all dangers alone. He would need as much advanced notice of danger as possible. He travelled cautiously, often checking his back trail and making sudden turns to the right, or left so that his direction of travel could not be easily predicted. He constantly smelled the wind and changed course often in order to smell and visually examine his back trail.

He had decided that he would travel south for two months in a zigzag pattern, which he measured as new moons, before he would approach other humans.

The first two months were spent traveling, hunting and exploring alone. He made mental maps of the areas through which he passed and noted the presence of game animals, possible caves that were fit for a clan and the presence of meat- eaters. When he had seen signs of other clans, he had avoided any contact with them. He had been able to find and kill other ponks, which seemed to be plentiful in this area. Toward the end of the two-month period, he could see rain clouds coming from the direction of the hills to the south. He had come to a wide river and decided that it would be wise to cross the river before the high water from the rain arrived. If he waited too long, the river would be difficult to ford, until the flood waters receded. The river was about one hundred feet wide and he found a place where animal tracks indicated that they had often crossed. He saw reindeer (conkut) and red deer (conk) tracks in abundance, followed by the ever-present meat-eaters, mostly large wolves, hyenas and giant cats. He knew that the river must be fordable here, since it was place where animals crossed. He tied his weapons to the backpack and laced the backpack sinews tightly, so as not to lose them in the crossing. He entered the river quickly with an eye toward the approaching rain. The water was very cold and his advance across the river was slowed due to the strong current.

The flash flood caught him when he was in chest high water in the middle of the river and swept him off of his feet. At first the backpack buoyed him in the water, as he tried to swim. He didn't fight the current, simply staying afloat on top of the water, as it swept him southwest. Time passed and he started tiring, as the backpack had become soaked with water. He considering letting his backpack go when the spirits-in-the-fire sent him something which would save his life. Coming toward him in the current, he saw a large tree that the flood had uprooted. He swam toward it with all of his strength and, just before it shot past him, he was able to grab a protruding branch and hang on. Slowly he improved his hold on the tree until he was able to get both arms over the top of a limb, which was just on the surface of the water. Luckily the tree was not rolling and he was able to maintain his hold.

He floated with the tree for what seemed like an eternity; but was probably only an hour or so. The tree finally stopped with a sudden jar and became caught on a sand bar, allowing him to escape the current and struggle to dry land on the south bank of the river.

He was tired and cold and decided to make camp, dry-off and warm up. First, he looked around and smelled the air for danger. He saw nothing; but caught the faint odor of horse. The wind was from the west; so, the horses must be in that direction. There was another odor mingled with the horse scent that he could not quite identify. He decided to forget the horses for now and find a campsite. He had landed on the side of the river where the forest was thick. Farther east up the river on the south side there was a series of cliffs that might be hiding a possible secure campsite. He headed in that direction.

His leather foot wraps were filled with water and he paused to remove the water. He removed the insulating grass from the leather foot wraps, which was now soggy and replaced the grass in the wraps and laced them over his calves. He knew that as the leather wraps dried, they would mold to his feet and be more comfortable. He again started for the cliffs, this time at a slow trot. He still had his back pack filled with ponk meat; so, he would not need to hunt right away.

When he arrived at the base of the cliffs, he could see that the river had carved out a path around the base of a high rock outcrop, creating a series of three cliffs about a hundred yards high. He examined the base of the cliffs to see if there was a ledge that he could use to scale the cliff face. There were several ledges that had been created over time by fissures in the rock aided by ice and water erosion. He examined the cliff face. He saw two possibilities for caves; one was half way up the middle cliffs face with a couple of ledges, which could be used to gain access to the cave entrance. He decided to try that one and headed for the first ledge that appeared to lead to the cave. He had to walk through a small, but roaring stream to get to the base of the ledge. After clearing the water from his leather bindings again, he started up the ledge. The ledge was about one yard wide at the beginning, but narrowed to about two feet wide running east to west across the face of the cliff. Another ledge intersected with it and continued up in a west to east direction. At one point the second ledge temporarily narrowed to about one and a half feet wide. Carefully he ascended the ledges until he was in front of an entrance about three four feet tall and four feet wide into the face of the cliff.

He crouched down in the entrance and sniffed the air as his eyes adjusted to the limited light in the cave. He did not smell any recent animal presence in the cave. There was only a musty smell, associated with dampness. With his thrusting spear at the ready, he entered the cave. His eyes had adjusted to the darkness and he could see that the cave would be a fine place to stop. It ran deep into the cliff; but there was a widened portion about ten feet wide at the entrance. There was water dripping down the back wall and a place where previous humans had built a fire pit near the entrance. The humans could not have been of the Nord Clan; since the fire pit did not have rocks placed in the four sacred directions of the world.

He quickly set about preparing a fire. He was shivering from the cold. He placed a round rock in each of the four directions around the outer edges of his fire pit. Then used flat rocks to build a wall on two sides of the fire pit to hold meat skewers and allow him to cook. He went back down the ledges to gather wood. He made four trips until he was sure that he had plenty of wood. Just as he returned to the cave from his last trip for wood, the rain arrived with crashes of thunder and lightning and gusting wind.

He took out his flint striking stone and fire rock and lay them near the fire pit. The bird nest that he carried for kindling was wet from the river crossing; so, he couldn't use that to start a fire. He looked around the cave. He found an old nest of some kind of rodent and took that to the fire pit.

It was very dry and worked perfectly when he used it to catch the sparks from the fire striker. Before striking the fire stones, he threw dust from the fire pit in all four directions. The Nord Clan believed that bad omens arrived from all four directions; but that the spirits-in-the-fire would protect the clan, if they were sufficiently respectful of them. In no time he had the fire burning brightly. He laid out his soaked skins and pouch contents to dry by the fire.

He had laid a spear-size piece of wood outside of the cave entrance on the ledge to soak in the rainwater and now used it to skewer the ponk meat from his backpack. Using the piles of flat rocks as support, he hung some cooked ponk meat high over the fire, so that it would keep and he could cut pieces of it to eat when he wanted.

It was raining very hard outside; but he was dry in the cave. The trickle of water at the back of the cave was now a steady stream of water flowing down the back wall and out a crack in the cave floor. He was starting to suffer from the cold; since he was still wet and he lay down as close to the fire as he could stand and drifted off to sleep.

When he awoke during the night the rain had passed and he was no longer wet and cold. He replenished the wood on the fire and slept until daylight.

Carni decided that he would use this cave as his camp for

a few days, while he explored the area around it. He was significantly further west than he had intended; but it really made no difference since his direction of travel was south and it was unimportant if he drifted east, or west.

He grabbed his thrusting spear and descended the ledges until he was in a position where he could see the hills. He knew that the hills protected the great mountain range to the south. He had been aiming at a break between two hills far in the distance; but he could tell that the river had taken him much further west and he could not see the break that had been his destination. After carefully examining the hills in the distance, he chose a new destination, which was another break between two hills that seemed broader than the previous one. He thought that he could see the mountains through that gap; but was unsure, since it could be just a bank of clouds.

He looked around close to the cliffs and found clumps of dead grass that he could use to replenish the insulation for his footgear. He pulled a large amount and carried it to the cave. He laid it near the fire to dry. With his cutting flint he cut a large piece of ponk loin and ate it, tearing off chunks with his strong teeth. He decided that he would begin his explorations of this area tomorrow. He made several trips to replenish his wood supply and then lay out his dried robe and went to sleep.

Carni's explorations of this area revealed that other clans had passed through while following migrating game; but none recently. He found campsites where fire pits had been made and entire clans had camped for several days. He knew that they were entire clans since he found the tracks of women and children. Often, he had seen tracks of hunting parties with few women and no children accompanying them. The Wonto had said that many of the clans were cannibals and that he would be able to recognize the cannibalistic clans by the bones they left in their fires. The Wonto had said that the cannibals could not be approached and that he should not plant the Nord Clan seed in their females.

Although the scavengers had eaten most of the bones left by the clans at these campsites, he found remnants of burned bones that he judged to be conkut bones and at least one ponk. The conkut were headed north and the clans and other meat- eaters were following them. Carni judged that to mean that these clans came from the area toward which he had set as his current destination.

His additional explorations of this area did not reveal anything of note. After consuming the ponk meat, he was able to surprise a conk and killed it with his throwing spear. He had cleaned, staked and scraped the new conk hide so that it was free of fat and would cure for long use. He intended to use it as a ground cover for sleeping.

As he passed time in the cave camp, he came to understand the weather in this area. The frequent thunderstorms arrived from the west and often stalled before entering the hills and possibly mountain range, dumping more than the average amount of rain on the area. He realized that this amount of rain would support vast plant growth attracting plant eaters. A clan could do very well in this area, he thought. He made mental notes of the area to pass along to the Nord Clan upon his return.

The days passed rapidly until two more moons had passed and the warm weather had taken hold. It was time for him to continue his southward journey.

CHAPTER 9

THE WONTU MAKES CONTACT WITH HIS FIRST CLAN

(Carni's dreams continue)

C arni dreamed of the time that he had prepared for his travels by killing another ponk and cooking its meat slowly until it was very dry. He had laced his conk-skin pack tightly to the pack frame containing the meat and his conk-skin ground cover and made sure that the pack could be carried comfortably. Using his cutting flint, he cut his large bear-skin robe so that; it was now only waist long.

His weapons were in good repair and ready for use. He would again travel with his thrusting spear at ready and his throwing spears carried in a pouch across his back. Just after daylight he descended the ledges from his cave and renewed his journey to the south.

He traveled at a slow trot, since he was still in the area that he had already explored while living in the cave and he knew of no impending danger, at least for a while. As he trotted, he maintained his previously developed method of travel, making sudden turns to check his back trail. During his first day of travel, he neither saw, heard, nor smelled the presence of any followers, or any danger. Occasionally, he caught a faint odor of meat-eaters, cats and wolves mostly; but it was too faint to cause him concern.

The area that he was crossing became wetter, where the forest consisted of very large trees surrounded by thick undergrowth. He suspected that there would be conk in this area and, if there were conk, there may be clans that hunted them. Because of the thick undergrowth, he was forced to travel on the existing game trails that animals had cut through the forest by centuries of movement to better feeding grounds and sources of water. He slowed his travel to a fast walk and became more watchful and more aware of his surroundings. At the slightest sound, or faintest odor, he stopped and listened, or smelled the wind to ensure that there was no danger.

He was now sure that he could see mountains to the south that gave the impression of a dark bank of clouds. Periodically, he stopped to look in that direction and to wonder what those mountains might be hiding.

He was on the sixth day of his journey when he made his discovery. As he was approaching a mid-sized river that ran from the direction of the mountains toward the northwest, he saw fresh indication of the passage of humans. On the north side of a large tree truck, there was a type of moss growing which he had seen a few times before; but only in this area. The moss was in a blooming stage and appeared to be a very light green color. What was different about this particular patch of moss was that humans had harvested some of it. He was certain that humans had taken this moss because he could see the tracks made by human fingers, as they stripped the moss from the tree trunk. He searched the ground around the tree where the moss had been harvested and found the tracks of a female. The tracks were recent, since the grass had not yet started to recover from the weight of the foot that made the track. He decided that the female had made the track on that very morning.

He decided to follow the female's tracks and see where they led. The tracks led further into the forest, where the female had stopped to gather mushrooms, which were a type that Carni did not recognize. He picked a small one and tasted it, spitting it out immediately. These were not edible mushrooms, he thought.

After gathering the mushrooms, the female had turned toward the river and was joined by another female who came from deeper in the forest. He closely examined the footprints of the two females. The one that had gathered the moss had a larger foot with a scar on the right heel. He judged this female to be older by the rough nature of her footprint. The second female had a smaller, smoother footprint and was probably a young woman. The younger woman had picked some berries. He had found a dark purple berry near the spot where her path intersected with the older woman's path. He could smell the women's odor mingled with the odor of the fresh berries. They had passed here recently and could not be far away.

The two women had turned and walked directly toward the river. As he followed their trail, he came to a point where they had stopped and turned back toward the forest, as if to listen, or look at their back-trail. They had started to run toward the river and Carni surmised that they were running from something in the forest.

As he followed the trail, the footprints of two men were implanted on top of the female's prints. He could tell that the men were also running after the females, because their prints showed only the balls of the feet and the toes with very little heel impression. After following the trail for about three hundred yards, he came to a clearing in the forest where there had been a struggle. He found very little blood; so, it did not appear that anyone had died in the encounter.

From the tracks he surmised that the two females had been ambushed by an additional three males and that the five men had attacked and captured the females. The group had departed the area of the ambush headed back away from the river and into the forest. The females were walking; so, they had not been harmed significantly.

The tracks led in a northeast direction and entered into a small stream. Carni found it difficult to locate the tracks after they had entered the stream. Apparently, the men were trying to cover their trail, if men from the female's clan should attempt to follow them. Carni was unable to find the point where the party had left the stream; although he had searched both banks up and down stream for several hundred yards. He stopped to contemplate what to do next.

He thought that if he were one of these men, he would exit on the side of the stream away from the direction of the clan from which the females came. He would exit on a rocky surface leaving no tracks and proceed in a direction at an angle from their desired route of travel. He would also want to check his back-trail to see if he was being followed.

Their initial direction had been to the northeast; so, Carni thought that was probably their desired route of travel. The wind was from the west so he surmised that they would make sudden turns to the north to check their back-trail. He decided to travel directly north until he was well north of what he thought would be their direction of travel. The wind would not carry his sent to the men and he might get an opportunity to see, or smell them, as they veered north to check their back- trail.

He traveled north at a trot for about an hour; then slowed his pace and turned northeast. He was very alert for the presence of the group that should be traveling more or less parallel to him. Occasionally, he stopped and turned into the wind, trying to get the smell of the group. He traveled in this manner for about two hours until he came to a long ridge that ran directly northeast as far as he could see in that direction.

As he exited the valley northwest of the ridge, he noticed that the wind was now blowing from the southwest and if he traveled along the ridge, he could continuously check for the group's scent. He varied his direction of travel to just below the top of the ridge and periodically looked over the ridge to the southeast and smelled the wind.

After following the ridge for about two hours, he paused to check the wind and smelled the distinct odor of men.

Carni's sense of smell was so good that he could tell that the odor was the same as the odor of the men's tracks that he had previously followed. He lay down behind the top of the ridge and carefully looked in the direction of the wind. Before his eyes lay a beautiful valley with a large river running through it; but he saw no one. He did catch the scent of an animal, a ronk (horse) he thought. He searched the direction that the wind was coming from; but saw no ronk. Just as he was about to change his position and move to the southeast side of the ridge, he heard a sound. It was some sort of call; he got the impression that someone was announcing their presence to a camped group; but there was no return call that he expected to hear. Then the small group came into sight; as they exited the trees and walked toward the river. They did not seem to show any cause for concern. He guessed that the men believed that the female's clan could not have followed them and that they were safe.

As he had suspected, there were five men and the two women. The two women looked tired and dejected. It was obvious that they were captives. The older female looked as if she had put up a fight; there was blood on her face and possibly her nose had been broken. The men had an olive complexion and dark black hair. They seemed to have something attached to their noses; possibly they had a bone pierced through their noses. He had seen this before, as he had watched a southern clan from hiding. As the group moved toward the river and away from the ridge where Carni was laying, Carni decided to circle to get in front of them, so that if the opportunity offered itself, he could ambush them. He moved swiftly through the trees that covered the side of the valley up to the ridge where he had been traveling. Just as he was about to try for a run across an open space toward the river, he smelled the stale smell of a spent fire. It was not a fresh smell; but there had been a fire here within the last couple of days. He crawled slowly toward the river until he came to the edge of a clearing where the group had stopped.

It was an old campsite with a large fire pit that still contained smoldering embers below the ashes. Apparently, the men's clan had been camped here and had moved, probably yesterday. They would not be far away; so, if Carni was going to take the women, he knew he would have to act fast. It was almost dark and the men started gathering wood to start a fire. It was obvious that they did not intend to follow their clan until tomorrow. Traveling at night could be very dangerous, even for a small group such as theirs. Carni decided that he would make his move after many of the men were asleep.

The men had eaten food that they carried with them and had not bothered to give their captives a meal. After eating, a large man, who was the apparent leader of the group, pushed a smaller man to a sitting position. It was obvious that the large man was telling the small man to stay awake and stand guard. The large man took the younger female's arm and hair and dragged her to his robe beside the fire. The other three men appeared to argue over who would get the older female and the argument soon came to shoves and blows. Finally, the large man jumped up and cuffed them all. He then pulled the older female toward his robe as well and had her sit on the ground near him. He returned to the young female, who was now sitting fearfully on his robe.

The other three gave up and accepted the fact that they would not get a woman and went to sleep. After the large man had his way with the young female, he tied the two females back-to-back and went to sleep. It was only a few minutes until the small man, who was standing guard, also fell asleep.

There was a new moon; so, there was not very much light to illuminate the camp, as Carni approached. He had used the cover of the trees to hide his approach, just in case one of the men awakened. He approached the camp with a throwing spear in the thrower. He had another two spears in his left hand. He hoped to get off three spears, before they could react.

He noticed that the old woman was awake. She made no sound, only looked directly at him, as he approached the group. Apparently, she awakened the young female, who also watched him, as he approached the group around the fire.

For his first target, he chose the small man who should have been standing guard. He threw his first spear; it hit the small man in the solar plexus and he grunted; but did not cry out. He quickly placed another spear in his thrower. He aimed that one at the large man who was the nearest one to the women. The spear entered his back and the point exited his chest. He let out a loud roar, not unlike that of a wounded cave-bear.

The other three men were quickly coming awake. His third spear caught the man closest to him in the throat. He would be dead in no time. The remaining two men charged him with their thrusting spears. He parried the first man's spear with his own thrusting spear and hit him in the jaw with the spear shaft. The man dropped like a dead man, unconscious before he hit the ground.

As the last man drove his spear at Carni, the sharp point of the spear caught him in the left side. He twisted such that the blow did not penetrate deeply; but cut a deep gash in his side. He drove his own thrusting spear into the abdomen of the man. It would take him a while to die; but he would be unable to fight any more. He writhed on the ground in pain, gasping for air.

Carni pulled his thrusting spear from the man's abdomen and hit the man a hard blow to the head with the spear shaft. Then he walked over to the unconscious man and drove the spear deeply into his chest, killing him with certainty. He checked all of the men and found that they were dead.

He looked at his own wound; it was bleeding badly. The old woman grunted and showed him her bound hands, obviously asking for him to untie her. He approached her and used the sharp edge of his spear to cut the leather bindings.

The old woman reached inside her pouch and took out a handful of moss. She placed the moss on the gash in his side and told the younger woman to tie a piece of leather around his waist to hold it on the wound. She then took out a curved piece of bone and some sinew. She motioned for him to lie down. He rolled the big man's body off of the robe and lay there, as the old female had instructed. When she was ready, she removed the moss bandage from the wound and used the sharp, curved bone to make holes in the skin on each side of the wound. When Carni winced from the pain, she grunted her disgust, causing him to cover up his discomfort.

Next, she took the lengths of sinew and forced it through the holes with the curved bone. Finally, she tied the sinew such that it tightly closed the wound. Carni was amazed that the old female used the sharp, curved bone and sinew to sew his wound closed and then covered it with more moss which she wet with water from the river. When she re-tied the leather bandage around it, he motioned to her to indicate what was the moss?

She understood and signed that the wound would close and become smooth again. She replaced her articles in her pouch and motioned that they must sleep. By gestures she made him understand that they must leave early in the morning before the other clan members looked for these men.

The next morning, they were up and awake before dawn. They searched the men's belongings for anything useful. From the large man's pouch Carni took a carved bone figurine of a cave bear. The man also carried an interesting device that Carni did not recognize. It was made with two leather strips attached on each side to a patch of leather. The big man also carried meat, which Carni did not recognize.

When the old woman saw it, she knocked it from Carni's hand and with a disgusted gesture, indicated that they should not eat it. She made the spear throwing gesture to indicate that the meat was a "hunter." Carni knew that these men were obviously man-eaters. He had heard about them from the Wonto; but had never seen one. He examined the ashes of the large fire pit that the clan had left and found the obvious small skull of another young human.

The women searched the bodies of the other men and found items that they wanted to keep, including what smelled like ronk (horse) meat.

They placed their respective items in their pouches and divided the ronk meat between them. They heard the sounds of approaching hyenas and decided to throw water on the fire so that the bodies would keep the meat-eaters busy, as they made their departure. They departed the camp just before first light. Carni was sore from his wound; but he still carried his thrusting spear at the ready. The old woman led the way and headed straight for the river.

They entered the shallow part of the river and waded downstream; occasionally exiting on the bank on a rocky surface and reentering the river. After traveling in this manner for about an hour, they came to a waterfall. The old woman led them through the water cascading over a cliff, where Carni saw the entrance to a cave. Without hesitation, the old woman entered the cave. She motioned for Carni and the young woman to follow. Using their hands to feel the left-hand cave wall they followed as the cave turned upward. After stumbling through the dark cave, which ascended at a very steep incline for what seemed like an hour, but was probably only a few minutes; Carni saw light ahead.

When they exited the cave, Carni saw that they were above the waterfall and on the opposite side of the river from which they had entered the cave. The old woman seemed to relax now; she led them southwest along the banks of the river. They traveled in this manner until about midday, when the young woman whimpered that she needed to stop. They stopped in the cover of a small group of trees that grew down to the water's edge and ate some of the meat that they had taken from the men. The old woman took Carni's bandage off and replaced the moss. The wound was not an angry red that would be a precursor to a more serious problem. The woman moved a large rock and dug a hole in which she buried the bloody moss before putting the rock back in its place. After this short break, the old woman motioned that they should go.

They traveled until it was almost dark, when the old woman motioned to the young woman to run ahead and signal their arrival. The young woman sprinted forward toward rocky cliffs along the south bank of the river. She made a sound which sounded like migrating geese, which was answered in the same manner from the top of the cliffs. In a matter of minutes, the little party was surrounded by short stout clansmen armed with thrusting spears.

CHAPTER 10

CARNI RECOVERS WITH THE RIVER CLAN

(Carni's dreams continue.)

After the clan had surrounded Carni and the two women, the old woman hastened to explain what had occurred. Carni understood many of her gestures; but not her guttural exclamations. She told the clan of the capture of the two women by the cannibals and about Carni's attack and killing of their captors. The clansmen were amazed that a single man could attack and kill five cannibals. The clan had experienced many encounters with the cannibal clan and had lost many people, who were most probably eaten by them. They stared at this strange man. He was much taller than, but not as heavy as, members of their clan. He also had a lighter complexion than the clansmen. They had never seen light colored hair and skin and wanted to feel its texture. When they realized that this strange looking man represented no danger, the women of the clan began to arrive and marveled at this tall, strange man.

As a group, they turned and headed back to the cliffs above the river, motioning for Carni to follow. Apparently, he had been accepted by the clan. As the group walked toward the cliffs, Carni motioned to the old woman, using the universal sign for clan and shrugged, asking what the clan was called. The old woman understood and pointed to the river and used a word, "hotu." The woman went on to gesture that the clan hunted in this river valley.

As the group approached the base of the cliffs, which were a few feet from the edge of the river, the remainder of the Hotu Clan came out of three caves in the face of the cliff to look at the tall stranger. Other members of the clan had carried them the news of the arrival of the tall, strange man and all came out to see for themselves. The clan members lined up along a path that approached the cliffs and reached out to touch Carni, as he passed.

Carni chose to carry himself tall, with a bit of a swagger. Because of his size and somewhat arrogant walk, the clansmen and clan women were either in awe of this strong stranger, or afraid of him. Most felt the latter emotion.

The men looked at the weapons that the man had used to kill the cannibals. Carni could almost see their minds working to understand how the weapons had helped this man kill five brutal cannibals. The women looked at his groin and gestured to each other in subdued fashion about his potential at mating.

Carni examined the details of the Hotu Clan camp site. There was a large communal fire pit in front of the cliff face. Apparently, the clan used this fire pit as a gathering place. A large fire was burning in the pit and there was a large number of ashes in the pit. Carni read this to mean that the Hotu Clan had been in this camp for some time. There were a number of bones in and around the fire pit. A cursory glance told Carni that the clan hunted fish and birds, as well as wild boar and red deer. The fire pit was surrounded by containers made of reeds and reed mats, which had been weaved together. Carni found these very interesting for he had never seen anything like them. He knew that he had much to learn from the Hotu Clan and vowed to learn everything they had to teach before he continued his journey.

He found the women to be very comely; most were very short, only five feet tall, or less. The clansmen were no taller than five feet four inches; so, this was a short race of people. However, the men were very muscular and obviously strong for their height. The clan reminded Carni of ants, very numerous, hardworking, energetic and strong for their size. The members of the clan even seemed to scurry about like ants.

The leader of the Hotu Clan had not come to meet Carni before he had arrived at the camp site. He now made a grand entrance, exiting the center cave and descending the slope down to the communal fire pit. He held himself to his entire five feet four-inch height and approached Carni, as if he was neither awed, nor afraid. He spoke loudly and gestured widely, possibly to hide his nervousness. Carni put him at ease by making a submissive bow and then standing to his complete six feet two inches of height. The leader seemed to accept the gesture and motioned to the women to bring food for their guest.

The women started preparing a meal; while men jumped and ran toward the river on some unknown tasks. In a matter of moments, the men returned with large reed baskets full of fish and gave them to the women to prepare.

The women set about preparing the fish by removing the innards and placing the fish on wooden spits that had been soaked in water. They cooked them over the communal fire pit. The innards were cleaned of their contents and placed on hot rocks around the fire, probably to be eaten as snacks, thought Carni.

The fire pit was not like a Nord Clan fire pit. There were no rocks to mark the sacred directions. The spits were supported by forked sticks which were set at different heights and which surrounded the fire pit. The women stuffed plants inside the fish, which gave off a delicious aroma as they cooked. From reed baskets the women took what looked like crushed nuts, or seeds of some type and mixed them with berries taken from another reed basket. The women wet their hands from water kept near the fire in deer stomach containers and molded the berry and grain mixture into flat cakes. They placed the cakes on hot rocks set in the edges of the fire pit and surrounded by hot coals. The cakes began to harden almost immediately.

Apparently, these cakes were a clan favorite for everyone became excited, when they saw them being prepared.

The leader led Carni to a position around the fire pit closest to the cliff. The leader indicated that Carni should sit on one of the two rocks located there. The leader sat on the other. Carni saw that this must be a position of honor and again he bowed to the leader. The leader beamed a giant smile, showing his pleasure at the gesture. The evening festivities lasted late into the night with the clan serving Carni all of the fish and berry cakes that he could possibly eat. The fish innards had been cooked until they were hard and were eaten before eating the fish. The berry cakes were delicious. The berries were obviously a black berry that Carni had encountered and eaten in this river valley. But the grain was something that he did not recognize. He intended to ask the old woman from where they had obtained it.

Carni passed his days with the Hotu Clan recovering from his wound, which was healing nicely with no infection. Carni had never understood why some people died from small wounds and others lived after suffering greater wounds. He wanted to learn how the old woman had fixed his wound and where she had obtained the moss. He surmised that the moss was the same moss that she had been gathering when the cannibals had taken her and the young woman captive.

Carni spent his time with the old woman, or with the clan leader, and learned what the Hotu Clan had to offer. The Hotu was a large clan, consisting of more than forty members. They were small in stature; but very strong. They did not practice the trotting methods of the Nord Clan when they moved; but traveled more carefully, keeping a watchful eye out for animal and human enemies.

The Hotu clan lived in two basic locations. This cave complex was their summer camp. During the warmer months they existed primarily on plants that the females gathered from the many varieties growing in the river valley and fish from the river, which were caught mostly with nets made from reeds. They also killed occasional geese and other water birds, which spent their summers along the river and a lake a day's walk to the west. They supplemented their summer diet with the occasional red deer, horse, or wild boar, which summered in the river valley.

The women used a method for trapping small animals and birds which Carni had never seen. In reality it was a common "deadfall" trap that was used to crush the prey. The deadfall used a leather strip and a stick as a trigger mechanism. Carni saw that it was easy to set and the River Clan women had developed methods which aided the trapping of squirrels, hares and some birds, such as wild pheasants. The old woman demonstrated to Carni how the deadfall trap was set. She tied one end of a leather strip to the lower end of a diagonal stick. The other end of the leather strip was tied to another stick about the length of a man's thumb. This stick was used as the catch stick. The strip was brought halfway around the vertical stick with the catch stick at a 90-degree angle. A bait stick was placed with one end against the drop weight, or a peg driven into the ground, and the other against the catch stick. When a prey disturbed the bait stick, the stick fell free and released the catch stick. As the diagonal stick flew up, the drop weight fell, crushing the prey. *(See Figure 6 in the Index of Drawings.)*

The old woman allowed Carni to set a deadfall trap for a mountain hare. He chose a rabbit run, which was used by a number of the large rabbits, as indicated by the tracks and eaten vegetation around the run. She showed him how to select the sticks that he would use from dead wood instead of freshly cut wood, which would ooze sap and possibly alarm the prey. Before he began to set the trap, she showed him how to cover his hands in mud to mask the human scent. As bait, the old woman showed him a plant root that the hare cherished as food and he placed it on the bait stick. The old woman indicated that he should choose bait that the desired prey in the area was accustomed to finding. Finally, she showed him how to construct a funneling fence from brush to channel the hare toward the deadfall trap. His first deadfall resulted in a catch during the first night after he had set the trap. Carni was very impressed with the River Clan's methods for obtaining small game.

During the fall, as the days grew shorter and the nights grew colder, the clan moved its camp southwest, until the river widened so much that men could no longer cross it safely. In this area the Hotu Clan occupied a large cave near where great herds of reindeer normally passed their winter, eating moss and other plants which were available in that area.

In the past, the winter months had never been as dangerous as the summer months. During the winter the local clans had staked out claims to various parts of the river valley where other clans entered at their peril. There were plenty of reindeer to go around; so, there was no real competition for food. The Hotu had never seen anyone from the northern clans, until Carni had arrived.

During the summer months the style of life available to the clan changed. The reindeer migrated north and many of the clans followed the reindeer migration and continued to exist on the food, clothing and tools supplied by the reindeer. Legend had it that the Hotu Clan had once tried to follow the reindeer herds; but attacks from other clans had caused the Hotu Clan to abandon this method of existence and they had adapted their life to harvest the game, fish and plants in the river valley the year around. As a result, the growth of the clan was slow and they learned little from interactions with other clans.

A few other clans had adopted this same strategy. However, that caused competition for the available resources during the summer months to become fierce. The Hotu Clan occupied their cave camps during the warmer months, as well as the winter months, because these caves allowed the Hotu to better defend themselves against other clans.

This less nomadic style of life impressed Carni and he planned to bring this innovative approach back to the Nord Clan.

During the summer months their primary nemesis was a cannibal clan, which lived in the woods along the northeast end of the river valley. The Hotu Clan had not been very successful in their fights with the cannibals; but the cannibals had been hesitant to attack the cliff dwellings, since the Hotu Clan could more effectively defend the caves. The cannibals chose instead to attack individuals, or small groups as they hunted, or gathered plants. The cannibals seldom ventured to the south side of the river.

The Hotu leader had also indicated to Carni that there was a clan from the east that occasionally threatened the Hotu. It had been a few years since they had been attacked by that clan, which he referred to as "Step."

Carni was able to understand how the Hotu Clan defended their caves from attackers. The leader had showed him how they stationed men on top of the cliffs armed with large rocks which they would rain down on the attackers to prevent them from scaling the cliff face. Other defenders were prepared to stop an attack on the ledges with thrusting spears.

The Hotu Clan also employed a weapon that Carni had

never seen. Cedar limbs about four feet long were split in the end and flat rocks were forced into the slit. The leader demonstrated that the rocks could be thrown with remarkable force and accuracy from the top of the cliff.

From the old woman Carni learned how to close a wound and the powers of producing a poultice of moss laced with plant leaf juices (probably *lantana camara or tridax procumbens)* and a paste made from mashed plant roots. She showed him where to find the moss, roots and plants from which to extract the healing juices. Finally, the old woman took him into a grassy meadow near the river and showed him the grasses from which the women had gathered the seeds to make the berry cakes.

After learning everything that the Hotu Clan could teach him, Carni had but one other task to complete. The women of the clan were very attracted to him, since he was so tall and strong with a fair complexion. They were very interested in his fair hair and fine beard. But most of all they were interested in his male anatomy. They discussed the possibilities among themselves, speculating on whether it was different from Hotu Clansmen.

After weeks of discussion among the women, it was agreed that one woman should get the honor of satisfying the man. This woman would become a hero to their clan. The leader's woman took the problem of choosing the lucky woman to the leader to decide.

The leader selected a comely woman, whose man had recently been killed in an encounter with the cannibals. In order to inform her of his decision, the leader asked her to walk with him to the river. During this walk the leader told her that she would go to the man, who called himself Carni, during the night and offer herself to him. He told her that she should make herself ready by swimming in the river, after which the other women would rub her body with fish oils.

Upon his arrival, Carni had been offered a bed around the cave fire of the clan leader. The clan leader's entire family slept around this fire. Carni's wound had healed nicely and he was contemplating the final step necessary for the completion of his encounter with the Hotu Clan, as he lay on his robe at the rear of the leader's cave. During the night he was awakened by someone slipping onto his robe with him. He reached out his right hand and felt the body of the person to see who it might be. But he recognized only the fact that it was a female. The other inhabitants of the cave were apparently sleeping. The female breathed rapidly showing her obvious excitement.

He felt her breasts and womanhood, as she sighed and became more excited. He drew her to him and to her surprise placed his mouth upon hers in a strong kiss that caused her to become light-headed and to almost lose control of her actions. He raised himself over her and entered her womanhood with a strong stroke that she met with equal force. Their mating culminated in multiple climaxes for the woman and Carni planted his seed in her body. He was sure that the seed would grow into a virile and strong Nord Clansman, who, one day, would lead the Hotu Clan.

Once he was spent, the woman stealthily left the cave and returned to her robe around her brother's fire. She felt very satisfied and could not wait to tell the other women of the strange man's kiss and mating prowess.

The following day Carni informed the leader that he intended to depart to continue his journey the following day. The leader was disappointed and urged him to reconsider, considering the dangers that a man alone must face. When he saw that Carni was not going to change his mind, he informed him that he would always be welcome in the Hotu Clan. As a gesture of goodwill, the Hotu leader gave Carni one of the rock-throwing weapons that the Hotu used.

The following day Carni arose early, packed his gear and secured it to his backpack. To his surprise the entire clan lined the path to say goodbye. He searched the women's faces to see if he could tell which one had visited him the night before; but he could not. As he passed each clan member, they grunted and gestured their farewells. The old woman gave him some berry cakes and some seeds that he placed in his pouch. Some of the children followed him to the edge of the clearing, where they stopped and watched him until he disappeared into the forest to the south of the cliffs.

When Carni entered a clearing where he had a view of the very distant hills and mountains, he located the gap in the hills that would be his aiming point. As he had done in the past, he started traveling with sudden turns to the left or right to disguise his route-of-march from any follower and to check his back trail. He was again alone and would need all of his cunning and skills to stay alive.

CHAPTER 11

CARNI AND THE CAVE BEAR

(Carni's dreams continue.)

C arni decided to travel to the foothills of the vast mountain range before he made contact with any other clans. The Hotu Clan leader had warned him about the clans to the south. He had indicated that they were fiercer than the Hotu and occasionally made raids into the river valley.

One such raid of the Hotu's summer camp had occurred three summers earlier. The raiding clan had been a larger people than the Hotu; but had not been able to dislodge the Hotu from their cave defenses. They had been able to kill two Hotu clansmen and had also succeeded in stealing one woman before giving up their attack and returning to the south. The Hotu warriors had followed the attacking clan to try to recover the woman; but had not been able to do so before the raiding clan had entered their own homelands and it became too dangerous to follow further.

The Hotu leader had advised him to go southwest instead of due south or southeast, since the Hotu believed that the attacking clan had come from the land near the mountains to the south and east. The leader also indicated that the eastern lands held the threats from clans that were cannibals. Carni understood the dangers; but felt that his destiny lay to the south. He intended to travel in that direction, regardless of the dangers that he might face.

Using his zigzag course of travel, Carni continued in a southern direction toward the gap in the foothills that led the way to the mountains that had become his aiming point. He traveled slowly, smelling the wind; listening to the sounds that the wind carried to him and sometimes climbing a tree to get a good view of what his course might hold. His travel habit was that in the late afternoon he would make camp, usually in a grotto or next to a deadfall that he could shore up to protect him on three sides.

The danger was greater when he was traveling than it was when he was camped. After he had been traveling for about three weeks, he came to a large spring that was full after a summer thunderstorm. His destination required that he cross the stream; but it was too deep and the current too fast to attempt a crossing at the point where he had intersected the stream. He looked upstream and downstream to see which way might offer the greatest possibility of a fording site. He decided to go upstream to the east, since there was an animal trail running along the bank of the river in that direction. He walked slowly along the animal trail, carefully examining the tracks of the animals that had used the trail recently.

He first saw the tracks of a red deer which had passed no more than a couple of hours earlier. The red deer must have been a female, since she was accompanied by a fawn born in the early spring, judging from the size of the hoof print. He continued to examine the tracks, as he rounded a bend in the stream. He looked up just intime to see a giant cave bear that appeared in the trail. The bear did not see him immediately, since she appeared to be following the red deer's trail and the wind was coming from the south off of the mountains.

Carni came to an immediate halt and tried not to move, so as to not attract the attention of the bear. The bear sensed that something was amiss and stood on its hindquarters and looked around. The bear saw Carni almost immediately and emitted a loud, "Humph!"

The cave bear returned to all fours and charged in Carni's direction, as if it was trying to scare Carni. Carni's first inclination was to flee; but he quickly realized that he could not outrun the cave bear and that his only choice was to stand his ground. He darted into the forest using the trees to gain time as he searched for a better defensive position. Finally, he came to a deadfall made from two trees that had fallen parallel to each other. These trees offered him some protection on two sides. The bear would have to attack him through a narrow opening possibly allowing him to use his thrusting spear effectively.

The bear was only about ten yards behind him when he turned inside the deadfall corridor. The bear did not slow down, as it made its charge through the entrance into the corridor, probably believing that his prey was trapped and wanting to finish it off quickly. Carni placed the handle of his thrusting spear against the ground and the bottom of the deadfall trunk, which formed a perfect stop for the spear handle. He pointed the flint-tipped spear head at the chest of the cave bear. The bear was accustomed to overpowering its prey and ignored the spear tip as he charged. The weight of the bear and the speed of the bear's charge caused the head of the spear to bury itself deeply of into the chest of the cave bear, just as the cave bear swatted at Carni with its huge right paw. The bear's claws raked the side of Carni's left shoulder cutting three deep gashes parallel to the ground. The cave bear roared its indignation at whatever had hurt it and started to swat at the spear to no avail. The bear withdrew from the deadfall corridor and retreated into the woods, growling intermittently with Carni's thrusting spear imbedded deeply in its chest.

For a moment Carni just sat in the dead fall corridor. He looked at the gashes in his shoulder and saw that he would need to stitch them up, using the method that the old woman had used to stitch up his side. He took out the materials from his pouch and gritted his teeth, as he made the holes for the sinew. Carni decided that only the center gash required stitching. He made six holes straddling the gash and threaded the sinew through the holes and pulled it tight. He placed a piece of the magic moss on the wound and tied a piece of leather over it before pouring water over the bandaged wound. He stood up and decided that he was set to go.

Carni debated whether he should follow the wounded beast. Wounded animals could be very dangerous; but it was a good thrusting spear and he did like to eat bear meat. He decided to follow the bear keeping downwind of the animal. He drew a throwing spear and the spear thrower from the pouch on his back and placed the spear in the thrower in order to be ready should the wounded bear attack him. A throwing spear might be too small to take down a cave bear.

The bear had retreated to the north and the wind was coming from the south; so, Carni circled to the west to get in front of the bear. He could smell the bear's acrid aroma easily. The smell was not getting stronger, nor weaker and he could hear no movement. He thought that it might have stopped. There was a small cluster of trees from where he judged the smell was probably coming. He held the spear thrower in the ready position and located trees that he could climb, if it became necessary to escape the bear. As he approached the trees, he could hear heavy breathing and a low whine. He saw the bear and recognized that it was a mature female. She was laying on her right side with the thrusting spear protruding from her body. He could see blood spurting out of the wound as her heart beat. He had seen this situation with other animals and he knew that it was only a matter of time until the cave bear died from a loss of blood. He sat down to wait.

A half hour passed before Carni judged that the cave bear was dead. He approached the bear cautiously and stuck it with a throwing spear. There was no reaction. The bear was dead. Now he had to worry about other meat-eaters. He built a large fire to keep the meat-eaters away for a while, as he cut the choice pieces of meat from the bear's carcass with his cutting flint. He took the tongue, the two front paws and a large piece of one rump and the liver. He cooked the meat over the fire. He wished he could take the hide but it was far too heavy of a burden to travel with. He also took the rear claws, which might be good trading material someday. The claws were at least three inches long and were very sharp. He had to cut his thrusting spear out of the bear's chest, since it was lodged so deeply and tightly. He decided to move his camp more to the south away from the bear's body.

He took the cooked meat and wrapped it in his back pack and started south. He thought he heard hyenas approaching from downwind and he sped up his trotting pace. He made his camp at the deadfall where he had battled the bear. He set a fire pit at each end of the corridor to discourage the approach of meat-eaters. He cooked the meat a little more and then ate his fill. Then he spread out his red deer skin ground cover inside the deadfall corridor and went to sleep. He awoke every two hours to replenish the fires. Tomorrow he would continue his travel to the south. He wanted to find a clan that he could observe for a while without making contact.

CHAPTER 12

CARNI FINDS THE STEP CLAN

(Carni's dreams continue.)

C arni continued his journey toward the gap in the foothills that slowly rose in the lands before the mountains; but he was more cautious after his encounter with the cave bear. He had crossed a river that flowed along the base of foothills north of the mountains and, after seeing old tracks of humans along a game trail, he no longer traveled on the game trails. Instead, he forged a path parallel to the game trails. Periodically, he would go to the trail and check for the recent passage of humans.

The game trail that he was following ran near the river and probably served the animals that used it as means of reaching a place to ford and for arriving at the rich grass lands in the areas where the river valley widened. During flood stage, the river had dumped fertile soil in this valley over the years that it had flowed. Many days passed and he did not find any signs of recent humans traveling along this game trail. He did find some older signs where a small group of about four men, which he surmised was probably a hunting party, had used the trail before the last rain. The last rain had been more than a week earlier; so, the tracks were more than a week old. These men had been proceeding in an eastern direction.

Carni decided to climb to the top of a cliff that overlooked much of the area to see if he could detect any signs of human presence from that vantage point. The cliff was about three hundred feet high and overlooked a place where the river and the river valley widened. There were numerous cliffs in the area which had been produced as the river flowed through the valley eroding the softer rock faster than the hard rock that composed the cliffs. Climbing was difficult since much of the rock face of the cliff was slippery and the wound in his shoulder made the use of his left arm painful. If he were to fall and seriously injure himself, he knew that he would die, or be killed and eaten by the meat-eaters.

Carni continued his climb, slipping occasionally; but never falling. When he arrived at the top of the cliff, he sat down in the shadow of a large boulder. He did not want to show himself against the skyline. Carefully, he examined the terrain that lay before him.

The cliff on which he was now perched was higher than the other cliffs in the area. The series of cliffs formed a wall between the river and the foothills that led to the mountain range to the south. From the cliff on which he was crouching, Carni saw a wide valley with the river running swiftly through it. The river did not run through the middle of the valley, but hugged the south side of the valley near the cliffs. To the north of the river a triple canopy forest covered the low-lying areas near the river. As the valley floor proceeded north from the river, the forest gave way to grassy plain with occasional wetlands, which seemed to be filled with every imaginable type of water fowl. He could see a small lake towards the north end of the valley. He saw red deer grazing near the edge of the forest and some type of large horned creature, the like of which he had never encountered, grazing across the green grassland. The creatures may be a type of elk; he thought. The Nord Clan hunted the elk, called "spos" in their language. He had heard tails of a large spos (Irish elk) that had been hunted by the Nord Clan; but had never seen one himself. He made a mental note to hunt one of these giant spos before he left the river valley.

Carni guessed that there should be a clan in this area since food would be plentiful. Slowly he allowed his gaze to examine the entire river valley. For more than half an hour he examined the terrain and found no signs of humans. That didn't mean that they were not there; it just meant that their presence was not obvious. Carni decided to spend the night on the cliff and see if he could see a fire after dark that would verify a clan's presence.

He located a small grotto which was situated near the top of the cliff on a broad plateau-like gradual slope and surrounded by giant boulders. He made a small fire from dry wood that would emit only a small amount of smoke and, because of the boulders, it should not be visible from any point on the valley floor.

He had killed a large snake that morning and he prepared it for cooking over the fire. Carni had often eaten snake meat during his journey; although, until he had arrived in the south, he had never tried it. Since it was too difficult to carry a large number of provisions, Carni had learned to exist on smaller game, such as squirrels, mountain hares, birds, snakes, fish, and, during the spring, bird eggs. There were a number of smaller animals that he had never encountered before his travels that he had learned to kill and eat. He occasionally ate lizards and turtles, which he found to be very appetizing.

He coiled the snaked around a spear sized limb; suspended it over the fire on the rocks marking the four sacred directions and allowed it to slowly cook. Periodically, he rotated the spear to expose parts of the snake to the fire that had not been exposed previously. When he judged it to be cooked thoroughly, he removed it from the fire and laid it on a rock to cool. After a few minutes he took the snake and broke the brittle blackened skin to reveal delicate, juicy white meat. He ate ravenously, until he had consumed the entire serpent.

He wiped his greasy hands on his robe and looked at the sky. It was completely dark now and the night sky was filled with stars. He had often wondered what those bright fires in the sky were. The Nord Clan believed that the stars were fire pits of Nord Clan warriors, which protected the clans of distant worlds from the meat-eaters. He was not so sure; but the Wonto had told him of the fires in the sky that could guide his way. The Wonto had shown him the fire in the sky that always pointed to the Nord Clan home and had emphasized that he could always follow that fire to guide his journey home.

Carni took a drink of water from his water bladder; rose and walked to the edge of the cliff to examine the river valley after dark. The first thing that he saw was far in the distance to the north, possibly on the northern rim where the river valley ended. There was a faint flicker of light. It was an obvious fire pit used by some unknown clan. Judging from the fact that he could see the fire from this great distance told him that it was a large fire pit, probably used by an entire clan. But the fire was too far north to interest Carni. He continued his search. At last, his search was rewarded. On the right side of the valley floor, he saw a reflection of a fire off of the face of a cliff. If he had not been so high above it, he would not have been able to see it. It looked like it might be a fire pit in front of the last cliff in the line of cliffs along the south bank of the river. Carni decided that he would get closer to that fire tomorrow and see if this was a hunting party, or a small clan.

After the sun had begun its rise in the eastern sky, Carni analyzed the terrain and decided that the best way to approach the fire that he had seen and remain undetected was to move along the top of the cliffs. He would have to be careful not to expose himself against the skyline. With his experience, Carni realized that any leader worth being a leader would realize that the ridgeline was a vulnerability and would post lookouts to spy anyone approaching along that route.

He picked up his back pack and started to move in the direction where he had seen the fire reflection. He moved slowly, crouching below the skyline and, periodically, looking through a break in the rocks in the direction of the last cliff in the line-of cliffs. He saw nothing; but continued to draw closer to where the fire that he had seen last night must have been. Finally, he was on top of the next to last cliff in the line-of-cliffs along the river. He eased forward to the edge of the cliff where he could see the base of the last cliff, where he judged that the fire must have been.

He saw no humans; but he did see evidence that someone had made a fire pit near the cliff face and spent the night. He examined the surrounding country side; but couldn't see any human movement. He decided to descend from the top of the cliff and examine the camp site.

Slowly he descended down the cliff face. There were many cracks in the cliff face that allowed him to carefully climb down; but the cliffs were composed of slippery rock; so, he had to descend very carefully. His shoulder wound felt better and was apparently healing well. He was able to use it in his decent with very little pain. He arrived at the bottom of the next to last cliff after a slow descent. He cautiously made his way through the large boulders which covered the ground at the base of the cliffs, until he was about ten meters from the fire pit that he had seen from the top of the cliffs. Without moving, he made an initial examination of the ground around the fire pit.

He saw bones that had been burned in the fire; but he could not determine the type of bones from that distance. The tracks around the fire indicated that there were about five men in the party and no females, or children. So, this was probably a hunting party, or a roving band of cannibals intending to prey on hunters, or gatherers from local clans.

He had been told of such roving bands of cannibals by the Wonto, who had said that these small, mostly-male clans existed primarily on human flesh. The Wonto had said that these clans were really remnants of southern clans that banded together for support.

Carni moved around, circling the fire pit until he discovered the direction from which they had arrived. They had come from the northwest; made camp and had departed toward the river to the east. He judged from the depth of their footprints that four of the men were carrying burdens. That probably meant that their hunt had been successful. He examined the bones in the fire pit.

"They might be spos (Irish elk)," he thought. The hunters had probably killed one of the elk-like animals that he had seen grazing in the grasslands of the valley. He also saw the tracks of a large cat that was following the hunters. Carni carefully examined the boulders and cliffs for any sign of the cat. He saw nothing. The wind was coming from the south; so, his scent should not carry to the hunting party, or the cat that was following them, since they were located farther to the east. He decided to follow their trail, but to keep a wary eye out for the giant cat. He could not risk the cat discovering him before he saw the cat. Carni knew that these giant cats liked to attack from above their prey; so, he resolved to keep a wary eye out for an attack from the top of a bolder.

It was easy to follow the hunters, since they were following a well-used animal trail and the four men with the burdens could not have hidden their tracks, even if they had tried. He estimated that he was less than half a day behind them, possibly much less. Each time that he crossed a clearing in the woods, he paused before crossing and listened, smelled the wind and searched the surrounding area for any signs of life.

He saw virtually nothing, not even the smaller animals that he sometimes startled with his passing. He surmised that all animals were aware of the passing of the giant cat and had either left the area, or were hiding. When the animal trail turned toward the river, he guessed that there must be a fordable animal crossing at that point. The hunters' tracks indicated that they did not follow the trail to the crossing, but instead veered to the southeast staying on the south side of the river. After exiting the animal trail, the men had paused to rest for a few minutes and then picked up their burdens and continued along the river bank. He found the giant cat's prints just off of the trail to the south; it continued to follow the hunters.

At a point near a bend in the river, the hunters paused and were joined on the trail by three additional men. Judging from the change in the depth of the prints of the new men, they had shared some of the burden previously carried by four of the first group of hunters. The cat prints changed direction and headed to the south and the hills in that direction. Carni believed that the cat had become discouraged when the size of the group had increased and had decided to look for an easier meal.

Carni followed the cat for a short distance to see what its

true direction was and its trail did not vary; he was headed due south. Carni turned his attention to the hunting party and their friends. Since the additional men had joined them, Carni judged that the clan's camp must be nearby. He looked around to see what high points might allow him to get a good view of the area. To the east there was the inevitable series of cliffs that seemed to periodically rise up on the south side of this river. He changed his course to go in the direction of the highest cliff.

Carni arrived at the base of the cliffs in about half an hour. He started to climb to reach a low ledge that would eventually take him to the cliff top. The ledge ran from west to east across the face of the cliff and, when it was about two thirds of the way to the top, there was a break in the ledge, such that the ledge stopped at a crack in the cliff face and started again about three feet higher up. When Carni arrived at the crack, he looked into the crack in the face of the cliff and discovered a cavern that ran about twenty feet into the face of the cliff. The floor of the cavern was covered with old bones.

"At one time," Carni thought, "this must have been the lair of one of those big cats; but not any longer. The bones were too old." He decided that this would make a good place to set up his camp while he searched for the clan.

He entered the cavern, which had more sunlight than most caves that he had seen, since the crack in the rock that formed the cavern entrance was very high and gathered sun light that reflected off of the west side of the crack. He examined the cavern floor and found very large cat foot prints in the soft sand near the west side of the cavern; so, he knew that the bones had been left here by a giant cat.

He examined the bones. He immediately found bones from several reindeer and red deer, at least one ponk and a hyena. Then to his surprise he found the bones of two humans. One was a fully grown man, he thought and possibly a young woman, or adolescent. The only recent animal presence in the cave was the small tracks of vermin. The bones had been gnawed and broken open probably to reveal the precious marrow to the meat-eater. Carni moved the bones to the back of the cavern and laid down his back pack and thrusting spear. There was no water in the cavern; so, he would have to depend upon his water bladder. Carrying his throwing spears and spear thrower in the case on his back, he turned and left the cavern and continued his climb to the top of the cliff.

When he had gained the cliff summit, he was careful not to show himself against the skyline. He placed his back against the cliff face and sat on the ledge, just below the cliff top. Slowly he started searching the river valley in front of him. The river to his right wound its way like a giant serpent in an east by southeast direction and the valley seemed to narrow as it moved further in that direction. To his left the river valley widened for a great distance before it appeared to narrow toward the western end of the river valley. Carni had come from the west and examined that direction to see if there was any sign of life on his back trail. He saw nothing.

He started to examine the valley to his right in the direction that the hunters had apparently taken. He started by looking at the river. All animals, including men, needed water; so, it was probable that if the clan's camp was in this area, it would be near the water provided by the river. Almost immediately he saw a whiff of smoke rising through the trees near the river. It was not a large fire pit; but appeared to be several small fire pits using very dry wood, so as not to produce a large amount of smoke. A small dry-wood fire was hard to see unless you had the advantage of height, as Carni did now. The wind was from the southwest, coming off of the cliff toward the camp site; so, even if he had been closer, Carni could not have captured the clan's scent.

Carni had learned to recognize the scent of different animals, as well as different clans. For example, the Nord Clan scent held a suggestion of reindeer and mammoth, the primary sources from which they obtained food, skins and tools. The river clan, on the other hand, included the scent of fish in their collective odor. He wondered what the scent of this clan would be. He judged the clan's camp site to be about half a day's travel from the cliff. He examined the surrounding area to determine how he could approach the camp without being detected.

The forest covered the entire area near the camp and there were the occasional cliffs on the south side of the river that rose above the trees. He decided that his best observation point would be on top of one of the smaller cliffs near the camp. Carni expected that the clan would have a lookout stationed on one of the cliffs, if the clan expected danger from any other clans in the area. If he were the leader of the clan and was stationing such a lookout, Carni decided that he would have sent the lookout to either the western, or eastern cliffs, or possibly both; but not the center one nearest to the camp site.

Carni decided to try for the center cliff. By closely examining the area from the cliff where he was currently located, he determined that he could gain access to the lower cliffs from which he should be able to observe the clan camp site without revealing himself. He would have to be careful as he passed the western cliff in case there was a lookout stationed there. He decided to spend the night in the cavern before proceeding to the cliffs closer to the camp site. Tonight, he would not make a fire; so, he ate cold meat and slept with his thrusting spear in his right hand.

Before the break of dawn, Carni was up and prepared to explore the lower cliffs near the camp site. He decided to leave his back pack and thrusting spear in the cavern and took his throwing spears with him. Carni judged that if he were discovered, he would be severely outnumbered and that his best possibility of survival would be to run. If he needed to run, he did not want to abandon the pack, or to be encumbered by the large thrusting spear. Carni reasoned that if this clan was anything like the River Clan, few people would be moving about at dawn. Activity usually waited until about an hour after the break of dawn; therefore, he used that time to sprint through the forest that separated his higher cliff from the lower cliffs near the probable camp site. When he arrived at the edge of the forest near the western cliff, he carefully and patiently examined to top edge of the cliff. His patience was rewarded when the lookout moved, probably just awakening from sleep while standing watch.

Making sure that he was out of site of the lookout, Carni circled to the south of the western cliff and was able to ascend the middle cliff without being detected by the lookout. From the height of the middle cliff, he examined both the eastern and the western cliffs. He saw the lookout that he had previously detected on the western cliff and he placed himself in a position where the lookout could not see him. He was unable to detect a lookout on the eastern cliff. Possibly the clan did not expect danger to arrive from the east; but thought it prudent to watch for the approach of enemies from the west. Carni wondered if the cannibals that the Hotu had told him about foraged this far south. He also had to consider the possibility that the clan that threatened this clan was the cannibal clan that had attacked the Hotu. Carni settled down to study the forest surrounding the camp site.

He could identify five, possibly six small fire pits. He surmised that this clan was organized around family units. He had seen other clans who were so organized. The Nord Clan was organized according to stature with important men, such as the clan leader and the Wonto, each having a separate fire and clan members most closely associated with them were members of their fire. Carni had been a member of the Wonto's fire, after his selection as a wontu. Before that he had been a member of the clan leader's favorite hunter's fire, as a young, respected hunter and warrior. The River Clan had a more communal organization, where there was one large fire that everyone shared and other fires were created to support a particular task.

These fires were too small to be attributed to either the Nord Clan, or the River Clan organizations. There were several small clearings in the forest near the camp site and Carni could observe their comings and goings, as members of the clan passed through the clearings. He started to mentally register the different clan members that he saw. He saw and recognized the hunters that he had followed to the camp site. They seemed to be boasting about their successful hunt. He saw a few children and several women. He also thought that he recognized the physical characteristics of one woman, who could be the woman that was stolen from the Hotu Clan. The woman was shorter than the other fully grown women of this clan and she appeared to be the subject of abuse from the other women. After observing the clan most of the day, he decided that the clan was larger than the River Clan and probably was composed of about fifty to sixty people. In Carni's experience, he had never encountered a clan with so many members.

Carni thought that it was very possible that this was the clan that the leader of the River Clan had referred to as the "Step Clan." The leader of the River Clan had said that they were numerous and used throwing spears in their attack. The River Clan leader knew that they were not cannibals, since they had not carried off the dead. They had stolen one woman in their last attack and had killed all of the wounded of the River Clan that they had discovered. The leader said that he believed that the goal of the attack had been to steal women.

As the days passed, Carni closely watched the clan and learned their numbers, hunting and gathering habits and many individual's routines. He decided that this clan was potentially too violent for a stranger to be able to safely approach them. He set his goal, regarding the clan, as selecting and stealing a young woman. As late fall approached, he wanted to have a woman that he could spend winter with and use her to spread the Nord Clan seed to the southern clans, as he had been instructed by the Wonto. In reality, although the Wonto's instructions were paramount in his decisions, he was also lonely for companionship and the comforts afforded by a female. If this was the Step Clan, then it would be an honor to plant the Nord Clan seed in such a powerful clan.

On one occasion he was able to hide in a reed patch in the shallow water of the river for an entire day and observe the females, as they came to the river to fish; collect water and gather plants in the forest near the river. There were perhaps three young women, who met his requirements for the type of woman that he desired. He reasoned that she had to be comely, strong and young enough that she had not been given to a man. Additionally, he wanted the woman to possess a sense of confidence to give the offspring that he intended to leave her with a strong spirit. After watching the three potential victims, Carni selected the one that would be his target.

She was small and perhaps thirteen to fourteen years old with raven black hair, which was typical of this clan. Most of the females of this clan had broad faces with strong brows and a flat nose. Unlike many of the women in this clan, this woman possessed more pleasing features, such as a narrower face and a more delicate brow. Her hair had a bright luster in the sun and she showed her teeth in a smile when she was pleased. She also seemed to exhibit a self-assurance, not often seen in females of her age and experience. She unhesitatingly went into the forest and along the river bank in the performance of her chores. When approached by one of the young males of the clan, she quickly rebuffed his advances and prepared to defend herself. He had heard the other women refer to her as "Kardi."

CHAPTER 13

CARNI AND KARDI TOGETHER

C arni awakened next to Kardi and felt strangely satisfied and content. "Perhaps this is the way the men with females feel each day," thought Carni.

He had planned out his intentions regarding the female before he had taken her. His goal was to use her to prepare for the winter, which they would pass in the grotto that they now occupied, and to plant his seed in her and deliver her back to her clan in the early spring, or late winter to raise her Nord Clan child in her clan. He needed her help to prepare enough provisions to be able to live through the winter, without the support of a clan, and to watch his back in case of attack from the ravenous meat-eaters that he expected to encounter during the winter. In normal winters, plant eaters were weakened by the sparse availability of food and slowed by deep snow. This made them easy prey to the meat-eaters. Therefore, food was more plentiful to the meat-eaters in the winter. The meat-eaters grew stronger from this increased availability of food. On the other hand, the cold and snow made travel and hunting more difficult for humans, also making them more easily hunted by meat-eaters.

He expected that the reindeer would return to the area for the winter and, of course, they would be followed by the clans that made their life following the reindeer migrations. Hiding from these clans would be paramount to his survival. Carni's plan to prevent detection when returning from a hunt was to hunt just before, or during snow storms. The snow storms would serve to cover his tracks when he returned to the grotto. Additionally, Carni had devised the large rock cover of the grotto entrance to conceal any fire that he needed, along with the fact that the smoke would exit the cliffs at the top above the grotto and be dispersed by a large grove of trees that grew on top of the cliff. The trees surrounded the crack in the cliff where the smoke exited from the grotto. This would make it difficult for anyone to pin point the location of their fire, should they smell the smoke.

Carni rose and stirred the ashes to allow the still hot embers that were buried under the ashes to ignite new wood that he had place on the fire. There was already a heavy frost in the air; so, winter was not far away. He wanted to get started hunting for winter meat, as soon as possible; but he was hopeful that the reindeer would soon arrive and give him plenty of opportunity after the snow covered the ground. He wanted to get some good fur that they could use as winter cover, because the winters in this area would undoubtedly be very cold. If he could get a spos (Irish elk), he would have a good fur and plenty of meat for a long time.

They would eat the fish today and he would take Kardi to the woods north of their grotto, where she could find useful plants and he might be able to kill a red deer, a spos, or a ponk. Kardi awakened; left the warmth of the robe and moved to the fire. She removed the remainder of the fish from a flat rock near the fire and placed them over the fire to warm. In a couple of minutes, she handed Carni three of the fish and she ate the last one.

After finishing two fish, Carni placed the last one in his pouch for later on the trail and through gestures made Kardi understand that they were going to journey to the forest north of the river to hunt for plants and meat. Kardi had nothing to prepare; so, she shrugged and indicated that she was ready. Carni decided that he would immediately start to teach Kardi everything that he knew; so, that when their child was born,

Kardi could pass on this knowledge to him. In Carni's mind, he knew that the offspring would be male for he was a fierce warrior with a strong spirit and the Nord Clan believed that strong warriors produced male off-spring. The Wonto had taught the wantu that if the babies were born as a result of Nord Clan seeds, the mother must be prepared to help the child became a respected member of their southern clan. There was no better way to ensure that the mothers could produce a child that would be respected than to impart knowledge that would make the child successful. Someday, the Nord Clan would journey south and may find an ally in a southern clansman that looked more, or less like them.

Carni rolled the large stone from in front of the grotto, so that they could exit. He checked the area for signs of danger and finding none; rolled the rock back in front of the grotto. He led Kardi north toward a dense forest that he had already explored while he had been observing the Step Clan. He knew that there were red deer and ponk in this forest and he had also seen some of the old woman's magic moss. When they were out of sight in the forest, he stopped and showed Kardi the moss, explaining through his gestures that the old woman had used it to heal his wound.

Kardi understood and took large hunks of the moss and placed them in her pouch. As they proceeded deeper into the forest, Kardi saw plants that she recognized. When she saw a broad-leafed dark green plant, she almost squealed with pleasure and leaped to harvest it. Carni was perplexed and did not understand her euphoria. She pulled one of the plants up by its roots, which were round and purple at the top. She motioned to Carni that one could eat the tops and the roots. She used the word, "kip," with a gathering gesture. Kip was a species of turnip highly valued by the Step Clan due to its ability to remain edible for a long period of time after it was harvested. The Step Clan had stockpiled these for winter eating. She brushed the dirt off of a kip root and started to eat it, motioning for Carni to do the same. He tentatively followed her lead and took a bite. He liked it and showed his pleasure by smiling at her. The root had a strong spicy flavor that caused his mouth to water, as he chewed. They finished the kip roots and looked at the rest of the plants growing in a cluster nearby.

The patch of kip grew in an oblong area about ten feet across in a clearing among tall evergreen trees and Kardi wanted to harvest it all. She looked around and motioned to Carni that she needed a skin from his pack. He took a large red-deer robe from his pack and handed it to her. She quickly started pulling the kip and placing them on the hide. When Carni saw what she was doing, he joined in to help her. It only took half an hour before the hide was covered with kip plants. She motioned to Carni that they needed to roll the hide and tie it for carrying. He removed leather strips from his pack and they rolled the kip plants into the hide and tied it so that it could be carried. She noticed that an animal had recently rooted the ground on the edge of the kip patch, apparently eating the kip.

Kardi's father had always told her that where you found kip, you would also find ponk (wild pigs). Kardi thought for a moment about how to tell this to Carni. She gestured toward where the kip plants had been uprooted by an animal and said "ponk" to Carni. He looked quizzical and then understood, as she pointed to the evidence of the rooting. He examined the tracks that the ponk had left to see in which direction it had gone. The tracks led north from the kip patch. He looked in that direction in search of a thicket that might serve as a daytime lair for a ponk. He saw a possible thicket further into the forest at the bottom of a brushy ravine.

Carrying the kip roll, Kardi followed him as he circled the possible ponk lair. On the far side of the lair, Carni discovered the tracks that a ponk had made entering the lair. He could smell the animal as the slight breeze met his face. There seemed to be only one unobstructed way into or out of the thicket without bursting through the brush barrier. Carni decided on his hunting strategy. He told Kardi to throw sticks into the thicket and beat the brush from the back side, while he waited to ambush the ponk as it tried to escape from the entrance on the other side of the thicket.

The wind was from the back side of the lair and Carni positioned himself behind a tree to the side of the lair entrance/ exit with his throwing spear ready. Carni knew that the ponk was aware of their presence and would be prepared to attack, or escape. He motioned to Kardi to start throwing the sticks. She began beating the brush with a club and growling. Carni heard a snort from within the lair and more loud snorting as the ponk charged out of the thicket toward him. The ponk had no intention of escaping; instead, he veered to the right to charge Kardi at the back of the thicket. Carni only had a moment in which the ponk's right side was exposed for a throw. He launched the spear and without waiting to see if it successfully landed, he loaded another spear in the spear thrower. The ponk squealed as the spear sank into its lower abdomen.

It was not a killing blow! The ponk continued to charge toward Kardi, the spear hindering his charge by striking the brush as it ran. As the ponk reached Kardi it swung its massive head to strike her with its sharp tusks. Kardi landed a blow to the side of the ponk's head with a club she had used to beat the brush which caused it to temporarily swerve exposing its left side to Carni, who had been chasing after the wounded animal. He threw his second spear, which struck the ponk behind the left shoulder. The animal immediately dropped to the ground and started kicking, as its life blood drained onto the ground.

The ponk was not a large one; it was as large as a small deer, possibly 120 pounds. Without hesitation, Carni began to prepare the ponk for transport back to the grotto. He wanted to act fast before other meat-eaters smelled the carcass. Using his flint cutting stone, he opened the ponk's abdomen, allowing the entrails to spill onto the ground. He intended to leave the entrails for the scavengers and just take the carcass. It should weigh less than one hundred pounds and he judged that he could carry it. Kardi salvaged the ponk's stomach to use as a water container. The two hunters shared the raw liver. As they tore off pieces of the raw liver with their teeth, the juices from the liver ran down their chins. Laughing, they wiped away the juice with bloody hands and continued to prepare the carcass. It was surprising how the captor and the captive had become so comfortable together.

Once the carcass was ready, Carni lifted it across his shoulders and kept his thrusting spear in his right hand. Kardi carried the hide roll filled with kip in a similar fashion. Carni took a surreptitious route heading first southwest, then southeast and returning to the grotto from the south after hiding their tracks by walking in a stream and exiting on rocky ground. The carcass had stopped dripping blood well before they entered the stream.

When they arrived at the entrance to the grotto, Carni rolled the stone from in front of the entrance and rolled it closed behind them. In the grotto, they began to prepare the meat for cooking. When Carni started to cut the meat into large chunks, Kardi stopped him. She showed him to cut it into thin strips, which were easier to cure over the fire.

After the meat was cut, Kardi told Carni through gestures that she wanted to go to the river. Carni agreed; since he wanted to replenish their water bladders. When they arrived at the river, they washed the ponk blood from their bodies and then Kardi went directly to where a patch of reeds grew in the water's edge and began to harvest them. Carni had seen baskets used by the River and Step Clans and he assumed that she was gathering the reeds for that purpose. After he had filled the water bladders, he helped her gather reeds until they had all that the two of them could carry back to the grotto.

They returned to the grotto, using the same type of surreptitious route that they had used before. Once in the grotto, Kardi set about the process of weaving the reeds into a crude basket of sorts. Once she had a basket completed, she turned it upside down and hung thin pieces of ponk meat inside the basket. Then she showed Carni that she wanted to hang the basket high over the fire to allow the meat to dry in the heat and smoke of the fire. Carni started building up the rocks on two sides of the fire pit until the baskets could be suspended over the fire using a thrusting spear. She repeated this process until late into the night. Finally, there were four such baskets hung to cure the meat. The baskets trapped the heat and smoke around the meat, smoking and drying it, without allowing the cooking process to burn it.

While she had been busy preparing the baskets and meat, she had placed a large piece of the ponk on a skewer over the fire to cook. They ate the ponk roast late that night before retiring to the robes that they would share. Carni decided to implant more of his seed in her. He had no idea how many times it was necessary to plant his seed before she would carry his child. It did not matter, he thought, since he enjoyed this part of his wontu adventure and he intended to repeat it as often as possible.

Preparation for the winter continued at a brisk pace for the unlikely couple. At about every two-day interval, the two lovers went on a hunt, which often became a hunt and plant gathering expedition. Carni showed Kardi his methods for finding and tracking animals, his methods for conducting a hunt and the "deadfall trap" for crushing small animals that he had learned from the old woman of the Hotu Clan. He also started teaching her how to use the weapons that he carried. The Step Clan prohibited females from using any weapon except a club, or a rock, as a matter of tradition; but the Nord Clan encouraged women to learn to use all hunting and defensive weapons. They stayed within a day's walk of the grotto, but occasionally were forced to camp out for one night, before returning to the grotto.

They were able to kill a large red deer during an ambush that they set up along a well-used game trail. They set out two deadfall traps on two rabbit runs that garnered them several mountain hares over a period of several days. But to their disappointment, they had not been able to find, nor kill an Irish elk. They were able to save all of the red deer meat and even the deer antlers. The meat was prepared in the same way as the ponk meat had been prepared. Once it was dried, it was stored in a reed basket that Kardi made. Carni also had a use for the deer antlers. He had seen other clans from the forest use antlers as the tips for their spears and he intended to fashion some throwing spears with antler tips. They scraped and cured the deer hide to use as a sleeping robe in preparation for the arrival of the severe cold, which both knew was only a few days away. The mountain hare hides were prepared in the same way. Kardi used the sharp-pointed bone and sinew that Carni gave her to create an upper-body cover for Carni and head covers for each of them from the soft mountain hare hides.

Each night they could smell and hear the sounds of meat-eaters outside of the grotto; sometimes they were close; but more often than not, they were far away. The meat-eaters that they heard, or smelled were mostly wolves and hyenas, although Carni did smell a giant cat at least one time. These were normal events; since most of the meat-eaters owned the night. They could not enter the grotto and even if one should try, such as a cave bear, the fire should probably keep them out unless they were desperately hungry.

Carni told Kardi of the Nord Clan hunter who had once killed a female wolf and discovered that she had been suckling wolf pups. The hunter had back-tracked the wolf to her den and discovered that one wolf pup was still alive. The pup's eyes were still closed and the hunter had taken the wolf back to the Nord Clan, with the intention of killing and eating it, when it was convenient. In the end, the hunter had developed an affection for the wolf pup and the pup had grown to a full-grown wolf that lived and hunted with the hunter. Carni indicated that this was the power of the Nord Clan spirit that was so strong that it could even control the wolf.

Finally, Carni announced that the following day would be dedicated to finding and killing an Irish elk.

CHAPTER 14

CARNI AND KARDI HUNT IRISH ELK

The following morning Carni and Kardi were up before the break of dawn. During a previous hunt, Carni had observed tracks that indicated that a few Irish elk fed at the edge of the forest in the early morning hours, when the mist was rising from the dew on the grass. It seemed that their preferred diet was composed of grass and the leaves of many trees and bushes that grew at the edge of the forest.

The Irish elk had a monstrous set of antlers, which some have compared to moose antlers of present times, only much larger. Their bodies were larger than any other deer-type of animal in the area. In order to carry such a massive set of antlers, the Irish elk (spos) had a huge neck and front shoulders, giving the appearance that they used the antlers in their defense.

In actual fact, Carni had observed two male spos during rutting season. Apparently, the female spos were attracted to the male with the most impressive set of antlers. However, during combat for the right to mate with a female, Carni had observed that the two males had tired quickly and the losing male had retreated from the battleground after only a few minutes of battle.

Carni had observed that after the spos had finished eating at the edge of the forest, perhaps a couple of hours after dawn, they retreated back into the forest to seek an appropriate bedding ground for the remainder of the day. They seemed to stay in groups of three to five individuals, which were led by an impressive male. Carni had also seen that the spos tended to keep to well-used animal trails instead of forging a trail through the forest. He surmised that due to the size of their antler rack, the animals probably could not easily get through dense forest, their antlers becoming tangled with the lower branches and impeding their progress. Carni decided that the first order of business for the day was to track a spos group to their daily bedding ground after they finished eating at the edge of the forest during the morning. He wanted to arrive at the forest edge an hour after dawn.

Carni had been demonstrating to Kardi how to use the various weapons in his arsenal. First, he had shown her the thrusting spear of which she was familiar from her time with the Step Clan. In reality the thrusting spear that Carni used was too large for Kardi to use effectively. She was also familiar with the throwing spear and spear thrower, although she had never used them. Carni demonstrated the way to most effectively use the spear thrower and then made her practice until she was capable of launching a spear about half of the distance of which Carni was capable. Carni had fashioned a spear thrower and four throwing spears with deer-horn tips for Kardi to use.

Kardi was extremely proud of her new weapon. Step clan

women typically were only allowed to hunt with rocks and clubs. It was believed by the Step Clan that those women who used men's weapons brought the wrath of the spirits down upon the clan. Therefore, women were not allowed to use weapons, such as spears.

Carni also had in his arsenal two additional weapons that he had to learn to use, as he was teaching Kardi. One was the split-end rock-thrower that he had taken from the cannibal clan members that he had killed when saving the females of the Hotu Clan. He had seen these used by clans before, but had never used one. The weapon was made from a branch with a split in one end of it. A flat rock was inserted into the split, allowing the thrower to use the branch length to create greater speed before the rock disengaged from the branch and flew toward the target. The keys for using this weapon were to understand at what point in the swing of a particular weapon that the rock would disengage from the branch and to time this disengagement such that the rock flew directly at the target at a greater speed and with greater momentum that a rock thrown without the use of the weapon. Carni called this weapon a "kawl," which meant a predator bird in the Nord Clan language.

Carni and Kardi had collected a large number of flat rocks, which were plentiful in the area surrounding the grotto. They had practiced using the weapon for several hours until they were both capable of hitting a tree trunk consistently from a distance of fifty feet. They both had excellent hand-eye coordination; Carni because of his experience using the spear thrower in the past and Kardi because of the fact the Step Clan women killed small animals, such as the mountain hare and birds, by throwing stones.

Finally, Carni had the strange weapon that he had taken from the pouch of the leader of the cannibals. It was made of a piece of reindeer hide with a hole cut in each of the four corners of the square piece of hide. Four narrow strips of leather had been run through the holes on each side. Then an additional narrow piece of hide had been used to wrap around the two pieces of hide, one on each side, creating only two strands of leather for the hunter to hold. Carni called this weapon a "lop." The word "lop," in the language of the Nord Clan, meant small animal. Carni surmised that the weapon was used to hunt small animals. After seeing the split-end rock-thrower used, Carni understood how a lop should be used. Through trial and error, Carni discovered how to use the lop and that round rocks flew in a truer direction to their target than rocks that were not round. Both he and Kardi became very skillful in the use of the lop. Carni had already killed a number of tree-living animals and several hares that he found living near the grotto. Kardi made her own lop, so that she could hunt with Carni.

For this spos hunt, they each carried a spear thrower and throwing spears and the lop. This meant that they could travel quietly and fast, if necessary. Both were capable of running long distances at higher speeds than most of the clans that they might encounter in the area.

They departed the grotto at a trot with Carni in the lead and Kardi trotting in his footsteps about three yards behind him. They headed initially northwest and then changed their direction periodically to northeast and then back to the northwest until they arrived at the potential hunting ground at the edge of the forest which lay to the north of the grotto.

As they crossed an open grassy clearing and arrived near the edge of the forest, Carni slowed to a walk and checked the direction of the wind. Kardi had learned to copy his actions; so, she slowed also and noted that the wind was from the west.

In order to be able to approach the spos undetected, they would need the cover of the forest and have to be east of their prey. Carni led the way into the forest and turned west to parallel the forest edge so that they had a good view of the grassland at the edge of the forest, as they traveled. Carni started his stalking walk, which essentially was a crouching walk with each step landing on the balls of the feet, feeling the ground before putting pressure from the step and preventing any sound from a snapping twig. Kardi observed his posture and copied his moves. The path Carni chose kept them deep enough into the forest, so as not to be seen by anything at the edge of the forest. At about two-minute intervals, he stopped to smell the wind. The wind had the faint odor of horse; but he saw none. He did not detect any odor strong enough to attract his attention. Kardi's sense of smell was actually stronger than Carni's, as was the case for all southern clan women. She slowly breathed in the aromas that the wind carried to her. She gestured to Carni that she recognized horse, a fox, squirrels and a red deer. Carni was impressed and smiled at her.

Again, Carni stopped to smell the wind. This time he picked up several faint odors including the red deer that Kardi had smelled. He judged that there must be an animal trail ahead. As he proceeded westward, he checked the ground for tracks. His diligence was finally rewarded when he came across an animal trail which ran south to north. He smelled the odors that the trail possessed, as he examined the tracks. The trail held the tracks of red deer; but the odor was faint. The tracks had begun to crumble on the edges and there were small wind- borne seeds in them, indicating that red deer had not used this trail for at least a couple of days. He also saw the tracks of some sort of clawed animal which he did not recognize. It was not a big cat and was too small to be a bear. It could be the animal the River Clan had spoken of which lived in burrows. Carni had seen a pelt of such an animal at the cave dwellings of the River Clan and it had been a black and white color. It held no interest to him today. Looking at the other tracks on the animal trail, he saw the cloven hooves of what he recognized as possibly three spos which had walked to the edge of the forest. Judging from the freshness of the tracks, Carni estimated that the spos group had passed along the trail during the night.

He followed the animal trail to the edge of the forest; but a close examination did not reveal the presence of spos. The tracks led toward the southwest as the group of spos appeared to be grazing along the edge of the forest. Kardi pointed out evidence that the spos were grazing on small shrubs that grew just outside of the forest. Carni returned to the forest and proceeded west as before, stopping occasionally to smell the wind. After traveling for about half an hour, Kardi caught the strong odor of the spos and motioned to Carni. He carefully smelled the wind and caught a faint odor of spos. He nodded to Kardi. He carefully led Kardi to the edge of the forest and scanned the area to the west along the edge of the forest. About a hundred yards to the west, he saw three spos grazing calmly on the brush that grew just at the forest's edge. Carni and Kardi quickly returned deeper into the forest and proceeded west to get as close the spos as possible.

As he was a little east and north of the spos group, he came across another game trail. Without actually entering the game trail, he examined the tracks and saw that there were old spos tracks headed both north and south. Carni surmised that the spos used these trails regularly and since it was about time for this spos group to find a bedding site for the day, they probably would use the trail to re-enter the forest.

He motioned to Kardi to follow him and he proceeded north through the forest east of the game trail. He selected an ambush site just east of the game trail, as the trail entered a small clearing. He and Kardi concealed themselves at the eastern edge of the clearing and waited with their throwing spears ready. It was only a few moments until Kardi detected the odor of the spos getting very strong and gestured this information to Carni. He nodded his agreement and simultaneously they heard the noise created by the massive antlers rattling against the branches, as the spos passed along the animal trail. The huge bull entered the clearing first and Carni motioned to Kardi to wait. The second spos to enter the clearing was a large female; again, Carni motioned to wait. The third spos to enter was a younger female that was about half the size of the giant male.

Carni motioned to Kardi that this was the target and simultaneously they stood and launched their throwing spears at the young female. As soon as the spears were in the air, they reloaded the spear thrower, Carni much faster than Kardi.

The large female was just entering the forest and was the first to notice the standing hunters, just as the throwing spears struck the smaller female. Carni's spear entered the smaller female spos just behind the right foreleg and Kardi's spear entered the center of her abdomen, both spears sinking deeply into the spos' body. The two uninjured spos broke into the forest making loud noise as their antlers struck tree branches announcing their progress, as the escaped through the forest. The injured spos ran north on the animal trail about fifty feet before falling onto her left side. Her legs continued to gyrate as if running, as she slowly died from loss of blood. From the look of the dark red blood, it was obvious that Carni's spear had struck her heart. Kardi's spear had not been a death blow and would have resulted in a long, slow death and possibly a loss of the animal, if Carni's spear had not hit its mark. Carni pointed this out to Kardi and told her to practice more.

The two hunters knew that it would be impossible to carry all of the meat to the grotto in one trip, since the animal weighed hundreds of pounds. They started dressing the animal. They took turns drinking the blood, as it ran from the spos body, until they had their fill. They would leave the innards for the meat-eaters and try to carry choice cuts, such as the loin and the liver and one hind quarter each. There were no rocks close by; so, they could not cover the remaining meat to protect it from the meat-eaters until their return. Carni decided to trust to luck and placed the front quarters, the hide, the head and the neck up two trees in a "V" in the branches about six feet high. It might be effective against hyenas; but not cats. They shouldered the meat and started their zigzag return to the grotto.

It took them about two hours to make the return trip to the grotto. They were very tired when they arrived and left the meat in the grotto; but they knew they had to make another trip as fast as possible, or the remaining spos meat would be stolen by meat-eaters. They rolled the rock back in place and made the return trip to the place that had left the spos meat up in the trees.

As they neared the area, they approached from the east since the wind was still from the west. Carni did not smell meat-eaters; so, they were in time, if they hurried. Carni quickly pulled the two front quarters and the hide from the trees and they carried them across their shoulders, as they retraced their steps back to the grotto. As they neared the grotto, a large bank of dark clouds was approaching from the northwest. They both knew that the first winter storm was on its way and tomorrow would be very cold, probably with heavy snow.

By the time the meat was safely in the grotto it was late afternoon and the sky was darkening. Carni knew that there was not enough time to retrieve the head and neck of the spos. He decided to let the meat-eaters have it. They set to work preparing the meat for drying and cooking. Once that was complete, they intended to prepare the hide to make a sleeping robe for their bed of boughs.

With the rock in place in front of the grotto, the fire could be larger than normal and a greater amount of smoke was acceptable since the snow storm would probably obscure it. They worked into the night cutting and smoking the meat.

Simultaneously, they had a roast cooking over the fire to eat as their evening meal. They had not eaten since they had shared the animal's blood after the kill. Before the roast was completely cooked, they stopped work and shared a small portion of it. The roast was gigantic and would be enough for at least five or six days.

The weather outside of the grotto had become a wind-driven, howling blizzard. As the wind blew over the crack in the top of the grotto, it made an intense howling sound that at first startled them until they understood its origin. They surveyed their preparation for the winter. They had plenty of wood to last a few weeks, if necessary; they had water at the back of the grotto and snow to melt, if needed. The reed baskets lined the grotto walls and were filled with plants, roots and smoked meat. They were both convinced that they could pass the winter with only an occasional need to supplement their resources by additional hunting.

Although there was no urgent need, Carni intended to kill a reindeer occasionally to provide fresh meat. He had seen the results of people who had tried to go an entire winter without the benefit of fresh meat. Many became ill, suffered and often died. He told Kardi of this and she agreed that fresh meat was a necessity. They were still covered with spos blood and they retired to the bed of boughs, where they licked each other until clean. Carni again planted the Nord Clan seed in Kardi.

CHAPTER 15

WINTER AND REINDEER

The blizzard lasted for two complete days. The wind blew unmercifully, driving the snow into snow banks which were ten feet high in places. The grotto was completely covered with snow; but the heat from the fire melted the snow above the rock blocking the entrance. Carni could not move the rock from in front of the grotto due to a blockage of snow. He was able to push it out about five inches so that he could see that a snow drift had covered the area where he normally rolled the rock.

He decided that after the weather improved, he would clean the snow away from the area where he rolled the rock and build a snow bank in front of the grotto entrance to block the snow from blowing a drift in front of the grotto. A snow bank would also help to provide concealment for the grotto entrance such that the contrast of the dark entrance to the white snow would not be so obvious.

In the meantime, Carni and Kardi busied themselves by making a robe and winter garments from the Irish elk hide. They wanted to first stake the hide outside to freeze before scraping it. But since the snow had them locked in the grotto, they scraped the hide after soaking it in water and stretching it out inside the grotto. Carni showed Kardi how the Nord Clan made their winter footgear, molding the soft, hairless side of the leather around the contours of the foot and wrapping the top of the foot and calves with the haired leather side out. Inside the foot gear the Nord Clan placed layers of dried grass to provide additional insulation. When they had them available, they sometimes used the soft down feathers from a goose's breast. When there was deep snow, the Nord Clan fashioned what they referred to as "snow feet." They used pine boughs to create a frame which they covered with reindeer hide. These snow feet were tied to the feet of the individual to spread his weight across a greater surface, thus preventing him/her from sinking into the snow.

The Step Clan foot gear consisted only of pieces of reindeer hide tied around the feet. During harsh winters, many Step Clan men suffered from frost bite on their feet. Carni and Kardi each made a set of foot gear, including the "snow feet" for themselves. Carni called these snow feet "muco."

On the fourth day after the snow began, the clouds disappeared and a strong sun appeared. The wind was blowing slightly from the northwest, making the day feel cold, if an individual was not properly dressed for it. Carni was able to move the rock blocking the entrance to the grotto just enough to allow him to squeeze out of the grotto and crawl on top of the snow drift that blocked the front of the grotto.

Using a large pine bough, he cleaned the snow away from the area where he needed to roll the entrance rock to open the grotto. Once that area was cleared of snow, he was able to roll the rock away from the entrance. He and Kardi then set about the task of clearing the area immediately in front of the grotto of snow and rolling rocks and large snow balls in front of the grotto to form a wall. It was hard work; but would pay great dividends in preventing the discovery of their grotto and helping to prevent snow from blocking the grotto entrance again. They worked all day, taking frequent breaks to return into the grotto to warm. Finally, the wall was finished. To enter the grotto, one had to go around the wall on the left side as you faced the entrance. The entrance rock blocked the right side. Before dark, the couple gathered additional wood for the grotto fire from trees that had lost their dead limbs due to the storm. They placed the wood in the grotto to dry before burning it.

Before returning to the grotto for the night, they made their way to the summit of the cliff to look across the valley. Spread out below them was an enormous herd of reindeer that had apparently arrived with the first winter storm. The reindeer were grazing near the river in groups of ten or more. They saw at least two packs of wolves along the western and northern perimeters of the herd. They saw no men and no other meat- eaters.

Carni indicated to Kardi that the next time that the weather turned very cold, so that other clans had to give up the hunt, they would put on their muco and hunt reindeer. The reindeer hunt was a staple of Nord Clan life and Carni couldn't wait to show Kardi how it was done.

Reindeer reigned supreme during the lifetimes of most northern clansmen that lived in the lands north of the great mountain range. Small game (rabbits, birds, and reptiles) and red deer were more regular food items for southern clans since the southern clans had for many years suffered continuous attacks from northern clans when the followed the reindeer herds. Reindeer hunting was a defining aspect of Nord Clan life in the northern plains, both economically and socially. An adult reindeer stood almost seven feet tall at the shoulders; therefore, killing one was a feat for which a good hunter could be proud. A northern clansman's prestige was often attributable to his ability to hunt reindeer.

In the autumn and spring, the migrating clans attacked the reindeer during their migration, as they forded rivers. In the winter successful hunting required more stalking. During the winter a successful hunt normally required hunters to slowly stalk the reindeer until they were close enough to use their weapons. In the case of most northern clans that made their living hunting reindeer, the throwing spear with the spear thrower was the weapon of choice. Some southern clans still used the throwing spear without the spear thrower; but these weapons were much less effective.

The Nord Clan also had a unique hunting technique that they used for reindeer that was very effective. Wearing a reindeer hide jacket, they carried reindeer antlers and moved very slowly toward their prey, as if they were a group of feeding reindeer. Using this effective camouflage technique, a hunter was often able to get within a few feet of the prey, if he was downwind of the animals.

The hide of the reindeer was just as important to the survival of a clan as the reindeer meat. After a winter kill, the reindeer hide was staked and stretched outside the cave, or tent, so that it would freeze as hard as rock. The next day it would be scraped to remove all the residual meat and often the fur. Then it would be left to cure in the cold. The Nord Clan used the reindeer hide for clothing and sleeping robes; while the nomadic clans also used the reindeer hide to cover their tent poles and provide shelter.

The reindeer population in the northern region had steadily increased over the years; since they were one of the animals that thrived in cold weather. As winter arrived in the far north, the reindeer herds migrated further south and as winter weather began to give way to warmer weather in the south, the reindeer herds migrated north. The clans of the north didn't have to travel far out of their normal dwelling areas to hunt the reindeer. These northern clans didn't have to carry the carcass very far, or invest a great amount of time butchering their kills at the kill site and carrying only certain parts of it back home. The Nord Clan filled themselves on everything from reindeer tongue to reindeer roast, as a result, and used the bones and antlers for tools. As a part of the Nord Clan diet, the bone marrow was viewed as we might view a desert in modern times. After the leg roasts were cooked in the fire and the roast meat eaten, the large leg bones were broken open with a rock, or flint cutting tool and the bone marrow hiding inside was shared by all members who were present during the meal.

On the other hand, the clans that lived closer to the great mountain range, who had developed a livelihood of following the reindeer migrations, were exposed to the ravages of outdoor living and the nomadic lifestyle. They could carry only a limited amount of resources and therefore based their way-of-life on a day-to-day existence, which required continuous hunting. This life style forced the migrating clans to remain small in comparison to the Nord Clan and other northern based clans. Many of the southern clans fell victim to the attacks from the larger clans of the north, such as the Nord Clan, and were weakened as a result. A collective defense was an essential element of their continued existence and only constant vigilance made a collective defense possible.

These reindeer migration followers were small clans; but they tended to form bonds between clans with similar ways of life to help each other defend against the attacks from the resident clans of the north. An attack on one migrating clan was often viewed as an attack on the other migrating clans. Northern clans had learned this lesson and made quick, hard-hitting strikes against the nomads and then retreated to their home bases, where defense was virtually guaranteed.

It had become commonplace for the northern clans to attack the migrant clans, killing the men and stealing their women, when an opportunity presented itself. However, the Nord Clan considered the migrant women to be inferior and would not accept them as members of their clan. Any female captured by the Nord Clan was made a slave and eventually worked so hard that they died. The Nord Clan traditions had developed such that they considered it their duty to plant the Nord Clan seed in the southern clan females and return them to their clan to help spread the Nord Clan throughout the known world.

It was several days before the persistent winter weather arrived with a vengeance. The second winter storm was a powerful blizzard which locked the area into a frozen state which would remain until the spring thaw. The blizzard wind had the force of a small hurricane and blew the snow in around the rock that closed the entrance to the grotto. Carni and Kardi kept the fire burning, but still needed to remain bundled up as protection from the cold.

Carni knew that, once the wind subsided, a deadly cold chill would stay in place over this land for a long time. He believed that most clansmen would not venture out to hunt until their food supply started running low; therefore, the best time for he and Kardi to get a reindeer without being discovered was in the early part of the day as soon as the wind allowed them to move about. Each morning he rose and listened to the howl of the wind and each day decided that now was not the time. Finally, after the fourth day of the blizzard, he awaked and discovered that the wind no longer howled. Quickly, he rose and went to the grotto entrance to check the wind and weather. The snow was still falling; but the wind had almost completely stopped

Their preparation of the rock wall in front of the grotto had been effective in preventing a massive amount of snow from drifting in front of the grotto. As a result, Carni was able to roll the rock to the side. He built the fire a little higher as Kardi exited the sleeping robes. She also had listened for the wind and knew that today was the day that they would hunt reindeer.

They used all of their clothing to dress for the weather and tied on their foot gear with the idea that they would later tie them onto the muco. This should allow them to walk on top of the snow, as opposed to sinking into it. Their foot gear was lined with dried grass, giving them some effective insulation for their calves, feet and ankles. They did not have a reindeer hide that they could use to make a reindeer jacket which would allow them to use the Nord Clan method for stalking reindeer; so, Carni had developed an alternative plan.

He felt that the reindeer were not accustomed to being stalked by hunters who could walk on top of the snow; so, he believed that they would not run until he was within spear thrower range. He intended to move slowly closer to the reindeer and before they considered that he was too close, he would sprint toward them and throw his spears. He hoped to be able to launch two spears before they were out of range.

Once they were dressed and both had their spears with the spear thrower, they departed the grotto. The air was icy cold; but the wind was blowing only a small amount. Carni rolled the stone back into place and they started to carefully pick their way down to the valley floor. The snow was about three feet deep. Once they were on level ground, they stopped and attached their muco to their feet. Kardi tried them out and almost giggled when she did not sink into the snow.

Carni led the way toward the nearest reindeer herd that they could see in the distance. The wind was blowing steadily at about 5 miles an hour from the north. The small herd that they were interested in was located north of the grotto, so the reindeer should not pick up their scent. Now it was just a matter of moving slowly, not going directly toward the herd, but first moving at an oblique angle to the northeast, then to the northwest and then again to the northeast, until they were within spear thrower range.

Carni had motioned to Kardi to stay behind him in relation to the herd. He wanted to present as small a profile to the herd as possible; because, in the eyes of a large reindeer, small was less dangerous. In the minds of these seven-feet-tall giants, wolves and bear were recognizable dangers; but a single man was not a recognizable danger. The herd slowly modified the direction toward which it was feeding to the north, to move slowly away from the hunters; but the reindeer were still not ready to run. Slowly the distance between the herd and the hunters decreased. Carni slowly turned back northeast for the fifth time and motioned to Kardi that it was almost time to charge the herd. He had told her that when he raised the spear thrower to shoulder level. they would charge.

She knew that he was about to charge when the muscles in his legs tightened. She prepared herself to follow his lead. Carni raised the spear thrower slowly to shoulder level and started running directly at the herd. Kardi followed a few steps to his left.

The reindeer realized that they had allowed the hunters to get too close and started leaping through the snow to escape to the north. Carni threw his first spear at the nearest reindeer and, without waiting for the spear to land, quickly loaded and launched his second spear at the next closest one. Kardi was able to launch only one spear before the reindeer were out of range.

Kardi's spear struck and embedded itself into the rump of the reindeer at which Carni's second spear had been launched. Carni's second spear had struck the reindeer in the abdomen. Neither of these wounds was effective in stopping the reindeer. The reindeer continued to leap through the snow to the north; but now the reindeer was splashing blood on the white snow. Carni's first spear had struck the nearest reindeer behind the left shoulder and had embedded itself deeply into the reindeer's chest cavity. It had dropped immediately and lay in the snow bleeding to death, as its legs quivered.

Carni knew that there was little time to waste, since there were at least two packs of wolves in the area. They went to the now dead reindeer and quickly started to cut the meat into transportable sizes. Carni decided that they would only be able to take select cuts, the two hind quarters and the hide. It took more than an hour of working feverishly to get the meat ready to carry. They were both covered in blood when they finished.

From the east they saw the arrival of the first wolf pack. Carni motioned that they should leave immediately while the wolves would be occupied with the remainder of the reindeer carcass and possibly the wounded reindeer. They carried their heavy burden to the southwest intending to head to the grotto in a zigzag pattern. They had reached the boulder field that was scattered before the grotto when a second pack of wolves showed up.

Carni motioned for Kardi to lay the meat down and load her spear thrower. They placed the meat in a V created by two very large boulders. From this position, the wolves could only attack them from one direction. The leader of the pack approached from the edge of the boulder on Kardi's side. Carni stood to his full height and growled like a cave bear. The wolves slowed their advance, as Carni launched a spear at the leader of the pack. The spear struck the wolf in the right side of his rib cage. The wolf went down with a loud yelp. He would be dead momentarily. Carni loaded another spear. The other wolves were more wary now and retreated after the loss of their leader. At first, they sat and watched, as the leader bled to death. Once they saw that he was dead, they decided to follow the blood trail back toward the remainder of the reindeer carcass that Carni and Kardi had left behind. They would probably go after the wounded reindeer, if the first pack did not get it before them.

The snow continued to fall as Carni and Kardi picked up their heavy load of meat and continued their trip to the grotto, keeping a wary eye out for other wolves. Within a few hours their trail near the grotto would be obliterated by the snow. The scene of the kill would remain detectable by the scent of the blood; but after the wolves finished their business, it would be impossible to determine which direction that the hunters had taken.

Once back at the grotto with the rock safely back in place and the fire burning nicely, Kardi began to prepare the meat. Carni staked the hide outside to freeze and covered it with boulders to try to keep the meat-eaters away from it. It would not take long to freeze solid, but he kept watch in case meat-eaters showed up. Once frozen he quickly took the hide into the grotto to clean off the remaining meat. He left the hair.

They worked late into the evening and then used melted snow to clean their bodies of the animal blood. The process made both of them excited and they finished the evening in passionate embrace on the pine bough mat.

To Kardi these sexual encounters were a natural part of what she believed was her new life. To Carni each sexual encounter was another opportunity to ensure that his task of planting the Nord Clan seed into the southern clans was successful. There is no doubt that Carni was fond of Kardi; but he had resigned himself to the fact that he would return to the Nord Clan alone after his year of exploration was complete. Carni was able to surmise how Kardi felt about their union and knew that he had to prepare her for his eventual departure.

The winter proved to be one of the coldest winters that had

struck this area in many years. Snow piled up high around the grotto. Carni and Kardi were fortunate in that they could hunt reindeer by using the muco, while the clans in the area had no muco and the deep snow hindered their hunts. Carni knew that they had plenty of food and therefore, he had only hunted reindeer on two other occasions, primarily to supplement their diet with fresh meat. These two hunts had been conducted using the same technique that Carni had used during the first hunt.

The second hunt had been even more successful than the first, since they had been fortunate to kill a reindeer not far from the grotto during a heavy snow storm with little wind. Because of the nearness to the grotto, they had been able to use the entire reindeer carcass, including the antlers.

The third hunt resulted in Kardi's first kill. Carni had allowed Kardi to throw her spear first and she had struck a small yearling in its most vulnerable spot, right behind the left front shoulder. The reindeer was dead minutes after it hit the ground. Because the reindeer had been small, they were again able to take most of the meat back to the grotto.

The remainder of the winter was spent hunkered down in the grotto during the frequent blizzards and outside near the grotto practicing with their weapons during the infrequent breaks in the weather. When their exit from the grotto was restricted, they worked on their equipment. Carni showed Kardi how to make spear points from flint rock and deer antlers and throwing spears by attaching the points to cedar shafts. He also made pouches for each of them for carrying both flat rocks for their kawls and round rocks for their lops.

As they worked, he taught Kardi many universal language gestures understood by most clans and told her of his wontu journey and the fact that he must return to his clan, or the clan would perish. He made her understand that in the end she would have to return to her clan; but that she would have an important life ahead of her. He told her that she would bear a son who would possess the abilities of the Nord Clan and that this son would become a leader to a people who would dominate the southern world. Her role was to teach the son everything that Carni had taught her and to protect him until he was a man, who was capable of assuming his role in the world.

At first Kardi tried to argue that they should be together; but Carni made her understand that it was not possible. She resigned herself to the inevitability that Carni would leave during the spring. In the meantime, she learned that her son's mission was to always look to the south; explore the southern areas and lead a people to dominate the southern clans.

CHAPTER 16

KARDI RETURNS TO THE STEP CLAN

The winter lasted longer than usual with frequent blizzards continuing to blow well into late March. Carni was getting anxious to be on his way; but two things prevented him from departing the grotto before the definitive end of winter. First, the reindeer migration to the north had not started. Carni needed that event to begin in order to open the way north. As the migrating clans followed the reindeer, Carni could pass through the area undetected. And second, and perhaps most important, he had to be sure that Kardi was safely returned to the Step Clan.

Although Kardi's pregnancy was not yet evident, Carni was sure that she was with child. The Wonto had told him of the signs that indicated that a female was with child. When a young, mature woman ceases to run the blood of life from her female parts, she was with child, according to the Wonto. Kardi had not run the blood for more than one new moon.

Carni instructed Kardi that when she returned to the Step Clan, she should tell her fellow clan members that she had been stolen by a northern clan and forced to work preparing the reindeer that they had killed during their winter hunts. She would show the Step Clan leader the muco that the northern clan used to walk on top of the snow. These muco would prove her truthfulness and show the Step Clan that her absence was in reality a reward to the Step Clan.

She would tell them that she had escaped during the night and had been able to steal their prized weapon, the kawl, to give to the Step Clan. She would explain to them that she had been able to escape by using the methods Carni had taught her to prevent the northern clansmen from following her. She would tell them of hunting for food during her journey using the kawl and about climbing a tree to escape wolves. She would show them how the northern clan used the kawl weapon. Carni convinced Kardi that the Step Clan would accept her back into their fold. Carni was convinced that she might be treated as a hero when she returned.

Carni further instructed her that she should insist on being awarded to a man as soon as she returned to the Clan, so that she could bear many Step Clan children. This should explain her bearing a child six to seven months after her return.

After the final blizzard occurred around the last week of March, the sky cleared and the days became exceptionally warm for that time of the year in the spring. The huge piles of snow began to melt and Carni knew that winter was finally over. The only problem with travelling now would be that the rivers would be bursting their banks with melted snow and even ice dams, as ice broke up following the remarkably cold winter.

The reindeer did not seem to fear these floods and had started their migration to the north, as if they knew that they had lost too much time and were intent on making that time up. As the reindeer migration got underway, the migrating clans, who had suffered greatly during such a harsh winter, rushed to follow. The migrating clans had had a very unsuccessful winter hunting the reindeer, due in large part to the massive snow piles which favored the reindeer and clans that understood how to use the muco. These migrating southern clans were hungry and hurried to catch up to the migrating herds.

In actual fact, because of the rush of the reindeer migration, these migrant clans were to face many hardships during this migration. The reindeer were capable of fording swollen rivers, although some of them would be lost to drowning. The clansmen, however, were not adept at crossing swollen rivers. In the past, these clans had simply delayed their journey north until the floods passed; but this year their need for food drove them to attempt crossings while the rivers were in flood. Many members of these clans would attempt the fording of flooding rivers and would drown in the process. Others would harvest the reindeer that had drowned during the fording, as their carcasses swept by on their way to the next big lake, or the ocean.

Carni decided that he and Kardi would slowly move south and west, where he expected to find the Step Clan. But Carni knew that they would have to take all precautions possible to prevent detection. He intended that they would follow their routine zigzag pattern; but not cross any dangerous rivers until it was safe to do so. There was no hurry; so, there was no reason to take chances.

They left the baskets that Kardi had made in the grotto, along with several robes and the weapons that were in excess of what they could carry. They rolled the large rock back into place to close the grotto entrance. Carni instructed Kardi to remember the location of the grotto, should she ever need a sanctuary.

As they departed the grotto, Kardi felt somewhat dejected. Her life now was uncertain and uncertainty was a fearful condition to members of the Step Clan. It wasn't until their path took them closer to old Step Clan hunting grounds and she saw a well-known Step Clan River that her spirits began to pick up a little. She realized that she would see her father, her brother and her friends for the first time in months. It was not normal for a clan member to be absent from their family and friends for a long period of time and then return.

Therefore, this would be a unique experience for her, as well as for the Step Clan.

Now Kardi knew where she was and did not really need Carni to guide her to the Step Clan. She was sure that they were still in their winter camp and she could find her way there alone; but she withheld that information from Carni in an attempt to delay his eventual departure. They would need to cross two rivers and an assortment of smaller tributaries that were in flood stage to get to the Step Clan winter camp.

They had crossed two smaller tributaries; but had found the current to be very strong and the water to be very cold. Carni decided that they would have to wait on the river bank until the water had receded some before attempting a crossing. He located a deadfall of several trees and that created a defendable camp site, where they could only be attacked from one side. He found enough dry wood to build a small fire in the opening of the deadfall lair.

The fire burned with little smoke and the triple-canopy forest dispersed whatever smoke was created, making it difficult for anyone to pinpoint the location of the fire should they catch its scent. Only someone who was very close to the fire would be able to pinpoint its location. The wind was from the southwest; so, Carni climbed a tree and examined the terrain to the northeast. After an hour of slow, meticulous observation, he did not detect the presence of any danger from the direction to which the wind carried their scent.

They made camp there for the next week, spending their time hunting with the kawl and lop. Kardi was becoming very skillful with both of these weapons. She brought down a running brush rabbit with the kawl, the flat rock skipping once on the ground before striking the rabbit in the neck and killing it instantly. As if to prove a point to Carni regarding the development of her hunting skill, the following day she killed a forest bird (similar to a pheasant) with one rock from her lop. She demonstrated to Carni that she could accurately hit a small limb on a tree with a rock launched from her lop from a distance of fifty feet. Carni supplemented their food supply by killing a newly born red deer fawn. Kardi used the fawn hide to make him a new pouch for his waist band.

After the seventh day, the flood waters had receded to the point that Carni felt that it was safe enough to attempt a crossing. They had scouted the river in both directions and had discovered a natural fording site that had been used by animals for years. At this point the river widened and, as a result, the water was not as deep nor as swift as in other places both up and down stream. They prepared for the crossing by securing their backpacks tightly and carrying a heavy thrusting spear to use to check the river bottom before attempting a step; but it was also used to help prevent a loss of footing, as the current became stronger.

It was slow progress and the water was very cold. At one point the water rose up to Kardi's neck. Carni gave her one end of his spear, so that he could pull her forward through the current. At one point during the crossing, they had to dodge a small tree that had been uprooted by the flood waters and was tumbling its way down the river. Eventually they completed the ford without mishap, other than a case of hypothermia, and quickly built a fire to warm up and dry their clothing and gear.

It was now early April and Spring was bursting forth with a vengeance after being delayed by a protracted winter. Plants were beginning to bloom and green shoots were springing forth from the soil in every direction that Kardi looked. As they proceeded southeast toward where the Step Clan winter camp was probably still located, Kardi gathered many of these tender greens and they ate them with the dried meat they carried, or the small animals that they were able to kill along the way.

After ten days, both Kardi and Carni realized that they were drawing near to the clan's winter camp. Kardi was the first to catch the faint scent of humans; but as Carni explored the scent carried on the wind, he decided that it was still very distant. Carni had taken precautions to ensure that their trail together could not be discovered; so, he informed Kardi that she must go the rest of the way alone. He instructed her to wade downstream for a significant distance and exit on a rocky surface to prevent the clan from backtracking her to their common trail. Carni would observe her from a distance until he was convinced that she was safely reunited with her clan.

Before they separated, Carni reminded her of their time together by touching their mouths together, as he had done so many times before during their mating rituals. Kardi shuddered, realizing that this was the last time that he would do that.

Kardi entered the stream and began to wade west. When she turned to look back at Carni, he was nowhere to be seen. She imagined that he was watching from the forest; but she could not detect him. After wading in the stream for about half a mile, she came to a place where the southern bank was composed almost completely of smooth rocks. The rocks led to the southwest which was her desired direction; so, she exited the stream and carefully walked in that direction. She wanted to leave no tracks, as Carni had instructed. Here her footprints would disappear in a couple of hours. She walked all day and the river that she was following began to look more familiar as she travelled along it. She did not come upon the Step Clan winter camp before it was becoming too late to travel. She made camp at a deadfall made by two trees and built a fire. The wind direction had change and was now blowing from the northwest. Clouds were gathering in the direction and she expected a spring thunderstorm. She gathered branches and boughs and with the addition of a reindeer robe covered her deadfall lair to help protect the fire and her from the rain.

In a matter of minutes after she had gathered a large amount of dry wood, the thunderstorm arrived. Lightning flashed and thunder crashed, as the rain plummeted down on her little sanctuary in the forest. The limbs and reindeer hide did their job well and the fire continued to burn. Although her robe protected her from the rain, which was able to penetrate her shelter; the light breeze was cold against her face. Eventually, she fell asleep. As she had been taught by Carni, she awakened every two hours to replenish the fire with the wood she had gathered.

The wood had gotten wet from the rain that penetrated her shelter; so, although it burned well enough. As dawn began to break and Kardi was still lost in sleep, the fire was emitting a large amount of thick white smoke. The fire was too large to allow the triple-canopy forest to disperse all of the smoke and the smoke rose above the tree tops and drifted southeast with the wind.

Kardi awakened about an hour after dawn and ate some of the fawn meat and greens she had been carrying. She went just outside of the deadfall lair and answered nature's call and then prepared her pack to continue her search for the Step Clan winter camp.

When she was ready, she started to walk southwest. She had walked only a couple of hundred yards when a man jumped onto the trail in front of her. Startled, she turned to flee in the opposite direction only to discover two additional men behind her. Before she could try to run to the south, she realized that she recognized one of the men behind her. It was her father, Kroli!

She was ecstatic, although he did not recognize her at first. She made the gesture of being lost and said her name and Kroli beamed, as he recognized her. They ran together and touched their greetings, as they were surrounded by the rest of the Step Clan party. They all appeared astonished to see Kardi, since they had resigned themselves to the fact that she was probably dead. If she had been taken by another clan, they knew that they would never see her again; so, it was the same as if she were dead.

There were five clansmen in the hunting party with Golik as its leader. They had seen the smoke, as they were returning from a red deer hunt northeast of the winter camp. The party was carrying the results of their hunt, a female red deer and her fawn. The five were able to carry the meat from the entire animal and had left only some of the intestines for the scavengers.

In unison the members of the hunting part began to gesture their questions to her about what had happened. Golik motioned for all of them to be still. He was the leader and he would ask the questions; he showed with his typical domineering demeanor. She looked at Kroli, as if to ask what she should say. He wanted to know himself; so, he gestured for her to answer.

She told the story that she and Carni had rehearsed. She had been stolen by a hunting party from a northern clan that had migrated south with the reindeer and she had been forced to go north to where the reindeer herds were spending the winter and work for the northern clan by cleaning and preparing their kills. When the reindeer herds had begun their migration north, she had finally been able to escape and she showed them the muco that she had stolen from her captors and explained that they were used for walking on top of the snow.

They all looked at the muco in puzzlement, as Kardi showed them how they were used to walk on top of the snow. Only Kroli understood how the muco would help the men hunt in the snow and he gestured that the men could travel faster on top of the snow rather than being bogged down in it and then they seemed to begin to understand. Golik quickly grabbed the muco and indicated that he was taking the muco as his own, since he was the leader.

Then she showed them the kawl (rock-thrower) and the flat rocks from her pouch. Again, they looked puzzled. She motioned for a young hunter named Conk to take a flat rock and throw it at a tree about fifty feet way. He looked puzzled at first; but then understood that his throwing prowess was being tested. He took the flat rock and threw it hard at the tree. The rock barely arrived at foot of the tree and missed it by about two feet to the left.

Kardi placed a flat rock into the split at the end of the rock-thrower and carefully aimed her throw and swung the rock-thrower in a 45-degree arc over her shoulder with a downward snap of her wrist at precisely the proper moment, releasing the rock in its remarkably fast flight toward the tree. The flat rock slammed into the tree dead center at about the height of a man's head with a force that would have killed a man. This feat astounded the hunters and, as if they were all one, they exclaimed, "Aahhh."

They wanted to know more; but Golik insisted that they start for the Step Clan camp. He felt that he would be a hero for discovering Kardi and orchestrating her demonstration of the muco and kawl. He took the kawl from her, as his right as leader. He wanted to make a grand entrance to the camp with him in the lead. He would be holding the kawl, as if he were skillful at using it. Then he would display Kardi and have her demonstrate the weapon and the muco and tell her story. This might be his chance to upstage Krumen, the Clan leader in the eyes of the other clan members.

He was accustomed to setting a trotting pace in their travels and he did so now, urging the other hunters and Kardi to keep up. Kroli and Kardi kept the pace easily; but the other hunters started to fall behind until Golik himself tired and slowed to a walk.

Their arrival at the clan's winter camp was a major event. The entrance went as Golik had planned; he was in the lead, followed closely by Kardi and Kroli. Kroli had stayed by her side, since she had returned, and seemed to be taking a protective position regarding her. The clan members all gathered around her, initially ignoring Golik to touch her with their hands in affectionate greetings. Most of the clan appeared to be in awe of her return. No one had ever returned to the clan from the dead and it was as if she were supernatural.

Krumen tried to assert his leadership, demanding to know where she had been and why she had left the clan. He shoved her to demonstrate his authority.

Golik interrupted, gesturing that he knew everything and he would tell the story. He started gesturing and recounting the part of the story that they all knew. He gestured toward Kropin and recounted her order for Mardi to go to the river to fish. He gestured toward Mardi and recounted her disobedience, when she had sent Kardi to fish in her place. And then he told the story of the northern clan stealing Kardi, as if he had been there. He alluded to the possibility that the northern clan had been cannibals; but wanted to use Kardi to work preparing reindeer, before they ate her.

When he told this story, the crowd hissed their collective fear of the cannibals and looked at Kardi even more in awe than before. Golik saw that the crowd had turned their attention to Kardi and hastily continued his story. He told of beatings that Kardi had to endure and of working and never sleeping. And then he recounted her journey, as the reindeer herds migrated south, until just before her captors were preparing a celebration to offer her as a sacrifice to the spirits-in-the-fire, she was able to escape during the night, while her guards slept.

Golik said that he had seen all of this in a vision that had told him to take his hunting party to the north east where he would discover something that would make the Step Clan more powerful. And then he showed the kawl (rock-thrower) with a flourish, as if producing something from thin air. The crowd looked puzzled and Krumen scowled.

Golik said that he would conduct a demonstration. The other hunters that had been with Golik were smiling. They were impressed with Golik's ability to effectively tell the story, even though they knew that much of it had been invented by Golik.

Golik turned to Krumen and gestured that since he was the Clan's greatest hunter, would he like to throw this flat rock, which he handed Krumen, at a distant tree? Krumen was wary; but Golik had recognized him, as the clan's greatest hunter. He took the rock and threw it at the tree which was about seventy feet away. The flat rock sailed about four feet to the right of the tree.

Golik then turned to Kardi and motioned for her to step forward. He handed her the kawl and gestured for her to try. She took a flat rock from her pouch and placed it into the split at the end of the rock-thrower and carefully aimed her throw and swung the rock-thrower in a 45-degree arc over her shoulder with a downward snap of her wrist at precisely the proper moment, releasing the rock in its flight toward the tree. The rock slammed into the tree at about the height of the head of a man. The crowd erupted into exclamations of awe. Krumen was astonished and realized that he had been upstage by Golik. His scowl deepened.

The clan members started picking up rocks and throwing them at the tree. The tree was too far away for most to be able to throw that distance. The ones that could achieve that distance missed the tree. In unison they began to discuss this new development. They were obviously impressed.

Some considered the fact that Kardi had returned to the Clan alive to be a supernatural event and for her to bring a new weapon and demonstrate how the weapon should be used was even more incredible. Women were not typically allowed to use weapons in the Step Clan, except for clubs and rocks.

Realizing that Kardi's situation possessed an element of the unknown, an element that most often struck fear into the hearts of Step Clansmen, Kropin, the leader's wife, stepped forward to address the crowd. She admonished everyone to tread carefully since no one knew what had brought Kardi back to the Step Clan and what spirits were in control of the weapon she had just demonstrated. With demonstrative gestures Kropin said that women should not use weapons; it had always been so in the Step Clan and the Clan was a success because of it.

She looked at Krufen as if to ask what he was going to do about it. Krufen honestly considered this new development. On the one hand, Golik had brought not only a lost clan female home; but had brought the Clan a new weapon, which could help the Step Clan improve their lot. If he, Krufen, took action against Kardi for bringing the unknown to the Step Clan, Golik might be able to sway the crowd to support him instead of Krufen. And, on the other hand, if he did nothing Golik would get the credit for bringing Kardi home and obtaining the new weapon and win an advantage in the eyes of the clansmen.

Krufen made his decision. He informed the clan that Kardi was a member of the clan and should be accepted back; but that she was a grown woman now and must be given to a man. Her man would have the responsibility of ensuring that the unknown that she brought to the clan by Kardi did not harm the clan. He announced that Kardi would be given to Golik.

Golik was shocked! He had a woman and the Step Clan rarely allowed a man to have more than one female. Only in the case of a brother's death, sometimes the dead brother's wife was given to the surviving brother. Golik knew that Krumen had beaten him. If fate delivered tragedy to the clan, that tragedy could be blamed on Kardi; Golik would be held responsible. Golik's face darkened and he moved to the outer circle of the crowd to sulk.

Krufen continued, gesturing that Golik would have the responsibility of training all of the clansmen in the use of the kawl; but that Kardi and other females would not be allowed to use the weapon. Golik was becoming panicked! He was being set up for trouble and failure! He didn't even know how to use the kawl!

Kardi listened to all of this with no show of emotion. She hated Golik, because he was so domineering. She pulled Kroli to the side and spoke to him in undertones, using gestures that could not be seen by the other clan members. She wanted Kroli to propose that after the ritual mating between her and Golik that she return to Kroli's fire and that he be given the responsibility for performing the kawl training for Golik.

Kroli understood and since he was the oldest clan member, he was always allowed to speak to the clan. He stepped forward and indicated that he wanted to speak. He was granted speech by Krumen with a nod. Kroli gestured that Golik was a far too valuable hunter and leader and far too busy to be saddled with the day-to-day responsibility for Kardi and the kawl training. He was a hunter and leader and his value to the clan was in this role. But he was also a strong man and could father other strong clansmen, if he were to mate with Kardi.

Kroli gestured that now that he was getting old, it was often difficult for him to keep up with the younger hunters (a story far from true). Kroli proposed to Krumen and Golik that Golik conduct the mating ritual with Kardi and hopefully father a male and then that Golik send her to Kroli's fire and Kroli would monitor her actions to ensure that no harm befell the clan. He would also assume the role of kawl trainer for Golik, as long as Golik wanted him to perform this task.

Golik nodded his assent and everyone looked at Krumen to get his decision. Krumen wanted to be shed of the responsibility and it looked like this proposal put all of the responsibility on Golik and Kroli; so, he also nodded his assent.

That night Kardi went to Golik's fire for the mating ritual during which she felt no pleasure. Her attitude toward the mating also gave no pleasure to Golik; so, he was relieved when she left his fire and returned to the fire of her father. It would only be a few weeks before Kardi would start to show her pregnancy. She had decided that she would call the baby Raka. She knew that it would be a boy and that he would grow up to be a man of great stature and a great hunter. She would teach him about his father, Carni, and the great clans of the north. She would teach him all of the skills that Carni had taught her and make sure that he understood that he was more than just a member of the Step Clan.

Kardi delivered her baby alone in early October. There was frost on the ground and an autumn chill in the air. Kardi had witnessed, and even helped with, a few births by clan women; so, she understood what to expect. When she began to feel the pains that she knew were birth pains, she gathered a deer skin robe and went to a nearby grotto that she had prepared in advance for this event.

The grotto was very small, only about six feet by ten feet with a roof only five feet high. She had placed water, firewood, rabbit and deer skins in the grotto a month earlier to be ready for the delivery. She was afraid that if the clan women assisted with the birth, they would see that the baby was not a clan baby and kill it outright, or at least tell Krumen. What Krumen would do was anyone's guess.

When she arrived at the grotto, she quickly built a small fire. The pains were coming closer together now and she knew that the birth was near. She squatted down on one of the deer skins and covered herself with another. It was cold and she wanted to protect herself and the baby from the cold.

The baby came out quickly after she squatted down on the deer skin. The pains came in rapid succession; until she had an enormous need to push it out. It popped out onto the deer skin. The after-birth followed a minute later. It was a boy. Kardi quickly took the infant in her arms and bit the cord off, as she had seen other women do. She wiped the blood and mucus from the baby's body with the soft rabbit fur and wrapped him in the fawn's skin that she had prepared for that purpose.

The infant had pale skin, a narrow face, very blond hair and blue eyes. Clan babies always had a wide face, light olive skin, black hair and dark brown eyes. Kardi decided that she would have to hide the baby from the clan in order to keep it alive.

CHAPTER 17

EXPULSION FROM THE STEP CLAN

When Raka was about two years old, as recounted earlier, Kardi was compelled to remove him from the animal skin wraps where she had kept him and to allow the clan to see him. Her efforts to disguise his appearance by applying an ash emulsion to his hair perhaps delayed the inevitable for a few months. But she could not hide the blue eyes, which drew the attention of all of the clan women, who carried the tale to their men.

After a few days Krumen confronted Kroli, who was responsible for Kardi. The confrontation occurred in front of the entire clan. Krumen asked Kroli to explain the blue eyes, since the Step Clan had never seen such a thing. Kroli responded by exclaiming his own consternation. Who could explain the mysteries of the spirits-in-the-fire? He pointed to another clan child that had been born with a large birthmark on his back and said that the spirits-in-the-fire have a purpose for these things.

Krumen did not want to be saddled with the responsibility of this unexplained event. He informed Kroli in front of the entire clan that if this strange child brought evil to the clan, Kroli would be responsible. Kroli nodded his assent.

From that day and throughout the following winter Raka played with the other clan children. Every couple of days, Kardi would put the ash emulsion on his hair, so that no one would notice that he was blond. The winter passed uneventfully; the clan went about its work, while they waited for spring.

The cold weather had again brought the reindeer to their valley; so, the men were occupied with conducting the reindeer hunts. The women assisted by cleaning and carrying the carcasses and hides and preparing the meat to eat and to preserve. The business of sustaining clan life was business as usual for everyone. Clan members became accustomed to Raka's appearance and accepted him as a part of the group.

Another four years passed and Raka had grown and was showing an athletic skill more advanced than the other children his age. Now more than six years old he ran like the wind and threw stones with remarkable accuracy. It was during his sixth year that Kardi and Kroli had begun to train him in the skills that he would need to survive.

He learned to make and to use all of the Step Clan weapons, the thrusting spear, the spear thrower and throwing spears, the kawl and the lop. When he was only six, he was deadly accurate in the use of the lop and even a smaller version of the kawl. His hand/eye coordination was remarkable.

Kroli took him out into the forest to teach him hunting skills almost daily. He concentrated on such skills as determining what weapon to use, the use of stalking techniques, conducting an ambush and tracking. He also taught him the skills that Carni had taught Kardi, such as covering one's tracks, checking one's back-trail and selecting and preparing a defendable camp site. When he was on these trips with Kroli, he was able to kill small animals, which he proudly brought back to Kardi to show his ability as a hunter. One important skill that Kardi and Kroli had imparted to Raka was the skills of treating a wound. Raka's father had taught Kardi and Kardi had passed on the skills to both Kroli and Raka. He knew what plants to use to treat an open wound and he could suture the wound to close it and stop the bleeding.

The seasons came and went and the Step Clan prospered, never straying from their normal hunting grounds. They avoided contact with other clans and, as a result, were able to avoid conflict with other clans. But as the years passed and the arrival of each winter preceded the arrival of the reindeer, the migrating clans began to trespass on Step Clan traditional hunting grounds in greater numbers. When these clans arrived, there was always the threat of attack. It seemed that with the arrival of each new year, more clans and fiercer clans arrived to hunt the reindeer after their migration to their southern feeding grounds.

When Raka was ten years old, the winter brought with it an even greater danger of conflict. The migrating clans, operating in what the Step Clan regarded as their traditional hunting grounds, had increased to numbers greater than ever seen before. Unknown to the Step Clan, there were many northern clans that had decided to follow the reindeer migration further south than ever before. Their purpose was to prevent the southern clans from returning to the north, when the reindeer made their traditional northern migration in the spring. The migrating southern clans that traditionally hunted to the west and north of the Step Clan had been driven into the Step Clan territory by attacks, or the threat of attacks, from the northern clans. Additionally, with the number of clans in the area increasing, the number of reindeer available locally had decreased dramatically. Competition for this source of locally available food and resources, which the reindeer represented, was becoming very competitive.

It was early winter when during one of the first reindeer hunts of the season, Kroli had been assigned the role of the stalker. He was sent to locate the reindeer herd and return and tell Krumen and the other hunters, so that a hunt could be organized. He had not found reindeer near the camp site; so, he had gone much further north than usual. He was tracking a large group of reindeer through a pine forest, when he heard the sounds of hunters making a kill. The wind was from the north; so, the possibility that the hunters could sense his presence was remote. Carefully, he moved forward using the trees, brush and snow banks for cover. Luckily, he was using a set of Kardi's muco; so, he did not sink into the snow and made very little sign of his passage.

At the point where the forest ended, he looked over a small valley with a small river running through it. Along the river bank he saw the blood and intestines that was evidence that a group of hunters had attacked the same group of reindeer that he had been following. As far as he could tell, they had killed three of the reindeer. He saw that the hunters were still on the river bank preparing the carcasses. He looked more closely at the hunters. They were very tall and those without head covers had light brown, or blond hair. Kroli knew from legends that he had heard that these were the feared northern clans. He had never heard tales of the northern clans coming this far south. He had once known a hunter who claimed to have seen a northern clansman, as the hunter's clan had migrated north following the reindeer. The hunter had gestured that the northern clans would attack and kill southern clans, as they followed the reindeer. The hunter had alluded to the possibility that these northern clans were cannibals.

Kroli returned quickly to his hunting party and told Krumen of what he had seen. Krumen decided that it was too dangerous to risk an encounter with the northern clansmen. To most Step Clan members, Northern Clans were giants and possessed by the spirits-in-the-fire. Krumen decided that the Step Clan would hunt further east in order to avoid these giant demons from the north. Krumen's hunting party hastened to move their hunt to the east. After several days of hunting, they were only been able to kill one reindeer which had been too old to keep up with the reindeer herd.

Hunting continued through the winter, but much further to the east than Krumen would have liked. The available game in that area was very limited. Often the men returned with only an arctic fox, a few hares, or, if they were lucky, an occasional reindeer that was too weak to keep up with the herd. They discovered that the large reindeer herds were much further west and only small groups passed through the lands to the east. The clan was becoming hungry for fresh meat.

Other than the constant presence of hunger, the daily lives of the clan seemed routine. Kardi had taught Kroli how to use the kawl. When Kroli was not participating in a hunt, he instructed the other hunters on how to use the kawl to hunt small animals, or as a defensive weapon. Meanwhile, Kardi helped care for the children and, in her spare time, made pairs of muco for the hunters.

Most of the hunters were now equipped with muco which allowed them to walk on top of the snow. They stood taller, proud to walk on top of the snow. A similar number had mastered the use of the kawl to the extent that it could be called a weapon. None were as good with the kawl as Kardi; but she was not officially allowed to use one. She had hidden one in the grotto that she had used for Raka's birth and, when she could, she would go there and practice. Raka's skill with the kawl at the age of ten was better than most of the adult clansmen.

Krumen was preoccupied with the inability of the hunting parties to find enough meat to keep the Clan fed. He finally announced that the Clan could no longer confine its hunts to the east. The reindeer herds were to the north and west and they needed to go where the reindeer were. Although the northern clan that Kroli had seen was still a concern to him, he felt that it would be possible to carry out a hunt and leave the area of the herds before the northern clans suspected their presence.

The following morning, he sent Kroli and Conk to scout for a herd to the northwest. They both wore Kardi's muco; so, traveling was much faster and easier. Kroli was very careful that they did not reveal their presence to anyone that might pass through the area through which they passed. They never showed themselves in clearings, or against the skyline and used the trees, brush and snow banks for cover. He found a large group of reindeer tracks that led into the forest that covered both sides of a frozen stream.

Carefully, the two stalkers crawled through the trees until they saw the reindeer. There were at least fifty of them and they were feeding on the lichen, brush and trees that lined the banks of the frozen stream. Kroli motioned to Conk that they should leave and get the hunting party; so, they re-traced their path and returned to the temporary hunting camp that Krumen had established to support the hunt. The party was composed of twelve of the clan's best hunters, including Golik. Krumen had also brought five women to help with the skinning and carrying of the meat.

After being told of the location of the reindeer, Krumen informed the hunters that they would split up into two parties. The wind was from the northwest; so, Golik would take six hunters and cross the frozen stream on the east side of the herd and attack from the east. Krumen would take the remaining five hunters including Kroli and Conk and attack from the southwest. Since Krumen's group had to travel the farthest, he would be the one to initiate the attack. The women would wait in the forest edge until Krumen sent for them. The groups split up and proceeded to implement Krumen's plan.

Of the hunters with Golik, only Golik and four others had been equipped with muco, so the travel was slower and more work than Krumen had anticipated when he had planned the hunt. Golik's party became strung out with the muco wearers outdistancing the hunters without muco by least two hundred yards. Golik and the muco wearers arrived at their anticipated ambush site and saw the reindeer herd calmly feeding on the banks of the frozen stream.

The hunters in Krumen's group were all equipped with muco; so, their travel was faster and they were in place even before Golik's muco wearers. Krumen saw the herd and assumed that Golik's group was in place. He decided to attack immediately. All of the hunters readied their throwing spears and after getting as close as possible by using the cover of the trees, snow and brush, they charged the herd in unison.

Golik was caught unprepared; but he and the other men with muco charged also. Throwing spears flew at the reindeer and five reindeer were hit; but only three were wounded severely enough to allow the hunters to kill them on the spot. Golik's group had not been able to sink one spear into their targets. As the herd escaped to the north, Golik's stragglers without muco arrived. Krumen told Golik to take his men after the two wounded reindeer that had escaped. Krumen sent Conk back for the five women, who were waiting at the edge of the forest. The other men of Krumen's group began to skin and quarter the reindeer.

The work with the reindeer progressed rapidly under Krumen's supervision. The three reindeer were almost ready to be transported after a couple of hours; but Golik and his group had not returned. Krumen told Kroli to go check on their progress with the other two wounded reindeer.

Kroli followed the hunting party's tracks as they followed the escaping herd and the blood trail left by the two wounded reindeer. Periodically, he saw a large amount of blood that the wounded reindeer had left. The trail continued north out of the little valley created by the frozen stream and over a ridge into a larger valley to the north. A river, which was not completely frozen, ran through this valley. Kroli surmised that the reindeer would have halted at the river and the healthy ones would be feeding there, unless Golik's group had disturbed them, when they killed the wounded reindeer. The trail looped through a large clear area, which Kroli did not want to cross. Since he was wearing his muco he easily stayed in the tree line and circled the clearing to the west.

The wind was blowing slightly from the northeast and, as he approached the river from the west, he could smell reindeer; but the scent of reindeer was mixed with another odor that seemed familiar, but one that he did not recognize. He assumed a stalking posture and moved east along the southern river bank. He stopped and smelled the wind again. He still could not place the odor mixed with the reindeer scent. He picked up another smell that he recognized. It was the smell of blood. Maybe they have finished butchering the reindeer, thought Kroli.

As he drew closer and the unidentified odor became stronger, he heard voices and he knew that they were not the voices of Golik's group. He knew each of Golik's men and would have recognized their voices immediately. He realized that the strange odor must be the odor of another clan. He dropped to the snow and crawled forward using the trees for cover. What he saw sent shivers down his spine.

On the snow before him lying in pools of red blood contrasted against the white snow was a dead reindeer surrounded by the bodies of what appeared to be all of Golik's hunting party. They were surrounded by very tall men with light hair. Kroli tried to read the sign to see what had happened. It appeared that the hunting party had been surprised while preparing the reindeer for transport. They had been attacked with throwing spears and all of them appeared dead. He judged the bodies to be all fingers on one hand plus two thumbs (seven); so, he knew that they were all dead. He judged the number of all men surrounding them to be more than all fingers on two hands. Apparently, Golik's party had been unable to kill even one of the attackers.

Slowly he backed away from the ambush site and, when it was possible, he walked very fast, even running in the muco, when possible, and returned to Krumen's group. He told Krumen and the other hunters of what he had seen and they knew that they were now all in danger since these tall men could follow Golik's trail back to find them.

Krumen ordered everyone to pick up their load of reindeer meat and without any subterfuge, or attempt to hide their tracks; they headed back to the clan's winter camp. The winter camp was in a cave which was a better place to set up a defense in the very likely event that they were attacked by the northern clan.

As unaccustomed as the men had become to travelling at a trot, they did their best with Kroli and Conk leading the way. Everyone was loaded with reindeer meat, or a hide and some of the women did not have muco to help walk on top of the snow. The hunting party struggled on. Krumen and two other men who were not as heavily loaded brought up the rear. They kept their throwing spears ready and maintained vigilance toward their back trail.

Kroli was not worried that the northern clansmen were closely following them since the wind was from the north and he would catch their scent before they got too close. He guided the men directly toward the cave, since he judged that there was no way that they could hide their trail from the northern clan anyway.

While the hunters were trying to get the reindeer meat to the cave before they were attacked, Kardi was involved in making additional muco for the clan. She was preoccupied with bending the boughs to the right shape; while Garki, her brother's wife, watched the children. The children were playing in the snow and Garki saw no harm in this, as long as they stayed on the ledge in front of the cave. The children were putting snow on each other and then running into the

185

cave to warm up. Raka was the recipient of most of the playful attention because of his blue eyes. The kids would cover Raka's head with snow and then all would run inside to warm up.

Had Kardi not been so pre-occupied with the muco construction, she would have noticed that as the snow melted on Raka's head and water ran down his back and face; the water was black with soot. His hair was slowly becoming a brown-blond color.

Meanwhile, Kroli continued the forced march until they were in sight of the cave and then he suggested that the group rest; while he went to the cave for help in carrying the meat for the rest of the way to the cave. Krumen agreed and sat down in the snow. He was exhausted.

Kroli trotted ahead until he saw the kids on the ledge in front of the cave. He gestured to one child, that was watching the hunters approach, for him to call one of the women. Krumen's wife Kropin came out on the ledge and Kroli gestured that she should bring five women to help with the meat. He also made the sign that there was tragedy. From this sign, Kropin knew that there was loss of life. She called for women and several jumped up to help, including Kardi.

They descended the ledge and followed Kroli to where the men and women were resting with the reindeer meat. While they were picking up their loads, Krumen told the story of what Kroli had seen and his fear of the northern clan was evident in his voice. The women started to wail; but Krumen shut them up with a look over his shoulder, as if to say, "They might hear you!" The additional women shouldered part of the load and the group carried the meat to the cave, as fast as they could.

When they arrived at the cave, they went immediately up the ledge and dropped their loads inside the cave. Krumen turned toward the entrance to give orders about posting lookouts to watch their back trail, when the sun reflected off of Raka's brown-blond hair. Krumen was startled and walked closer to see what had attracted his attention. As he approached Raka, Kardi realized that Raka's hair was no longer black and jumped in between her son and the clan leader. The entire clan turned to stare at Raka.

Krumen looked puzzled. His simple mind was trying to grasp with the fact that this boy had light-colored hair, when Kropin began to chant to ward off the evil that had come to the clan. The other women picked up the chant and the entire clan, except for the members of Kroli's fire, moved away from the boy. Kropin began to gesture that it was the boy that had caused the death of Golik's hunters and they would all die at the hands of the northern demons, if something wasn't done.

Kroli tried to calm everyone and said that Raka was only a child; but his words fell on deaf ears. Men had been killed by an evil clan that was a race of giants with light-colored hair and these giants must have had magical powers. How else could they have killed a brave hunter like Golik and all of his men?

Another screamed and gestured, "The demons killed Golik and his men and none of the demons were killed. They had to be magic! Even Kroli had said that they were giants with light-colored hair! Raka has been changed into one of the demons to kill us in our sleep!"

As if in unison all of the men and women in the clan reached for a weapon and started toward Kroli, who was standing in front of Raka. Every member of Kroli's fire grabbed weapons and stood between Raka and the angry, frightened clan. The unknown had always been something that brought fear to the clan and the only way that the clan had ever dealt with the unknown was to either hide, fight, or to run.

Krumen stepped to the front of the mob and gestured to Kroli with his thrusting spear, "Kroli, either you give the demon child to the clan women to deal with, or you will threaten the lives of all of us."

Kroli knew that he was saying that the women would kill Raka and save the clan, or Kroli would be the cause of what ever happened. Kroli was a reasonable man and he tried reason, again gesturing, "I will keep the child at my fire and he will harm no one."

Krumen's woman gestured wildly, "It's the child and the mother; both must go, or we will all be killed by the demons! If Kroli defends the demons, then he is also a demon!"

Krumen's mind was searching for a way out; but he too was frightened. He saw Kroli and his group armed and ready to defend the demon child and he saw the rest of the clan armed and ready to fight Kroli's group in order to kill the demon child. Many more would die, if he did not stop the fight. He decided that it was more than he could deal with.

Faced with the flee-or-fight decision, Krumen decided to flee. "Kroli," he gestured, "The Clan will leave this place where the demons kill us and you and your fire must rid the clan of the demon child, or you cannot go with the Clan." He made the pronouncement with an air of authority that he did not feel.

He looked at the faces of his people and they seemed to relax, confident that he had come to a solution that would save the Clan. He looked at Kroli and saw a look of resignation and he knew that the problem of the demon child was solved.

Again, he gestured to Kroli, "Will you kill the demon child, or will your entire fire be banished from the clan and be left for the meat-eaters and demons to devour?"

Kroli seemed resigned to killing the child in order to save

188

the rest of his fire, until his eyes settled upon Kardi's face. Her scowl was fierce and she had armed herself with a kawl. He knew that she would defend the child with her life and she knew how to use the kawl better that anyone in the clan. He knew that there was only one way to end this.

He gestured to Krumen, "My fire will stay and not bring more danger to the Step Clan."

Milka, Kroli's son and Kardi's brother stared at Kroli in wonder at his bravery, while his wife Garki looked at him with a mixture of disbelief and fear. Kardi was resigned to her fate and knew that she must risk her life by being banished, or lose her life defending her child against the rest of the clan. She was amazed that her father and the others of her father's fire had decided to share her risk. She felt warmth inside her with which she was not familiar. She placed her hand on Garki's shoulder as a sign of support and solidarity. Garki relaxed and returned the gesture.

Krumen knew that this solution might not last; so, he quickly started gesturing to the rest of the clan to prepare to leave this place of danger. The clan worked furiously gathering their belongings, food, including most of the reindeer meat they had recently brought to the cave, and weapons. No one came near, or looked at the members Kroli's fire, who sat closely around the fire, appearing to be in a state of bewilderment. No one at Kroli's fire knew what to do next. They watched as their clan, their extended family and friends, disappeared over the horizon to the east. The fear of the unknown began to rise in each of them.

The clan had chosen to go to the east since the northern demons were to the north and west and the ice-covered mountains blocked their path to the south. Before it disappeared over the horizon, Kardi noticed that the clan had not settled into their familiar marching order. Kroli's fire normally travelled in the middle of the order-of-march and

Golik and his warriors normally led the march and brought up the rear; but now both were missing. Krumen led the group and there did not seem to be any recognizable march organization. No one appeared to be responsible for the defense of the rear of the column and performing the important task of watching their back-trail.

Kardi felt a chill, as if this might be the last time that she would see her clan. Kroli expressed the general fear of the unknown with a gesture that indicated that the clan had chosen its fate. He didn't add the feeling inside of him which told him that the clan had also sealed the fate of his fire.

The clan had disappeared over the horizon less than five hours earlier when Kardi saw Brom returning to the camp at a brisk run. When he arrived at the fire, he gestured wildly, indicating that the northern demons had ambushed the clan and killed, captured, or scattered everyone.

Kroli quickly snapped out of his depression and insisted on details. Brom replied that he was bringing up the rear of the march and had fallen back about five hundred yards due to having killed and skinned a mountain hare, when he heard the attack. The northerners made no noise during the attack. The only sounds that Brom heard were the screaming of the clan members. Brom gestured that he had left the trail and surreptitiously approached the ambush site through a stand of trees to the north of the trail.

"The scene was horrible," Brom gestured. The warriors from the north had already killed most of the men in their initial attack. They had used spear throwers in the initial attack and were in the process of running down the rest of the men, women and children and clubbing them to death, when Brom arrived. He saw them pounce upon Krumen, who had been felled by a spear, and club him to death. Kropin was killed outright when she tried to help him. All of the men were dead and many of the women. A few of the children were also killed; but the attackers seemed to be ignoring the children at first. He thought he saw a couple of the children escape to the woods further east; but he could not be sure.

When he saw that there was no hope for the clan, Brom did not know what to do. When the attack was finished, the attackers raped the few women left alive and then killed them with a blow to the head, as Brom lay hidden in the forest. He couldn't watch it and he couldn't seem to get the courage to run until he saw the men from the north gesturing toward the direction of the Step Clan's old camp where Kroli's fire remained.

He knew that they would go there next and find Kroli's fire and kill them all. It was then that Brom summoned the courage to run and warn Kroli.

Kroli did not hesitate any longer. He gestured that they would have to leave immediately; but Kardi interrupted. Kardi remembered how Carni had taught her to cover her direction of travel and to check her back-trail. She also knew where they could go until they could find a better place.

She would take them to the grotto that she and Carni had used to pass the winter. She gestured for them to gather what they could carry and to follow her.

Without waiting for agreement, or descent, she gathered two robes, a pack, weapons and what food she could carry and motioned for others to do the same. All complied, including the children. Raka, the ten-year-old, armed himself with his small kawl.

Kroli's fire included Gruma, Kroli's woman, and their eleven-year-old child, Mok, Kardi's older brother, Milka, and his woman, Garki, and their twelve-year old child, Bot, and a woman named Brow, whose man had been killed with Golik. It also included a young man about 14 years old, who had been given to Kroli to teach, named Beoh. Finally, it included Kardi and Raka.

Kroli's fire would now have to be a small clan and would include Brom. Kroli knew that their first task was to escape the northern warriors. But Kroli also knew that it would be a challenge for such a small group to stay alive and that they would need all of their combined efforts and knowledge to live just one more day, much less one more season. With the northern warriors after them, Kroli was unsure if he was the right man to lead this new clan.

As Kardi led them from the camp site, they were all startled to see three more members of the Step Clan running toward them from the east. It was the woman, Kosh, who had been a member of Golik's fire. Her man had also been killed with Golik and she was leading a young girl about twelve years of age and a boy about seven years old.

She told of the atrocities that Brom had recounted and indicated that she had escaped the attack and discovered the two children running toward the old camp site. Kroli gestured for each to get what they could carry and to follow Kardi. They complied immediately.

Kardi led the way west toward the river; then she entered a stream that fed the river and motioned for all to follow. After walking up the stream for a few hundred yards, she found a rocky formation on the north bank and gestured for all to exit. Kroli checked to make sure that they had left no tracks. She changed her course to Northeast and gestured to Kroli to check their back-trail. He detected no one on their back-trail yet. Perhaps they had left early enough to allow them a chance to escape the northerners.

Kardi led the little group northwest until she came upon another larger stream. She gestured that they should follow her west in the shallows of the stream; but she was careful to leave signs of their passage. After about a hundred yards she motioned for all to follow into the deeper current of the stream and she turned east headed upstream. She led the group east for several hundred yards before exiting on another rocky surface on the north shore and turned northwest.

They passed over a small hill and Kroli surmised that the hill might be high enough to allow a view of their old camp site. Kroli decided to check the back-trail again. Again, he saw no one following closely; but he summoned Raka to his side and gestured that he should climb a tree to see if he could see the old cave camp site.

Raka easily climbed the tree until he was well above the top of the forest. What he saw, he would remember forever. He could see that the northern clansmen were at the cave and they seemed to be searching the ground for signs. Raka saw that they had hair that was light-colored, like his; but he couldn't see their other features, except that they seemed very tall. He descended from the tree and gestured to Kroli and the others what he had seen. When Raka communicated, he used Step Clan gestures; but he also used the more verbal words that accompanied the gestures more often that other clan members.

Having verified that the northern clan was on their trail, Kroli gestured to Kardi to resume their flight. Without further delay, Kardi continued to lead the group in the zigzag pattern designed to disguise the direction of their travel.

She entered one more stream, a stream that she recognized from her travels with Carni, before exiting on a familiar rocky north bank of the stream and turning north toward the cliff containing the grotto.

When they arrived at the grotto, Kroli backtracked to obliterate any sign of their passage, as Brom and Milka moved the stone from the grotto entrance. To Kardi, this felt very much like a homecoming. Of course, Carni was not here; but she had used the knowledge that she had gained from Carni to at least temporarily save her family. She could feel his wisdom guiding her.

She had taught Raka all of the skills Carni had taught her. First, she had taught Kroli and then Kroli had taught others, including Raka. Both Kardi and Kroli knew that Raka would be their future, if there was to be a future.

The grotto was almost as she had left it, years earlier. Rodents had had gnawed the baskets and had eaten all of the food stuff that they had left in the cave. They had left several robes and lengths of leather which were mostly intact, with minor damage from the rodents. The fire pit was the same as she had left it and there was still a large supply of dry wood that they could use. The meat skewers still hung above the fire, ready for use. They had left some extra weapons, which they could not carry at the time. There were three kawls and two spear throwers with a large supply of throwing spears that Carni had made trying to make the perfect spear. The spear heads were made from antlers instead of flint rock. These might prove to be useful, if they had to fight the northern clansmen. She pointed them out to Kroli, who immediately squatted down to examine them. Brom joined him, hefting a kawl to test its balance.

She gestured to everyone to indicate that the fire must be very small and that the smoke would filter out a crack in the grotto roof and disperse through the trees at the top of the cliff. Kroli stopped her and told them all that they could not risk a fire just yet. Once they did start a fire, the rock would be kept in place when the fire was burning. Their most immediate priority was to prevent discovery by the northern clansmen.

As if she were the matron of the cave, Kardi started

gesturing to all the tasks that needed to be performed right away. Wood had to be gathered; but carefully, so as not to be seen by the men from the north. They needed food; but hunting would have to wait until the threat from the northern clansmen had passed. They needed to repair the baskets and they needed to post lookouts to be alert for danger.

The grotto was defendable; but not against a strong attack. This group was too small to fight off a determined attack and their safety would depend upon their ability to hide. Kroli motioned that only he and Brom would exit the grotto, until it was safe. He stationed the young Beoh at the grotto entrance to watch for the enemy, or other dangers. Beoh had been given his name, which meant "water bird," due to the fact that he had developed a reputation as an expert in the use of the lop to kill water birds.

Everyone jumped to their tasks, because they all realized that they were indeed alone without the protection of numbers to which they were accustomed. Brom and Kroli left the cave to gather wood and look for meat; everyone else started gathering the wood in the cave for a fire, when they could safely start one. Others started gathering rocks piled in the grotto to use with their kawls. They only had a couple of hours left before the night would be upon them.

Just as night was falling, Brom and Kroli left the cave to gather more wood and look for meat. Everyone else started to prepare sleeping mats using pine limbs just outside the grotto entrance. Others started gathering rocks piled in the grotto to use with their kawls.

Brom and Kroli had been able to kill two hares with their kawls. They would have fresh meat tonight and be able to save the food that they had brought with them. Tomorrow would be another day and there was much to do, if they were to stay alive.

They passed the first few hours of darkness huddled together for warmth inside their robes. Finally, at about midnight. Kroli decided to risk a very small, dry fire for warmth and to cook some of the fresh meat.

The little Kroli clan would be the smallest clan that Kroli had ever known, consisting of eight adults and six children. It was composed of three adult males (Kroli, Milka and Brom) and five adult women (Kroli's woman, Gruma; Milka's woman, Garki; a woman named Brow; a woman named Kosh; and Kardi). The six children included Gruma's child (Mok), Garki's child (Bot), the two children that Kosh had saved (a seven- year-old boy (no name) and a twelve-year-old female called "Kuo," which meant sun in the Step Clan language, Beoh, who was a young man of fourteen, and Raka, now ten years old.

The little group was now snugly hidden in a grotto, which the northern clan had failed to find during their first day's attempt. The northern clan would probably have to cease their search during the night. Kroli thought that they might continue the next day; but would soon give up the search, if they did not find them quickly. They would assume that the survivors would run to escape the pursuers instead of hiding nearby.

The group talked in hushed voices and gestures until late into the night. The fire was allowed to burn down to a red glow of coals. Well after midnight and after everyone had eaten fresh meat, most of the clan fell asleep, except Kardi, who also woke Raka. She took him to the grotto entrance, now closed with the boulder rolled in front of the entrance. She pointed to the cracks surrounding the edges of the boulder and motioned for Raka to look out of them for danger and to smell the air entering the grotto. They detected nothing; but her teaching point was made. They retired to their robes to sleep.

CHAPTER 18

THE KOPSUT CLAN

Kroli did not allow anyone to exit the grotto the next day. He did roll the entrance boulder slightly open, so that one of the adults could stand watch at the entrance continuously. They did not build a large fire; but kept the smoldering coals burning beneath the ashes. They did not see any of the northern clan; but did see a small pack of Kopsut (wolves) that showed a fleeting interest in the grotto; but moved on after a moment of observation.

Kroli gestured to the group that the presence of the wolves meant that there were no humans nearby. This was a good sign; but he insisted that they remain hidden. They ate some of the food that they had taken from the Step Clan cave, when they had made their escape. This food would last another couple of days; but soon they would have to hunt.

Kroli announced that their new clan was much like a kopsut pack and that the visit of the kopsut had been a sign that the Kroli Clan would be called the Kopsut Clan. The Clan would be cunning, fierce and loyal to each other, much like the kopsut.

The days were beginning to grow warmer and the reindeer would soon start their migration north. Kroli thought that they might be able to get a reindeer before the migration began; but they would have to be alert for the northern clansmen. The danger of discovery might be too great to attempt such a hunt.

They awakened on the fourth day in the grotto to an unexpected early spring snow storm. There was about six inches of snow on the ground when they awakened and the snow was still falling very hard. Flakes were as large as the rocks they used for their lops. Kroli looked at Kardi, remembering her relating the story of Carni using the snow storm to cover a reindeer hunt and hide the tracks of their return to the grotto.

He quickly stirred the fire, building it up to produce a small amount of warmth in the grotto. He gestured to Brom and Mardi that they were going reindeer hunting. Beoh insisted on coming along and Kroli knew that it would be important for Beoh to get experience hunting reindeer; so, he agreed. He cautioned everyone to follow his lead. Everything they did during the hunt could potentially bring the northern clansmen to their trail.

They each took a warm robe and wore a pair of muco to allow them to walk on top of the snow and carried a spear thrower and four spears. They rolled the boulder away from the entrance and then rolled it back in place.

Kroli led the hunters northwest, until they were some distance from the grotto; then he turned due north. Kroli surmised that the reindeer may have started drifting to the north in preparation for their annual migration. His guess was correct. They came across the tracks of a large herd of reindeer, perhaps fifty, or more, followed only by a small pack of wolves. He found no tracks of humans. He examined the reindeer excrement and judged that it had been left during the night.

Kroli examined the surrounding landscape. To the north there was a rise in the land which disappeared into a valley over the horizon. The snow was falling hard and it was impossible for him to see very far.

"There would probably be a river, or stream running through that valley," thought Kroli. The reindeer tended to feed along the frozen stream beds, or in frozen marshes. Kroli gestured to the other hunters that he expected to find the reindeer in the valley ahead.

The hunters proceeded toward the valley carefully using the forest for concealment, as they slowly stalked toward the rise to the north and entered the valley. As Kroli had suspected, there was a small river flowing through the valley and it was partially frozen. The reindeer were feeding along the southern bank of the river; but the snow obscured most of them. There was no wind; so, Kroli decided the best hunting tactic was to drive the reindeer toward hidden hunters to launch an ambush. He sent Mardi to circle the herd and to approach the herd from the west. He expected the herd to attempt to escape to the east along the southern bank of the river. He stationed Beoh slightly to the south of the herds projected escape route and he and Brom hid themselves in the snow along a game trail which paralleled the river bank.

As Milka approached from the west, the herd caught his scent and began to drift to the south and east along the game trail where Kroli and Brom were hiding. The herd sensed the presence of Beoh to the south and headed straight east along the game trail. As the herd arrived at the hiding place that Kroli and Brom had selected, the hunters jumped up from beneath the snow and launched their spears. Their two spears struck a large reindeer buck and it dropped immediately, thrashing onto the snow and quickly colored it red with his blood. The spears had pierced an artery and the buck was dead in a matter of minutes.

The group wasted no time, ripping the abdomen open with their cutting flints and removing the animal's intestines and organs before dressing the meat for transport. They knew that they needed to return to the grotto before the snow stopped in order to cover their tracks back to the grotto. Normally, the Step Clan used all of the various pieces of a reindeer carcass, including the intestines. Today, due to the distance that they had to travel and the need to obscure their trail, they intended to take only the four quarter sections, the head, the hide, the heart, stomach and liver. The reindeer weighed about five hundred pounds after it had been dressed.

Brom carried a front quarter section and the head, Milka carried a rear quarter section and the hide, while Kroli carried a rear quarter section and the selected innards and Beoh carried a front quarter section. Each man carried more than a hundred pounds. It was very hard work and they stopped a few times to rest. Their trail was initially covered in blood which dropped from the carcass; but the carcass pieces eventually froze and the snow continued to fall to cover their tracks. By the time they had secured the meat in the grotto, they were dead tired and covered in reindeer blood.

The men washed the blood off of their bodies using snow; while the women prepared the meat to cook and dry. The snow continued to fall, as the men entered the grotto and closed the boulder in front of the entrance. The snow had reached a height of about two feet and continued to fall. The fire was built up higher, since there was little chance of it being discovered during such a heavy snow storm.

The women started to cook a reindeer roast over the fire and to prepare most of the meat for drying using the basket "smoke catchers" that Kardi had left in the grotto from her time there with Carni. The meat was cut into thin slices which were hung in the baskets which were then suspended upside down over the fire. The grotto was filled with the delicious aroma of cooking meat. The warmth from the fire and the smell of food created a festive atmosphere in the grotto, which was a welcome change from the fear and uncertainty that had gripped the little group for the past few days.

Kroli felt content, as he sliced a piece of roast off of the cooking reindeer rump with his flint cutting tool. He shared the piece of roast with Raka, as they sat by the fire.

"Perhaps it was a time to recount a legend," thought Kroli.

Legends to the Step Clan were the way they passed history and the lessons in life from generation to generation. They were usually told in the evenings around a cooking fire. They normally included dangers and heroes and always the fear of the unknown. Kroli decided that he would tell the legend of the death of the Step Clan, which would be told to the descendants of the Kopsut Clan forever from this day forward.

To tell a legend, Step Clan tradition required that the teller hold a stick of wood, while it burned, so that the listeners could see the teller's face. Kroli reached into the fire and took the un-burning end of a burning stick and held it in front of him and started to hum slowly. Everyone became instantly quiet, knowing that Kroli was going to tell them a legend. Legends were exciting, very entertaining, as well as very instructive.

Kroli's humming became deeper and louder and was

picked up by the onlookers. Kroli began to gesture and speak of the events that led up to the death of the Step Clan, as the on- lookers continued to hum in a low monotonous tone. Kroli's gestures and words told this story:

The Step Clan was led by a mighty hunter, who was known for his feats of great strength. His name was Krufen. He had been fathered by the greatest of leader of all times, who was respected by all clansmen and feared by other clans, the great Kruf. (The group nodded their agreement with this statement.) The spirits-in-the-fire blessed Krufen with Kruf's strength; but Krufen had no use for the old wisdom of his father. He led the clan in new directions that were unknown to the clan and filled with dangers that the clan could not understand. The clan no longer travelled from place to place at a running pace, as they had always done, when Kruf had been the leader. Krufen often dispatched small hunting parties to unknown places instead of hunting in larger groups in familiar hunting ranges.

Because of the new dangers, the clan was not able to hunt in its old, accustomed ways and meat became scarce. The clan grew hungry. They turned to their leader and asked what can we do to get meat? Krufen was a brave hunter and not afraid of man, or meat-eater. He led his people unafraid to the lands where the reindeer played among the people of the north. The people of the north were giant demons, who hid among the reindeer and waited for the southern clans to come hunting and then sprang upon them and devoured them. (The group nodded their agreement at this statement.)

The Step Clan found the reindeer, led by their most able stalker, Kroli, and killed more meat than they could carry. But Krufen did not observe the wisdom of his father to keep his clan together and to train his clan for

202

quick movement. The Step Clan was surprised by the demons from the north; who were able to divide the clan due to Krufen's failure to follow his father's wise counsel and keep the clan together. Outnumbered in separate battles, the clan was slaughtered leaving only the fast and smart ones to escape. (The group smiled at this statement and nodded their agreement.)

The spirits-in-the-fire smiled upon the small group that had once been part of the mighty Step Clan and rewarded them for their bravery and sent them a new clan to be called the Kopsut Clan. The fire spirits gave them a savior female who knew the ways of the northern clans and who could use the weapons of men and who had a son who was a warrior child. (The group looked at Kardi and Raka and smiled their agreement.)

But most importantly, the fire spirits gave the new clan a new leader with vast experience and gave this new leader new and old wisdom to follow. (The group was fascinated by this pronouncement and listened in rapt attention.)

The spirits-in-the-fire told the new leader that the new clan must adhere to the old wisdom and to the new wisdom. This is the old wisdom Kroli gestured – the clan must not be divided and must run when the clan must move, making the clan strong in numbers and faster than other clans. The spirits-in-the-fire told the new leader that the clan must also adhere to new wisdom. Women will no longer be prohibited from using hunting weapons; but will be trained to use the same weapons that the men use, making the clan stronger in battle and more successful in the hunt. The new wisdom also said that the clan must find a new hunting ground far to the south away from the reindeer and the northern clans, where only death and destruction can be found by southern clans. This is the legend of the destruction of the Step Clan and the birth of the Kopsut Clan. All must remember!

Kroli started humming again and it became deeper and was picked up by the onlookers, until he sat down by the fire and placed the burning branch back into the fire.

The little clan was excited by the legend and many stayed awake late into the night and discussed it among themselves. As a group, the mood had improved and was much more optimistic. They understood a path forward and had confidence in their leader; so, the difficulties that lay ahead were ignored. They would face these problems tomorrow; but today they had survived. The Kopsut Clan had been born and they felt good about the clan's direction.

CHAPTER 19

THE LAST REINDEER MIGRATION

T he snow stopped falling after it had dumped almost three feet of snow on the area. Without muco it would have been impossible to move about in this snow. On the day following the snow storm, the weather started to become more spring-like. For the next few days, the clan stayed near the grotto; the men venturing out to hunt just after daylight and covering their tracks, both when leaving and when returning. They restricted their hunts to the southeast and were able to kill a number of water birds at a small nearby lake, four hares and a very large red deer.

They saw no signs of other humans in the area; but knew that the other clans would most likely be nearer to the reindeer herds. Kroli decided to make one last attempt to kill a reindeer before the reindeer herds started their migration to the north. Again, he took Brom, Milka and Beoh and closed the grotto entrance after their departure.

While they were gone, Kardi organized the women to make backpacks like the one that Carni had used. She wanted to have one backpack per person, including the children. Raka was upset that he had not been allowed to go hunting with the men. He considered himself a warrior now, since he knew that he could use the kawl, the lop and to some extent a small spear thrower, as well as many adults.

The snow was melting; but the snow drifts were still three to five feet high in places. The hunters used the drifts to help their concealment, as they moved northwest toward where they expected to find the reindeer herds. The muco allowed them to move over the snow without breaking through the crust. Crossing of the streams and rivers was a challenge, since the snow melt had started to fill them to flood stage.

They found the first reindeer herd on the same river where they had killed the reindeer during the snow storm. It was probably the same herd; but now it was in the process of moving across the river to the northern bank. The herd was split with about half of the herd on the south bank and the other half on the north bank.

Kroli decided that there was little time to waste, since he did not want to risk crossing the river. He gestured to the other hunters to sneak as close to the herd on the south bank as possible and then charge the herd in unison. He surmised that the herd would bolt across the river and that they would get the chance to throw their spears, as the reindeer entered the river.

The wind was from the west; so, the hunter's scent was not carried to the reindeer until they were close enough to jump from their concealment positions and charge the reindeer. They were well within spear thrower range when they charged and launched their spears. All four spears hit their targets, just as the reindeer entered the river. Kroli's deer dropped immediately in the shallow part of the river and died moments later, kicking the shallow water into a bloody froth. Brom's spear mortally wounded his prey; but the deer ran east in the shallows about a hundred yards before dying. The two deer that Mardi and Beoh were able to mortally wound were able to enter the deeper part of the river and their carcasses began to float downstream.

Kroli motioned for the hunters to run down stream to try to retrieve the two deer that were floating with the strong river current. There was a set of rapids where one of the deer became temporarily lodged among the river rocks and Brom was able to secure a hold on the deer's leg and hold it until the other hunters helped him pull it into the shallows, where they could prepare it for transport. They were unable to stop the fourth deer from continuing its float downriver. Brom and Beoh began to field dress this reindeer, as Kroli and Milka returned to the location of the first two kills and began the dressing of those carcasses.

Kroli decided to leave two of the carcasses in the river weighted down with large rocks and try to return for them later. The scent of the carcasses would be hidden from meat-eaters by the water; so, he expected that they would be safely hidden. The hunters each carried a quarter section of one reindeer, the hide, head and choice organs, as they followed a zigzag pattern, careful to cover their trail, in returning to the grotto.

They turned the meat over to the women and noted that it was too late to return for the other reindeer before dark. Kroli told the hunters that they would return for the other carcasses the following day. The remainder of the day was devoted to preparing the meat. The women had become very organized in the effort and involved the children, as well. The men cleaned the blood off of their bodies with snow.

Everyone was very tired from a hard day of physical labor and there was little talking after they retired to their robes. To Kroli it seemed that he had just fallen asleep, when he awakened. He saw that a faint light was showing around the entrance boulder; so, he knew that it was time to go for the other two reindeer. It would take two trips unless he took some of the women. He decided to take four women and the teenagers and leave Garki to watch the children. In this way they would be able to make just one trip.

For this trip, the men, women and teenagers used the backpacks that Kardi and the other women had made. This would allow the transport of additional weight more comfortably. Again, they made the trip using the zigzag method through streams to cover their tracks. They did not encounter any signs that would indicate that other humans were aware of their passing yesterday.

When they arrived at the river, they found that the meat had been preserved well in the cold water and that meat-eaters had not discovered it. However, the tracks of at least a pack of wolves and a small group of kops (giant hyenas) were found at the kill site. These animals had devoured the entrails that the hunters had left behind. Kroli gestured that everyone should be alert for these beasts in the event that they discovered the little group during their trek back to the grotto.

Retrieving the meat from the river was a little more difficult than anticipated, since the level of the flood waters from the snow melt had risen, leaving the meat below about five feet of water. The current was strong and the water was cold. Kroli asked that Brom and Marti strip naked and enter the water to retrieve the meat, while they held onto a branch which the others held to keep them from being swept away by the current.

When the meat was retrieved and Brom and Milka had gotten out of the water, Kroli took a moment to build a small fire and allow them to warm up before they began their trip back to the grotto. The trip took longer that yesterday's trip due to the difficulty of crossing flooded streams. The flooding streams offered the advantage of helping the hunting party to hide their trail. Even with the necessity of hiding their trail, they were able to reach the grotto before nightfall.

Again, everyone was exhausted; but there was an upbeat mood that comes after a sense of accomplishment.

Kroli decided that it was still possible to get another reindeer before the northern migration began and he gestured to the group that the four men would hunt reindeer again the next day. The other men groaned for they were tired and there was food; so, they could not see the point of such a quick hunting trip. It had not been normal for the Step Clan to continue to hunt in the spring unless the food supply was short. It was normal in the late summer and fall, but not the spring.

Kroli heard the groans and gestured that the reindeer would soon be gone and it would be too dangerous in the future to remain near the reindeer; so, they must use this last opportunity to get another reindeer. The groaning stopped, as the men accepted the task for tomorrow.

Raka approached Kroli and gestured that he should be allowed to go on this hunt. In his normal adult-like way, he reasoned that he needed to become a hunter more quickly than the Step Clan youth; so, that he could contribute to the small Kopsut Clan's survival.

Kroli smiled at this reasoning and was about to gesture that he was too young; when Kardi interjected by gesturing that Raka needed to learn quickly and asked that Kroli consider this request. Raka was almost eleven years old; but, physically and mentally, he was more like a fourteen-year-old. Kroli reasoned that he would allow it, if Kardi came along to keep an eye on Raka; so that Kroli and the other men could concentrate on the hunt. So, it was settled; Raka would go on his first large game hunt at the age of ten, an unprecedented occurrence for members of the old Step Clan.

Raka was so excited that he could hardly sleep through the night. He was the first one up the next morning and had a small fire going, when the other hunters rose from their robes. He had prepared his gear, consisting of his lop, his kawl and his small spear thrower. The men, Kardi and Raka donned their robes; picked up their weapons and left the grotto, after closing the entrance boulder enough to allow the women to come and go, as needed. Open in this manner, the entrance to the grotto could not be seen except when very close to the grotto.

Kroli directed that the group walk in single file and step in his footprints to mask their numbers, should their trail be discovered. Using what had become their standard zigzag manner of travel, they made their way northeast toward the area of yesterday's hunt. Kroli led the procession and Brom brought up the rear. Raka was silently attentive, soaking up everything that Kroli did.

When Kroli decided to change the direction-of-march, Raka wanted to understand why he chose to change at that particular place and time and he gestured these questions to Kardi. Kardi explained the reasoning that Carni had used when he explained these things to her. At one point, Kroli knelt behind a clump of brush and examined a clearing in the forest for a few minutes before deciding the circle the clearing to the east rather than crossing it or circling to the west. Raka gestured to Kardi asking why he did this. Kardi explained that he was searching the clearing for evidence that men, or meat-eaters had passed and then he searched the forest near the clearing to the same thing. Kroli had seen birds in the trees to the west of the clearing which would possibly fly into the air if they passed that way and announce their presence to anyone who was within sight of the clearing. Therefore, he chose to circle to the east, thus decreasing the possibility that they would scare up a flock of birds and announce their presence to possible enemies.

When the group of hunters arrived at the location of yesterday's kills, Kroli knelt in the edge of the forest and examined the area for a good half an hour. He saw no conkut (reindeer), but he did see the tracks of kopsut (wolves) and kops (hyenas) in the area where they had left the innards of the reindeer. From the edge of the forest, he could tell that the reindeer had crossed the river to the north and that the meat- eaters had followed them. He saw no human tracks in the area; but he wanted to examine the terrain closer to the river. He gestured this information to the other members of the party.

He led the party to the bank of the river and examined the footprints on the bank and in the shallow water and saw only the presence of conkut, kops and kopsut. He showed Raka the tracks and asked him how many animals there were and how long ago they had passed this way.

Raka studied the tracks for a moment and gestured that there were many conkut, at least five kopsut and four kops. Kroli was impressed; that was his estimation also.

Kroli gestured to the group that they would need to cross the flood swollen river to follow the conkut. This area was a natural animal fording point; so, the river was not normally extremely deep; but it was very wide and deeper than normal due to flooding. Kroli motioned for everyone to hold the spear handle of the person in front. He would lead and Brom would bring up the rear.

The river current was very strong; but Kroli chose a crossing direction that allowed the party to face into the current at a 60-degree angle. The water at its highest point was chest high to Kroli; but very cold. The party crossed without mishap and built a small fire to warm up before proceeding on their hunt. They kept the fire small and used dry wood to prevent detection.

Kroli led the hunting party on a line parallel at to the east of the conkut tracks. Occasionally, he would take Raka to the conkut tracks and discuss what the tracks meant. After they had been on the trail for several hours, Kroli motioned to the conkut tracks and asked Raka what the tracks told him. Raka studied the tracks only briefly and gestured that the conkut had increased the speed of their travel.

They were coming to a cliff that overlooked another much larger river and Kroli gestured to the party that they would climb the cliff to get a good view of what lay ahead to decide if crossing this river was feasible. The cliff was over a hundred feet high, but they were able to scale it by climbing the steep slope on its south side. From the top of the cliff the hunting party was afforded a view of a very large river valley. It was immediately evident to the hunters that the conkut migration had begun. As far as the eye could see, there were groups of conkut, varying in size from twenty to over one hundred, moving steadily northward. Kroli examined the landscape and was able to point out three groups of humans that seemed to be traveling with the conkut. The humans were separated by several miles; but he was convinced that the western most group of humans was a northern clan, probably the clan that had destroyed the Step Clan.

Kroli also pointed out to Raka the two packs of kopsut, which were operating on the southern edge of the massive migration. As the hunting party was watching the migration, Brom exhaled forcefully and pointed toward the western edge of the conkut herds. There was a group of hunters attacking a small herd of conkut. From their high vantage point, the hunters could see another group of humans approaching the men involved in the conkut hunt. It was only a matter of minutes until the second group of men attacked the conkut hunters, using throwing spears.

After a quick end to the battle between the two groups, the victorious attackers appeared to butcher the fallen warriors from the conkut hunters and it became apparent to the little group watching from the cliff that the attacking clan was cannibals.

This attack brought back terrible memories to the group and Kroli gestured that they would turn back without trying to get any more reindeer.

Kroli saw that hunting the conkut was becoming far more dangerous for the southern clans due to the increased presence of northern clans and cannibals. He reasoned that his clan was too small to compete for food from the reindeer herds and he needed to find an alternate hunting ground, hopefully where there were no northern clans. Kroli gestured to the other members of the hunting party that this was probably the last conkut migration that they would see.

Brom gestured his question to Kroli, "Conkut are good game; why will we not see the conkut next season, like all seasons?"

Kroli hesitated to reply and finally gestured, "I have been given a legend, which I will share with the Kopsut Clan when the spirits-in-the-fire tell me to share it."

With that pronouncement, Kroli turned south and gestured to the group to follow him. The hunting party's return to the grotto followed what had now become routine zig-zag procedures for hiding their trail. They entered three streams in an effort to hide the tracks of their return and felt secure in their belief that no other humans would find them.

The group arrived at the grotto well after dark and gestured what they had seen to the other members of the clan. There was a general air of fear which sprang from the apparent continuing assault of the northern clans on the clans of the south. The discovery that the attackers were cannibals that were intent on killing and eating other humans was very unsettling. Kroli knew that in order to sustain the morale of his little clan, he would need to do something quickly. It was time for the legend which he had mentioned to Brom.

As the little clan gathered around the fire sharing cuts from a conkut rump roast which was suspended over the fire, the air in the grotto was filled with a delicious aroma of cooking meat. Kroli reached into the fire and took the unlit end of a burning branch; held it in front of his face and began to hum in a low voice. Everyone immediately became silent for they knew that Kroli was going to tell a legend. The members of the little clan picked up the hum and Kroli stood before them his face shining brightly in the light of the burning branch and began the legend.

Kroli began the legend by gesturing that the Kopsut Clan was blessed by the Spirits-in-the-Fire with an old and wise leader to lead them to a new way of life that would allow them to overcome the adversities created by the aggressive cannibals from the north. (The faces of the listeners changed from worry to hope when these gestures were delivered.)

This leader was sent a vision, as he looked over the migration of the conkut to the north and the land of the northern cannibals. In this vision the leader saw the conkut luring the unsuspecting clans from the south to the northern cannibals to be slaughtered and eaten like so many mountain hares. (The listeners nodded their agreement.)

In the vision the leader was told to take the Kopsut Clan south away from the conkut that lure the southern clans to the northern clans to be slaughtered. The leader was told that the future of the Kopsut Clan lay to the south; so, the clan must find hunting grounds near, and in, the great mountain range, near the ice, in order to escape a world dominated by northern cannibals.

The new hunting ground would give the Clan many conk (red deer), large spos (Irish elk) and baskets of krop (fish) to fill their stomachs. To receive these gifts from the Sprits-in-the-Fire, the clan needed to move quickly south, as the last snows were melting and find a secure camp where other clans did not hunt. (The listeners humming became louder to show that they agreed with the speaker.)

The clan should carry all of its goods to their new camp and they would do so using transport logs. (Kroli had seen how the northern cannibals had carried their victims tied to poles with one porter on each end of the pole.)

The vision had continued to show the leader that all of the clan must do their part, men, women and children. During the next moon (month), the Clan must plan and prepare for the journey south. The Clan must leave the grotto on the first day of the new moon.

This is the legend of the journey of the Kopsut Clan to the south. All must remember! (There was a determined look on the faces of the listeners and Kroli knew that he had accomplished what he intended and pointed the Kopsut Clan to what he knew was the only way to give the Clan a chance to survive.)

Kroli placed the branch back in the fire and silently sat down, as the rest of the clan slowly ended the hum that had accompanied the telling of the legend.

Everyone started gesturing at the same time. The primary conversation was about where they would go and what they would find when they reached their new hunting grounds.

CHAPTER 20

THE KOPSUT CLAN MOVES SOUTH

P reparation for the journey to the south began in earnest the next morning at daybreak. The clan knew that they would need to travel light; but they had come to like the idea of staying in one place and accumulating tools and food stuff.

Kroli advised everyone that they must carry their own possessions and for every two personal possessions they carried, they would have to carry an item of food.

Kardi set the standard for the other members of the clan; she separated her animal skins, robes, garments, weapons, baskets and tools into two piles. She intended to carry the first pile with her when the clan departed the grotto, while the second pile would be left in the grotto and possibly retrieved someday. When she attempted to load her intended cargo onto her backpack, she found that it was too heavy to carry any appreciable distance; so, she moved some of her gear to the second pile, until the weight of the backpack seemed appropriate for a long journey.

Other clan members followed her example until, by the end of the week, most of the clan members knew what they would take and what they would leave behind.

Kardi and the other women had made backpacks for each clan member, including the children; so, each member realized that he, or she, must carry what it took to sustain their life.

In accordance with one of Kroli's new "wisdoms," each clan member, including the women, must carry at least one weapon. Kroli advised each individual that it was always prudent to carry a primary weapon and at least one secondary weapon. Kroli, for example carried throwing spears and a spear thrower, as his primary weapon and a thrusting spear as his secondary weapon. Not content with two weapons, he also had a kawl and a lop with appropriately sized rocks for the lop. For the kawl, he only carried one rock and would have to find appropriate rocks, when he needed them.

Raka was proud of the fact that he carried his small spear thrower and spears, a small kawl and his deadly accurate lop. Kardi carried a spear thrower, a kawl and a lop. Each clan member decided what weapons they were best at using and carried them.

Finally, Kroli and Kardi showed the members of the clan how they would transport much of their load using thrusting spears and two pole bearers per spear. They used a large animal hide robe which was attached as a sling under the thrusting spear poles and one person on each end of the pole. The end of the pole resting on each pole bearer's shoulder. After the clan members had hefted the weight of the poles and loaded robe, they took some of their intended items from their backpack to be left at the grotto.

As the group continued their preparations for the journey, Kroli announced that he and Brom would scout the area to the south and determine the route that they would travel for at least the first few days of their journey, even if their final destination would still be unknown. In this way, he gestured the night before their departure, they could preplan their overnight camps in secure locations.

Raka announced that he would accompany them since he wanted to learn how such a route reconnaissance was performed.

Kroli was surprised by this adult-like pronouncement and was preparing to deny Raka this opportunity; but a glance at Kardi showed that she wanted Raka to go with him. As a result, Kroli nodded his agreement. He resigned himself to the fact that Raka was now to be treated as an adult. Brom was astounded, since it was not like a Step Clan leader to allow a child to decide such things. Krumen had not even allowed children to speak directly to him. But Brom had also seen the determined look on Kardi's face and, therefore, accepted the decision.

Kroli and Brom were up and prepared to depart before dawn. With no urging, Raka was awake and had prepared his small backpack and weapons. The other members were still sleeping when Brom rolled the rock from in front of the grotto. The small group checked their surroundings and detected no danger. They exited the grotto and rolled the rock back in its place. Kroli led the way; first heading in a southwestern direction with Raka in the middle and Brom bringing up the rear. Of course, they used the clan's zigzag pattern of travel to head south.

Kroli and the other members of the clan had never ventured more than a couple of day's travel to the south; so Kroli knew that they must be especially watchful for danger and careful not to leave evident signs of their passage. He intended to scout out at least three campsites which the group could reach in a day's travel. As they started the journey Kroli explained his plan to Brom and Raka.

He first explained the intent of using the zigzag pattern to disguise their direction of travel. Kardi had learned this skill from Carni and had taught Kroli. He also showed his two companions how the clan would travel; stepping in each other's footprints to disguise the size of their group. He explained how the leader of the march must guide the group over hard packed ground while avoiding clearings and using streams to throw off any followers. Finally, he explained the skill that Kardi had learned from Carni for checking the back trail to watch for followers.

Kroli had been the Step Clan's most skilled stalker and he knew how to follow a trail better than anyone. That allowed him to know how to avoid detection better than anyone. As the little group travelled, Kroli told them how he intended to set up the marching-order of the Clan.

He informed them that Brom would be the first in the order-of-march, allowing Kroli the freedom to scout ahead of the Clan and hopefully discover danger before it discovered them. Brom would be responsible not only for choosing the correct paths to follow, but also for the defense of the front of the column. The front of the column was the most likely to encounter unexpected danger and Brom was the most skilled warrior in the Clan.

The rest of the order-of-march would be alternated, a female after each clansman. Kroli insisted that skilled spear-throwers must be spread out throughout the order-of-march. The children would each be assigned to a female, who would be responsible for the child's protection. Kroli announced to his two companions that Milka would be last in the order-of-march.

Milka had developed into not only a very brave man, but also a very observant one. He would be responsible for the defense of the Clan's rear during a march and it would also be his duty to check the back-trail for followers.

Raka asked Kroli, "Where is my position in the order-of-march?" He gestured that he would not travel with the females and children! To his delight, Kroli informed him that he would accompany him as a scout to learn stalking skills.

The little group settled into a silent mode of travel, each absorbed in his thoughts and plans of how he would perform his duties when the journey began.

Kroli led the little group in the familiar zigzag pattern southeast toward the mountains. They saw no signs that other humans had passed this way and, as their journey progressed, the ground slowly rose. The forest became more thickly populated with evergreen trees and fewer deciduous trees. They saw abundant mushrooms, which Raka recognized as edible from Kardi's teachings. Kroli and Brom were unimpressed by the abundant supply of mushrooms; since they preferred meat and seldom ate the mushrooms gathered by Kardi. Mountain hares were everywhere and they used their lops to kill several for their meals during their journey. Kroli also crossed game trails which were replete with tracks of red deer and Irish elk. Kroli pointed out the "golo" (cave lion) tracks that followed the game trail to Raka.

It was apparent that the large cat was stalking a red deer that had passed during the night. Kroli gestured to Raka that once the golo had been very abundant in the Step Clan's former hunting ground; but now a hunter could only occasionally encounter one of these giant cats.

After traveling all day, the little group came to a narrow, very swift river, which they would have to cross. Kroli decided that this would be their first camp site. He searched the rock cliffs on the southern side of the river and noticed a shadowy smudge on the granite cliff face that indicated a possible cave or grotto. He gestured to Raka and Brom that they would camp on the north side of the river tonight and check the grotto/ cave out the next day. They found a deadfall near the river that would give them some protection on three sides and they set up camp there.

Raka built a fire at the entrance to the deadfall-protected area, while Kroli and Brom gathered wood and improved the deadfall protection by dragging additional logs and re-enforcing the sides of the deadfall and creating some overhead protection. When the deadfall camp was ready, Brom cleaned several of the mountain hares and began to cook them over the campfire.

They ate their fill and each slept between the fire and the deadfall trees with their spears by their side. During the night a small pack of Kopsut approached the camp having crossed the trail of the humans and followed it to the campsite. Kroli was awake, as the leader of the pack sniffed the rear of the deadfall enclosure. Kroli could smell the Kopsut almost as well as the Kopsut could smell him.

He looked at Brom and Raka. Both were wide awake; Brom had his hands on his thrusting spear and Raka had his kawl raised to use as a club. Kroli eased himself out of his bearskin robe and moved to a position just to the right of the campfire, his thrusting spear at the ready position. Brom took a position on the left side of the campfire. Raka was limited to staying behind the campfire near the deadfall tree-trunk. The campfire had burned too low and Kroli added a couple of logs, hoping that the fire would grow quickly.

The Kopsut circled the deadfall enclosure and arranged themselves across the entrance to the enclosure facing the small fire. There were four Kopsut in front of the enclosure. When they made darting attempts to attack the men on each side of the fire, the men parried their attacks with their spears, injuring one of the Kopsut, but not gravely.

A fifth Kopsut leaped on top of the deadfall enclosure from the rear and launched himself down into the enclosure. Raka had been aware of this Kopsut, since he had heard the animal as he landed on top of the deadfall. Raka stepped toward the animal and swung his kawl as hard as he could at the animal's head. The kawl blow landed behind the animal's right ear, killing it instantly. Kroli and Brom were occupied defending the front of the enclosure and only glanced briefly at Raka long enough to see that he had killed the Kopsut that had entered the enclosure.

The Kopsut pack made another attempt to get at the humans through the front of the enclosure and this time Brom was able to sink his thrusting spear deep into the side of one of the attackers. As his spear became locked in the body of the Kopsut, a second animal attempted to attack Brom. Brom fell back away from the attacker having no weapon, as Raka leaped forward and swung his kawl, hitting the Kopsut on the left side of its head knocking the Kopsut into the growing campfire. The animal screamed in pain, as it withdrew from the attack. The remainder of the pack also withdrew, having become convinced that there was easier prey to be had elsewhere.

The men added more wood to the fire and began to skin the two Kopsut that they had killed. Raka was ecstatic! This was his first battle with meat-eaters and he had killed one and saved Brom from at least a severe injury. Kroli and Brom gestured that Raka was a brave hunter and would be recognized by a legend when the clan was able to set up a long-term camp.

The Kopsut fur would make very good winter head covers and the men would eat as much of the meat as possible and carry as much as they could on their journey. Kopsut meat was considered a rare treat for the clansmen and they would make the most of this opportunity.

After the fire was sufficiently large to keep meat-eaters away, they went back to sleep, since it was still some time until daylight. They slept until well after daybreak and then prepared as much of the Kopsut meat as they could eat and carry. At about mid-day, they decided to cross the river. Kroli led the group southeast upriver until he found a place where a giant pine tree had fallen across the river. Tracks indicated that other animals, including Kopsut had crossed the river using this fallen-log bridge. The clansmen crossed the river single file until they reached the northern side of the river and headed toward the cave/grotto that Kroli had seen the day before.

When they arrived at the base of the cliff below the entrance to the cave or grotto, Kroli examined the approach to the entrance and noted that there was a ledge that led to the entrance from left to right. He told Brom to check it out and Brom immediately started up the ledge. The entrance was about fifteen feet above the base of the cliff and the ledge was only about four-feet wide, making it somewhat easy for a clan to defend it from a larger force. Brom smelled the air and listened for sounds from inside the entrance. He smelled stale air and possibly some small animals. He tossed a stone into the cave and heard only the stones vacant rattle as it bounced around. He ventured through the entrance and after his eyes were adjusted to the low light level inside, he saw that this was a shallow grotto that had probably been created by the river flow during flood stage. It was about twenty feet deep and ten feet wide and would be suitable for a temporary clan camp. He descended the ledge and told Kroli what he had seen and Kroli ascended the ledge to see for himself. He was satisfied that this would suffice for a few days campsite, as the clan migrated to the south and east. Kroli decided that the little reconnaissance group would return to the clan and bring them to this site before reconnoitering any further.

The group stayed the night in the grotto carrying in a significant amount of wood and rocks for their kawls. They built a campfire pit and ate their fill of Kopsut meat. Raka made the fire pit the way that his mother had told him that his father used with a large rock marking each direction, north, south, east and west. They would have to carry water from the river; so, they would need to use their animal stomach water bladders. Kroli resolved to make sure that they had plenty to withstand a siege in the cave, if that should occur. That night they slept in the grotto and rose before daylight to retrace their trail back to the clan. Kroli was satisfied that things were going well for the Kopsut Clan and he did not want the clan to be split up any longer than necessary.

The journey back to the Clan was uneventful. The Clan had stayed in and around the grotto as instructed and had only ventured out in the nearby forest to collect wood, mushrooms, greens and roots. Kardi and the other women and children had collected two baskets of mushrooms, greens and roots, while Milka had been able to kill several mountain hares and Beoh had killed several birds with his lop.

The return of the reconnaissance group was a festive occasion and the entire clan was looking forward to the move to a new hunting ground. The women prepared a feast to eat as much of their store of food as possible, so that they would have to carry less. As the feast was drawing to a close, Kroli again picked up the burning branch and started to hum, telling everyone that he was about to tell a legend. The clan picked up the humming as they listened with rapt attention as Kroli recounted his legend.

Kroli began the legend by gesturing that the Kopsut Clan was blessed by the Spirits-in-the-Fire with a young warrior who would be a wise leader in the future to lead them to a new way of life when the old leaders had joined the Spirits-in-the-Fire. (The faces of the listeners were quizzical, wondering where this legend was going.)

Kroli recounted the encounter with the kopsut pack saying that the Spirits-in-the-Fire had sent the kopsut pack to test the skills of the Kopsut Clan's young warrior and how Raka had killed one kopsut that had entered through the top of the deadfall enclosure and had prevented the injury of Brom with his attack on a second kopsut. His legend continued that the Spirits-in-the-Fire had made Raka a warrior long before his natural time since the Spirits-in-the-Fire knew that the small Kopsut Clan would need warriors more badly than a larger clan. (The listeners nodded their agreement.)

Kroli continued by gesturing that the Spirits-in-the-Fire had told him that from this day forward Raka would be considered the clan leader-in-training and that all members of the clan should take it upon themselves to teach Raka all of the knowledge that they possessed to prepare him for the day when he would assume his responsibility as the clan leader.

This is the legend of Raka and the kopsut pack. All must remember!

There was a look admiration on the faces of the listeners and Kroli knew that he had again accomplished what he intended and established Raka as the future leader of the Kopsut Clan to ensure the Clan's survival.

The clan departed the grotto two days later using the order-of-march that Kroli had established and following the route that the reconnaissance group had followed before. The going was slow due to the burdens that they carried and it took the clan more than three days to travel the distance to their new temporary camp in the grotto by the river. Kroli set a hard marching speed and by the time they made camp each night, everyone was very tired. No one complained and each night there was no absence of volunteers to stand watch since their camp sites were not in protected locations and would be hard to defend against a determined attacker, meat-eaters, or humans.

On the fourth day they crossed the fallen log bridge over the river and for the first time saw the grotto that would be their home until they departed on the next leg of their journey to new hunting grounds. Kroli had told the clan that this location was still too close to other clans and when the time was right, they would continue their journey.

The clan started preparing the grotto for comfort and defense by carrying logs, boughs for sleeping mats, rocks for their kawls and the fire pit and water for drinking and cooking. By nightfall they were settled into the grotto.

Oddly enough, the Step Clan leader, Krufen, had never shared his plans with the clan until it was time to act upon them. Kroli was of a different mind and liked to share his plans in advance to allow the clan to become accustomed to the idea before it was time to act upon the plans. Kroli told the clan of his plan for the immediate future.

CHAPTER 21

THE KOPSUT CLAN'S MOVES INTO THE MOUNTAINS

Kroli wanted to determine if this new hunting area would be suitable for the Clan. To make this determination, he needed to explore the area and he decided to take Brom and Raka with him. Milka would remain near the grotto with the clan until the group's return. Before venturing away from the grotto, he wanted to get a general idea of what the area looked like around the grotto and along this narrow river. It seemed that the weather was warmer than usual and the river was running high with water melting from the snow and ice in the mountains.

Kroli climbed to the top of the cliff that housed the grotto and overlooked the river to see the lay of the land around the grotto. After he had arrived at the summit of the cliff and had begun to survey the surrounding area, he saw that Raka had followed him up the cliff and was just completing the climb up behind him. In a way that pleased him, for it showed an adult confidence, not normal in one so young. But in another way, he felt that such an independent act without his approval was an affront to his authority as leader.

"Well," Kroli thought, "the young man wants to be involved in everything." So, he let it go. He pointed out to Raka that there were actually two forks to this river and that they connected east of the grotto. The river traversed across the front of a deep canyon which ran far into the mountains.

The canyon floor appeared to be covered with forest. The fork where the two rivers connected was at the eastern edge of the front of the canyon. The tributary that formed the fork ran through the canyon along the eastern wall and exited the canyon just before it met the river. From the top of the cliff, it appeared that they could gain access to the canyon by following the south bank of the river until the opening to the canyon appeared and turning right to enter the canyon. From the look of the two forks of the river, Kroli expected that there would be plenty of fish and a forest, such as the one in the canyon, should be full of bush deer, red deer and other forest animals. It was possible that a small clan such as the Kopsut Clan could winter in this area and have plenty of game to hunt.

Kroli gestured to Raka of his thoughts and indicated that they would begin their exploration of the area the next morning. They climbed down from the top of the cliff. It was a little disconcerting to Kroli that Raka arrived at the bottom of the cliff well ahead of him. He was agile as an ibex. Even at almost eleven years of age, Raka was as tall as Kroli; but much leaner. It was already apparent that Raka was going to be much taller than the other Step Clan descendants.

Members of the clan reached maturity much earlier than humans in modern times. A male normally reached physical and sexual maturity by at least fourteen years of age, while females reached maturity between twelve and fourteen. It appeared that Raka might reach maturity by thirteen years of age, a surprising development.

Brom was waiting for them when they climbed down from the cliff and he gestured to ask what they had seen. Kroli gestured and sounded about the two forks of the river and the forest in the canyon. He told both Brom and Raka that he needed to think in order to plan their activities for the following days. Kroli left the two and went to find Kardi. He had found that he did his best thinking and planning while talking with Kardi.

Kroli found Kardi down by the river. He gestured to ask her what she was doing and she gestured back that she was looking at the possibility of catching fish. She said the current was strong and the water level was high; but she could see many fish and believed that they would be able to catch many of them.

Kroli explained what he had seen from the top of the cliff and told Kardi that he wanted to take Raka and Brom to explore the canyon and possibly hunt a deer. Kardi thought for a moment and asked herself what Carni would have done in this situation. She concluded that Kroli was on the right track and gestured as much to Kroli, adding that she would take Beoh and Milka to set deadfall traps, like the one Carni had showed her how to build, for small animals in the forest near the grotto.

Kardi's mind for organization was in high gear. She would ask Garki to take the children Mok, Bot, Kuo and Kosh's seven-year-old ward and gather reeds to start making baskets. She would suggest to Gruma, Brow and Kosh that they try to catch some fish.

Kardi had been toying with an idea for catching fish in this river with a strong current. She had seen how the fish tended to congregate at the bottom of the small falls near the grotto. Her idea was to make reed baskets attached to leather strips that could be placed in the water below the small falls and when a fish moved over the basket, the woman could quickly pull the basket up, hopefully catching the fish in the basket. She told Kroli of her idea and he nodded his agreement.

In the meantime, Kroli and Kardi decided that they needed to gather wood for the fire, boughs for sleep mats, rocks for the fire pit, flat rocks for ammunition for their kawls and poles for spearing through the meat that they hoped to bring home after tomorrow's hunt. Kroli gestured to the men to gather the rocks and Kardi to the women to gather the wood and pine boughs. Kroli indicated that no one should leave the grotto alone. Raka and Beoh took their lops and kawls and went hunting for small game.

The other children, supervised by Garki, started to dig a hole in the rear of the grotto. Kardi remembered the natural depression in the back of the grotto that Carni had found which had been a convenient source of water. She had asked Garki to make one for this grotto. They would have to carry the water from the river; but they could store much more in the depression than their water bladders would hold.

By the time everyone had finished their tasks, it was growing dark. The fire was burning brightly in the fire pit toward the front of the grotto. Raka and Beoh had killed several squirrels and two forest hares; so, the clan would have fresh meat for the evening meal. The meat was cooking over the fire and the clan members were lounging around the fire waiting to eat the meat. The women were grooming the children's hair, looking for lice and the men were gesturing about the trip to their new hunting ground.

Kroli decided it was important to make a teaching point. He gestured to the fire and to the area in front of the grotto, communicating that the fire could not be seen by anyone unless they were directly in front of the grotto. Tomorrow, he wanted to stack rocks in front of the grotto to prevent the illumination from the fire from escaping the grotto and being seen by other humans. If their clan had been as large as the Step Clan, he would not have taken this precaution, since the clan would have been large enough to defend the grotto. But Kroli understood that the best defense for such a small group was to prevent discovery. He also gestured that the fire during the daytime must be small and should burn only dry wood to prevent the smoke from being seen far from the grotto.

Everyone nodded their agreement and looked at the meat to see if it was ready to eat. The women started removing the meat from the fire and passing it to the other members of the clan. Step Clan tradition had allowed the men to eat first, then the women ate and finally the children. The Kopsut Clan continued this tradition. Raka and Beoh were fed with the men, a significant gesture which placed them in the category of men, not children. Kuo ate with the women, indicating that she had been accepted as a woman and would be treated as such from this day forward.

As the people ate, Kroli decided to take another step toward establishing his authority over the Kopsut Clan. He turned to Kosh and gestured that her seven-year-old ward needed a name. He surmised that the boy was strong for his age and would make a good hunter someday. His father had been part of Golik's fire and was called "Bunt," which loosely translated in the Step Clan language as ferret, or weasel, when used with a gesture with the hand of an animal darting left and right. Kroli announced that the boy would have his father's name, Bunt, to keep his memory alive and add the quickness and cunning of the weasel to the Kopsut Clan. Kosh and the boy seemed proud that he had been given his father's name.

The members of the clan slowly retired to their sleeping mats. The clan now had five men and, when they were in a potentially dangerous area, in accordance with the old Step Clan tradition, the men slept on each side of the fire, while the women and children slept behind the fire. The men slept with their thrusting spears near their hands and awakened often to replenish the fire.

During the night Milka rose; checked the night for signs of danger and, when finding no danger, moved behind the fire to Garki's sleeping mat. As the others slept, Milka mated with Garki before returning to his mat at the side of the fire.

The next day began as the sun rose. Raka was the first to rise and put more wood on the fire and left the grotto to relieve himself. As he exited the grotto, he surveyed the area for danger. Since the annihilation of the Step Clan, everyone was constantly vigilant for danger. As he returned to the grotto, the other members of the clan were exiting and going into the trees to relieve themselves.

The matter of relieving one's self was an important aspect of the clan's ability to hide its presence. Much like the wolf, members of the clan buried their scat under leaves, or dirt after relieving themselves. In this way the clan did not attract the attention of other clans so easily. If not buried deeply enough, the scat could be smelled, but not for a great distance.

In the grotto, Garki had started to heat some of the old meat that the clan had brought with them, so that everyone could eat before proceeding with today's plans. Brom, Raka and Kroli grabbed pieces of meat and quickly consumed it until they had eaten their fill. Kroli announced that it was time to depart.

They each took their weapons and a water bladder, as they left the grotto heading east along the southern bank of the river. Kroli was in the lead, Raka in the middle and Brom bringing up the rear. They travelled a well-used animal trail which hugged the bank of the river. The forest was very dense and travel off of the animal trail would have been difficult. The trail led slightly uphill, but became steeper as they came closer to the fork in the river.

They travelled for about two hours before the animal trail that they were following forked. The right-hand fork headed into the canyon interior; while the left-hand fork continued to follow the river. Kroli considered which fork in the trail to take and decided to take the right-hand fork into the interior of the canyon. They had begun to startle small animals along the trail, as well as several deer, which had obviously never been exposed to humans and showed more curiosity than fear. Many of the bush deer stopped to watch the hunters well within the range of their spear throwers. Kroli wanted to kill a deer; but decided to wait until they were returning to the grotto, so that they would have to carry the deer less distance. The deer in the canyon were larger than the deer that they had killed so far on their journey and there seemed to be an abundant food supply for them.

The trail curved first left toward the eastern canyon wall and then back to the right toward the western canyon wall. It seemed that the trail meandered through the canyon, occasionally entering small grass covered clearings. From the evidence that they were able to observe, the deer ate the leaves from the many varieties of bushes and small trees that grew under the larger evergreen trees. At the edges of the small clearings, they saw berry bushes and several small trees that were covered with some type of purple fruit. The fruit was new to Kroli. Kroli picked one of the fruits and first smelled it. It had a pleasing odor; so, he tasted it. It was sweet and probably edible. Kroli and Brom ate mostly meat; but they did like fruit on occasion. Kroli and Brom each ate a couple of pieces of fruit; while Raka, who always ate fruit and greens, when possible, ate four pieces before they continued their exploration.

They continued toward the interior of the canyon until well after midday. Kroli estimated that they were still only about a third of the way into the canyon; but the forest prevented him from seeing the rear canyon wall. Kroli was satisfied that the area would support the Kopsut Clan for a long time and decided that they should turn back and try to get a deer, as they returned to the grotto.

After they had travelled about two hours toward the grotto, Kroli assumed his stalking posture; so, the other hunters knew that they would begin the hunt for a bush deer. It was another hour before they came upon a large buck deer with a massive rack of antlers. The buck was alert; but did not run. He watched curiously, as the men approached well within spear-throwing range. Each of the men had a spear in their spear throwers. As the men tensed to launch their spears, the buck sensed the danger and prepared to run. Brom and Kroli launched their spears simultaneously, striking the deer in its exposed right side. Brom's spear went deeply into the animal's chests, piercing the heart. The bush deer made three leaps before landing and collapsing immediately to the ground. It was only a few minutes until the deer ceased to move.

Brom hit the deer another time with a spear to ensure that it was dead and then the three men quickly opened the abdomen with their flint cutting tools and shared the raw liver. As Brom and Raka dressed the deer, Kroli built a fire to protect against any meat-eaters that should arrive. Kroli had seen little evidence of meat-eaters; but he knew that where there was such an abundance of plant eaters, there would be an equal abundance of meat-eaters. Kroli did recall seeing old tracks of a cave-lion where the trail had forked into the canyon; but those tracks had followed the other fork in the trail.

They decided not to skin the deer. Gutting the deer took about an hour and that was enough time for Kroli to decide how they would be able to transport the entire deer. The deer was quite large; weighing about 250 pounds, after it was dressed. Kroli decided to use a thrusting spear as a transport pole and two men would act as pole bearers, while the third would lead the way and be prepared to defend against any meat-eater attack. Brom tied the feet of the buck to the transport pole. He and Kroli were the strongest; so, it was decided that they would be the pole bearers, while Raka led the way with his throwing spear at the ready position.

The journey was difficult; but it was downhill; so, they

made good time. Raka gave each of them a short break, as pole bearers; but he was not as strong and could only carry his end of the deer for a few minutes. As Raka was giving over his duty as pole bearer to Kroli for the third time, he glimpsed movement over Kroli's shoulder at the edge of a small clearing. His attention to the movement alerted the other two hunters and they dropped the deer and pole and loaded a spear in their throwers.

At that moment a small, gaunt cave-bear crossed the clearing and headed straight for the hunters and the deer carcass. As the bear neared the hunters, it rose on his hind-legs and roared, a typical ruse that these bears used to frighten other meat-eaters away from a carcass. When he stood on his hind legs all three men launched their throwing spears, hitting the bear in the chest and abdomen. The spears sank deeply into the bear's chest area, cutting an artery near the heart. The bear sat down on its rump and emitted a loud, "humph." He tried to rise; but could not and started to whimper, much as Kroli had seen small cubs act when they called their mother. The bear fell onto its side; the spears preventing its fall onto its stomach. Blood was already collecting in a puddle around the body. Kroli decided to wait for the bear to die. He built a fire to keep other meat-eaters away and visually examined the bear.

He wondered why the bear was so thin, when there was so much food in this area and then he saw that the bear only had one good eye. Something had destroyed the bear's left eye. The right eye had also been injured and there was a grey film covering it; making it difficult for the bear to see well enough to hunt.

The men discussed how they could save all of the meat; they were still at least two hours from the grotto. Kroli decided that two of them would stay with the meat, while the third went for help in carrying the meat. A lone man could run the distance in about an hour. Returning at a trot would take an addition hour, so there should be enough daylight to carry the meat back to the grotto. Raka volunteered to return for help.

It was agreed and Raka started toward the grotto at a medium fast run, while Brom and Kroli dressed the bear carcass. Raka was careful as he ran; alert for what lay ahead and occasionally stopping to listen and smell the wind. He covered the distance to the grotto in just over an hour. Milka had just returned to the grotto and saw him running up the trail before he arrived.

Raka explained what they needed and Milka indicated that he, Kosh, Gruma and Brow would go back with him. Milka told Kardi that they might not be able to make it back before night; so, she told everyone who was left at the grotto to go into the grotto. They would build up the fire and wait for the hunters' return tomorrow morning.

During the day, Kardi, Milka and Beoh had been able to set three deadfall traps and had already killed two rabbits. Kardi had also discovered some of the fruit that Kroli's group had sampled and had picked a large amount and placed it in the grotto.

The five men and women immediately started up the trail at a slow trot. Brow was the slowest; so, they set their pace to match hers and arrived at the site of the bear kill after about an hour and forty-five minutes. Kroli and Brom had prepared the carcass for transport; but it was now getting late and Kroli decided that they would have to wait until the following morning to return to the grotto.

They moved their camp fire next to a very large deadfall tree that would provide protection on one side and built up the fire. The fire was larger than Kroli would have liked; but they were in the canyon; so, he estimated that the only place that the fire could be seen from was from the canyon rim.

Kroli said that they would need a guard all night; so, they took turns staying awake.

The night passed uneventfully and Raka, who had the last watch, woke the group at dawn. The group made preparations for the return trip by using poles to carry the meat. They were able to carry it all, although they were heavily burdened. Kroli led the way and Brom brought up the 'rear of the column. Raka teamed with Kroli as a pole bearer and the others paired up as well.

They arrived at the grotto in mid-morning, very tired from the work of carrying the meat. Although Kroli had been concerned about the remainder of the clan being left alone at the grotto, he felt that Kardi would ensure that all possible precautions had been taken. Kardi had also set up guards during the night and had burned the fire higher than she would have liked, had the clan not been separated.

Everyone set about preparing the meat and making more reed baskets that would be used to smoke and dry some of the meat. It seemed that each member of the clan was falling into a natural duty position, without being ordered to do so.

Kroli and Raka were viewed as the leaders and, as such, planned the day's activities, usually in consultation with the other members, especially Kardi. Kardi always tried to envision what Carni would have done, when giving her advice.

Kardi, Raka, Brom and Milka had proven to be the most successful hunters of large game. They often took the younger men, Beoh and Bot with them to give them experience in the hunting of large game. A hunt with Kroli was always an instructional event in which he taught the other hunters the techniques needed to track; find; stalk and kill large animals. To their delight, they had found that this forest was full of bush deer and there were even a few red deer. They had seen one set of prints of an Irish elk; but these prints had been old. As they had found out during the last hunt, there were bear in this canyon and they had seen the signs of large cats. There were signs of forest kopsut, a large breed of kopsut; but they had not yet seen any.

Kardi had accepted the responsibility of setting and running the deadfall traps. They now had three traps set out near the grotto and she wanted to set out many more. She used Brow, Beoh, and Bot to help her with this task. The deadfall traps were set within an hour's walk from the grotto to prevent meat-eaters from stealing the dead animal before they were able to get to it.

Garki and Gruma had the task of making read baskets and fishing in the river. Kuo and Kosh often helped them. Kuo and Kosh also had the responsibility of cooking and watching the children. The children helped at all of the tasks near the grotto.

Life for the Kopsut Clan settled into a comfortable routine. They were always vigilant for meat-eaters; but so far, there were no signs that humans had ever visited this area before the Kopsut Clan. About once a week, Kroli and Raka would climb the cliff after dark to see if they could detect any signs of a fire. Each time they were relieved that they did not see signs of fire.

The clan began to accumulate food stores for the winter. There was an abundance of bush deer, red deer and smaller animals. The clans hunting expeditions, fishing efforts and plant gathering work were extremely productive. They found many types of fruit, plums and berries mostly, a large number of edible mushrooms and many types of edible green. Kardi was sure that there would be more food for this winter than any winter that she had experienced with the Step Clan. This canyon was simply teeming with plant and animal life. Most of the greens were eaten fresh; but the fruit and mushrooms were dried on hot rocks near the fire in order to preserve them for eating during the winter months.

Kroli decided that it was time to explore a larger portion of the canyon. He wanted to take the fork of the large animal trail which led along the eastern wall of the canyon, paralleling the canyon fork of the river. He chose Raka and Brom again to accompany him.

The three explorers intended to make this trip what had been referred to in the Step Clan as a "long hunt," which meant that the hunting party intended to stay away from the grotto for at least one night. Milka would be in charge at the grotto and Kroli encouraged everyone to stay near the grotto and only venture away from the grotto in groups of three.

The hunters travelled light, taking only their weapons, a deer skin robe, water bladder and dried food. They intended to travel light and fast in their outward journey and to hunt on their return trip. Brom took the lead, with Kroli bringing up the rear, since Kroli was not in the best of shape anymore. Due to Kroli's age, his strength was waning and he was suffering from illnesses attributable to a gum disease. He often rubbed his gums with the moss that Kardi had said would help heal the gums. It seemed to help; but did not cure the problem.

They started out on the animal trail headed east at a slow trot. They arrived at the right-hand fork in the trail after about an hour of trotting. They had previously explored part of the fork to the south and now wanted to explore the left-hand fork in the animal trail. Now they slowed to a walk and proceeded more cautiously. The leader of the group gave the most of his attention to the area in front of them and Kroli in the rear was responsible for their back-trail. Raka watched both the right and the left of the trail for danger.

They made steady progress, as the trail followed the fork

of the river that hugged the eastern canyon wall. The river was brimming with water, as the ice in the mountains melted and flowed west toward the sea. This year was becoming the warmest year that Kroli had ever experienced and was resulting in an increased melt of glacier ice. The river was full of rapids and small waterfalls. The hunters could see an abundance of fish in the pools below the small waterfalls. In some places the river had exited its natural banks and had spread out into the canyon floor, forming a shallow lake that they had to go around. Other animals had also travelled around the lake, indicating that the lake had been there for a long period of the warm weather. They saw tracks of bush and red deer and even a rare Irish elk. These tracks were accompanied by a large pack of kopsuts. Due to the large number of tracks, they realized that kopsuts were very abundant in the canyon; so, Kroli called the canyon "Kopsut Canyon."

The little group stopped in the late afternoon and ate some of their dried rations. They had arrived deep into the canyon and had come to realize that the canyon proceeded very deeply into the mountain range. Raka climbed a tree to look at the trail ahead of them and saw that the canyon veered to the right so far that he could not see the end. He told Kroli and Brom that the rim of the canyon to the south appeared to be covered with ice.

They startled many deer and forest hares; so, they knew that food was very abundant here. A thought had begun to form in Kroli's mind that deeper into the canyon might be a better hunting ground for the Kopsut Clan, since it would be further from other clans and there was an abundance of food available. They had also noticed many edible plants that the clan typically used to supplement their diet. Raka had begun to gather and eat some, as they travelled. Brom and Kroli abstained, since they were more partial to meat.

As the evening began to arrive, they killed two forest hares and decided to make camp. Brom found a good camp site that was protected by the river on the east side, a large boulder on the north side and a large deadfall tree on the west side. They could easily defend this camp from meat-eaters and they were convinced that there were no other humans in the area.

Raka built the fire pit, as Brom skinned the rabbits and Kroli gathered wood for the fire. After the fire was burning well, Kroli and Raka gathered pine boughs to use for sleeping mats as Brom cooked the rabbits. The clan members preferred to sleep on mats of pine boughs, not only because of the cushioning affect, but also because in the cold winter it was warmer. The aroma of cooking rabbit filled the air around the fire pit, as the men squatted beside the fire.

Kroli began to gesture his idea that they should find a better site for their clan deeper into the canyon to be further away from other clans and to have better defensive possibilities. Brom and Raka agreed. It was decided that they would start the search the following day, even if it meant that they had to stay away from the grotto an extra day.

They ate the rabbits; built up the fire and slept with their hands on their thrusting spears. As normal, they awakened every couple of hours to replenish the wood on the fire. In the distance they could hear the lonesome howls of kopsuts, as they talked to each other across the canyon. The kopsut were not near the camp; but they knew that the kopsut were aware of their presence, since they could easily detect their fire.

The following morning, they were up at dawn and continued their exploration of the canyon to the south at a stalking pace. The animal trail continued to follow the bank of the river and the course of the river stayed against the eastern wall of the canyon. They encountered a series of small waterfalls, as another tributary joined the river from a steep canyon which ran into the mountains to the east. They continued to see many bush and red deer and an inordinate number of forest and mountain hares. Raka killed two more with his lop and strung them around his neck. When they stopped in the afternoon, he intended to clean them. They would eat them this evening.

Kroli stopped the exploratory journey just after midday and they ate dried meat. Raka had continued to find edible plants and fruits and ate them as they travelled. The break was a short one, because Kroli was intent on seeing how deeply this canyon ran into the mountains. They had still not found the end of it. By nightfall, they decided to spend another day exploring to the south and they made another camp near a small deadfall next to the river. They cooked the rabbits and ate them before falling asleep. The kopsuts howled the entire night and their howls were closer than the night before.

The following afternoon they arrived at what appeared to be the rear wall of the canyon. Raka climbed a tall tree to get a view of what he hoped was the river headwaters. The river made a sharp turn to the southwest and the rim of the canyon wall ran as far as Raka could see to the southwest. There appeared to be a point where the west canyon wall met the wall running across the rear of the canyon; but Raka could not be sure.

Kroli decided that they could stay away from the clan no longer; he gestured that they would start their return tomorrow morning. They scanned the canyon wall on the other side of the river and saw what looked like a cave about half way up the face of the cliff. To check the cave out, they would have to cross the river. The river was not extremely deep; but had a very strong current. It would be virtually impossible for a man to try to wade across it. They searched the river bank upstream and it didn't take long to find a natural deadfall bridge which they could use for the crossing.

They crossed the deadfall and examined the cliff to see if

there might be a way of getting up to the cave. There was a steep ledge leading to just below the cave entrance from right to left. Kroli knew that the narrow ledge would make defending the cave an easy matter. He gestured this to Raka. They all proceeded up the ledge to get a look at the cave. When they arrived in front of the cave entrance, Kroli threw a rock into the entrance and listened for any responding noise. He heard none and they each agreed that there was no smell of a dangerous animal coming from the cave. They stepped through the ten-foot-wide entrance and allowed their eyes to adjust to the limited light in the cave. The entrance to the cave continued about ten feet wide for a short twenty feet and then it opened into a large high-ceilinged area about forty feet wide and sixty feet deep.

The first thing that they saw was an enormous pile of bones that had been picked clean by meat-eaters. They examined the bones and saw that they included deer and ibex. Kroli examined the tracks that still remained in the silt on the cave floor and announce that the meat-eaters had been a pack of Kopsut. He gestured that the cave had not been occupied for a few years; so, these bones were from animals killed years earlier.

There was a small corridor where the cave continued into the rear cliff wall. Air was coming through this corridor; so, Kroli supposed there was an opening at its end.

Against the right wall of the cave a small pool of water had been formed in a trench by water trickling down the cave wall. This would make a good base for the Clan, thought Kroli, since there was water, a good defensive location and possibly another exit.

Kroli made his decision. He gestured to the others that they would move the Kopsut Clan to this cave when they returned to the grotto. They made their camp for the night in the cave. Raka and Brom left the cave before dark had closed in and were able to kill five squirrels, which they cooked with the hares for the evening meal.

They rose at daybreak; ate leftover meat and started their journey at a trot back to the grotto. Since they were no longer exploring Kroli felt that they could arrive at the grotto after two hard days of trotting.

After a very hard day of travel, they camped for the night at the location that they had used for their first camp. They ate remaining hare meat and continued their journey as dawn broke the next morning.

CHAPTER 22

THE CLAN IS BEING FOLLOWED

Kroli's exploration party had been gone for three days and Kardi was becoming concerned that the small party may have encountered trouble. She had expected them to be gone only a couple of days. She conferred with Milka and it was decided that Milka would climb to the top of the cliff to see what he could see from that height.

It was early morning when Milka climbed up the cliff. He looked in the southeastern direction, which Kroli's party had taken. After careful study, he could not see any evidence of a fire. He really did not expect to see a fire, since Kroli typically kept the fires so small that detection was problematic. Milka thought that they probably had already put the fire out at this time of the morning. Milka turned and started to climb down from the cliff, when something to the northwest caught his eye.

The northwest was the direction from which the Kopsut Clan had travelled to Kopsut Canyon. In the distance Milka could see a very small wisp of smoke from a fire. He would not have been able to see it, if he had not been so high. He knew that the fire was man-made since it remained small for several minutes. Milka judged that the fire was about three days travel from the grotto.

He climbed down the cliff and gestured what he had seen to Kardi. Kardi knew that they would need to leave this location, when Kroli returned. She called everyone together and informed them of the danger. Now they needed to wait for Kroli to return to decide where they should go.

Meanwhile, Brom had killed a bush deer about an hour away from the grotto and they had slung it using a thrusting spear as a pole to carry it back to the grotto. They entered the clearing in front of the grotto in the evening of their fifth day of absence. Milka had sent Beoh to the top of the cliff to watch for their return; so, the entire clan lined the path, as they entered the clearing with the bush deer.

Normally there would have been happy greetings and rejoicing at the thought of eating fresh meat from the bush deer; but everyone was reserved and waited until Milka gestured about what he had seen from the top of the cliff two days before.

Kroli and Brom dropped the bush deer on the ground and Kroli gestured for the women to begin dressing the animal. He gestured that they would discuss the events over the evening meal. He, Milka and Raka climbed the cliff to see if the fire could be seen at dusk.

The sun was just setting as they reached the top of the cliff. Milka pointed in the direction which he had seen the fire. Far in the distance they could see the faint glow of a small fire. In Kroli's judgment, it was perhaps two to three days journey from the grotto.

Kroli gestured to Milka to ask if this was the same location where he had seen the fire. Milka gestured that it had moved further east and south closer to the grotto. It was obvious to Kroli that whoever had made the fire was following the trail the Kopsut Clan had followed. He could not be certain that the Kopsut Clan was being tracked; but it was obviously a possibility. It was dark; therefore, climbing down from the cliff was dangerous. The group climbed down from the cliff by feeling the rocks and handholds before committing. They approached the fire where the clan had gathered to wait their return before starting to eat the bush deer roasts that cooked on spits over the fire pit. Raka was famished and the deer smelled great!

Raka was growing faster than other youngsters in the clan. The diet of most young members of the clan consisted mostly of meat; whereas, Raka supplemented his meat diet with fruits and other plant products, as much as possible. This varied diet fed his young body like a good rain feeds the plants. He was now taller than any member of the clan, although his muscles were elongated instead of bunched like other clan members.

As the clan gathered around the fire and cut off and ate pieces of the venison roast, Kroli began to gesture the story about another clan following their trail. Kroli indicated his fear that the following men were from a northern clan and very well might be cannibals. He had laid out his plan for preventing the followers from finding them to Kardi and Raka and they had made suggestions to improve the plan.

It was agreed that they would need to obscure their trail and prevent the followers from crossing the narrow river. Kroli and Raka planned to cross the river tomorrow morning and obliterate any sign of human presence. After that, they would cross back over the river and, with the help of the other clan members, they would push the fallen-log bridge into the river, thereby eliminating the closest crossing to the grotto. The river was still running full from the ice which was melting in the mountains. The log would be carried away and there would be little sign that humans had crossed there. This summer had been very warm relative to previous years and the melting ice had caused perpetual flooding along the rivers. Kroli gestured adamantly that the Kopsut Clan would forever remain south of this river because only danger from the northern clans remained north of the river.

After this part of his plan was agreed, Kroli announced that the clan would move to a new location that he, Brom and Raka had found deep in the Kopsut Canyon. In this way it would be easier to hide their presence from other humans north of the river. They would make their move starting after they had destroyed the fallen-log bridge and would move all of their stores in several trips. From this day forward, all fires at the grotto would only be hot coals, so that they would not give away their presence to the followers.

Everyone was excited with the idea of a move and taking action to foil the followers. They gestured and talked late into the evening and then slept.

The following morning Kroli's plan was executed and they began their move to the Kopsut cave deep in the Kopsut canyon. The move required four trips to carry all of the stores that they had amassed for the winter.

On the evening of the final return to the grotto, Kroli and Raka climbed the cliff to see if they could detect the followers. Raka was the first to see the faint sign of a fire. The followers seemed to still be following the animal trail which paralleled river on its northern bank. However, the fire seemed to be farther to the north than the river that the Kopsut Clan had begun to refer to as the "North River."

Kroli surmised that the animal trail had branched to the north after it had passed the place where the fallen-log bridge had been. It was apparent that the followers had not discovered the trail where that had crossed the river. If they had discovered the trail, Kroli gestured to Raka; they would have stayed close to the river looking for a place to cross.

The clan left the grotto for the last time the following morning and travelled to their new home in the Kopsut Cave along what was now referred to as the Kopsut River.

CHAPTER 23

LIFE IN THE KOPSUT CANYON

L ife in Kopsut canyon was good for the Kopsut Clan. They were the only humans in the canyon; edible plants were in abundance; the canyon and river valley were full of red and bush deer and forest hares. The only dangers that they routinely faced were from the weather, disease and the meat-eaters that were most prominently Kopsut packs.

They prepared for their first winter in their new home by hunting both red and bush deer and smaller animals and gathering large amounts of fruit, nuts, roots, mushrooms and edible greens. Kardi had introduced the clan to many edible plant products that she had learned from Carni. She had also found some edible grains that Carni had told her about; but they were not in great abundance in the canyon and therefore, served only as a delicacy. She mixed the grains with dried fruit and heated them on hot rocks to form a small dried paste similar to a modern-day cookie. Another delicacy that the clan enjoyed was bone marrow. The women often cracked the large bones of a deer leg roast with a rock to reveal the succulent marrow inside. The clan members typically ate the bone marrow after a meal of deer meat, much as modern humans might eat a desert.

The women smoked and dried the meat and some of the plant products. They made reed baskets to use for the smoking process and in which to store their dried food. They constantly had skins staked out in the sun to dry and to be scraped clean for making robes and other garments. The cave became packed with baskets of food stuff and cured hides and robes. Never had the clan seen such an abundance of resources than they had found in this Kopsut canyon. The remarkably warm winter and the lack of competition for resources in the canyon had created an ideal hunting ground for the clan.

The children helped the women in the food and hide preparation processes. Since the clan was small, everyone had several jobs and everyone was armed, wherever they went. Kroli had directed that no one go anywhere away from the cave alone. Usually, if they left the cave area, they went as a group of least three adults.

Raka and Beoh were now men; so, they hunted with the men. They also had the additional duty of checking and baiting the many deadfall traps that the clan had set near the cave. When they found animals in their deadfall traps, they used a thrusting spear to bring their catches back to the cave, where the women cleaned them. They often returned with many hares and an occasional forest weasel. Due to the abundance of edible plants in the forest, there were many forest and mountain hares feasting upon these plants. Squirrels were also very plentiful due the availability of fruit and nuts. Raka and Beoh used their lops to kill several each day, as they made their rounds to check and re-bait the deadfall traps.

The children were given the task of collecting the nuts that the squirrels feasted upon. The clan members ate the nuts by cracking the shells with their teeth; or the women would mix the nut meat with fruits and make the dried pastes on hot rocks. The clan loved the pastes and looked forward to these treats after a large meal of meat. Edible greens were used as supplements for the meat. Clan members had found that eating greens with their meat helped prevent stomach pains.

The cave became the clan's first home for a long period of time. Since the tradition of the Step Clan had been to live a nomadic life following the game to summer and winter hunting grounds, the clan had never become accustomed to gathering large amounts of stores, except to pass the long winter months.

Now with the abundance of food available in the canyon and river valley and the non-existence of a threat from other humans, the clan made a conscious decision to stay in the cave through all four seasons. They began to collect possessions and store food stuffs.

The clan tended to gather in family groups called a fire, although the clan shared only one actual fire in the cave. Each family group (fire) had its own space in the cave. Kroli, as leader of the clan, settled his group at the rear of the cave along the left wall in a high spot on the cave floor. Milka's group occupied the right rear wall near the water pool, while Brom and the clan members that had no family group filled in the spaces toward the front of the cave. Food stores in reed baskets and other possessions lined the cave walls.

Kroli had Brom and Raka explore the cave as it continued into the cliff. They discovered that the opening in the rear wall of the cave ran toward the surface at the top of the cliffs and opened into another large chamber. This chamber opened into another entrance/exit which allowed a remarkable view of the mountains and the canyon below the cliffs. This second exit/entrance might become important, if the clan ever faced a siege of their cave from the canyon below. The opening at the top of the cliff was marked by large boulders and a small stand of evergreen trees. Discovering the opening from the outside would probably be too difficult for potential enemies.

The winter temperature was mild, relative to past winters; but the winter brought an immense amount of snow to this canyon. Contrary to past winters that the clan had experienced north of the canyon, there were many winter days when the snow melted and filled the river that ran through the canyon to its brim even flooding in places. The Clan gathered around the fire in the evening on these cold days and told legends about the reindeer. They wondered aloud about where the reindeer herds would be at this time of year in their old hunting grounds. They wondered if the northern clans had followed the reindeer south again, as they had in previous years, and if their old hunting grounds were now safe, or still dangerous, as they had been when they had left.

There was no way for the clan to know; but this year the reindeer herds had not migrated as far to the south as they normally did, due to the fact that the winter temperature was extremely mild. However, the northern clans had returned and were operating on the southern edges of the reindeer herds, as opposed to the northern and western edges, where they had hunted in the past few years. It would have been a shock to the clan to know that the northern clans had become more interested in finding and hunting the southern clans than in hunting the reindeer.

The southern clans that had migrated north with the reindeer herds in the spring had spent the winter being attacked many times by the northern clans and had not had a very successful hunting season in their northern hunting grounds. The necessity for them to focus on their collective defense decreased their ability to hunt. The northern clans had killed many of their members and had taken many of their women as captives.

As the reindeer herds had started their southern migration in the fall, the migrating southern clans had hoped that the northern clans would remain to the northern and western edges of the reindeer herds. But they soon found that the dangers that they had faced from the northern clans in their traditional hunting grounds in the north had followed them south with the reindeer. The southern clans were being routinely hunted by the northern clans and systematically killed. Additionally, many of them were attacked by northern cannibalistic clans and served as one of their sources of food. Captives were often used as slaves until their usefulness diminished and they were killed and eaten.

But the Kopsut Clan knew none of this and their life was good. Although the snow was deep at times, the weather was mild and the Kopsut Clan used their muco to travel on top of the snow and, much like their namesake, the wolf, they were able to kill many deer and the occasional Irish elk and ibex; so, food was plentiful. The melting snow and ice in the surrounding mountains caused the river that ran through the Kopsut Canyon to overflow its bank and fill the small lake at the southern end of the canyon with water.

The fall and early winter were the traditional times that the Step Clan had planted their seed in their females. The Kopsut Clan maintained this habit and Kroli's female (Gruma) and Milka's female (Garki) found that they were with child.

Brom felt a strong primal need to mate with a female. He approached Kroli and gestured his desire to be mated with a woman. He, Brow and Kardi had been spending time together at the river catching fish for the clan and Brom felt a strong desire to mate with Kardi. He gestured this desire to Kroli and asked to be given Kardi as a mate. This was a new situation for Kroli, since as leader of the clan; he had never contemplated his authority in such matters. He told Brom that he would think about it.

Kroli sought out Kardi and discussed Brom's request with her. Kardi also felt a strong urge to mate with a man and gestured that the clan needed new babies, if it was to survive and that she desired to have Brom's baby. She suggested that Brow should also be given to Brom as a mate. Kardi suggested that Kroli inform Brom of this decision that he would be given two females as his mates for his fire. She also said that Kosh needed a man and since Milka was young and strong; he should take Kosh as a second mate and have Bunt and Kuo added to his fire, along with Bot. Brom's fire would now include Brow and Kardi. Raka would remain at Kroli's fire with Gruma, Beoh and Mok, since he was being groomed as the future clan leader. She also suggested to Kroli that Brom should move his fire to the large chamber of the cave near the upper entrance, close to the top of the cliff. This would help to defend the cave, should that become necessary.

During the next evening meal, Kroli informed the clan of his decisions. The clan members seemed happy with his decisions and celebrated by eating some of the dried fruit pastes that Kardi had made.

Brom wasted no time after he was given two females as mates. Females made separate sleeping mats of boughs and the male chose where he would sleep during the night. After moving his fire to the upper chamber of the cave, Brom first mated with Kardi in the early evening and then, during the early morning hours, went to Brow's mat and mated with her. Both women became pregnant in the early winter.

Milka planted his seed in Kosh at the same time; so, the new Kopsut Clan was expecting five new members to arrive by late summer. Life for the Kopsut Clan was good and their daily lives were very pleasant, when compared to their previous experiences.

Raka and Beoh rose on an overcast day in late winter and put on their muco to perform what had become their routine of almost daily checking and baiting of the deadfall traps. They used kips to bait the traps that they had set for hare and squirrel meat to bait traps set for smaller mammals, such as the weasel and the fox. Since the first snow, they had killed three weasels, four fox, something that looked like a martin and another animal which looked like a small bear (probably a wolverine). The clan had no name for this bear-like animal, so Raka gave it the name "carnini," which meant little bear to him. He used no gesture when referring to the animal, only the word "carnini."

The clan was very pleased with this new meat and had made head covers with the hide for the three older men. Today Raka hoped to get another of these animals and maybe a kopsut. He had seen tracks in the area of one deadfall trap which indicated that a kopsut pair was hunting in the area. To kill a kopsut, Raka knew that his deadfall traps would need to be especially large and well camouflaged. He set the trap for the kopsut in a run normally used by hares with a large fallen tree blocking each side of the hare trail. The deadfall log would fall hard and fast on top of the kopsut, as it took the bait. Jumping out of the way of the falling log would be prevented by the logs on each side of the hare run. For this deadfall trap he had used a wounded hare as bait. The hare's back had been broken when Raka had hit it with a rock launched from his lop. Raka had tied the front feet of the hare to prevent it from struggling and setting off the deadfall trigger. The hare's back legs were inoperable. The hare was tied to the deadfall trigger and lay essentially still and made squealing noises during its plight, which should attract the kopsut.

Raka and Beoh set out to run their traps with Raka in the lead. Each carried their unloaded spear throwers in their left hand. Both were quick at loading and throwing a spear, if needed. They also had their lops ready with a round rock; should they see a smaller animal during their journey. The going was not difficult, since their muco allowed them to walk on top of the snow.

Their traps were set in a rough semi-circle around the cave site, extending along the river to the south, then turning west into the forest, then back to the north and finally east to the river and south back to the cave. They started their check of the traps in the reverse direction to the north. The time normally required to run the traps was less than half a day, depending upon what they found.

The first trap was a hare trap, baited with a kip; but there was nothing in the trap, although the kip bait was gone. Beoh reset the trap making sure that the trigger was sufficiently set to allow a hare to easily trigger it, when it took the kip bait.

The next trap was also for a hare and it had not been triggered. At the next two traps, they removed two large forest hares and reset and baited the traps.

Now they were deep into the forest and the next two traps were meat traps, set for small meat eaters, like a fox. These traps were baited with squirrels and had not been disturbed.

As they approached their final trap, which was the one they had set for a kopsut; Raka saw kopsut tracks in the snow. He examined the tracks and saw that the edges were still intact, indicating that the tracks had been made during the night. As time passed, especially during the day, the edges of the tracks would begin to crumble. Raka took his stalking stance; loaded a spear in his thrower and moved toward the trap and Beoh followed his lead. As they approached the area where the trap had been set, Raka could see that the trap had been triggered, since the deadfall tree had fallen between the two trees that blocked the sides of the rabbit trail.

Raka and Beoh quickly ran to the trap and saw that they had killed not one kopsut; but two with the same trap. Raka checked to make sure that both kopsut were dead and noted that they were, although their bodies were still warm. He and Beoh lifted the log off of the kopsuts and examined the carcasses. One was male and one was female. Raka saw that the female had recently given birth and based upon the evidence of her full breast, she was nursing three baby kopsut. They were both large, almost black kopsuts with yellow eyes, weighing about a hundred and twenty pounds.

He picked up the female carcass and placed it across his shoulders, as Beoh did the same with the male carcass. Beoh started in the direction of the cave, when Raka noticed the footprints that the kopsut had made when they had arrived at the trap. The tracks had come from the direction of the cliffs near the river to the east.

Raka halted Beoh with a grunt and indicated for him to follow and he started following the kopsut tracks toward the cliffs next to the river. Beoh understood that Raka was following the kopsut, but he did not know why. He gestured as much to Raka. Raka didn't know why; but he was drawn toward the kopsut lair. He remembered his mother's story of his father's clan that had tamed the spirit of the kopsut and, somehow, he wanted to do the same. Maybe it was a connection to the father that he had never known.

He gestured to Beoh that they would try to find the kopsut pups; so Beoh understood that they were after the succulent kopsut pup meat.

The trail led directly to the river. The kopsut pair had probably heard the hare's cries and gone directly to it.

When they arrived at the river, they found that the river was full to its brim with melted snow and very deep. The current was too strong to consider entering the water to cross it. The tracks turned south along the river bank and stopped at a fallen log that formed a natural bridge across the river. The water was only inches below the log. It appeared that the kopsut had crossed this bridge many times for most of the snow had been knocked off of the log by their passage. The log was about two feet wide. He saw what appeared to be a crack in the cliff face about ten feet high. "This could be the kopsut lair," he thought.

Raka laid down the kopsut carcass and took off his muco. He gestured to Beoh for him to wait with the carcasses and crossed the log bridge to the other side of the river. As he neared the crack in the face of the cliff, he saw that it was in fact large enough for him to enter. He knelt in front of the entrance and listened intently as he sniffed the air from what seemed to be a small grotto. He smelled the kopsut and heard a weak whimper.

He took a spear to use for defense, if there were other kopsut in the lair, and slowly began to crawl through the entrance. His eyes adjusted to the limited light in the den and he saw that the grotto was in fact only about ten feet deep. At the end of grotto were three little balls of fur that were huddled together in a nest of dried grass and kopsut fur. He crawled toward them and picked one of them up. The pup's eyes had not yet opened. Raka had the smell of their mother upon him; so, he was accepted immediately by the pup and the pup began to search for a teat to drink its meal. The other two pups had opened eyes and bit his hand with their small, but sharp teeth, as he reached for them. He experienced only a scratch from the bites.

He gathered up the three kopsut pups and backed out of the den. He crossed the log bridge and showed them to Beoh. Beoh immediately picked up a pup with opened eyes and was rewarded with a bite and growl. He quickly killed the pup by smashing its head against a tree. Raka took the pup with the closed eyes and kept Beoh from killing it; however, Beoh killed the third one in the same way.

Raka took the last surviving pup over to its mother's carcass. The mother kopsut's teats were full of milk and he allowed the pup to drink. Apparently, the teats still worked and the pup drank its fill. Raka dumped the water from the water blabber that he always carried and filled it with the milk from the other full teats by squeezing the teats. He surmised that the pup might survive, if he could give it its mother's milk. Raka placed the pup in his pouch; where it instantly fell asleep.

The young men had too much meat to carry individually; so, they used their two thrusting spears as slings for the kopsut carcasses, the kopsut pup carcasses and the hare carcasses. They carried the ends of the spears on each shoulder and began the trip to return to the cave. They made steady progress, since these two young men had developed an enormous endurance and strength from their time spent checking, baiting and setting the heavy deadfall traps. The young men normally ran from trap to trap, finishing this chore early in order to be able to go on hunts for larger animals with the older men. Today, they would be a little late; since they had wasted time with the kopsut pups and had been burdened with the large kopsut carcasses.

When they returned to the cave it was approaching early evening. They gave the carcasses to the women, who immediately prepared the two kopsut pups and the hares for eating along with a partial deer rump roast remaining from the day before. When the meat was ready and the clan had gathered around the one communal fire, an event that had become the clan's habit, the live kopsut pup was shown around. Most of the clan, including Kroli, expressed the opinion that the last surviving pup should be killed and eaten. It was not considered appropriate to have a meat-eater near their fire. What if the meat-eater lost its fear of fire and grew into an adult kopsut and later devoured them? But Kardi related the story that Carni had told her of the Nord Clan and the kopsut that lived among them. She explained that the kopsut had hunted with the clan and lived as a clan member, making the clan more feared by other clans because of its ability to tame the spirit of the kopsut.

Raka chose this moment to tell his first legend. He reached into the fire and withdrew a burning stick and held it in front of his face. The clan members knew that he was about to recount a legend; but such an occurrence by someone so young was an extraordinary event. An expectant hush descended around the fire, as Raka began a low hum. The on-lookers picked up the hum, as Raka stood before them. He used more words and fewer gestures than was the habit of the other clan members, as he told his story.

The clan has been blessed by the spirits-in-the-fire as they helped the clan escape the northern clan hunters. The spirits-in-the-fire named the clan after the most cunning of the meat-eaters, the kopsut. They guided the Kopsut Clan to the Kopsut Canyon where they have found a home that is hidden away from the dangers of the northern clans. Food animals are plentiful and there are many plants that the clan can also eat and enjoy. All of this abundance is protected by fierce kopsut packs, who could challenge the clan for the right to eat the plant-eaters, if they were so inclined.

But the spirits-in-the-fire chose to tell the kopsut not to bother the Kopsut Clan; but instead to send one of their own to join the Clan. The spirits-in-the-fire guided the kopsut parents to the deadfall trap; where they were both killed to fill the stomachs of the Kopsut Clan. Every hunter knows that the kopsut is cunning and hard to kill by a deadfall trap; but the spirits-in-the-fire caused two kopsut to be killed by one trap. (The on-lookers nodded; they had never heard of two kopsut being killed by one trap.) By eating the meat from the cunning kopsut parents, the Kopsut Clan will be given the kopsut courage and cunning by the spirits-in-the-fire.

The spirits-in-the-fire guided the brave young hunters Raka and Beoh to the kopsut den; where they showed Raka three kopsut pups and told him to select the one that would become a member of the Kopsut

Clan. Raka looked into the hearts of each kopsut pup. (The crowd was silent, intent upon what was being told. They knew that Raka had strong medicine and believed that he would now reveal something about his strength.) He saw that two of the pups had hearts filled with the blackness of meat-eaters and he allowed Beoh to kill those two. The heart of the final pup was filled with a desire to hunt and showed no desire to kill men and eat them. The spirits-in-the-fire told Raka to select that kopsut pup that would become a part of the Kopsut Clan forever more. All members of the Kopsut Clan must teach the kopsut pup the ways of the Clan and feed it, as a mother kopsut would feed the pup. This is the legend of the kopsut and all must listen and remember.

Raka placed the burning stick back into the fire pit and sat down. Kroli was impressed and knew that Raka had learned the art of molding the opinion of the clan. He now felt more comfortable with his decision to declare that Raka would be the future leader of the clan.

Kroli knew that his time as leader was drawing to a close. He was no longer as strong as he once had been. His body was growing stiff and ached at the end of each day. He could no longer run fast and far and the spears he threw often failed to kill the prey. During the cold weather, he could no longer run after the large plant-eaters, as he had always done during his adult life.

In the following days, when the kopsut mother's milk was exhausted, the women accepted the task of feeding the pup broth made from animal fat. The pup adjusted to this diet well and grew rapidly. He started eating meat much earlier than a kopsut pup raised by its mother might have and, as a result, grew into a very large adolescent kopsut, as large as a normal fully grown kopsut.

The clan called the pup "kop." Its nights were spent with Raka, curled up on the skin that had once been its mother. When it was still a pup, it spent its days with the women and children, as they performed their chores near the cave. He went to the river with Kosh and Kardi to catch fish and observed that the women were there to catch fish. He quickly started learning how to jump into the water and try to catch a fish. He was not successful most of the time; but after many tries, he caught his first fish and carried it to Kardi, as if it were a prize.

As he became an older adolescent, Raka began to take him on his runs of the traps. Kop learned how the traps worked. Raka showed him the bait and growled at him to indicate that he should not touch it. He saw Raka and Beoh take the animals from beneath the deadfall logs and seemed to understand. While on these trips, they often saw hares and squirrels and Kop would lunge after them. After a few unsuccessful attempts, he caught a hare and brought it to Raka. Raka skinned it and gave Kop half of it to eat. After that it became routine that Kop would go hunting with Raka.

They developed a means of communication that was based upon looks and body language. If Raka took a stalking stance, Kop did the same. A minute gesture from Raka would cause Kop to stop and remain still. Another minute gesture would send Kop after an animal they were hunting. During a deer hunt, Kop became the member of the hunting party that drove the deer toward an ambush conducted by the other hunters. Usually, the hunting party consisted of at least one female, Kroli, Brom, Milka, Beoh and Raka. The women were becoming very adept at the use of hunting weapons. Kardi was still the most skilled; but the adult women were with child and only came along on the hunts to help skin and carry the kills.

When Kop was with him, Raka ran more than ever. The wolf loved to run and would run in front of Raka unless a minute gesture from Raka pulled him back toward him. The animal and the young man became inseparable. As the weather grew hot, the wolf no longer slept on its mother's hide; but sought out a crevice near the cave that he reached by means of a narrow ledge. The crevice was only about three feet deep, but it provided shelter from the rain and was cooler during the summer than the cave where the men kept a fire burning.

As the Kopsut Clan completed its first year in the Kopsut Canyon, the wolf had become an accepted member of the clan. He acted independently, killing his own food and sharing it with Raka. Other members of the clan could approach it; but if they attempted to touch him, Kop would move away. He allowed Raka to touch him and, in fact, often came to Raka, as if he wanted to be touched by him.

When he was about a year old, Kop heard the call of a distant kopsut and attempted his first howl. The mournful wail was answered from three different directions. The answering howls seemed to call Kop to join them; but he remained near the cave. It was not until his third year, when Raka was fourteen, that Kop left the cave in answer to the calls from the distant kopsut.

Kop was now an immense adult male kopsut. He weighed more than one hundred forty pounds. No one knew what happened when he joined the kopsut pack; but he was gone for almost a month until one morning, when Raka was running his traps, Kop showed up beside him. He had a few healing wounds around his head and neck; so, whatever the encounter had been, he had successfully defended himself.

Raka did not realize how much he had become attached to the wolf until Kop had gone missing. He was happy to have him back. As it turned out Kop would disappear for days at a time, only to return to Raka. On one occasion, he returned accompanied by a female kopsut that refused to approach the humans and no amount of coaching from Kop could get her to come close. Eventually, they disappeared together and Kop returned a few days later alone.

Life continued to be good for the Kopsut Clan. Five new babies were born, although Kosh's baby died a few days after birth from an unknown ailment, which caused the baby to run a high fever. Garki's baby developed a breathing disease when it was about one year old and it also died. The other three babies developed normally as the Kopsut Clan developed a repetitive routine for life in Kopsut Canyon.

Kroli could no longer climb the cliffs and run with the hunters. He started to stay with the women and children and Raka, or Milka led the hunts. Every couple of days Raka would climb through the tunnel at the back of the cave to the top of the canyon wall, where he could see not only the entire canyon, but also far to the north. He never saw evidence of fire pits; but every few days, during all but the coldest winter days, he checked anyway.

Just before the first snow arrived, Bunt, who was now eleven years old was given the duty of accompanying Bot and Beoh to run the traps. As had become Beoh's routine, he led the group out at a trot, until they arrived at the first deadfall trap. The first trap held a hare, which was given to Bunt to carry, as Bot re-baited the trap. They trotted to the next two traps which did not contain a catch. They began their trot to the fourth trap with Beoh in the lead, followed by Bot; as Bunt brought up the rear. Bunt was not a strong runner and dropped behind the group about a hundred yards. Bot thought that it was a fun trick to leave him behind; so, he said nothing to Beoh. As the two leaders rounded a bend in the trail, they heard a startled scream from behind them that ended abruptly. They rushed back down the trail to see that Bunt had been attacked by a giant cat (golo). The golo had Bunt in his mouth and was easily carrying him through the woods.

Bot and Beoh gave chase and threw their spears at the cat too early, their throws falling short. The golo dropped its prey and attacked the two hunters, as the attempted to load their spear throwers for a second throw. Beoh's spear glanced off of the golo's back as he swiped at Bot with his large right paw, slicing into Bot's right side. The golo left Bot where he fell and charged Beoh. Beoh threw his third spear which penetrated the left rear hip of the golo and then fell to the ground, causing the golo to turn, biting at the wound and stopping the attack. The golo returned to Bunt's carcass; picked it up and proceeded through the forest. The golo had escaped with Bunt's carcass. Beoh checked on Bot's condition and saw that he had two deep gashes in his left side that were bleeding profusely. He took some of the moss Kardi made all hunters carry and tied it over the wound with a leather strip. Beoh considered attempting to follow the golo; but the first snow of the year had started and soon would hide the trail, probably before he could discover the golo's lair. Bunt would be the first casualty from an attack in Kopsut Canyon. He needed to get Bot back to the cave, so that Kardi could treat his wounds.

Bot could not walk, so Beoh carried him across his shoulders, as he had carried game many times. He took a direct path through the woods and arrived at the cave after about an hour and a half.

Kardi quickly examined the wounds and smiled at Beoh when she saw that the moss had almost stopped the bleeding. She washed the wounds with water and placed more moss on the wounds and bound them tightly. She poured more water over the moss to release its healing powers.

Beoh and Bot recounted the details of the cat's attack to the Clan and it became obvious that Bot had made a mistake to allow Bunt to fall so far behind him and Beoh.

The next morning the clan awoke to find Bot was delirious;

making strange noises and attempting to fight an imaginary golo. The fever lasted four days before Bot died of his infected wounds.

The clan fretted for days whether these two deaths were an omen of things to come. Was the Kopsut Canyon now a bad place for the Kopsut Clan? In a large clan the loss of two men would not be so important; but the Kopsut Clan was small and this loss meant that fully one quarter of the males of the clan had been lost.

Kroli decided that it was time for another legend and he discussed the possibility with Raka. Raka agreed to tell the legend of the loss of Bot and Bunt. When the evening meal had been consumed, Raka picked up a burning piece of wood from the fire, stood and held it in front of his face. He began a low hum, which the crowd picked up as he began to speak. As was his habit he used fewer gestures to tell his legends than other clansmen.

The great spirits-in-the-fire has given the Kopsut Clan a great bounty of food in the Kopsut Canyon. They have fed the Clan and given the Clan new babies to train in the Clan traditions. But they have become angry that many in the Clan did not heed the rules that they had been given to follow. They were never to become separated. In unity there was strength. The spirits-in-the-fire decided to punish the Clan

for their disobedience by giving Bunt to the meat-eaters and causing Bot to die in the Clan's presence to prove the strength of the spirits-in-the-fire. From this day forward, the Clan must only hunt as a group of at least three. No one will be away from the cave alone. This is the legend of the Bot and Bunt; all must listen and remember.

Raka placed the burning branch back in the fire and sat down.

The legend did not dispel the doom that the clan members felt; but their sense of fear told them to follow the guidance that the legend provided. As the individuals slowly retired to their sleeping mats, there was a tendency to huddle together more than normal. Kop sensed the fear and slept near Raka in the cave that night.

The next morning Kroli remained near the fire. He had contracted some kind of illness which was causing him to feel chilled. He told Raka and Kardi that he would stay near the cave since he felt weak this morning.

Raka did not have a sense of confidence that he normally felt. He decided to go through the cave rear tunnel and climb to the top of the cliffs and to get a good look at the canyon and beyond. He exited the tunnel and climbed to the top of an outcrop of rock that gave him a clear view of not only the canyon, but of the area across the river that ran in front of the canyon to the north. The ground was covered with the season's first snow, which was only a couple of inches deep.

He slowly searched the entirety of the Kopsut canyon. He saw two red deer males battling for supremacy just to the west of the cave near the lake that had filled at the southwestern corner of the canyon. There were water birds in the lake and he made a mental note to talk to Kardi about trying to catch some of them before they flew south of the mountains. His eyes continued to search the area around the cave, slowly searching the areas farther away from the cave. In the end, he saw nothing out of the ordinary in Kopsut Canyon.

His eyes began to search the area north of the river outside of the canyon. He thought he saw a wisp of smoke far to the north. Raka thought, "This would probably be a southern clan since it was too early for the reindeer herds to have migrated this far south."

Then he saw two other thin columns of smoke west of the

one that he had originally seen. He had never seen three separate fire pits at once. What could this mean? He decided to discuss this with Kroli and Kardi. He returned through the cave tunnel to find Kroli sitting by the fire shivering, as Kardi was giving him a piece of hare to eat.

CHAPTER 24

THE MEANING OF NORTHERN FIRES

R aka went to the fire where Kardi was giving the shivering Kroli a piece of meat. Kroli was uninterested in eating and Kardi continued to gesture for him to eat, until he finally took a small bite. He chewed and swallowed with difficulty, as Raka looked on. His face was flushed and he shivered continuously. He motioned to Kardi that Raka wanted to discuss something; so, Kardi stopped her insistence for him to eat and turned her attention to Raka.

Raka squatted across the fire from Kardi and Kroli. He explained his trip to the top of the canyon wall, telling them about the fighting male red deer and seeing the many water birds on the lake. He asked Kardi if she thought that she, the other women and maybe some of the men could get some of the water birds before they migrated south. Kardi responded that she could and that she would take Brom, Kosh, Kuo and Mok. All were very good with the lop and Brom and Kardi could use the kawl well enough to kill water birds in flight, or in the water.

Kroli nodded that that was a good plan and Raka agreed. Kroli knew that the water birds were not the reason that Raka had approached him at the fire. If that had been the only issue that he wanted to discuss, he would have discussed it with Kardi later. He gestured to Raka to continue.

Raka explained that after he had searched the canyon and seen nothing out of the ordinary, he had looked north across the river that ran in front of the canyon mouth. Far in the distance to the north he had seen a thin ribbon of smoke that had to be a fire pit. As he continued to look in that direction he saw evidence of two additional fire-pits separated by at least a half day's run, perhaps more.

"What does this mean," he asked Kroli? Kroli pulled the bear skin robe more closely around himself to try and stop the shivering. He could not get warm. He thought over what Raka had seen. Kardi watched, as her father seemed to be lost in thought.

Finally, Kroli gestured his thoughts. It is too early for the reindeer to have migrated this far south. The northern clans always follow the reindeer herd migration. So, the fires must have been made by southern tribes that did not follow the migration north in the spring. Usually, you do not see so many southern tribe fires in the same area until the reindeer return in early winter. Kroli weakly gestured, could Raka have been looking at a larger area than they had ever seen before? Raka gestured that he had looked at this area many times throughout the summer and had never seen so many fires, so close together, nor so close to Kopsut Canyon.

Kroli shivered under the robe and after the shivering subsided, he weakly gestured that maybe the southern clans had left the northern hunting area early, before the reindeer migration. Maybe the northern clans had made their lives so dangerous that they had left ahead of the reindeer migration?

For the first time during this conversation, Kardi acted as if she had something to contribute. She asked Raka, "Were the fires large enough to indicate a clan communal fire, or small like a hunting party might make?"

Raka thought about her question. Slowly he explained that from the distance from which he was observing, it was hard to determine the size of the fire pits. The fires were definitely fire pits created by humans and the fires seemed to be about the same size. He said that the fires were about the same size as their own fire when you looked at it from the top of rear canyon wall. Raka said that if there had been a small hunting party fire pit in that same area, he believed that there would not have been enough smoke for him to see it from that distance.

Kardi thought for a moment and gestured to Kroli, "Would hunting parties, or raiding parties build so large a fire as to attract the attention of other humans?

Kroli's breathing was labored as he gestured that he did not thinks so; it would be too dangerous. For three such parties to make the same mistake of building such a large fire pit would be very unlikely. It had to be entire clans that made the fire pits. Their numbers were probably large enough for them not to fear other humans. That meant that there were probably at least three large clans close to Kopsut Canyon before the arrival of the reindeer herd. They were probably southern clans and since they had not followed the reindeer migration, they might be cannibals.

What should we do, gestured Kardi?

Kroli was becoming weak, he gestured toward Raka, dismissing the decision and turned away from Kardi and pulled the robe over his head. He immediately was either asleep, or unconscious.

Kardi looked at Raka and gestured the same question.

Raka thought for a minute and indicated, using only a few gestures, that these clans would probably spend the winter months at locations they were familiar with and the Kopsut Canyon had not previously shown signs of human presence. Raka indicated that they were probably not familiar with Kopsut Canyon. The canyon also was not that easy to access.

They would probably hunt the reindeer, when the migrating herds arrived and red deer before the reindeer herd arrived. Therefore, during the winter, they would stay far to the north of the canyon. It was likely that they would not be disturbed by these clans at least until spring, if at all. In the spring the clans might migrate north with the reindeer.

There was no way that Raka could know that the first fire pit that he had seen from the canyon wall had been made by a large northern clan. The clan had left its traditional hunting grounds in search of southern clans, which had become the target of this clan's hunts for the past few years. This clan was called the Clan of the Golo and it was a traditional cannibalistic clan. Hunting southern clans had become one of the steps that a young hunter must complete to become a man and be declared a Golo Clan hunter. The Golo Clan was led by a giant warrior named Aksot. Under the leadership of Aksot, the Golo Clan had become the most feared enemy of all southern clans. He had made the hunting and killing of southern clansmen the Golo Clan's eternal quest and he had been very successful.

Although the Golo Clan hunted and ate all large animals, hunting the southern clans had become an integral part of the clan's identity. Clansmen who killed a member of a southern clan were embraced as great warriors and given positions of honor in the clan. This clan, and others like it, had been very successful in their attacks on the southern clans that had followed the reindeer north. Many of the southern clans had already been destroyed or widely scattered by their attacks, resulting in a situation in which hunting them was no longer an easy task.

The clan preferred to conduct its attack on a southern clan just at dawn. Their attacks were invariably a surprise and the only survivors were the individuals who could run. The southern clans seldom were able to make an effective defense. The Golo Clan had killed and eaten most of the southern clan members from the River Clan, which had been their most recent attack. There were two exceptions, two young women whom they now used as slaves. They too would be killed and eaten at some point in the future, after their use as slaves was no longer needed.

With the elimination of the southern clans, the Golo Clan had considered attacking a northern clan and had gone so far as to send a scouting party toward a northern clan camp to determine the feasibility of such an endeavor. The scouting party had returned to indicate that the northern clan appeared to be very strong and ready for such an attack.

The other two fires were made by two other northern clans that had decided to precede the reindeer migration to move south and occupy the best hunting areas before the arrival of the reindeer. The reindeer hunts had provided these two clans with an abundance of food and they had decided that life in the warmer south might be better than the frigid north. Neither of these two clans was cannibalistic. These two clans were friendly with each other and both had seen the signs of the passage of the cannibalistic Golo Clan. If it was convenient and relatively safe, either of these two clans would attack the cannibals, realizing that the Golo Clan would always pose a threat. These two clans traded with each other routinely and shared the information about the Golo Clan. Each clan posted sentinels at night to guard against an attack from the Golo Clan.

Raka continued his discussion with Kardi. They would need to keep their fires small with little smoke; so, it was important to carry large amounts of old wood to the cave in order to keep it dry. Wet wood made white smoke and new wood made black smoke and both could be seen from a great distance. Dry old wood gave off less smoke and if the fire was small could not be seen from very far away.

Kardi said that she would inform the clan and ensure that

everyone followed Raka's order.

Raka was surprised to learn that he had given an order; since he was so accustomed to orders being given by Kroli. He turned away from Kardi and approached Brom, Milka and Beoh, who were preparing their weapons to go on a red deer hunt. Brom was chipping the edges of a throwing spear point to make it sharper; Milka was reattaching a spear point to a spear shaft which had become loose. Beoh was gathering round rocks for his lop, in case they startled a hare during the hunt.

Raka gestured for them to come and he explained their situation regarding the clan fire pits that he had seen north of the canyon. Beoh became excited by the news; while Brom and Milka looked concerned. Raka suggested that that they confine their hunts to the southern end of the canyon; but that they visit their old grotto camp first to make sure that there were no signs of their presence to attract the attention of any clans that might discover the canyon. They decided that today's hunt would be delayed and that they would visit the old grotto and hunt on the way back. This would make the hunt at least a five-day trip and possibly six. They all spent the rest of the day preparing their weapons.

Raka decided that Milka would stay at the cave, since Kroli was ill and Brom, Raka and Beoh would make the journey to the grotto. The journey would take them two hard days of travel to get to the grotto and one day at the grotto to ensure that they left no signs of human presence. It would probably take three days to return; since they would hunt on the way back. So, they would be gone six days. Milka agreed to keep everyone close to the cave until they returned. They had enough meat and lots of fruit and other plant products. They could check the dead-fall traps close to the cave and might get some fresh meat from them.

The next morning Raka, Brom and Beoh were up before

dawn and at the break of day started their journey to the old grotto camp. They traveled at a slow trot, which ate up the distance remarkably fast. Since they knew the trail, it was easy to avoid possible ambushes by meat-eaters while continuing to make steady fast progress.

They camped the first night next to the river which was full to its brim, as usual. The river had been full to overflowing since early spring, as the remarkably warm weather melted the ice and snow in the mountains. Crossing the river had been a risky task all year and Raka knew that the high river water could help the Kopsut Clan avoid contact with the clans that were approaching from the north.

They made their camp in between two fallen trees and built a small fire using only dry wood. Any smoke that the fire made was dispersed by the thick canopy formed by the tall trees along the river. Kop had decided to accompany Raka and he disappeared into the night, as the men rolled up in their robes to sleep on boughs that they had cut from the smaller trees. The night brought the howls of kopsut packs that lived in the valley. Raka recognized Kop's answering howl and wondered if the wolf would leave again on one of his extended absences.

When the men awoke at day break the next morning; they saw Kop sitting near the glowing coals of the fire. When the men rose from their mats, Kop retrieved a hare that he had killed and dropped it near the fire. The men gestured their praise for him, as Raka stoked his head. Beoh cleaned the hare and cooked it over the fire. They all shared it with Kop before departing at their customary slow trot.

They arrived at the grotto about an hour before dark and found little had been disturbed. A kopsut pair had used the grotto some time before and there were prints and bones scattered about to attest to that fact. They built a fire in the fire pit and slept for the night. Tomorrow they would search the area near the river and the canyon entrance to remove as much of the signs to indicate their presence in Kopsut canyon as possible. It would be virtually impossible to remove all signs; so, their intention was to hide it as much as possible.

Before retiring for the night, Raka climbed the cliff above the grotto to see if there was any sign of human-made fires in the area. He saw the faint glow of two fires; one about a day's run directly north of the canyon entrance and another more than half a day's run further west. The fires were large enough to indicate a communal fire pit for large clans. He knew that they had drawn closer to the canyon since he had detected them a few days earlier from the canyon wall. Raka carefully climbed down the cliff and told the other two men what he had seen. They all slept lightly, awakening many times to check outside the grotto, but seeing nothing out of the ordinary. Kop spent the night away from the grotto; the men had no way of knowing where he went, or what he did.

They rose after daylight and Raka led them away from the grotto to the east along the river. His intention was to check for possible fording locations. They traveled for two hours before Raka was satisfied that humans could not easily cross the river in that direction. The river was full; water was deep and swift and there were no fording locations.

Raka then led the group back to the west for the same purpose. When they came to the location that the Kopsut Clan had used to cross the river, he saw that the fallen log bridge that he and the other men had pushed into the river was completely gone, carried away with the surging flood water. The group continued west until their path was blocked where the river hugged a cliff wall. Raka was satisfied that it would be very unlikely that other humans would find the Kopsut Canyon unless they specifically decided to explore Kopsut Canyon.

Raka was unaware that the Golo Clan had developed a

method of creating a fallen log bridge across a narrow river by felling a tree near the river bank. The method called for the setting of a ring of fire at the base of the tree until it fell across the river.

They returned to the grotto and slept. Before departing the next morning, they eliminated all signs of human presence in the grotto and did not remove the signs left by the kopsut pair. They ran in the direction of the cave for a day and half of the next day. Kop joined them when they stopped for a mid-day rest. Then they started their hunt for red deer. Raka saw the giant red deer stag first and gestured for Kop to circle the animal and drive it toward the hunters, who hid themselves in the brush along an animal trail. As the stag bounded down the trail, Raka rose and threw his spear. Both of the other hunters followed with their own throws. Raka's spear was a killing blow, striking the animal behind the left foreleg and sinking deeply into the stag's chest. Beoh's spear hit the animal in the abdomen and Brom's spear sank into the animal's neck. The deer ran a few bounds after being struck and fell onto its right side, its legs continuing to gyrate, as if it was still running. The leg movements slowed and then stopped as the animal lost consciousness and then bled to death.

They dressed the deer and then cut it into three portions, which could be carried. They ate the liver and heart raw and gave Kop the rest of the internal organs. Then they shouldered their loads and made the journey back to the cave.

CHAPTER 25

ENTERING THE GREAT MOUNTAIN RANGE

P reparation for the winter passed uneventfully. The Kopsut Clan was able to store enough food supplies to get them through the cold months of the winter with no problem, since game was so abundant in Kopsut Canyon. Winter snows were light and, once again, the winter was comparably mild. Snow and ice in the mountains continued to melt during the warmer days and the rivers remained at or near flood stage. This boded well for the Kopsut Clan, since there was less of a possibility that the clans north of the canyon would cross the river and discover their Kopsut Canyon.

Kroli never recovered his strength after developing the chills in the fall and he coughed constantly, often spitting up blood. His time was spent huddled near the fire in a robe. When he had the strength, he talked to Raka about the threat from the clans to the north of the canyon and advised him to scout the valleys and canyons deeper into the mountain range in case they needed to escape to the south.

He ate less and less, as winter closed in on the canyon; until, one morning during the middle of the winter, the Clan awoke to find him missing from his sleeping mat near the fire pit. Raka and Brom followed his tracks in the snow until they came upon his body, sitting beside the river without his robe and frozen solid. They brought his body back to the cave and placed in a deep crevice that was located in the passage leading to the top of the cliff. They covered it with rocks to keep it from the meat-eaters.

Kardi was despondent for days afterward. But she finally returned her attention to her new baby and her attitude seemed to improve with the passage of time.

Winter passed, changing into an exceptionally warm spring. Flowers bloomed; plants sprang to life and animals were in abundance. Kop became Raka's constant companion and hunting partner. They both ran like the wind and Raka often violated Kroli's rule and hunted alone with Kop. Raka and Kop communicated with imperceptible movements and became more effective hunters than a kopsut pack. They seldom failed to bring home game.

The clan had plenty of food and enjoyed a tranquil period until Raka was seventeen years old. At seventeen, he had grown into a man much taller than anyone in the Clan had ever seen. He was strong in a much different way than other Clan men. His muscles were elongated, where other Clan men had bunched, larger muscles. Other Clan men could lift greater loads; but Raka could carry a load faster and longer before tiring. The temperature continued to moderate and the rivers were always full of melted ice and snow.

Toward the end of the Clan's fifth winter in Kopsut Canyon, Kosh and the babies belonging to Kardi and Brow were stricken with the red-spot disease (rubella) and all died after a few days. The babies were buried in the crevasse with Kroli.

The red-spot disease had become a common killer of the young of southern clans; while most of the adults had developed immunities to the disease. Kosh had been the exception. Only Gruma's baby remained of the five Kopsut Clan newborn. Kardi was more depressed than ever after the death of her baby and seemed to have no appetite. Raka attempted to get her more involved in decision making; but she simply accepted whatever he wanted to do.

At the beginning of the next spring, the Kopsut Clan consisted only of five adult males, Milka, Brom, Beoh, Mok and Raka. There were five females considered to be adults, Garki, Gruma, Brow, Kuo and Kardi. There was only one child left in the Kopsut Clan, Gruma's baby, which was now four years old.

Raka was now a seasoned clan leader at almost seventeen years of age. As leader, he gave Gruma to Milka, as an additional mate and gave Kuo to Mok. The clan was so small that they all occupied the main cathedral space in the cave and Milka no longer made his fire in the large cathedral at the upper end of the tunnel.

Raka kept himself from taking a mate, since the available females in the clan seemed more like sisters, or mothers to him.

At least once a week, he went through the tunnel to the top of the canyon rim and searched the area to the north of the canyon for signs of fire pits. During the warmer months he normally did not see any evidence of other clans. This was not surprising; since most clans followed the reindeer migrations to the north. This year was an exception; during the hottest month of the summer, he had seen two thin ribbons of smoke that could only mean the presence of other clans, or at least hunting parties. He kept up his vigilance; until, during the middle of autumn, he climbed to the canyon rim to see four fires which were much closer than he had ever seen them. He knew that it was time to follow Kroli's advice and explore more deeply into the mountain range.

The first snow of the coming winter had not yet arrived; when he took Kop and explored alone toward the southwest. His journey lasted more than two weeks and he found that he could access a long mountain valley from the southwestern corner of Kopsut Canyon. The valley was about a week's journey from the cave. He found and explored a possible cave in this valley that could be used by the clan. It had a natural pool of water and ran deeply into the mountain; but he could not tell if there was a rear entrance/exit. The presence of water in the cave was important; but was seldom found.

Raka examined the signs that had been left in the cave by previous tenants. There were piles of old bones; but no sign that a fire had ever been built in the cave. He examined the bones. They were bones of ibex and a small dear-like animal, smaller than the deer that Raka was familiar with. There were also bones of hare and fox. He found tracks that indicated that both a cave bear and a golo had once occupied this cave.

The Game in this valley should be sufficient to support a small clan, Raka thought. There was less game in the valley than they had found in Kopsut Canyon; but Raka was convinced that it would be adequate for at least a year. He returned and told the other clan members of his discovery.

He indicated that there was no way to hide their presence in Kopsut Canyon from clans that might come from the north, once they discovered the canyon. They would have to keep a watchful eye on the mouth of the canyon and, at the first indication that the canyon had been discovered, they would need to move to the new cave in the valley. Raka called the valley the "high valley," since it was so high in the mountains.

The winter passed uneventfully. The weather continued to be warm, compared to other winters, and the rivers were full of melted snow and ice.

Raka climbed to the canyon rim more often now and always saw several fires. He had no way of knowing that these fires were made by several northern clans. One of the fires was the communal fire of the Golo Clan, a clan that had preyed on the southern clans almost exclusively for many years. There were other northern clans which also attacked and killed the members of southern clans; but not as successfully, or as continuously, as the Golo.

One northern clan which was located not far from the Golo Clan was the Nord Clan. The Nord Clan did not typically prey on other clans; but it was a warrior clan, taller than many others and unafraid to battle other clans, if necessary to secure resources. Other clans referred to the Nord Clan as the "Tall People."

The Nord Clan was particularly wary of the Golo Clan; since they knew that the Golo were cannibals. They were watchful should the Golo Clan set their sights upon them. The Golo Clan had depleted the supply of southern clans in the area and they were increasing their search area to find other southern clans to fill their desire for human flesh. They too were aware of the northern clans in the area, including the Nord Clan; but knew that the northern clans were more formidable than the southern clans and, as long as there were southern clans to hunt; they chose to leave the northern clans alone.

The Golo clan had no way of knowing that constant attacks, disease and lack of resources had all but eliminated the southern clans north of the great mountain range. Attacking the southern clans had become a way-of-life for the Golo and it was impossible for them to imagine life without their preferred pray.

Unknown to the Golo Clan, the last remaining southern clan was the Kopsut Clan, which was secreted in Kopsut Canyon and could only be discovered by crossing a deep, fast flowing river. Time would tell whether northern clans would discover the Kopsut Clan; but the stress on the life of the Kopsut Clan secreted in the mountains was also taking its toll on the Clan.

Raka climbed down from the canyon rim and told the other members of the clan what he had seen. He emphasized again that the clan fires had to be small and made only of dry wood. The smoke that he had seen could only mean several large groups of humans that were unafraid of being discovered.

The smoke was close enough that they could not take the risk that their fire might be seen.

Raka decided that it was time to start preparation for moving their camp to the high valley, which he now referred to as "ahop." The word "ahop," when used with a hand gesture above the head meant "high" in the Step Clan language. They would take some robes, tools, weapons and dried meat to the ahop cave. This was done as a precaution should they have to abandon the Kopsut Canyon cave on short notice.

The entire clan made the trip to the ahop cave, since Raka did not want to separate the clan. They carried all that they could carry and the trip took a little more than a week. When they neared the ahop cave location, they killed an ibex (mountain goat), for which they did not have a name. They carried it to the cave and that became their first meal consumed in what might become their new home.

Everyone loved the taste of the ibex; even Kardi broke her reluctance to eat and ate sparingly. This new valley would offer a new type of game; excitement once again filled their cave. They decided to stay at the new cave for a week and hunt other game. They were able to kill a spo, another ibex and two bush deer. They also killed a carnini and two foxes. Most of the meat was smoked and dried and the hides were cleaned. They left everything in the new cave, hanging well above the cave floor on poles. This would become their emergency rations, should the clan need to escape to the ahop valley.

After almost a month-long absence, they returned to Kopsut Canyon. They found nothing disturbed in their cave and they were all relieved to be back in a familiar place.

Raka's first task was to climb to the canyon rim and see if the fires had changed position since their trip to the ahop valley. He first examined the area around the cave and found nothing out of the ordinary. As he looked north toward the mouth of Kopsut Canyon he was startled to see a fire which seemed to be coming from this side of the river more, or less at their old grotto camp site. The fire was large and that meant that a large clan had discovered and entered Kopsut Canyon. Further north he saw three additional fires that were closer to the canyon than he had ever seen before. Raka knew that he had to take the Kopsut Clan out of Kopsut Canyon as soon as possible.

CHAPTER 26

THE GOLO CLAN

The Golo Clan had changed their hunting grounds to coincide with the modified migration habits of the southern clans. Since the southern clans typically followed the migrations of the reindeer herd and hunted on the southern edges of the reindeer herd, the Golo moved further south and hunted the southern tribes, as they hunted the reindeer.

Once the southern tribes had started to migrate south before the reindeer migration to escape the attacks of the northern clans, the Golo Clan did the same. The Golo Clan enjoyed immense prosperity using these migration habits and were able to kill southern clan members with relative ease. The Golo also hunted reindeer, when the migrating herds arrived.

The Golo enjoyed the warmer weather and, since they were such a large and aggressive clan, had relatively no major threats to fear in these southern lands.

Other northern clans noticed the fact that the Golo Clan had modified its migration times and hunting grounds and many of them soon followed suit. The Nord Clan, led by the great Wonto, Carni, was one of these clans. The Nord Clan maintained a distance from the Golo Clan of at least a day's travel away in order to limit their exposure to the Golo, as much as possible.

The Golo Clan, led by the giant Aksot, had continued to

hunt further and further south after they failed to find more southern clans further north. The River Clan had been the last major clan that the Golo had been able to attack. That attack had occurred more than a year earlier and they were hungry to find others.

They had occasionally found very small groups of southern clansmen whose clan had been destroyed; but these sporadic opportunities did not satisfy the Golo Clan's need for the killing of southern clansmen to advance their young men into manhood and warrior status.

Aksot had sent hunting parties south in search for signs of southern clansmen. Invariably, these parties returned with little evidence of southern clans. They had found old evidence of campfires north of the narrow river near the mountains; but the fires were very old and may have no meaning. Although most of the fires were years old, they had found two fires that led toward the river near the mountains. Aksot wanted very badly to believe that the southern clans had escaped to the south; so, he moved the Golo Clan south with the intention of crossing the narrow river near the mountains to find where the southern clans had secreted themselves.

As he neared the river, he was aware that other northern clans had stayed relatively near his clan, but farther to west and north. He warily posted guards in those directions to ensure that the Golo were not surprised by an attack.

Aksot still had two River Clan females that he kept as slaves and these females were required to work for the Golo Clan women and suffered horrible abuse from those women during the day and were given to the men for their entertainment during the night.

It was the late summer when Aksot had called his chief lieutenants together around the campfire to decide what the clan should do next. Aksot sent for the River Clan females, as the Golo Clan arrived at the river near the mountains. One of the females was a young woman and the other was quite old. Aksot asked the females if they had ever known of southern clans that lived along this river, or further south than the river.

The old woman had a broken nose and one eye was swollen shut. Her body was covered in bruises. The young woman was also covered in bruises and both had been subjected to continuous rapes and beatings. They were very dejected and had come to believe that death would be a relief.

The young woman looked at the old woman and waited for her to answer. The old woman gestured that there had never been a clan farther south than the River Clan. Aksot slapped the old woman to the ground and turned to the younger woman. He gestured that he knew that the old woman's reply was a lie. If the young woman maintained the same response, they would both serve as a celebration feast for the Golo Clan that evening.

The young woman responded that there had been once been a clan farther south than the River Clan. It had been called the Step Clan; but the River Clan had not seen evidence of that clan since it had been attacked by the Golo many years before.

Aksot slapped the young woman to see if she would change her story; but she did not. He sent the two women back to their work and turned to his lieutenants. He informed them that everyone knew that the Golo Clan had not killed the entire Step Clan. The remainder had to be south of the river near the mountains. He told his lieutenants that they would camp along the river and conduct hunting trips to replenish their food supplies with deer meat. They would find a way to cross the river and look for the remainder of the Step Clan. They had five young Golo clansmen that needed to be passed to warrior status and they needed to find and attack a southern clan to allow that to happen in accordance with long-standing Golo traditions.

Some of the Golo conducted daily deer hunts; others searched the banks of the river looking for a way to cross and a few were sent to keep tabs on the northern clan nearest to the Golo. When they found no way to cross the swollen river, Aksot decided to create a fallen log bridge at a narrow point in the river.

They found a likely candidate tree that grew on the northern bank of the river and was already leaning in the direction across the river. They set small fires against the tree trunk and kept the portions of the trunk that were higher up wet, as the fires slowly burned the base of the tree. After burning almost all day, the tree was felled by the clan members as they pushed to cause it to fall across the river. The men only needed to trim away the branches to be able to cross the river. The trimming took most of the following day.

Aksot ordered that the old River Clan woman be sacrificed and served in celebration before they crossed the river to look for the southern clans. She was killed with a blow to the head using Aksot's battle ax, which had a flint head. The young female cowed at the edge of the fire light, as the Golo Clan roasted and ate her friend and relative.

In the meantime, the Nord Clan had discovered that the Golo Clan had been sending scouts to check the Nord Clan's camp sites. The Nord Clan was aware that there were no southern clans in the area to keep the Golo Clan occupied and, therefore, was very cautious concerning possible Golo Clan intentions toward the Nord Clan.

Carni, the Nord Clan Wonto, had become the effective leader of the Clan. He decided to keep a close watch on the Golo Clan; so that at the first sign that the Golo had an interest in the Nord Clan, the Nord Clan could attack them.

To accomplish this objective, Carni ordered two of his best warriors, Sart and Gomp, to conduct periodic espionage trips to the Golo camp.

As fate would have it, Sart and Gomp were hidden in a nearby clump of dew berry vines when Aksot killed the old River Clan woman. Sart was incensed by this type of treatment of even a slave and indicated to Gomp that they should do something to save the other River Clan female. They waited until the Golo Clan members were asleep after their celebration and feast on the body of the old woman.

The Golo Clan guards were not as attentive as they might have been, had they not participated in the feast. A guard was stationed on the northern, eastern and western sides of the camp. Gomp saw that that left the southern side of their camp open for penetration.

The two Nord Clan warriors circled the camp and entered the camp perimeter from the southern side near the river. The young River Clan woman was sleeping near the river in the care of a Golo warrior who had been given her services for the night. The Golo warrior was fast asleep on his sleeping mat with his arm draped across the back of the woman, who was lying on the ground next to his mat. She was not asleep and Sart was able to get her attention and gestured to her that they were there to save her from the Golo. She indicated that she understood, as Sart and Gomp crept up to the Golo warrior. He must have sensed the woman's movement for without rising, he grabbed a handful of her hair and dragged her closer to his sleeping mat. Sart and Gomp remained still until the Golo seemed to fall back to sleep. The Golo and the woman were sleeping in relative privacy about twenty feet from the closest clan member.

Gomp planned to use his battle ax to kill the Golo. The only sound would be the blow and should not be heard by other members of the Clan. As Sart stood ready with his throwing spear, Gomp hit the Golo directly on his right temple. The blow was probably not hard enough to kill him; but it did render him unconscious and there was virtually little noise from the blow. The woman started to rise, but Gomp indicated that she should stay down.

The three of them slowly crawled toward the river. Sart saw the fallen-log bridge in the faint moon-light that the Golo had created and pointed it out to Gomp. He indicated that they should make it seem that they had crossed the bridge and headed south. The group made an obvious trail to the bridge and then entered the ice cold, swift-running river and allowed it to carry them downstream for about four hundred yards, until Gomp decided that they could no longer take the cold. They exited the river on the north bank on top of a rocky finger of land sticking out into the flooded river. They quickly entered the forest and started returning to the Nord Clan camp using a zigzag pattern to disguise their direction of travel. After running a few minutes, their bodies warmed and the cold from the river was forgotten.

At daybreak a Golo woman discovered the unconscious body of the Golo warrior and the missing River Clan woman. Aksot and his lieutenants examined the tracks that the woman and Nord Clan warriors had left. They followed them to the fallen-log bridge and decided that the group had escaped to the south. To Aksot it was obvious that a southern clan had crept up from the south to save one of their own kind. He was now completely convinced that this was proof that a southern clan lived south of the river. Tomorrow they would begin their search for the southern clan. He felt that it should be relatively easy to drive the southern clan toward the mountains and eventually kill them, as the Golos had done countless other times with other southern clans.

In the meantime, Sart and Gomp returned to the Nord Clan camp with the woman. Carni treated the woman's many injuries and told her that she would be the Nord Clan slave;

but she would not be harmed. The woman was relieved and happy to serve the Nord Clan. She immediately started gathering wood for their fire to show her value.

Carni huddled with his leading warriors. They discussed what this situation might mean to the Nord Clan. Carni felt that although Gomp's attempt to disguise their direction of travel was admirable, it would be foolhardy not to assume that the Golo would discover the Nord Clan's participation in the woman's escape. Carni directed that the Nord Clan prepare to strike the Golo Clan.

While the Nord Clan was preparing their attack, the Golo moved their camp across the fallen-log bridge and discovered the old grotto camp that the Kopsut Clan had previously used. Aksot ordered the Clan to camp at the grotto; although it was too small for the entire Golo Clan. It was a safe camp site since the river protected them from the north and the cliffs protected them on their southern side. The camp could only be approached from the east or west. Aksot set up lookouts in both of those directions; and placed one lookout at the fallen-log bridge, which was down river about two hundred yards from the grotto camp.

The following day Aksot sent out exploring parties to see what the land south of the river was like and look for game and signs of the southern clan. He was convinced that they would find fresh signs of the southern clan near the river.

It took the Golo almost two weeks to kill sufficient game to keep the Golo Clan fed for a while and determine that the only direction the southern clan could have taken was into Kopsut Canyon. They also found many old human prints. Following their careful searching, they found bones and old animal skins that the Kopsut Clan had hidden to obscure their occupation of the grotto camp site.

Aksot decided to take a large party of warriors deep into

Kopsut Canyon, not only to look for the southern clan, but also to find a camp site for the Golo further into the canyon. He left a few warriors, most of the women and all of the children at the grotto camp. They would be responsible for hunting and defending the clan camp site at the grotto.

When Aksot and his remaining warriors departed the Golo grotto camp site, Gomp and Sart were watching from across the river and immediately carried the information to the Nord Clan. Carni was waiting for a good opportunity to attack the Golo and this looked like a very good opportunity.

CHAPTER 27

THE GOLO CLAN FINDS THE KOPSUT CLAN

R aka gathered the small band together that made up the Kopsut Clan and explained to them the danger that they now faced from the clans that seemed to be entering Kopsut Canyon. Raka explained that it was inevitable that these followers would discover the signs that the Kopsut Clan had left in their old camp site at the grotto. He asked Brom, Kardi and Milka what they thought the clan should do.

Milka wanted to move the camp to the Ahop Valley, as did Brom. Kardi was slow to gesture her opinion. She asked Raka what he knew about the followers. Raka could not tell her very much, only what the smoke had told him.

There were several large fires which probably indicated several clans. One fire was at least in front of the canyon and may be already inside it. Since the clans had discovered the canyon with little loss of time, the Kopsut Clan had to assume that the followers knew of the Kopsut Clan presence in the canyon.

Kardi advised that the Clan needed to know more about the followers and, at the same time, they needed to start the move to the Ahop Valley. Raka saw the logic in her reasoning; but the Clan was too small to risk splitting the adult males into two groups.

Raka was now confident in his role as clan leader. He informed the group of his decision. The group would depart for the Ahop Valley in two days, using deception to make it appear that they were following the river toward the southeastern corner of the canyon. Raka knew that the river could be traced southeast until it reached its headwaters in a box canyon. The Clan would actually travel toward the southwestern corner of Kopsut Canyon, which eventually opened into the Ahop Valley. Everyone nodded their agreement with this plan, as Raka continued.

Raka surprised the group by saying that while Milka and Brom led the Clan to the Ahop Valley, Raka and Kop would scout the followers to learn more about them and what the Kopsut Clan was facing. Kardi immediately gestured her disagreement and Milka and Brom agreed with her. It was too dangerous for one man to scout the followers, Milka insisted.

Raka showed a calm determination in justifying his decision. He insisted that if more men went on the mission, not only were the scouts in greater danger; but the entire clan was also. One man with the aid of Kop could avoid detection and be safer than two men. Then, Raka acted like a seasoned leader and said that he would talk no more about it. The decision was made.

Kardi was dejected; but there was much preparation before they departed for the Ahop Valley. Everyone began preparations by repairing backpacks and two-man poles under which they would sling as much of the resources that they could carry with them.

Milka and Brom huddled with Raka to map out the best route to take to their new home. They would make a false trail back toward the southeast corner of Kopsut Canyon using the animal trails that ran along the river and backtrack to the trail that led to the southwestern corner. Raka believed that the followers would most likely follow obvious signs of human passage on the trail near the river. After turning west on the animal trail, the clan would try to cover their trail without leaving sign and head for the southwest corner of the canyon, where they could access the pass to the Ahop Valley. Raka stated that such a diversion might gain a week, or more time before the Golo Clan was able to find their true direction.

When the clan had finished preparations, Raka talked again with Milka and Brom and told them that he would try to catch up to them before they reached the Ahop Valley; but if he was unable to do that, they should not stop; but should continue to the new cave site and place a lookout where they could watch the entry into the valley in case the followers were able to pick up their trail.

With those final directions, Raka said his farewells to everyone and spent a moment convincing Kardi that the clan needed her leadership, until he was able to return. He warned her to give her counsel to Milka and Brom and ensure that everyone was alert to dangers. The Ahop Valley was a relatively unexplored land and might hide dangers that they did not expect.

Raka called to Kop and they departed down the animal trail that headed west across the canyon. His intention was to help make another false trail back toward the canyon entrance by turning north at the trail crossing.

Raka watched Kop, as they ran. He knew that Kop would sense the presence of danger before he did. The wind was directly from the north, so he did not believe that the followers would be able to smell him before he was able to pick up their scent carried to him by the wind. As Raka trotted down the trail, Kop ran ahead of him, returning to Raka occasionally, as if to assure him that he was still with him. As Raka ran, he searched for flat rocks suitable for use in his kawl. Barely slowing his trot, he picked up and discarded several before collecting four perfectly-shaped rocks and placing them in his pouch. Since he intended to leave sign of his passage, he could move much faster.

He arrived at the split in the trail in the early afternoon and, after ensuring that he left tracks showing that he was headed north, took some dried deer meat from his pack and ate it, as he continued to walk toward the canyon entrance.

He decided to camp off of the trail at a dead-fall that gave him protection on three sides. He did not build a fire and Kop seemed to sense their vulnerability as he curled up between the entrance to the dead-fall enclosure and Raka. Raka slept lightly with his hand on his thrusting spear.

He awakened before daylight and immediately looked for Kop. Kop was nowhere to be found; so, he rose; ate some meat and continued his trot toward the canyon entry. He had heard several kopsut howls during the night and wondered if Kop had answered their call. If Kop did not return, he would be much more vulnerable to discovery by the clan that was following them.

At about noon time, Kop returned to Raka and trotted close by his side. Raka had learned that when Kop stayed so close it was an indication that there was danger ahead of them. He recognized the area that he was in. He was not too far from one of the dead-fall traps that he had used while the clan lived at the grotto camp site. He slowed his progress to a walk and closely watched Kop, as he walked a few yards in front of Raka. After about an hour in the middle of the afternoon, he noticed that Kop slowed his advance and his ears were pointed forward, as he smelled the wind from the north. Raka did not smell anything out of the ordinary; but he continued to stop occasionally to sniff the wind.

Kop turned to look at Raka and Raka recognized his demeanor. He was asking what he should do. Raka again sniffed the wind and caught a very faint odor of what might be a fire, or it might possibly be a human that carried the smell of smoke on his body. He assumed his stalking stance and moved forward cautiously. Kop followed his lead. Now Raka got a good whiff of the odor that the wind carried to him. There was the smell of smoke mixed with the stale smell of sweat. The odor also contained the acrid smell of a cooked meat that Raka did not recognize.

From the direction of the wind and Raka's knowledge of the area, he thought that the human that he smelled might be near an old dead-fall trap that he had used when the Clan had been at the grotto camp. Raka left the trail and cautiously approached the area where he remembered setting the dead-fall trap. Kop spread out to Raka's right much nearer to the animal trail. As they drew near the trap, Raka noticed that Kop's body had stiffened and his ears were pointed toward the trap. Raka listened attentively and thought he heard the sound of a low conversation. Dropping to his belly, he crawled closer until he could surreptitiously look around a tree truck and see where the old dead-fall trap had been.

There were three large men sitting on the log that had once been the killing mechanism of the dead-fall trap. The men had an olive-colored skin, dark hair and dark eyes. The most noticeable thing about them was that they had what looked like human finger bones piercing through their noses and some type of dark drawings of animals on their arms.

The men were looking closely at the dead-fall trap and discussing it. One of the men was examining the old footprints and other signs that surrounded the trap. Raka knew that the area would be full of old signs, since he had used the trap for several years. They should not only find footprints of at least three different people; but might find old bones, pieces of animal fur and possibly a broken spear point. The men were engrossed in their study of the trap and its surroundings.

Raka considered the situation. He was ready to assume that these men were from a cannibal clan and that the clan knew of the Kopsut Clan presence. They probably could determine that the Kopsut Clan was a small, weak clan by studying the grotto campsite. Raka felt that he needed to slow the cannibal's search by making them more cautious. Such a delay would allow Milka and Brom more time to get the clan to the Ahop Valley. He made his decision.

He motioned to Kop to circle behind the men and he loaded his spear thrower and held a second spear in his left hand for a quick reload. When he knew that Kop had had time to get in position on the other side of the men, he crouched ready for his throw.

The men smelled the kopsut and became alert, looking in the direction away from Raka. Raka rose and released his first spear and reloaded his second in one swift motion. He threw his second spear just as the first one struck. He reached for his loaded kawl.

The first spear struck the closest man to Raka in the center of his back and passed through his body. As the injured man uttered a muffled "humph," as the second spear struck the man to Raka's left front in the right side in his chest area. He screamed a piercing "Aheee," as he fell to the ground. Raka grabbed his kawl and prepared to attack the third man, who had started his escape toward the animal trail. The trees prevented Raka from getting a good line-of-sight for his kawl; so, he leaped after the man. As the man entered the animal trail and turned left running back in the general direction of the grotto, Kop leaped from the forest. His powerful fangs sliced through the running man's right hamstring, as Kop passed behind the man. The man ran two more steps until collapsing in the trail. His scream stopped in his throat, as the rock from Raka's kawl shattered his skull. Kop immediately ripped his throat out for good measure.

Raka studied the dead man. The man was very large and tall. He had to be a northern clansman. Southern clansmen were never so tall. The bone in his nose was definitely a human finger bone. The acrid meat smell was probably the smell of cooked human flesh. The man had a drawing of a golo on his left forearm. Raka had never seen a tattoo before. There were other tattooed symbols on his upper legs and chest. His body also showed scars from battles and possibly ceremonial proofs of his strength. He opened the man's robe and saw vertical scars on his chest that were obviously inflicted intentionally. His left arm had a large scar that could have been a spear wound. The man wore a short robe made from reindeer hide and a lower body cover that went to his knees. He had a pouch tied around his waist.

Raka looked in the man's pouch. The pouch contained meat that had the same acrid smell that Raka had first detected. Raka threw the meat to Kop, who began to eat it. There were three spear heads made from antlers, a bone carving of a golo, some sharp bone tools and a flint ax head. The man carried a throwing spear, but no spear thrower. He also carried a flint- headed battle ax. Raka took the golo carving and left the rest.

He decided to move the body off of the trail and obliterate the signs of the battle. He hid the body behind a fallen tree and carefully spread dirt over the signs of the battle. He left the footprints of the man running down the trail; but obliterated his own foot prints. He also left Kop's prints.

Raka returned to the other two bodies. There would be no way to disguise the fact that these two men had been killed by a warrior; so, Raka didn't try. When he examined the other two men, he saw that they also had their bodies tattooed like the first man and they had the same finger bone pierced through their noses. They had similar vertical scars on their chests. The larger of the two men had a scar on his left abdomen that looked like a spear wound. In their pouches, he found similar bone carvings of a golo. Raka placed those golo carvings in his pouch also. The larger man also carried what looked like golo incisor teeth. Raka also took those. Both men carried bone tools, leather strips and a hunk of human flesh. Again, Raka gave the meat to Kop.

Raka considered what this "Golo" clan would read from the signs that he had left. It would take them some time to find all three bodies; but they would find them. They would believe that a kopsut had killed the man near the animal trail and, when they found the other two, they would realize that they had been killed by a warrior. They would also be able to determine that he was alone.

He decided to make them guess about the numbers of attackers. He made several prints as if there had been several attackers and carefully modifying the prints to look like different sizes of feet, occasionally adding a scar to the print. Then he made a false trail to make it seem as if the attackers had gone through the woods north toward the canyon entrance and the grotto campsite. Then he entered a small stream and hid his tracks, as he headed south toward the Ahop Valley.

Meanwhile, Aksot had taken his war party along the left fork of the animal trails through the center of the canyon and made a camp where the trail looped around to the left. He had sent one of his lieutenants and two scouts to search the right-hand fork of the animal trail with instructions to return to the group as soon as possible. The signs that they found along the left fork in the animal trail indicated the very old passage of a group of humans. The size of the prints indicated that the humans were southern clansmen. The numbers could not be determined; but Aksot knew that the group was small. Aksot was waiting for the return of the men that he had sent to search the right fork before deciding his next move.

When the men did not return to the campsite before dark,

Aksot was not concerned because he assumed that the men had searched too far from the campsite to return in one day. When they did not return on the second day, he became concerned. He sent a group of four warriors to check on the other three who had conducted the search of the right fork in the animal trail. It took them three days to find the men and return. The story that they brought to Aksot caused him to reconsider what he was planning to do.

The returning men told Aksot that the group of three had been attacked by several warriors that left large narrow tracks. The tracks did not have the appearance of southern clansmen. Krip and Got had been killed first by thrown spears. The warrior Bak had been killed later by a kopsut, as he tried to escape along the animal trail. They also told him that the attacking warriors had seemed to be going toward the grotto camp at the entrance to the canyon after the attack. Aksot was concerned, not only because the attackers had appeared to be headed toward the remainder of his clan; but also, because, like all humans at the time, he feared the unknown.

He needed to know what he was facing. If the clan he was following was not a southern clan, what was it? Could it be a northern clan? He did not think that the northern clans that had followed the Golo Clan to the southern hunting areas could have made the tracks they had found in the canyon. He knew that some of the old tracks that they had found in the canyon were the tracks southern clansmen. So, this new group of attackers must be a completely different clan. Maybe it was a northern clan that had preceded the Golo Clan into this area years earlier. He decided that for safety, he needed to keep his clan together. He decided to return to the grotto camp and get the remainder of the clan before continuing his search in a more cautious manner and sending out stronger scouting parties. If they were attacked, the scouting parties would be a large enough group to defend themselves.

The sign on the left-hand animal trail indicated that the southern clan had passed in this direction long ago. The other mysterious clan had shown its presence along the right fork. Aksot decided to avoid the right fork and the mysterious clan and follow the signs of the southern clan along the left fork in the animal trail. He ordered his men to prepare to return to the grotto campsite to get the rest of the clan. Then they would follow the left fork in the animal trail and set up a camp deeper into the canyon, such that they could search for the southern clan.

CHAPTER 28

THE NORD CLAN ATTACKS THE GOLO CLAN

The Nord Clan sent its scouts to locate the Golo Clan camp site. They found the Clan's encampment at the grotto across the narrow river in front of the entrance to the Kopsut Canyon. Carni moved the Nord Clan camp to a location which could be defended and was within striking distance of the Golo Clan. Carni ordered the clan to limit their fires to prevent detection. Carni was a hands-on leader and personally reconnoitered the camp from a concealed position across the river.

Carni recognized that the Golo Clan was still split into two groups. There were fewer warriors at the camp than had been previously reported by Gomp. The fallen-tree bridge that the Golo had used to cross the river was guarded by only one warrior, who did not appear to be very alert for danger. He was lounging on the southern end of the tree bridge, apparently looking at the women and children as they went about their chores in the grotto camp. Occasionally, the lookout would lie back onto the tree bridge and stare at the clouds. He was armed with a battle ax and throwing spear.

Carni judged that it should be possible to kill this warrior with a thrown spear, allowing the swift-moving Nord Clan attackers to cross the river before additional defenders could reach the bridge. Carni knew that he could get enough men across the bridge to overwhelm the Golo before an effective defense could be organized.

Carni critically examined the Golo Clan's preparation of their camp for defense. He knew that if he had been creating a fallen-tree bridge, he would have made it closer to the camp so that it could be defended quickly by the camp dwellers without running the two hundred yards or so to the location of the bridge. He also knew that the Golo should have positioned at least three warriors at the bridge to gain enough time for re-enforcements to arrive.

Carni judged that the decisive part of the battle would be fought on the south side of the river between the bridge and the Golo Clan's cave. If the defenders were able to retreat to the cave and there was no rear exit, they would be trapped and could be surrounded until they chose to battle their way out of the cave. Carni did not know if the cave had a rear exit; but he intended to inflict as much damage on the Golo as he could before they escaped.

Carni planned his attack to be conducted at the same time of day that the Golo had typically made their own attacks on the southern clans, at the break of dawn before the camp was completely awake. Carni directed the attack to take place the following morning after he had conducted his final scout of the camp. He wanted to catch the Golo before the other group of warriors returned to the grotto encampment.

Just at the break of dawn, Gomp led the attack on the fallen-tree bridge. He killed the bridge guard with a thrown spear without alerting the other camp dwellers since the bridge was so far from the camp. He sent fifteen warriors across the bridge immediately since the narrow space between the cliff and the river allowed only about fifteen men to fight without getting in each other's way. He positioned an additional ten men to follow the first attack in a second wave.

The first resistance that they encountered was at the edge of the campsite. Three warriors were just beginning to walk toward the river to get their morning drink when they saw the attackers. They raised the alarm, as they drew their battle axes.

Other warriors around the camp fire grabbed their spears and rushed to meet the invaders.

Using their spear throwers, the Nord Clan attackers had the advantage of being able to engage the Golo before the Golo were close enough to use their throwing spears. They dispatched the closest three warriors before these three Golos could get close enough to use their battle axes. There were ten additional Golo warriors that rushed to defend the encampment armed with their throwing spears and battle axes. After the Nord Clan attackers launched the first wave of spears, the closeness of the battle diminished the effectiveness of the Nord Clan spear throwers and the battle became a more even contest. It quickly became apparent that the Nord Clan warriors were more skillful at this type of fighting than the outnumbered Golo. The Golo were driven back toward the grotto.

As the battle raged on, many of the Golo women and the children recognized the danger of being trapped in the grotto and escaped down the animal trail, running toward where the rest of the Golo Clan and their leader, Aksot, had gone days before. The defending Golo were driven past the grotto and back down the animal trail. They could not afford to turn their backs on the attackers and run for fear that the attackers would use their spear throwers to kill them all. They had to give their women and children time to escape.

By the time that the battle was over, the Nord Clan had taken the encampment and killed most of the men and several of the women. Only two wounded men escaped to follow the women and children down the animal trail.

The Nord Clan stopped its attack and prepared for a continuing battle. They brought the remainder of their clan across the river and set up camp at the grotto.

Carni examined his losses. He had only three men who were wounded and were receiving treatment. The fact that no men had been killed was a good omen in Carni's eyes and he intended to pursue the Golo further into the mountains. He climbed the cliff behind the grotto and surveyed the direction toward which the Golo had retreated. It appeared to be a canyon and could possibly be a box canyon, which would mean that the Golo would not be able to escape the Nord Clan.

Carni and his men examined the signs around the grotto camp. Most of the signs were made by the Golo, but Carni found footprints in the silt along the grotto walls that were made by a southern clan. He examined these tracks closely. He believed that he recognized one of the footprints. If he was correct, the footprint had been made by the woman he knew as Kardi. For some reason, he felt a thrill at this discovery.

It was apparent that the Golo were in pursuit of the southern clan and quite possibly had focused their attention on finding and attacking the southern clan instead of defending against an attack from the Nord Clan. Carni felt that this was an indication that the Golo leader was not a great leader. The first priority of a good leader is a clan's defense. After the defense is assured, the clan can shift its attention to other objectives.

Carni posted one lookout at the top of the cliff to watch for any danger that approached from the canyon, or across the fallen-log bridge. He then posted six warriors to cover the canyon entrance in case the Golo should mount a counterattack. Just to be safe, he posted two warriors at the fallen log bridge with instructions to remain out of sight.

The Nord Clan started to make their camp comfortable, as Carni briefed the men on his plan for going after the Golo.

They would proceed after the Golo the next day. He had concluded that the Golo leader would probably not expect such a swift follow-up attack. Typically, after a successful attack, an attacking clan would celebrate their victory; while the losing clan would lick their wounds and plot a revenge attack. Carni did not intend to allow the Golo a minute's respite; since, he knew that if they had time to prepare a response, the Golo would be very formidable.

Meanwhile, Aksot and his men started their journey back toward the grotto camp to retrieve the remainder of their clan. They traveled until early evening when Aksot ordered the men to camp near the river. As the camp was being set up and fires were just large enough to start cooking meat, one of the lookouts that Aksot had posted at the northern edge of the camp sounded the alarm. When Aksot arrived at the lookout's position, the lookout said the he had smelled humans approaching on the animal trail from the north. Aksot smelled the wind which was lightly blowing from the northwest. He detected a distinct human odor. He carefully examined the odor until he recognized the smell of the Golo Clan. He cuffed the lookout across the shoulders and berated him for sounding the alarm for one of their own.

As Aksot turned to return to the camp, he heard a woman call his name. Turning he saw several women and children approaching along the animal trail. They appeared agitated and tired. Other women and children followed them toward Aksot. There were two men being assisted by the women. Both men were caked in dried blood and appeared to have been wounded by spears.

When the first of the straggling group reached Aksot, they all started to speak at once and the only thing that he was able to understand was that there had been an attack. He silenced them all with a raised hand. He pointed to one of the wounded men who was the closest to him and indicated for him to talk.

The man related the events that had occurred including the fact that the attacking clan had been the Nord Clan and that the attack had been a complete surprise. All of the other men had been killed and the women and children had only escaped because the dead men had fought hard to give them time to get away. They had traveled the remainder of the day of the attack and the entire night to reach Aksot and warn him.

Aksot was livid. No clan had ever been courageous enough to attack the Golo Clan before. He knew that he should have attacked the Nord Clan when he had considered it; now, he had lost a large number of men. The men and women appeared to be demoralized. He knew that he needed to act to prevent further demoralization. He stood with his battle ax raised and addressed his clan.

"We will take revenge on the Nord Clan and eat their hearts in a celebration feast before we continue our search for the southern clan," spoke Aksot.

He turned to the five youths that were waiting their opportunity to kill a southern clansman and become warriors. "You child warriors will kill a Nord Clansman and become men and warriors during our attack. Now everyone should rest and prepare their weapons for the coming battle. We will take one day of rest and then send our scouts to seek out the Nord Clan in preparation for our attack. The Golo Clan will destroy the Nord Clan before there is a new moon," Aksot spoke confidently.

While the Golo Clan rested and made its preparations to attack the Nord Clan and the Nord Clan started its pursuit of the Golo Clan, Raka had discovered that there were now two fires inside the canyon. When Raka arrived at the point where the north/south animal trail intersected with the east/west animal trail, he climbed a tree to examine his back-trail. What he saw was somewhat disturbing. He saw a large fire near what had been the Kopsut Clan's grotto campsite and a large fire on the animal trail near the river. By the sizes of the fires, he surmised that the followers were either one very large clan that had split into two groups, or two large clans. Raka decided that he needed to know what these two fires signified. He took the east/west animal trail to scout the fire near the river. He sent Kopsut ahead, as he trotted along the trail.

CHAPTER 29

RAKA SCOUTS THE GOLO CLAN

Raka traveled at a slow run for the entire day in the direction of the river that ran along the canyon's eastern wall until the early evening. He came to a spot that he had often used for an overnight camp and decided to spend the night there. He made his camp about three hundred yards off of the animal trail near a dead-fall trap that he had once set out to catch hare. The dead-fall served to provide a small degree of protection on one side. Kop was with him; so, he was not too concerned that he would be surprised by meat-eaters, or humans. He camped without a fire, fearing that he might be too close to the followers to safely build even a small a fire pit without it being discovered.

At the break of day, he continued his journey and came to the north/south animal trail near the river at about noon. There was no sign that the followers had recently passed down the trail; so, he knew that the followers had not arrived this far south. He slowed his pace of travel and sent Kop ahead again, as he turned north on the animal trail. Since he was headed toward the enemy, he saw no reason to hide his tracks.

After another hour of travel, Kop returned to his side and looked at Raka, as if to ask for instructions. Raka knew this demeanor as an indication that there was danger ahead. He slowed his advance to a walk and continuously checked the wind for an odor that would explain Kop's concern. Finally, Raka decided to climb a tree and see if he could discern what lay ahead.

The tree that he selected was the tallest tree in the area and he climbed to some of its highest limbs. Looking to the north, he immediately saw two fires. They seemed to be in the same positions as the fires he had seen two days before. The nearest fire was not more than a day's journey down the animal trail and seemed to be located past the lake about midway from the lake to the grotto camp site. Raka surmised that this was probably a hunting, or war party and that the rest of the clan was camped at the grotto. He had no way of knowing that there were indeed two separate clans; nor that these two clans were enemies. Raka's assumption led to his belief that the threat to the Kopsut Clan was very grave. It was very important to Raka to know what the threat from the closest fire represented. He climbed down from the tree and sent Kop ahead, as he stalked down the animal trail toward the closest fire.

Occasionally, Raka trotted cautiously, frequently sniffing the wind and watching for Kop's return. After about four hours of steady travel, Kop returned to his side. Raka stopped and slowly sniffed the wind. He smelled the odor of only small animals and plants. He assumed his stalking demeanor, which was copied by Kop. They continued to move north on the animal trail; but did not reveal themselves on the trail until Raka was sure that there was no danger close at hand. He sent Kop about a hundred yards in advance and watched his body language, as they moved down the trail.

It was in the early evening that Raka saw a change in Kop's body. He tensed his muscles and looked down the trail with his ears facing forward and sniffed the wind. Kop looked back at Raka for instructions. Raka motioned for him to return and both stalkers melted into the forest on the west side of the trail.

Raka began to stalk forward through the forest. Raka

gestured to Kop to lead the way. The wind was from the northwest; therefore, it was unlikely that the followers would be able to pick up his scent. He slowly picked his way through the underbrush, as Raka followed in his footsteps. When they had traveled about an hour, Raka picked up the distinct acrid odor of humans. He slowly tasted the odor and considered what it told him. The odor was the same as the men that he had killed at the dead-fall trap. He dropped to his stomach and moved slowly forward through the brush toward the odor. As he came close to a clearing near the animal trail, he began to hear raised voices. He crawled forward until he could see movement through the trees and brush. He was lying prone in a thicket of underbrush. He looked to his right and Kop was in the same thicket looking toward the movement.

From his hiding place he could see that this was a large clan that included by his estimate five hands of warriors and as many, or more women and children. They were gathered around a large fire-pit and were involved in a heated conversation. The men all had a finger bone pierced through their noses and had the body markings similar to the men that he had killed. A large man was gesturing with his battle ax and pointing north. The other men used similar gestures as the large man raised his voice. It seemed to Raka that the men were building up their courage for a battle. The women also had dark markings on their bodies; but did not have the finger bone pierced through their nose. These people were taller than the southern clansmen that Raka had seen and not as muscular, except for the large man, who was probably their leader.

It was starting to get dark and Raka decided to remain where he was and withdraw after the clan was asleep. He noted that the clan posted three guards on the trail to the north and two on the trail to the south. He saw the leader send a man into the forest to the west also. The eastern side of the camp was protected by the river.

317

Raka considered the clans vulnerability to attack. If he were planning to attack this clan, he would follow the river bank until he could attack from the east. They would not expect an attack from that direction.

The large man had stopped gesturing and lay down on a leather robe near the fire. Other men were doing the same while some of the men were still chewing pieces of meat that they cut from a roast which was still cooking over the fire-pit. The women and children seemed fearful and huddled together in groups on the side of the fire-pit closest to the river. A few of the men approached a female and took her from the group of women and children to their robes at the edge of the firelight. It became obvious to Raka that they intended to mate.

After the moon was high in the sky, most of the men, with the exception of the guards, had fallen asleep. Raka decided to withdraw to a safe distance and eat some of the dried meat that he had brought with him. He slowly crawled back to the south and then circled the guard which was posted to the west until he was at least six hundred yards to the south west in the forest. He chose a dead-fall tree and made a sleeping mat of boughs against the truck and sat down for his meal. He had to watch the wind to ensure that a shift in its direction did not carry his odor to the followers. It wasn't long until he fell asleep.

The Nord Clan had decided to approach the Golo camp from the west through the forest. Gomp had scouted the Golo and had informed Carni that there was a lookout in the forest to the west and more to the north and south along the animal trail. He had also told Carni that the Golo did not appear to be expecting an attack; but seemed to be working up their courage to counterattack the Nord Clan.

Just before dawn was about to begin, Carni spread his men out along the western perimeter of the camp. Gomp had quietly killed the lookout stationed in the western edge of the forest with a quick blow to the temple and a spear through his throat. Now the Nord Clan warriors were prepared to attack. When it was just light enough to see, Carni motioned for the warriors to attack.

The attack was silent at first. The first sound made was the sounds of many spears simultaneously striking the bodies of sleeping men. Then there were screams among the Golo and roars from the mouths of the attacking Nord Clansmen. After throwing their spears, the Nord Clan attackers used their thrusting spears and an occasional kawl to take down, or finish off the startled Golo men. The women and children ran toward the river to seek a place to hide from the onslaught.

Raka was awakened from his sleep before the attack by a low growl from Kop. He looked at Kop. Kop was looking over the dead-fall log to the northwest. He quickly loaded a spear into his spear thrower and silently moved to the west through the forest. His eyes were adjusted to the low visibility and he could see the shapes of trees and brush. He took hold of Kop's tail and motioned for him to move west. Kop guided him to the west, until he picked up the odor of humans. This was a new smell that he had never encountered. He thought that he smelled the full-bodied odor of red-deer and the rank odor of another animal mixed with the stale odor of perspiration emitted only by men. This odor was not from a cannibal clan; since, they did not emit the acrid smell that the clan in the camp emitted.

Raka realized that this group of men was not the same group with the bones in their noses that had been following the Kopsut Clan. Since they were approaching the clan with the bones in their noses from the forest, it was obvious to Raka that their intention was to attack.

Kop stopped completely still as a shadow passed about ten yards in front of him. Raka dropped to his stomach and

319

crawled into the underbrush that formed a thicket near a large tree.

Another shadow passed in front of him and he realized that he was much too close to these attackers. He was afraid that they might pick up his odor. Kop crouched by his side as his eyes silently followed the movement of the shadows. His worry appeared to be unfounded as the attackers continued to move stealthily past Raka and Kop toward the Golo Clan camp.

As the attackers passed by, Raka decided to creep forward to observe what he was sure was an attack on the followers with the pierced noses. He arrived at the edge of the camp just as the Nord Clansmen through their first spears. Light was just beginning to break, as Raka found a hiding place in the edge of the forest.

As Raka settled into a thorny thicket of underbrush and motioned for Kop to move to his side, the attackers in unison threw their spears at the men in the camp. Many of the men in the camp were killed, or severely wounded by the first onslaught of spears. Those that had not been downed by a spear jumped from their robes and grabbed their battle axes just in time to meet the roaring attackers.

Aksot was one of the men who had not been hit by a spear. He grabbed his battle ax and sprang upon one of the attackers, striking him a heavy blow on the shoulder. Before Aksot could finish this man off, he was forced to defend himself from another attacker. He and the other able-bodied Golo Clansmen were being driven toward the river. It quickly became apparent to Aksot that there was no hope of survival, if they became pinned against the river. He screamed at his men to follow him and he began to battle his way south along the animal trail.

The women and children had run toward the river; and

upon reaching the river, they realized that there was no place to run to the east; so, they turned their flight south along the river bank. As the battle raged on along the animal trail with Aksot leading his men south, the Golo Clan women and children ran out of the forest and onto the animal trail about two hundred yards ahead of Aksot and what remained of his men. Aksot saw them and urged his men to fight a delaying battle to give the women and children a chance to run south.

Raka saw all of this from his hiding place on the western edge of the camp. He saw that most of the attackers had light colored hair, much like his own. He focused on the tall man who appeared to be directing the attack. The man was very tall and no longer young. He stayed to the rear of the attackers and only made selected throws with his spear thrower. Each throw struck one of the clan with the pierced noses. As Raka saw how the battle was developing, he decided to use the confusion of the battlefield to withdraw from the area.

He motioned to Kop and they crawled out of the thicket, receiving many thorn scratches for his trouble. After he was about two hundred yards west of the camp, Raka started to run south in a parallel line to the animal trail. It was rough going, since the forest was very dense in this area. He intended to follow the escaping clan with the pierced noses to see where they stopped their flight.

The Nord Clan stopped their attack, as the Golo Clan was about half a mile south of the camp site. Carni indicated to his men that they would follow at a deliberate pace and destroy the remnants of the cannibals. As his men searched the possessions of the Golos, Carni counted the dead and wounded. No Golo had been left wounded on the battleground. Those that were initially wounded were quickly killed by the Nord Clansmen. Carni counted fifteen dead Golo Clansmen and three women. The Nord Clan had four men with severe wounds and one dead. This was the greatest victory that the Nord Clan had experienced in recent memory.

After Aksot and his remaining men had run for about three miles south on the animal trail, he ordered a halt to rest. The men had overtaken the women and children and all were exhausted and frightened. Aksot examined what remained of the Golo Clan. He had thirteen men, three of whom were wounded badly enough to affect their ability to fight. There were twenty women and about fifteen children. For a clan that had been one of the strongest clans in the area, the Golo Clan had been reduced to the size of a weak clan. Aksot knew that they had to find a place that they could defend against the Nord Clan.

After a few minutes rest, he ordered the clan to move south on the animal trail. He told his men to be on the lookout for a defensible location.

Raka had caught up to the fleeing Golos and watched from the edge of the forest. He felt a strong hatred for the big leader of the cannibals. This man most probably led the cannibals that preyed on the southern clans, Raka thought. If allowed to live, this man would eventually find the trail of the Kopsut Clan and they would never be safe from attack. Raka intended to find a way to kill him.

Carni let his men rest until the following morning. He sent the wounded back to the grotto and kept the remaining twenty-six men with him. Carni knew that he had to decimate the Golo Clan to protect the Nord Clan from a future revenge attack. The Golo were notorious in their attacks on other clans.

As Raka was scouting the remainder of the Golo Clan, Carni planned his pursuit of the same group. He intended to send a large scouting party led by Gomp about three hundred yards ahead of the main body. He thought that six warriors should be enough to ensure their safety. The main group of warriors would be close enough to respond, if the scouts were attacked. The Golo would not be able to travel very fast since they would be encumbered by their females and children. Carni decided to also send a group of six warriors led by Sart to circle to the west through the forest to get in front of the fleeing Golo and set up an ambush. That left him fifteen men in the main body of the pursuers.

The following morning, Sart departed with his men at daybreak. He was an excellent stalker and was the best choice for setting up an ambush. Gomp led his men out of the camp three hours after Sart departed. The remainder of the Nord Clan, led by Carni followed shortly after had Gomp departed.

After a few hours of fast progress headed south on the animal trail, Gomp paused to examine the Golo Clan tracks.

From the signs, it was obvious that the clan was no longer fleeing uncontrollably at this point. He expected to find a camp soon. He did not believe that the Golo would try to put distance between them and the attackers by traveling through the night. The Golo would assume that the Nord Clan would pause their pursuit long enough to celebrate their victory.

Gomp's thought process was correct. He came upon a place just off of the animal trail next to the river where the Golo had camped for a large part of the night. He found traces of blood from their wounded. He examined the fire and the excrement left unburied by the clan. Judging from the warmth of the coals and the excrement, Gomp estimated that the Golo had departed the campsite before daylight. They had been gone at least half a day. He decided to speed up his pursuit.

Raka had slept near the Golo camp in a thicket with his hand resting on Kop's shoulders. He knew that Kop would alert him, if danger approached the thicket. The night still covered the canyon when Kop stiffened and Raka came awake. He could here movement in the camp. He crawled closer to the animal trail and saw the shadows of the clan members starting to travel south on the animal trail toward what had once been the Kopsut Clan's cave campsite. Raka knew that if the Golo reached the old Kopsut Clan cave, they could mount an effective defense against the attackers. He decided to get there before the Golo and prevent their use of the cave. He and Kop backed into the forest and started a fast trot through the forest circling toward the cave.

Aksot sent a man ahead of the clan to try to find a defensible site before the attackers caught up with them. Then he started the clan movement south on the animal trail, well before day light. He knew that he had to take chances now, or the clan would be destroyed by the Nord Clan. The scout returned when the sun was at its highest point in the sky. He told Aksot that he had found a cave across the river that could be defended. He also said that there was evidence that a southern clan had made a long-term camp there. It was now empty, the scout told him.

This was a good omen thought Aksot. He would be able to mount a defense for the clan and pick up the trail of the southern clan. After the Nord Clan abandoned their attack, the Golo Clan would find the southern clan and destroy it. Since the loss of so many men, Aksot wanted to capture some slaves. He motioned to everyone to speed up their pace.

Raka arrived at the cave just as the scout sent by Aksot was checking it out. He considered killing the man; but decided to let him report back to Aksot that the cave was not occupied. After the scout left the cave and headed north up the animal trail, Raka crossed the fallen-log bridge and entered the cave. It was exactly as he had left it when the clan had departed for the Ahop Valley. There was still a large stack of flat rocks that could be used in his kawl. There were also several throwing spears that had been left, as excess to the clan's needs. He placed the spears and the rocks near the entrance to the cave. There was even some dried meat hanging over the fire pit. He cut pieces of meat for himself and Kop. He had eaten the food that he had carried with him. He motioned to Kop to exit the cave and go into the forest across the river. Kop hesitated; but understood and entered the forest. He hid near the edge of the forest and watched the entrance to the cave, where Raka was waiting.

Meanwhile, Sart had led his group in a wide circle to get ahead of the Golo. As luck would have it, he set up his ambush just to the south of the cave, which, if the Golo occupied the cave, would be too far south to have any effect.

Aksot could smell the Nord Clan as they pursued the Golo. He knew that they were getting closer. The clan arrived at and crossed the fallen-log bridge without hesitating. The river was not very wide at this location; but it would help in the defense of the cave. He and the other Golo warriors pushed the bridge into the river and watched it float downstream. Aksot motioned for the clan to scale the cliff to the cave.

Raka recognized Aksot's order to enter the cave and stepped out onto the ledge with his spear thrower. He aimed his first spear at Aksot. The sharpened antler spear point struck Aksot in the throat and pierced his jugular and severed his spine. He dropped immediately to the ground and would be dead in seconds.

The clan members were looking at Aksot, when the spear struck. Screams from the females and children filled the air. They ran right and left trying to hide in the cliffs and boulders on each side of the cave entrance. Raka launched three more spears; each struck a Golo warrior before he could get out of his line-of-sight. The bridge was gone; so, it would not be easy to get back across the river. One warrior who was wounded was too slow to find cover and Raka killed him with a well-placed rock from his kawl. Raka crouched in the entrance; he would be able to see anyone who tried to get to the cave entrance well before they were a threat.

Sart heard the screams that the females had made when

Aksot was killed. He guessed that the main body had overtaken the Golo and had decided to attack before they reached his ambush site. He told his men to advance carefully north through the forest parallel to the animal trail. He arrived at the site of the cave, just as Gomp and his men arrived from the north. Neither man knew what was happening. They saw the dead Golo and the Golo that were trying to find cover on each side of the cave. They thought that there must be other Golo in the cave; but could not understand why the Golo remained outside of the cave in plain sight of the Nord Clan. Sart and Gomp joined Carni who had just arrived across the river from the cave. Quickly, they decided to take advantage of the vulnerability of the Golo and started throwing their spears at them across the river.

They were easy prey since there were few places to hide in the cliffs on each side of the river. They killed females and children indiscriminately. In an attempt to escape some of the Golo jumped in the ice cold, swiftly flowing river. The Nord Clan ran along the river bank and hit the people in the water with spears. In a final attempt to try to save themselves three of the Golo warriors decided to try to take the cave. They rushed up the ledge toward the cave entrance.

Raka stepped out on to the ledge in front of the cave entrance, sidestepped a spear thrown by one of the Golo and threw a spear striking the first man of the three. He fell off of the ledge, as Raka used his kawl to strike the other two with rocks, causing them to fall also. The Nord Clan warriors finished them off at the bottom of the ledge.

The members of the Nord Clan, including Carni, Gomp and Sart, were shocked to see the tall light-haired man in the cave entrance. They did not know what to expect; but they knew that he was not a Golo. His hair made him look much like a member of the Nord Clan. He had killed many of the Golo; so, Carni assumed that he was not a cannibal.

Carni held his right hand up toward Raka without a weapon in it. This was a universal sign that no harm was intended. Although Raka knew the meaning of this universal sign, he did not respond. He simply looked at the Nord Clan warriors. Raka knew that it was impossible to trust warriors that killed the females and children of a clan. He squatted on the ledge in front of the cave entrance with his kawl in his right hand and his spear thrower and spears near his left. A pile of flat rocks for his kawl were also near his right hand.

Again, Carni signaled the sign that he was harmless. Raka looked at Carni. From his appearance Raka saw that the tall man could be an older version of the man his mother described as his father. Raka dismissed the thought. Carni touched his chest and said the words, "Nord Clan." Raka understood that that was the name of his clan.

A group of the Nord Clan warriors began to shout and point to the right of the cave entrance. Raka glanced in that direction; but only saw the bodies of several females. As the warriors continued to shout and began to lob stones across the river toward a spot to the right of the cave among some small boulders. Raka looked more closely and saw the dark head of a small child. The child was sandwiched between two female bodies and a boulder about two feet high.

The warriors across the river had no direct aiming point at the child; but they were attempting to hit it with stones cast to arch down on top of it. Raka jumped to his feet and with his kawl in his right hand he scrambled down the ledge toward the child.

The Nord Clan warriors apparently thought he was going to kill the child for they began to cheer him and point to where the child was hiding. Raka ran to the spot and looked at the child. It was a boy and clothed in a reindeer robe which was tied in place by leather straps. He was apparently less than two years old with brown eyes, black hair and an olive-colored skin; a typical Golo baby. One of the females had used her body and the boulder to protect the child from the spears. There were two spears protruding from the female's body. Raka looked around at the battle ground. The Nord Clansmen had used most of their spears in the attack. He looked at the Nord Clan warriors, as they gestured for him to kill the baby. Some made motions of bashing the baby's head against the boulder. Only a few of the warriors had a throwing spear in their hands.

Raka picked the baby up by its feet. The baby began to whimper in fright. He walked toward the ledge and quickly climbed to the cave entrance where he placed the baby just inside the cave. The warriors realized the Raka was not going to kill the last Golo and two of the warriors through spears at Raka. Raka sidestepped one of the spears and used his kawl to parry the second. He swiftly launched a rock from his kawl striking one of the spear throwers in the left shoulder. The rock had broken the warrior's left arm near the shoulder and he dropped to the ground.

Carni growled and motioned for the warriors to cease their attack. Raka noticed that there were only two or three spears left in the hands of the Nord Clan warriors. He withdrew into the cave and examined the baby. It was not injured except for a bruise on the left side of its face and arm. Raka thought that it was probably hurt when its mother fell.

Raka looked out the cave entrance and saw Kop still watching him from the edge of the forest behind the Nord Clan warriors. He made a minute gesture to Kop and Kop swiftly headed south through the forest. The baby was whimpering, almost silently. Raka cut a piece of meat off of the dried piece hanging over the fire pit and gave it to the boy. He took it eagerly and began to suck on it and chew it.

Raka examined the cave and saw an old back pack that Kardi had discarded after she had made a larger one. He took the pack and examined it. He could use one of the old robes left in the cave to fashion a pouch to carry the boy in. He took a bone cutting tool from his pouch and proceeded to cut the robe into the proper shape. He made holes in the robe for the boy's legs. He tied the robe to the backpack with thin strips of reindeer hide that he cut from the robe. There would be extra space in the pouch with the baby. He decided to take the dried meat and began to cut it into smaller pieces.

The boy had finished the piece of meat that he had been given and Raka gave him another to chew on. Raka looked out of the cave entrance. It was getting dark and the Nord Clan warriors were preparing to camp on the other side of the river. Carni was gesturing to some of the warriors. The warriors were placing wood around the base of a tree that was growing near the river and leaning out over the water.

Raka surmised that their purpose was to create a fallen-log bridge. Although their purpose might be to retrieve the throwing spears, which were a valuable commodity, Raka had to assume that he would not be safe in the cave. He would be unable to defend the cave by himself. He decided to exit at the rear entrance to the cave which exited at the top of the ledge above the cave. If he departed now, he would have to travel in the dark; but he had no choice. He strapped on the backpack and picked up his weapons and stooped low through the passage way to the rear exit to the cave. He had to climb and, in several places, it was difficult to pass through with the backpack on; so, he removed it until he exited the cave.

He looked down at the fires burning across the river. The men had made three fires and one was being used to fell the tree for the bridge. The warriors were sitting around the fires obviously waiting and eating what smelled like spo meat.

Raka looked south into the canyon; but saw no sign of Kop. He retreated below the edge of the canyon rim and raised his voice in what sounded like an authentic howl of a Kopsut. He moved south just below the canyon rim and howled again. This time the howl was answered by a kopsut in the forest to the south of the cave. Raka recognized the howl as Kop's answering howl. Because of the change in location of each of his howls, Kop would know that he was moving south along the canyon rim.

Carni heard the howls and recognized that the first two howls were from the top of the canyon rim. He did not know that it was not a kopsut that had howled; but he did think that it was strange for a kopsut to be on the canyon rim. He went to check on the progress that his men were making in creating a log bridge. He decided that the bridge would be ready for use just after daybreak.

He wanted to retrieve the throwing spears; but he also wanted to try to reach the blond man in the cave. He hoped that they could take him alive. He thought that it was possible that the blond man was the child that he had left in Kardi, when he had returned her to the Step Clan. There was no way that a southern clansman could be a member of the Nord Clan; but he thought that he could be a slave. He would have to convince the young man that it would be a good life. Maybe they could capture the remainder of the Step Clan, including Kardi, and have them also as slaves. He was excited at the possibility. He sat by the fire and slept. He would be rested when they crossed the river. He would first try to talk to the young man and, if that didn't work, they would attack the cave. There was no way that one man could defend it.

There was a full moon and Raka could see well enough to make his way along the canyon rim toward the box canyon, which was the headwaters of the river. It would take him the entire night and most of the next day. From his former exploration of the box canyon, he knew that there were at least two spots where he could descend to the bottom of the box canyon. The river at that point was narrow enough that he could ford it. Every half hour or so, he emitted another howl which was answered by Kop, always a little closer than before.

It took Carni the entire next day to determine that Raka had exited to cave at the top of the canyon rim. They very cautious, as they explored the passage way to the cave exit, because it could be easily defended by one man. When he realized what Raka had done, Carni decided to bring his clan to the cave and make camp, while his men tried to find the remainder of the southern clan. The men gathered their spears and tossed the dead Golo into the river.

CHAPTER 30

RAKA RETURNS TO THE AHOP VALLEY

Raka descended to the floor of the box canyon and crossed the river before the Nord Clan realized that he had escaped the cave. Kop joined him and they started their journey to the Ahop Valley staying off of the animal trail. He did not want to leave a trail that the Nord Clan could easily follow. On the second day of his journey, clouds began to arrive from the north. It would only be a few minutes until a summer rain arrived. From the looks of the clouds, Raka could tell that it would be a strong storm.

Raka decided to return to the animal trail and increase his speed in the rain. The rain would cover his tracks and he wanted to make as much fast progress as possible. He adjusted the robe cover of the backpack so that the boy got only his lower legs wet. As he ran, the rain did not feel cold due to his exertion. When he saw that the clouds were beginning to clear in the north, he again exited the animal trail and entered the forest. As he ran through the forest, he startled numerous animals and decided to get some fresh meat for a meal. He used his lop to kill a hare and then found a dead-fall, which offered not only protection on three sides; but also, a covering of limbs that decreased the amount of rain that penetrated the enclosure.

He found some dry wood that had been protected from the rain under the dead-fall trunk and used that to build a fire at the entrance to the dead-fall. Kop lay in front of the fire, as Raka showed him the boy. Kop sniffed the boy's entire body and then seemed to accept him as part of his pack. He lay down near the boy and the boy played with his ears and giggled. Raka gave Kop a large piece of the raw hare meat and then cooked the rest. He curled up in his robe behind the small fire with the boy against his stomach to share the warmth of his body. The night was becoming cool after the rain. The fire dried his robe and other possessions. Finally, he was comfortable again.

It took him four days to arrive at the entrance to the Ahop Valley. He was traveling on a well-used animal trail; when he sent Kop ahead to scout the trail. Kop returned to his side at midday and looked at him for directions. Raka knew that Kop had found something ahead. So, he assumed a stalking mode and went forward. Kop was looking to the left of the trail where there was a stand of trees that Raka knew would make a good hiding place for a lookout who might be keeping an eye on the valley entrance.

The valley was very high in the mountains, making travel in the area more tiring than in the Kopsut Canyon. Raka was winded, when he crawled into the stand of trees. There were no sounds of small animals, or birds in the trees. Raka knew that this could mean the presence of a meat eater, especially a human. There was only the buzz of insects, as they swarmed about his head. There was a biting fly that was trying to make a meal from a piece of Raka's skin. With his right-hand Raka caught the insect in one swift movement and quashed it. He lay still until he finally heard a slap, as someone slapped an insect. The sound came from a tree on the northern edge of the stand of trees. Raka carefully examined the tree and finally saw the lookout. He was perched in its limbs about halfway up the tree. Raka saw that it was Mok. He stood up and made the sound of a song bird, causing Mok to look in his direction. When he saw him, Mok slid down the truck of tree, as adept as any squirrel, and landed on the ground in front of Raka. Raka admonished him for the slap of the insect that had given his position away to Raka.

Then Mok led him to the cave that was now the new home of the Kopsut Clan. Mok was ecstatic at Raka's return. He gestured that Brom had insisted to anyone who would listen that Raka was obviously dead, since he had not returned when the Clan had expected him to return. His insistence stopped only after Kardi had grunted a warning to him. For the first time Mok saw the baby boy in Raka's backpack. He gestured a question to the effect of asking, "Whose baby was that?" Raka indicated that he would tell him at the right time.

The Ahop Valley was a high mountain valley that had only been free of ice during the summer months for a few years. As a result, the forest was composed of smaller trees and spots of thick brush. There were many areas that were free of trees and brush where grass grew thickly. As Raka and Mok moved toward the cave, which was at the southern end of the valley, Raka searched for signs of animal life. He saw an occasional track of a deer-like animal that he had never seen before and many tracks of what he believed were ahop-conk (ibex or mountain goats). Midway in their journey through the valley, Raka discovered the unmistakable tracks of a golo and later a cave bear. There were also signs of mountain hares and their arch enemy the white fox. The clumps of thickets were often filled with berry bushes. Raka was satisfied that the clan could find food in this valley in preparation for the winter.

When Raka and Mok were a couple of hundred yards from the cave, Kuo, Mok's female, saw them coming up the valley and greeted them with a loud kopsut howl. The clan members had learned to mimic the kopsut howls after Kop had been adopted by the Kopsut Clan. It had become their way of communicating with each other over long distances. Kop raised his head and answered with a long mournful howl of his own. The entire clan came to meet them, as they arrived in front of the cave. They all nuzzled each other in familiar greetings. Brom was the first to notice the boy in Raka's backpack. Everyone gestured the question at the same time, "Whose baby is that?"

Raka gestured that it was getting late and he and the boy were hungry. Was there food? Kardi, Gruma and Brow were balls of energy, building up the fire and moving a roast that was partially cooked back over the fire. In order to cook a roast, the clan typically ran a sharpened, wet limb through a piece of meat and placed the ends of the limb on top of rock mounds on two sides of the fire such that the meat hung low, close to the fire. In order to cook other sides of the meat, the limb was turned. In order to cook with less heat, the coals were moved away from the meat, or the meat was moved closer to the edge of the fire.

Raka motioned for the females to keep the fire low. He would explain later. Gruma quickly moved to the fire pit and spread the wood in the fire out to reduce the flames. The boy began to grunt anxiously, as he smelled the cooking meat. Raka took him from his backpack and sat him in front of the fire. Everyone examined him. The boy would be tall; gestured Kardi while she pointed at his long fingers and feet. He had coal black hair and very dark, piercing eyes. His features were more angular than a member of a southern clan and he did not have a pronounced brow, as southern clan babies had. After her examination, Kardi announced that the boy was of a northern clan. Everyone looked their questions at Raka; but he simply ignored them and moved a piece of wood under the meat. Everyone knew that the more quickly they ate, the more quickly Raka would answer their questions.

As it began to grow dark, the clan began to gather around the fire. There were fewer insects near the fire, due to the heat and smoke. At this height in the mountains, the most annoying insect was a biting fly that made its home in the forest and would bite a piece of skin out of most animals, including men. These flies did not venture near a fire. Raka saw that the clan had left the place of honor, the spot nearest the cave, for him. He took the boy into his arms and sat in the place of honor. He cut off a piece of the cooking roast and gave it to the boy. The boy ravenously began to chew it and to suck the juices from the meat. Raka asked the group in general who had killed the ahop-conk (ibex).

Milka pointed to Brom and said that there were many ahop-conks in the valley and the surrounding mountains and that they were not difficult to hunt. They had already killed five and were preparing meat for the winter. Kardi and the women had set three dead-fall traps and had been able to kill several mountain hares and a white fox. There was a bird in the valley that they had never seen before and Mok had killed several. The bird looked similar to the birds that eat the dead animals, but seemed to eat seeds and berries.

"They were delicious," exclaimed Milka.

Kardi indicated that the women had also been able to gather many berries, that they had dried into the berry paste, and about two baskets of mushrooms. There were still many mushrooms that they would gather. A small river ran through the valley. It was fed by the melting ice and snow from the surrounding mountains. Kardi was sure that there were fish in the river; but she had not been able to fish yet. Kardi also indicated that there were no reeds to make baskets. Gruma was trying to use brush twigs to make a basket; but it was more work and took more time than using reeds. Kardi looked disapprovingly at Gruma. Gruma lowered her eyes and sat silently, embarrassed at Kardi's criticism.

Kardi started the meal by cutting a piece of roast off of the cooking meat and giving it to Gruma, obviously as an apology for her criticism. Everyone began to cut off pieces of roast using flint cutting stones. Occasionally, each of the women cut off a small piece and gave it to the baby boy. He seemed to revel in all of the attention that he was getting. When all had eaten their fill and were sitting around the fire pit, Raka reach for a burning piece of wood and held it in front of his face. He began a low hum, which the group picked up, as he began to speak. As was his habit he used few gestures to tell

337

his legends.

> *The great Spirit-in-the-Fire has given the Kopsut Clan a new life in the Ahop Valley. These great spirits have protected Raka from the great dangers from enemy clans from the north. The Spirit-in-the-Fire guided Raka to be able to discover three members of the northern clans who were following the Kopsut Clan alone. While they were examining one of the dead-fall traps that Kardi had set near the old grotto camp, the Spirit-in-the-Fire told Raka that he must kill these men and make it seem like a larger force had killed them. The spirits guided Raka's spear to the hearts of two of the men and guided the rock from Raka's kawl to the third man's head, as Kop tore out his throat. The men were carrying these carvings of the fierce golo; he passed around one of the carvings. They were also carrying meat that was not the meat from any animal that the clan has ever seen. The meat was from a man. The Spirit-in-the-Fire told Raka that this clan was a cannibal clan and probably the one that had destroyed the Step Clan. The members of this clan had human finger bones pierced through their noses. The Spirit-in-the-Fire called this clan the Golo Clan.*

> *The Spirit-in-the-Fire then guided Raka across the canyon to the remainder of the Golo. When Raka discovered these fierce Golo, they were being attacked by another fierce northern clan. This northern clan must have been guided by the Spirit-in-the-Fire since they were quickly and easily victorious and drove the Golo Clan south on the animal trail. The Spirit-in-the-Fire told Raka that the Golo would try to find a defensible location and that that location would be the Kopsut Clan's former cave, since it was the closest defensible position along the animal trail.*

> *With the help of the Spirit-in-the-Fire, Raka arrived*

at the cave before the Golo. In their haste to get to the cave before their pursuers from the north, the Golo did not check to see if the cave was occupied. The cannibals crossed the fallen-log bridge and then pushed the bridge into the river to protect them from the attackers.

They were caught between Raka and the attacking northern clan before they realized their predicament. The northern clan used spear throwers from across the river and the Golo could not find a hiding place and could not enter the cave, since Raka was defending it. The northern clan killed everyone, including women and children. Only one child was saved from the slaughter. The last boy of the Golo Clan sets before you now. He will now be a member of the Kopsut Clan and will be called "golo," after the fierce meat-eater. He will be strong and cunning, like the golo, and will serve the Kopsut Clan well.

The northern clan was led by a tall man with light hair and brown hair on his face. He made the sign that he meant no harm to Raka, as he sought to take the baby boy from Raka and kill it. He had said the words, "Nord Clan," to indicate that that was the name of his clan. (Kardi turned pale as she heard this pronouncement. She wanted to interrupt and ask Raka questions about the leader; but it was unacceptable to interrupt a legend.)

The Spirit-in-the-Fire told Raka that the Nord Clansmen were killers of children and not to be trusted. The Spirit-in-the-Fire led Raka through the darkness with the baby boy in his backpack and back to the Kopsut Clan in the Ahop Valley.

The Spirit-in-the-Fire gave Raka new wisdoms to guide them. The first wisdom was that the Nord Clan were killers of children and must be avoided. (Kardi's face showed her disappointment.) The second wisdom was that the Kopsut Clan must continue to move south through the mountains to escape these northern clansmen who would kill and enslave the Kopsut Clan and prevent us from exiting the mountains to the north. The mountains will protect the Kopsut Clan and all members must hear these words and obey!

He replaced the burning branch into the fire and silently took the boy into the cave to a sleeping mat that Kardi had prepared for him. He and the boy slept side-by-side, covered with the same robe. The other members of the clan discussed Raka's legend well into the night and agreed that the legend told the truth. They must move south through the mountains. Everyone, that is, except Kardi. She had nothing to say; but sat in silence lost in her thoughts of life a long time ago, when she had known Raka's father Carni. She was disappointed that this chance to know Carni again would be lost.

The next morning Raka discussed the clan's future with the other members of the clan. It was the early fall and it was not wise to travel further into the mountains until the next spring. Raka knew, that trying to pass the winter as high in the mountains as they were, would be difficult. Raka counseled the group that the Nord Clan would have the same reservations of moving further into the mountains and would probably be unable to locate where the Kopsut Clan had gone until the spring. Raka decided that the Kopsut Clan would stay for the winter in the Ahop Valley, before moving further south into the mountains. There should be enough food here for a small clan like the Kopsut and he wanted to prepare as much food as possible, since the winter snows would probably be much worse in the Ahop Valley than Kopsut Canyon.

The members agreed on their tasks to prepare for the winter. Milka, Brom and Raka would hunt ahop-conk. Mok and Beoh would set and run dead-fall traps and hunt small game. Gruma, whose child was still alive and the only other child in the clan, would watch Golo and her child and help Garki make baskets from bush twigs. Brow and Kuo would gather mushrooms and late berries, while Kardi would see if there were fish to catch from the river and the small lake in the Ahop Valley. Mok would return to his lookout spot to make sure that the Nord Clan did not surprise them. Mok always was able to bring home small animals from his trips to the lookout location. Everyone proceeded on their assigned tasks.

Mok had a long way to travel and started out early, carrying a large piece of meat to eat later. Raka gestured to Kop to go with Mok and the two of them departed at a trot toward the northern entry into the Ahop Valley. Kop ran ahead of him, as was his habit, unless there was danger close by. His return to Mok would be an indication to Mok that there was danger ahead.

The Kopsut Clan hunted with remarkable energy and found enough game to properly prepare for the winter. Their store of dried meat and an enormous number of mushrooms was large enough be adequate to get them enough the winter. They hoped to supplement their diet with fresh white fox and hare meat during the winter. A long stay in this valley, even for a small clan, would be impossible over time as the game became scarcer, as a result of the clan's hunting activities.

Winter arrived early, although again this year it was not an inordinately cold winter. The little river that ran through the valley did not freeze completely over. It snowed an immense amount and often banked up so high that the clan could not safely travel even with muco; so, they stayed in the cave. There were several breaks in the snow storms in which the days were beautiful and sunny. During one such break, using their muco the women traveled to the dead-fall traps to see if they may have killed a hare, or fox. Raka, Milka and Brom decided to try to hunt an ahop-conk near the river, while the

341

other men repaired their weapons. The hunting party returned empty- handed, Kardi, Kuo and Brow returned with a white fox and a mountain hare.

Everyone looked around for Gruma. She had not returned with the women. Raka asked Kardi where she was. Kardi lowered her eyes. She knew that she had made a mistake to allow Gruma to wander off alone. Kardi had asked Gruma to gather bush twigs to be used to make baskets. Gruma had been near the river when she had last seen her. Raka gestured to Brom and Milka to come with him and they departed to check the area near the river for Gruma.

They followed her tracks until they were near the river. Near a thicket of brush where the signs indicated that she had been gathering twigs, they discovered a large amount of blood which stained the snow. The tracks indicated that she had been attacked by a large golo. From the looks of the scene, the golo had surprised her from the rear. The golo had probably broken her neck with its first blow. The Golo had carried her body to the south toward the cliffs that formed the southern border of the mountains. Raka thought that the golo probably had a lair in those cliffs. Typically, a golo might eat much of its prey at the scene of the kill and take the remainder to its lair. In the winter a golo was vulnerable to an attack from kopsut; therefore, it was not out of the ordinary for a golo to take its prey to a safe place before eating it.

There was a storm arriving and Raka knew that Gruma would be dead. So, they would not be able to save her, nor would they be able to complete a hunt for the golo before the storm hit. They returned to the cave and told the other members of the clan what they had discovered. The clan mourned through the night. Raka awarded Gruma's child to Garki. He had already given the Golo child to Kuo and Mok to mother and father. Mok had already started to teach Golo to use the lop.

The remainder of the winter passed uneventfully. The clan ate frugally, careful not to exhaust their supply of meat and mushrooms. On rare occasions, Kardi would allow them the pleasure of eating a small piece of her berry pastes. Throughout the winter the clan was watchful for the golo and occasionally from a distance they saw a golo, as it stalked prey near the river in the valley. Raka wanted to hunt it; but decided to wait for spring, when they could run without being encumbered by the muco.

The entire clan practiced the use of their weapons near the cave, when the snow prevented other activities. All of the clan adults had become experts in the use of the spear thrower, the kawl and the lop. Raka and Brom were capable of hitting a limb on a tree fifty yards away with their kawl while running parallel to the target. Milka could throw a spear further than anyone, except Raka, who also was more accurate. Mok was the most expert with the lop; and when he was checking the dead-fall traps, or going to and returning from his lookout post, he brought down many hares and squirrels. Brom was the strongest hunter and Raka was the fastest runner. Raka could run at speed farther than anyone. Although Kop stayed with Raka whenever he could, if directed by Raka, he would hunt with any of the men.

The winter was warmer than the previous year; but there had been a large amount of snow. Some days the sun would shine and much of the snow in the valley would melt. The little river always ran full throughout the winter. Spring arrived early in this high valley and the clan members were able to kill many water fowl as they landed in the gorged lake to lay eggs and raise their young before continuing their migration north. When the young could fly, the birds migrated to the far north for the remainder of the warm weather.

Kardi showed the other females how to roast a bird over the fire after stuffing it with spice plants, which was better than just roasting it over the fire. All of the women learned the young spring plants to collect that could be eaten with the meat.

As the snow melted away, Raka began to send Mok and/ or Brom to perform lookout at the valley entrance. Brom had reported that he occasionally saw smoke from a fire at a location which was probably their old cave campsite. Raka assumed that the fire was made by the Nord Clan. The only reason that the Nord Clan would have remained in the area through the winter was to find the Kopsut Clan when the weather permitted. Raka decided to explore further south into the mountains; so, that when the Nord Clan found the Ahop Valley, the Kopsut Clan would be ready to move.

On a beautiful early spring day, Raka took Kop with him and headed southwest to take a look at possible southern routes out of the Ahop Valley. At the point where the Ahop Valley ended there was a very high pass between two mountains. The pass was narrow and had once been covered by glacier ice. Now, only occasional patches of grass were growing between the scattered boulders. An ice wall still lined both sides of the pass and water was running off of the ice on both sides into large streams that flowed into the river, as the glacier continued its recession.

The pass turned due south and rapidly descended into a long narrow valley with a full, strongly flowing river running through it. Raka called this valley the Ahop-Conk valley because he saw many of the ahop-conk feeding between the glacier ice and the river. The sides of the valley were more cliff- like than the pass with many grottoes and caves in the cliffs. He saw tracks left by cave bears and golos and assumed that this was an area where the cave bear hibernated through the winter.

Raka found a cave at the south end of the valley that could serve as a defensible camp for the clan for a short time; but

344

he intended to take the clan further south, where game and plants were probably more plentiful. He knew that the Nord Clan would also eventually find the Ahop-Conk valley.

When Raka returned to the Ahop Valley, he had been gone for more than three weeks. The clan had started to believe that he was dead. The night of his return was a cause for celebration. Although Raka did not tell another legend, he did tell the clan what he had discovered and informed them that he wanted to move to the Ahop-Conk Valley, as soon as possible.

Early summer arrived without any evidence that the Nord Clan was searching for the Kopsut Clan. Then on a late summer day Brom and Mok returned to the cave and told everyone that they had seen a fire much closer to the entry into the Ahop Valley than previously seen. Raka thought about this revelation and stated that they had to assume that it would only be a matter of days until the Nord Clan discovered the Ahop Valley. With that discovery, the Nord Clan would easily find signs leading them to the Kopsut Clan cave. Raka announced that they would depart the Ahop Valley the day after tomorrow.

CHAPTER 31

THE JOURNEY SOUTH

Thereわ was no way to leave a diversionary trail, since there were only two ways to go out of the Ahop Valley, north (where the Nord Clan was) and south. Raka decided to make it appear that the clan had moved to the western side of the valley where a large and very deep cave was located. He thought that the Nord Clan would be delayed for a few days searching that area. They left clear tracks to the cave and set up what looked like a clan camp there and then left that cave and moved toward the south by hiding their tracks in the river. The water was very cold and he was only able to keep everyone in the river for about two hundred yards. They exited onto a rocky surface and continued their journey to the south.

They carried a large number of supplies in baskets hung from two-man poles and each person carried a backpack and two weapons. They made good time since everyone was very strong from the hard work required to sustain a small clan such as theirs. They exited the Ahop Valley and entered the high, narrow pass after a four-day journey.

As they entered the pass, Raka stopped to examine the ice cliffs on each side. Far above the ice cliff to the right side of the pass was a large over-hang of ice and rocks, which appeared to be teetering precariously over the river. As he examined the ice walls, he could here noises emitting from the walls. The sound was a squealing sound like a dying hare. The members of the clan thought that the sound was spirits-in-the-ice and wanted to leave immediately. Raka knew that the teetering mass of ice and boulders would eventually fall and dam up the river behind the mass of ice and rock. He thought that the noise might be the ice moving against other ice, or the cliff granite. If the ice and boulders fell, Raka knew that the river would eventually cut a path through the blockage; but initially the pass should be closed.

Raka turned to Milka and Brom. He gestured to them an explanation of his idea to make the ice-rock over-hang fall and asked them how could it be done? Both said that it could not be done unless there was a large rock at a higher level above the over-hang that could be dislodged. They slowly examined the face of the ice cliff above the over-hang. As they were watching a chuck of ice dislodged from the ice cliff face and tumbled into the river.

Raka realized that they were in danger and had to move quickly through the pass, or they might be caught in an ice/rock avalanche. He gestured to everyone to speed up. They began to move through the pass at a fast trot. They were heavily loaded with their backpacks and the baskets carried suspended using the thrusting spears as two-man poles; so, their progress was slow and labored.

The clan members were tiring. As they went through the pass to a point where the overhang was behind them at least two hundred yards, Raka felt that they were no longer in imminent danger of being caught in an avalanche. He ordered a halt to allow everyone a few minutes of rest. Most of the group was breathing, as if they had completed a long run. As they caught their breath and sat in a rough circle discussing the over-hang and how long it might be until it fell into the pass, Raka examined the terrain in the pass. The floor of the pass was littered with boulders; many of them were as large as a mammoth. However, most came to about the height of a man's waist and had been rounded by water and ice action. The glacier ice and running water from the melting glacier

348

had created the rock-strewn floor of the pass over a long period of time. The river was now so full of the melted-ice run-off that in places it covered almost the entire width of the pass. Only a few trees and bushes were able to cling to life near the river. The ice walls on each side of the pass contained many boulders protruding out of the ice as it melted. There were several over- hangs on both sides of the pass. Raka saw where an overhang on the west side had collapsed at some point in the past and had created a partial blockage of the pass a few hundred yards north of where the group was resting.

At this point the pass began to slope down toward the south and also started to slope down toward the north just a hundred yards to the north. Toward the north, because of the partial blockage from a past avalanche, a bowl affect had been created, which caused the development of a small lake where the clan had only been able to pass by hugging the eastern pass wall. Raka was sure that the pass would be closed during the winter by ice backing up and filling the pass at that point.

Raka gestured to everyone that it was time to continue their journey. Everyone shouldered their loads and the march south continued. When the group was about half a mile from the pass, they heard a loud cracking noise followed by a loud roar from the pass. They stopped and could see a cloud of mist, or water vapor rising from the pass.

Again, Raka ordered a halt. They saw a wall of water coming toward them and they retreated toward the east wall of the pass which was higher than area to the west side of the pass. The wall of water passed below them in a matter of minutes.

Raka and Brom ran north toward the pass to see what had occurred. When they arrived at the pass, what they saw astonished them both. The pass was filled with ice and boulders. Both walls had caved in to create an impassable barrier. The water in the river no longer flowed south. No doubt the flow would start again as the ice continued to melt; but for the immediate future the flow was stopped.

Although Raka had no way of knowing it, the area on the north side of the blockage was filling with water and would become a large natural lake, effectively blocking the pass.

While the Kopsut Clan was moving through the pass, the Nord Clan had continued their attempt to find the Kopsut Clan. They arrived at the Ahop Valley a week after the Kopsut Clan had departed and wasted three days determining that the clan had not moved their camp to the cave on the west side of the valley; but had exited the valley to the southwest. They arrived at the pass ten days after the avalanche. The water already blocked them from getting close to the ice and boulder blockage and Carni realized that he would not be able to follow the Kopsut Clan to the south. He ordered his men to turn around and return to Kopsut Canyon.

After the cave-in of the pass walls, Raka felt that the immediate danger from the Nord Clan had passed and he slowed the pace of travel and began searching for a new home for the Kopsut Clan. The new home would need to be in an area with sufficient game to support their small clan and would need to be located in a place that allowed such a small clan to mount an effective defense, if attacked.

The Clan continued to travel south, and often southwest when natural passes turned them in that direction. They travelled starting just after daylight and only stopped early enough to build a fire and set up camp. During their travel they watched for chances to kill small game with their lops and often were able to kill squirrels, hares, and birds to eat. Rarely, Brom, Raka, or Milka was able to run down a deer with Kop's help. They travelled in excess of a new moon before they saw that the mountains were not as high as earlier.

As the clan began to exit the highest part of the mountain range, the last pass led them into a long wide valley. From the high vantage point at the end of the pass, Raka thought that he could see that there was a smaller valley that ran to the southeast, reentering the mountains, albeit not as high as the mountains that they had previously passed through.

They traveled six days through the large valley staying near the eastern valley wall before they arrived at the entry into the smaller valley that Raka had seen. As the Kopsut Clan entered the valley, Raka saw ample evidence that there were many red and bush deer in the valley. There was a wide animal trail that led into the valley. Raka, Milka and Brom studied the tracks left on the animal trail. Besides the tracks of bush and red deer, they also saw signs of ahop-conk and spo. He did not see any indication that humans had ever entered this valley. The valley was heavily forested with a wide variety of very tall trees, which indicated that the glacier ice had not covered this valley for a very long time.

During their first night in the valley, they heard the mournful howls of a pack of kopsut. Kop became very interested in these howls and answered them before disappearing for two days. He returned showing small rips in his skin around his neck and ears. It was obvious that he had gotten the injuries from having been in a fight. He did not leave Raka's side for the next few days, as Raka searched for a defensible location for their camp.

After traveling for five days east through the valley, Raka found a high set of cliffs on the north side of the river that ran through this valley. Raka examined the face of the cliff and at first did not see anything to suggest a possible cave, or grotto. He walked toward the cliff and, as he got closer, he noticed that behind a very large spruce tree, there appeared to be a dark spot on the cliff face. Looking closely through the spruce boughs, he saw that midway up the face of one of the cliffs was an opening that represented either a cave, or grotto.

There was a ledge about three feet wide that should allow access to the opening. Raka examined the ground around the bottom of the ledge and found the very large tracks of a cave bear. The tracks were not fresh; perhaps at least a few months old and almost obliterated by rain. It was too late in the year for a cave bear to still be in its hibernation cave; so, Raka was relative sure that it was safe to check out the cave, or grotto.

Cautiously, he approached the entrance by climbing the ledge, as Kop followed. Raka sent Kop forward to check the entrance out first. Kop showed no sign that he detected danger; so, Raka entered the opening and waited for his eyes to adjust to the poor light. The cave was damp; but there was no musty smell. As he had first suspected, Raka discovered that it was a large cave and not a grotto. Raka knew that there must be an opening toward the rear of the cave because air was gently circulating from the rear of the cave toward the entrance. The air current carried the odors of vermin, but no other animals. The entry to the cave was very low, only about four feet high and six feet wide. After about ten feet, the entry tunnel opened up into a large room, about twenty feet wide and thirty feet deep with a ceiling about ten feet high. The room was covered with bones and there was an area to the left rear of the room where a depression had been excavated and a mat of course brown hair had been deposited.

"This was probably the place where the cave bear had hibernated," thought Raka. Kop smelled the hair and bristled at the offensive odor.

Brom had followed Raka into the cave and he and Raka knelt to examine the bones. They were from all types of plant-eaters. The larger bones were from bush or red deer. Many of the bones were from smaller deer, indicating that the bear had hunted young fawns more often than adult deer. At the rear of the room was another low tunnel about the same height as the entry tunnel. Looking through the tunnel, Raka could not see the rear wall; but he knew that there was another room there.

He decided to call the rest of the clan to come up and build a fire to better examine the cave. They would at least stay the night in this cave. Lately, they had been eating primarily small animals such as snakes, hare and squirrels and Raka wanted to mount a hunt for larger animals. He decided that, if this cave was not suitable as a long-term camp; it would at least suffice until they found a better one.

When the other members of the clan arrived in the cave, Kardi started to build a fire pit a few feet from the entry tunnel. With the gentle flow of air from the rear of the cave out the front entrance, Kardi assumed that the fire smoke would exit the front entrance. The spruce tree in front of the entrance would help disperse the smoke from the fire so that, if they kept it small, it would not be visible from very far away. Everyone else started to carry in wood and to cut boughs to make sleeping mats.

After the fire was burning, Raka took a burning branch from the fire and entered the second room. The other clan members followed him into the room. The light from the burning branch lit up the cave room with a sparkling light. Light sparkled off of the walls, which were composed of a hard rock with occasional crystals dotting the walls. This dazzle of lights was amazing to the clan members and they all stopped to stare. Once they became accustomed to the sparkling walls, they looked around the room.

It was larger than the first room; but the ceiling was only about five feet high. On the right rear wall, a trickle of water seeped down into a pool which was about a foot deep and covered about a 20 square foot area along the entire right side of the room. Raka and the other members tasted it. It was clear, cold and pleasing to the tongue. Water would be plentiful, Raka declared.

353

On the left rear wall of the room there was a crack in the rocks which led upwards. The crack was too small for a man to pass through; but air was gently blowing from the crack. Another crack was evident in the left wall of the room. A small amount of air also came from this crack. This crack was large enough for a man to pass through; but was partially filled with rock debris. Raka thought that he might check this tunnel out when he had nothing better to do. It would be good if there was a rear exit to the cave. The Clan was always concerned about not being able to flee from danger because of their extremely small size.

Kardi announced that the front room would be for sleeping and the rear room for storing supplies. She gestured that if they were going to prepare for the winter, they did not have time to marvel at the sparkling walls. They needed to explore the area to see what food was available. They would need more baskets and they needed to hunt.

Brom and Mok left to see if they could find meat before dark. The small animals in this area were not used to seeing humans and Mok found that it was easy to kill squirrels with his lop. He killed six before Brom was able to find and kill a mountain hare. They also were lucky to find a serpent about four feet long sunning on a rock. Brom smashed its head with his thrusting spear.

They returned to the cave with their bounty and began to skin the hare and squirrels. The snake would be roasted in its skin. The females began to roast the meat, as each carcass was ready and the entire clan sat around the fire pit discussing their luck at finding such a good cave for a new camp site.

After the meal, Milka and Garki retired to their sleeping mat, as did Brom and Kardi and Mok and Kuo. Only Raka was without a female. He felt alone at times like these and settled down on his sleeping mat with Kop at his side and went to sleep.

354

CHAPTER 32

THE NEW KOPSUT VALLEY

T he days before the onset of winter were numbered and the clan had much to do in order to prepare for the onslaught of cold weather. They were in an unknown area and the unknown had always instilled a bit of fear into their lives. In order to rid themselves of this fear of the unknown, the clan had to get to know their surroundings and be able to control the key factors in their lives that determined if they lived, or died. On the first morning of their lives in this new valley and new cave, Raka assembled the clan members to agree on their way ahead.

As had become his custom, he asked each member what they needed to do to prepare for the winter in this new valley. Kuo was the first to speak, although, as a rule, she seldom had anything to say to the group. Kuo proposed that the first thing that they should do was to name their new valley. Everyone nodded their agreement; so, Raka turned to Kuo and asked what she wanted to name the valley. She looked surprised that she had been asked; but immediately replied, "Kopsut Valley!" The clan was very proud of its name and the fact that they had their very own kopsut. Everyone grunted their agreement; so, it was settled; they would call this valley Kopsut Valley.

As the clan sat around their morning fire and ate the leftover meat from the previous night's meal, without being aware of it, they developed a plan to prepare for the winter. Raka and Kop would explore deeper into the valley to see what food resources it held and determine what dangers may be waiting for them from meat-eaters, or human inhabitants. Raka and Kop would also attempt to get a kill of a large animal before returning to the cave. Raka told the group that he would limit his time away from the clan to five days (the fingers on one hand).

Milka and Brom would hunt within half a day's walk from the cave to see if they could locate and kill some large animals without traveling too far from the cave. The odds of only two hunters getting a large animal were not very good; but Raka felt that it was necessary for the time being. Kuo would watch the two children and assist Garki and Brow to gather reeds to make more baskets. Kardi and Mok would set dead-fall traps near the cave. Mok would also check out the river and other waterways to see if there were waterfowl that could be harvested. Brow would also check the river to see if catching fish was possible. Raka reiterated that no one was to go anywhere alone. Even Raka had Kop with him, which in fact made him as strong as three men.

It was understood that everyone needed to be alert for meat-eaters. They had seen the signs of cave bear, golo and kopsut; so, there would be the potential of attack from those animals.

Everyone would also keep their lop, or kawl handy to try to kill small animals, or birds during the performance of their tasks. Everyone had become an expert with these two weapons and the women had perhaps surpassed most of the men in the use of the lop. Kardi was in fact as good with the kawl as any man, except Raka. Mok was still the most accurate at a distance with the lop. Raka remained the champion with all weapons except the thrusting spear. Brom was stronger and, by virtue of his strength, he was better at the use of the thrusting spear. Everyone could use the spear thrower with great skill; but Raka could accurately throw a spear twenty yards further that the second best, which was

Brom. Evenings were often spent practicing the use of their weapons and showing off to the others. Little Golo had been given his own small kawl and he imitated the adults during the events.

Raka rose at the break of dawn. Before beginning his exploration, he wanted to get a birds-eye view of the valley. He climbed the cliffs in which the cave was set, until he was about two hundred feet high. From this vantage point, he had a marvelous view of most of the valley. To the south, he could see that the valley ended and passed through a narrow pass through the mountains into another river valley. The river in that valley seemed to be fed in part by the river that ran through the Kopsut Valley. To the northeast the valley extended several miles and then turned north. He could not see very much of the valley after it turned north. He could see intermittent breaks in the forest cover and apparent evidence of an animal trail near the river. A pair of eagles soared over the valley as he watched. There was a large lake toward the northeast and apparently the lake extended into the north end of the valley. The eagles varied their flight over the lake and continued their hunt until Raka could no longer see them. Raka slowly climbed down from the cliff. He was ready for his exploration of the Kopsut Valley.

Raka shouldered his back pack; took his weapons; motioned to Kop to come and departed east on a well-used animal trail that followed the river that ran through the valley. He had decided not to carry food, but to survive on what he could hunt during his exploration. He carried his kawl in his right hand; it was loaded with a flat rock in the split. In his left hand he carried his thrusting spear. In a pouch slung on his left shoulder, he carried his spear thrower and five throwing spears. His backpack hung beside the pouch and contained only a robe for ground cover. His waist pouch contained the tools, other than his weapons, that he cherished the most. The pouch contained a cutting flint, two spearheads made of flint, two spearheads made from deer

357

antlers, a fire sparker (iron pyrite), a bone piercing tool, a bone chipping tool, medical moss, a few thinly cut leather strips and a length of sinew. The pouch also contained the four golo carvings and two golo incisor teeth that he had taken from the Golo Clansmen that he had killed. The teeth were useful for making holes in leather.

Raka sent Kop ahead on the trail and began his exploration at a steady walk. He was very attentive to his surroundings and made mental notes of everything of consequence. The valley appeared to be more than a mile wide at its center and about twenty miles long. It ran east and turned north at its center. Its sides were very steep and partially covered with ice. The ice cover began about midway up the eastern and northern sides and near the top on the western and southern sides. Where the ice ended, evergreen trees had taken hold. Smaller trees dotted the sides of the valley near the ice and became taller and more thickly populated further down each side.

As Raka watched the sides of the valley, he detected movement and stopped to closely examine it. He saw several groups of ahop-conk walking in single file through the smaller trees near the ice. He slowly examined the sparse forest near the ice and saw a total of five different groups. It was obvious that this valley was populated by an abundance of ahop-conk. The clan should be able to kill many of them before the cold weather set in. The ahop-conk would probably spend the winter in the lower parts of the valley; so, Raka was convinced that they could also get fresh meat throughout the winter.

The river that ran through the valley hugged the western side, which was steeper than the eastern side. Raka looked at the river at a point near the animal trail. The river was running fast and was full of runoff from the melting ice. Raka estimated that it was deeper than a man's head at this point.

The floor of the valley was covered with a thick evergreen forest, which was spotted with many clear areas devoid of trees and covered in grass. There were a few deciduous trees that grew near open meadows. Many of the trees were at least a hundred years old; therefore, it was evident that the glacier ice had not covered the valley floor for over a hundred years. The animal trail on which Raka was trotting followed the river and occasionally made turns into the forest and into the clearings, which were great places for plant eaters to graze.

Every few minutes Raka stopped and examined the tracks in the animal trail. There was an abundance of fresh tracks that had been made after the last rain. Of course, there were many ahop-conk tracks; but he also found tracks made by several different kopsut, red deer, a spo, a fox, a carnini, a golo and a cave bear. Smaller animals were also in abundance, including hare, squirrels and large forest birds, such as pheasant. Game was very plentiful in this valley. At one point, Raka found that golo tracks seemed to be following a red deer. The tracks of three kops (giant spotted hyenas) also entered the trail and followed the golo. The kops were obviously following the golo in the hope of robbing a portion of the golo's kill.

Because of the presence of golo, kops and cave bear, Raka decided to bring Kop back closer to him. He made a low-pitched howl that was immediately answered by Kop from some distance in front of him. The clan members had all learned to communicate using kopsut howls and Kop had come to understand them, as well as the clan members. Generally, the lower pitched howls signified normal communication about location; whereas higher pitched howls signified danger and urgency. Raka used a low-pitched howl to inform of his location. If he wanted to call Kop, or a clan member to come to his location, he would raise the pitch of the howl slightly. He would use two, or three similar howls as he moved his location toward Kop, or the clan member to indicate that he was coming to the hearer's location, and so on.

Mok had taken the use of animal sounds to a new level. At night he used the sounds of an owl when he wanted to communicate from a closer position where a kopsut howl might be out of place. He used a squirrel's chatter for the same purpose during the daytime.

Kop returned to Raka's side; but showed no indication of danger. Raka motioned for Kop to move forward along the animal trail, as he trotted. They settled upon a separation of about fifty yards. Raka could see Kop and, based upon Kop's body language, Raka would be able to tell if Kop sensed danger.

Raka and Kop continued to follow the animal trail, as it turned north with the river. After he had traveled north about a half hour, he noticed that Kop came to a sudden stop; his body stiff, his ears pointed toward the north and his nose testing the wind, which was coming from the north. Raka assumed a stalking posture and eased forward along the trail for another fifty yards and then with a quick motion to Kop, they both melted into the forest on the side of the trail away from the river.

He stalked forward slowly, continuously smelling the wind, listening for sounds and most importantly, watching Kop. As Kop came to a gentle rise that bordered a small stream that fed into the river, he lowered himself to the ground and slowly moved to a position in a clump of bushes on the stream bank. Raka followed suit and crawled into the bushes, until he could see over the rise.

The stream cut across the animal trail as it flowed into the river. Raka could see three kops hidden in a dense clump of bushes on the other side of the stream. They were watching something just inside the forest near the animal trail about a hundred yards from the stream. Raka adjusted his position until he could see what was drawing the kops' attention.

First Raka saw the shore of the lake that he had seen from the cliff above the cave. It appeared to be a large lake and the animal trail curved to follow the lake shore.

A giant golo was devouring the carcass of a small red deer near the lake shore. From the looks of the deer, it was probably born this year and would have been easy prey for the golo. The golo had already consumed a large amount of the deer and seem to be searching for the choice pieces, such as the liver. A low whine from one of the kops alerted the golo and it looked toward the sound.

The kops gave up their attempt at concealment and

cautiously approached the golo snarling ferociously. A pack of kops were often successful in taking another animal's kill by showing their ferocity. The kops separated, so as to threaten the golo from three sides. The golo seemed to consider the advisability of taking the carcass to a safer dining area; but as it lifted the carcass, the kops growled more loudly and edged closer to the golo. The golo growled and stood defensively over the carcass; but the kops continued their approach. One of the kops darted toward the golo from its rear and nipped its hip before retreating. The golo swung around to face the threat from its rear and the other two kops surged toward it nipping its hips before jumping clear of the golo's swipes with its massive front paws.

The golo realized that he was not going to save this meal and in fact was in danger of becoming a meal for the kops. In one strong leap the golo cleared the kop to its rear and growled its scorn, as it disappeared into the forest along the lake shore the north.

The kops quickly jumped to the carcass and began to tear pieces off of it. They often fought over pieces, until the most dominant female seized control of the carcass and ate her fill. When the dominant female had eaten its fill, the other two, a smaller male and a young female, began to eat. They shared the carcass without rancor. Kops were devastating meat-eaters and Raka knew that if these kops remained alive, they would reduce the amount of game available to the clan by a large amount. He decided to try to eliminate them.

Raka chose the moment when the two kops were eating and the dominate female was lying nearby to launch his attack. He gestured to Kop and quickly stood and threw a spear at the dominant female. As Raka's spear entered the body of the female, Raka's second spear was already on the way toward a second kops. It hit one of the remaining kops in the left side and passed through its body. At that moment Kop leaped at the last kops, who was distracted by its wounded companion. Kop's fangs sank deeply into the young kops' throat and held on as the kops struggled to free itself.

Under normal conditions, a kop was more than a match for solitary kopsut. In this case, given the effect of surprise and the inordinately large size of Kop, the initial victory was to go to the kopsut. Raka rushed over to where Kop was struggling with the kops and quickly killed the kops with his thrusting spear. He looked at the other two kops and saw that although they were not yet dead; they were dying. He used his thrusting spear as a club and finished their struggle for life with a blow to the head.

Raka knew that the golo might still be in the area; so, he remained alert and watched Kop to see if he sensed danger. Raka was debating with himself about whether he should try to save all three kops' carcasses. A kop weighed over a hundred pounds and it would be difficult to get all three carcasses back to the cave. Raka decided to dress the carcasses to reduce their weight.

He built a large fire and started to remove the skin and innards from the carcasses. He saved the liver, heart and kidneys and allowed Kop to eat some of the remaining innards. After he had completed the task, he placed two large pieces of kops meat over the fire to cook. He went into a stand of trees near the lake and cut two limbs about twelve feet long and three inches thick. He cut thin strips from one of the kops skins and used those strips to secure two feet long cross pieces to the two long poles that he had cut. He tied the three carcasses and the skins to the makeshift travois with strips from the kops skin. Raka decided to stay the night in this camp and start his journey to return to the cave in the morning.

He built the fire up larger than he would have normally liked since he was in the open with no protection on any side. He went to the lake and washed off the blood and dirt off of his body and returned to the fire. He ate one of the pieces of kops meat that he had roasted and saved the other for tomorrow. Kop slept just outside of the firelight, as Raka curled up in his robe near the fire. He awakened several times to noises of meat-eaters prowling nearby. Kop had moved closer to the fire and Raka placed more wood on the fire. He smelled a golo and a kopsut pack as they searched for a safe way to get the meat, or the prey that was near the fire. It wasn't long until the meat- eaters departed for more productive hunting grounds.

Raka decided to delay his departure until a couple of hours after day break. That should give the night-prowling meat-eaters time to bed down for the day. He had fashioned a strap from leather and tied it to one end of the travois. He placed the strap over his shoulder and pulled the travois down the trail. It moved with relative ease, leaving two parallel groves in the soil on the trail. Kop preceded him and occasionally disappeared, as he checked out the trail back toward the cave.

Raka's travel was slowed by the effort required to pull the travois and he was forced to make another camp the next night. He was pleasantly surprised that he could transport more weight with less effort using the travois. He had gotten the idea from watching Kuo and Mok using a thrusting spear as a two-man pole to carry their gear during their travel to the new cave. Mok had become angry that Kuo was not moving fast enough. Kuo responded in anger and dropped her end of the pole. Indignantly, Mok continued to pull the pole forward and did so for a couple of hundred yards with, what seemed to be, no additional effort.

It was thundering and threatening to rain, when he stopped to make camp. He chose a location next to a dead-fall tree which had fallen against another large tree and allowed him to stretch his ground cover robe over a limb, forming a makeshift lean-to. He gathered a large amount of wood and placed it inside his lean-to. He built his fire pit just outside of the entrance to the lean-to, where the dead-fall leaned against the other tree, forming a V. The trees would provide the fire some protection from the rain. He placed the travois with the meat in the rear of the lean-to near the large tree trunk. It started to rain after he had finished his preparations and he ate the kops meat that he had cooked the day before and shared it with Kop. Kop slept to the left of the fire under a large branch of the dead-fall, as Raka curled up in his robe between the meat and the fire. Before Raka fell asleep, he remembered the eagle pair that he had seen hunting together. He felt a surge in his loins and thought that he needed to find a mate. He slept with dreams of having his own female. In his dreams the face of the female was obscured and he could never make out her face. In his dreams, he always saw her female body clearly, but when he looked at her face; it was always a blur. His dreams stopped, as he periodically awoke and added wood to the fire every couple of hours.

The rain stopped during the night and, when the morning light began to appear, water vapor rose from the wet vegetation creating a low ground fog that covered the entire valley. As Raka stood his head was just above the ground fog, but everything lower than his head was obscured by the fog. He decided to wait to continue his journey until the sun burned off some of the fog.

In mid-morning enough of the fog had dissipated to allow Raka to see the trail and he shouldered the travois strap and continued his journey toward his new cave in the new Kopsut Valley. Kop preceded him on the trail and periodically returned to Raka, as if to reassure him that all was well ahead. On one occasion, Kop returned with a large mountain hare and Raka chose that moment to stop and cook the hare.

After they had eaten, they continued their journey. Night was approaching and Raka estimated that they were still a couple of hours from the cave. Raka decided upon spending another night in a camp away from the cave. He chose a location next to the river where a dead-fall formed one wall and the river formed a protection across from it. He built two fire pits, one at each end of the entry into this protected area, and placed the meat loaded travois in the area with him. Kop slept outside of the area. During the night there were many sounds of meat eaters approaching the camp. Members of a pack of kopsut were calling to each other and Kop responded with his own mournful howl.

Later during the night, Raka could see the eyes of the kopsut, as they circled the camp site. Kop ventured away from the fires to confront the kopsut and was attacked by several. He held his own in the battle, using his superior size to dominate them individually. As a group, they would eventually get the best of him, so Raka stepped outside of the protected area with his thrusting spear and joined the battle. He used his spear as a club and landed blows on two of the attackers, giving Kop the chance to rip the throat of a third. There were five in all and they retreated after Kop had killed one of their pack.

Raka skinned the dead kopsut and added his carcass and hide to the load on the travois. After the ground fog had lifted the next morning, he continued his journey. He arrived at the cave before midday and, since Kop had run forward to announce their arrival, everyone, except Mok and his family, was there to meet them. Mok had set off early with Kuo and little Golo to check deadfall traps and set a new one.

Brom and Milka were astounded that Raka had killed so many meat-eaters. Their experience with kops had been such that the only times that they had been able to kill one had been in defense of an animal carcass. Most often the kops were kept at bay by the use of fire. They typically ran in packs of five, or more.

The women took charge of the meat and hides and Milka showed Raka the hide of the giant spo that he and Brom had killed very near to the cave. The meat was being smoked and dried over the fire. The spo had been a massive bull and there was meat to last for a long time. Kardi complained that they needed more baskets. She had found some reeds at the river which they could use for that purpose; but many of the reeds had already been harvested and were lying in a pile in the second chamber of the cave.

Kardi showed Raka where she had placed his sleeping mat. She had cut a large number of a soft, gray evergreen boughs with a clean fragrant smell. The mat was too large for one person and Raka gestured as much.

Kardi looked quizzically at him and gestured that he must soon find a mate for the good of the Kopsut Clan. Without thought, Raka nodded his agreement. He had been of the same mind for some time. He gestured that when spring came, he would venture into the lands to the south in search of a clan that might be suitable to provide him a female.

Kardi agreed; but insisted that he take Kop and that he observe the clan before making contact to ensure that they were not cannibals. Neither Kardi, nor Raka had contemplated the idea that there were no other humans south of the mountains; although they had not yet found any indication that other humans inhabited these lands.

Preparations for the winter continued at a brisk pace. The clan was able to kill many large animals including red and bush deer, spo, ahop-conk, fox and hare. They had made many baskets which were filled with smoked/dried meat, mushrooms, wild apples, grapes, berries, nuts and edible roots. Kardi had also found that the river and, by assumption, the valley lake were teaming with fish. They knew that the fish were there for the taking and in the late fall they supplemented their diet with an occasional fish. Fish was a treat after eating red meat for days. Garki and Brow had also discovered a large patch of grass grains that Kardi had often used to mix with berries to make her delicious pastes. They gathered two baskets full of the grains; but it was too late in the year to find fresh berries. They were able to gather older berries that animals had failed to find.

The first snow arrived comparatively late this year; but it was a forceful storm. The clan's movement was restricted to the area near the cave for more than a week. The wind whipped through the cave entrance and made the front cave chamber uncomfortable on extremely cold days.

Raka remembered how the entrance to the grotto that Kardi had taken them to, after the destruction of the Step Clan, had been blocked by a rolling rock. He considered how the clan might be able to accomplish the same thing for this cave. There were many boulders in the area; but none appeared suitable to roll in front of the cave entrance. He gestured to the others that they could use the boulders to build two walls in front of the cave entrance to make it more narrow and use a spo hide robe to cover the entrance and thus block most of the wind.

Everyone agreed and they set to work, as it continued to snow. The job was finished in less than half a day and the snow banked up against the boulder walls, effectively sealing the walls, such that wind could not pass through it. The spo hide was suspended from poles placed on top of the walls, weighed down by rocks and draped down over the front entrance. Two poles were inserted in the center to cause an inclined tent affect, so that the snow would not gather on top of the hide too much that it caused the hide roof to give way to the weight of the snow. The front chamber of the cave was now more comfortable. The fire was constantly burning; but now it was lower than it had been before the entrance had been blocked. The Clan had gathered an inordinate amount of wood to store both inside the cave and just outside the entrance.

Kop chose to sleep just inside the entrance tunnel; but as far away from the fire as possible. He often disappeared outside and, on many occasions, returned with a hare, or a fox which he delivered to Raka and was given a portion as a reward. Everyone now had head covers made from a fox's fur, except Raka, who had made his head cover from a kopsut skin.

During this winter the life of the Kopsut Clan members was very good. Brom announced that Brow had ceased to run the blood of life from her female parts; so, according to tradition, he knew that she was with child. Brom's exultation caused Milka to mate more often with Garki in the hope of creating a child of his own. Mok and Kuo did not appear capable of producing a child, although they continued to try. They did have Golo as their child and he slept with them on their sleeping mat.

The men went out on a hunt, when the weather permitted, although there was plenty of dried meat. They were able to kill several ahop-conks and a red deer; but had to be careful of the large kopsut pack that roamed the valley. The kopsut pack was made up of over ten members. During the winter the kopsuts became stronger due to the availability of large animals that were weakened due to the fact that the snow limited the available food and slowed their ability to escape from the kopsut pack. Mok and Kuo accepted the task of checking and baiting the dead-fall traps. They normally were accompanied by Kop, who ranged near them and was always interested in what they found in the dead-fall traps.

When hunting was not possible because of an impending storm, Raka organized a weapons practice session near the cave. Everyone's skills remained sharp and each member tried to impress the others with their favorite weapon. The females were becoming as good with the kawl as the men and were also adept at the use of the spear thrower. Little Golo could use the lop well enough to hit a tree thirty yards away.

Mok was anxious for him to kill his first animal and took him squirrel hunting, when possible. Golo finally managed to kill a ground bird which was huddled beneath an evergreen tree for protection from the snow. Mok showed him how to clean the bird and Kuo cooked it for him. He was very proud of himself and strutted around the cave like a full-grown hunter.

There had been no dangerous situations throughout the winter and, as the winter gave way to early spring, Raka decided to inform every one of his intentions to journey to the lands to the south in search of a mate.

The spring plants were sprouting throughout the valley and the river was full of melting snow and breaking ice, as Raka broke the news to the clan members. He did so in the form of a legend. As the clan was gathered around the fire after a filling meal of red deer roast, Raka picked up a burning branch from the fire and held it in front of his face and began a low hum. The clan members became quiet and joined him in the hum. Raka began to speak.

The great Spirit-in-the-Fire has given the Kopsut Clan a great new home in the new Kopsut Valley, which possesses a great bounty of food and a defensible cave. The Spirit-in-the-Fire has told Raka that the Clan needs new babies to train in the Clan traditions. Raka was told to search for a female in the lands to the south. In a vision, Raka was shown many clans roaming the valleys south of the mountains and told to seek one out that can provide a strong mate, who will join the Kopsut Clan and give Raka many babies to join little Golo to keep the clan alive. The Spirit-in-the-Fire taught us that in unity there is strength. So, your leader is asking your blessing in going on this search for a fitting female. Any among you that does not believe that the Spirit-in-the-Fire yearns for Raka to find a mate must state your position now. (No one stepped forward to talk, since everyone was aware that Raka suffered from loneliness and needed a mate.) The Spirit-in-the-Fire has spoken and Raka will depart within this new moon. While I am gone, Milka will lead the clan and with the help of the Spirit-in-the-Fire, no harm will befall the clan while I am gone.

He put the burning branch back into the fire and started humming and then drew silent. Everyone began to speak at once. Many wondered what kind of female Raka would find to join their clan.

CHAPTER 33

RAKA'S SEARCH FOR A MATE

I t was still briskly cold in morning with layers of fog filling the valley when Raka and Kop departed on the search for Raka's mate. They traveled through the pass that controlled entry into the new Kopsut Valley from the south and found an animal trail that led along the bank of the river that ran to the southeast from the mountains. A careful examination of the tracks that had been left in the animal trail revealed the presence of conk, ahop-conk, spo, ponk and many different meat-eaters; but there were no tracks of humans. Raka decided to follow the animal trail, as long as it led to the southeast. He sent Kop ahead and started traveling at a fast walk. It was mid- morning before the fog began to dissipate. After a long day of travel, Raka found a hollow tree where a dead-fall had fallen over the hollow entrance. He decided to make camp there and built a small fire below the dead-fall in front of the hollow. The hollow would protect him from the rain. The sky was covered with clouds and he expected it to start raining, and possibly snowing, at any moment. Kop had killed a hare during their travel; so, Raka cooked it and they shared the meal before bedding down. It rained and sleeted throughout the night and was still raining when morning arrived.

Before continuing their journey, they ate some dried meat. Raka decided to trot for a couple of hours to warm up. Kop enjoyed running with Raka and would often circle him at a very fast run. They traveled in this manner for more than a week, camping near the rivers and streams and not finding signs of other humans.

After another day of travel, Raka came to a clearing in the forest where two animal trails crossed. Raka examined the tracks left by the trail's users. The trail on which Raka had been traveling had tracks of many types of animals; but nothing new and no recent meat-eater tracks. He moved to the trail that crossed the trail on which he traveled. This trail came from across the river and ran almost due south. Raka examined the tracks on this trail. At first, he found only the tracks of the animals that he had consistently seen on the trail that he followed. All of the tracks had been made before the rain. After careful examination, he found a partial print protected by a low bush branch that had been made by a human, an adult male. The print was almost obliterated by animal prints that had passed this way after the man. Raka estimated that the print had been made at least two weeks earlier, before several rain showers. By the orientation of the print, Raka estimated that the man was headed south along the trail. Raka continued to examine the trail, as it proceeded south. After about a hundred yards, protected under tree foliage, he found another adult male human footprint. Raka decided that it might be the same man that had made the previous print that he had found. This print also made it evident that the man was traveling south.

Raka decided to follow this tail farther to the south and sent Kop ahead of him. As he came to a pass between two high cliffs, he decided to climb one of the cliffs and see what the way ahead looked like.

He climbed the highest cliff on the right of the trail and, since it was almost evening when he reached the summit of the cliff, he decided to spend the night and see if he could see any fires after dark. To the south there were foothills, cliffs and an occasional mountain towering above the hills. He could not see past the hills. There were large birds of prey circling the hills and a river ran through the valley nearest to him. The river's headwaters were somewhere in the mountain range to the north between two snow-covered hills. The river was very wide and fog hung low over it, as it splashed its way from between the two foothills. The river was full and occasionally spilled over its natural banks and flooded the valley floor.

As night closed in around Raka, he wrapped himself in his robe and with Kop at his side waited for the full dark of the night. Finally, he was able to scan the land to the south. His body stiffened and he became alert as he saw the light from a fire possibly twenty miles away and apparently near the river. This was the first indication that he had seen of other humans south of the mountains. He stared at the fire for a long time and contemplated what types of people were sitting around that fire. Tomorrow he would go in that direction and with luck in a couple of days; he would be able to see these people up close.

It was cold and damp; so, Raka was clothed in a soft leather upper garment made from deerskin and a thicker, courser wolf skin tied around each leg with strips of leather. When the weather warmed during the day, he removed the lower garment and placed it in his backpack. He also had a large robe made from bearskin, which covered his head and torso and hung below waist. His feet were encased in a leather wrap, tied around his calves with strips of thinly cut leather. Raka had stuffed dried grass into the leather to provide insulation.

In his pouch Raka carried a piece of flint rock used for cutting, a piece of flint used for scraping and three spearheads made of flint rock and a couple of spearheads made from deer antlers. Also, there was a golo tooth which he used for making holes in leather and chipping the flint rock into the shape that he needed. There was also a piece of flint that would someday be shaped into a spearhead, but now was used it as a striker to start a fire. The second element in the pouch which was essential for fire making, was a piece of iron-pyrite. The pouch also held a dry rat's nest, which he used as kindling for starting a fire and a ball of sinew; which he used as lace, when needed. Finally, he had five smooth, round rocks for use in his lop. The pouch also held a ball of moss soaked in what the clan believed was magic plant juice for treating injuries. The moss was wrapped in a thin piece of rabbit skin. The last items in his pouch were the two bone carvings of a golo, which he had taken from the Golo.

Raka drew the robe around him and fell asleep. He dreamed of finding his mate; but as hard as he tried in his dream, he could not see her face. He was sure that she would be pleasing to the eyes. In his dreams her body was well formed and, in his dream, when he tried to touch her, she disappeared into the fog.

Raka was anxious to find the clan that had made the fire; so, as soon as it was light, he descended from the cliff and trotted down the animal trail with Kop about a hundred yards ahead of him.

After trotting for most of the day, Raka stopped and examined the tracks on the animal trail. He found many human footprints, which had been made by different men and at least one woman. He knew that he was getting close to their camp. He decided not to follow the animal trail anymore; but to follow the river and use the forest for cover. Making his way through the forest, he had to clear massive spider webs that had not been disturbed all spring. Although there was very little wind, it was coming from the northwest. This worried Raka, since the clan, that he wanted to find, might be able to pick up his scent before he could pick up theirs. To prevent that situation, he traveled as far to the east as the river would allow him and he sent Kop ahead of him. As night was approaching Kop returned to his side and his attention was focused a few hundred yards west and south of Raka's location.

Raka decided to wait for the morning to explore further and sought a safe place to spend the night. He found a large dead-fall with a massive branch spread. He moved through the branches until he was enclosed inside its branches. He dug out a depression under the truck of the dead-fall and wrapped himself in his robe before he drifted off to sleep. Kop had left his side after he was asleep and stealthily crept up to the edge of the forest next to the camp and watched the humans, as they sat around the fire and, one by one, fell asleep.

Raka had spent the night without a fire and, as a result, his sleep was often interrupted by the slightest sound, or movement in the nearby forest. During the night Kop had returned to the dead-fall enclosure and had slept next to Raka.

At dawn Raka, with Kop in the lead, assumed his stalking mode and moved toward the smell of the fire pit. When he judged by the smell that he was near enough to the camp to be seen, he crawled forward on his stomach. The first thing that he saw was that the fire was smoldering; but not burning. He searched the area around the fire with his eyes and sampled the air with his nose; but neither saw, nor smelled anyone. Carefully, he moved toward the fire and examined the area around it. He saw at least six different tracks of adult males and one woman. There were no children. Raka surmised that this was a hunting party which was returning to the clan camp. He examined the footprints which led south out of the camp. He found four that made a deeper impression in the moist soil and, therefore, Raka judged that these men, and probably the woman, were carrying burdens. They were probably carrying the carcasses killed during their hunt. Raka smelled the area around the fire and picked up the distinctive odor of ronk (horse). He looked at the bones that the group had left in the fire pit. In the fire pit ashes, he only found the small bones of forest hare. He looked around the fire more carefully and found ronk hair on a bed of pine boughs that one, or more of the party, had used as a bed mat. Raka decided that the ronk smell came from a hide the group had used as a ground cover. He also detected the odor of conk and spo. Raka decided that the burden they were carrying was probably hides. Raka decided to follow this group to the rest of their clan.

Judging from the fire which was still smoldering, the group had departed from the camp at dawn and had continued south on the animal trail on which they had previously been traveling. Raka decided to give them some time in case they were checking their back trail. He decided to spend the remainder of the day and the night in the camp and sat down by the fire and added a couple of small pieces of dry wood to the fire pit and stirred the ashes. The fire quickly began to burn; but created very little smoke. He cooked and ate a squirrel that he had killed with his lop the day before. He gave the bones and a piece of the meat to Kop, who swallowed them without fanfare. He motioned to Kop to hunt, and Kop disappeared north on the animal trail. Raka began to sharpen the spearhead on his thrusting spear, as he waited for Kop to return.

Kop returned a few hours before nightfall with a forest hare carcass. Raka cleaned and prepared the hare, then gave half of it to Kop and cooked the other half. It tasted like sage. That meant that there were sage plants south of the mountains. That would make his mother happy. She used sage to prepare most of the meat she cooked. After dark, Raka built the fire higher and rolled up in his bearskin and slept. During the night, he heard the howls of kopsut and the fierce screams of golo. None were near his camp; but he kept the fire burning high and watched Kop for signs of danger.

An hour after dawn he began to follow the group that had made the fire. They were at least a day ahead of him. He guessed that they were not traveling fast; so, he also took his time. From the tracks he could tell that the clan members

378

were large. The female was also a large woman with broad feet. Raka judged from the depth of her tracks in the moist soil that she was carrying more weight than the men.

Raka traveled all day and made another camp under a couple of dead trees. The dead-fall enclosure had only one entrance and Kop positioned himself between the entrance and Raka. Raka decided not to make a fire for fear that he was too close to the clan that he was following. He drew Kop closer to him, as he fell asleep. During the night Kop alerted at a danger in the night by rising from his prone position and facing down wind. Raka picked up his thrusting spear and waited for whatever it was to attempt to enter the dead-fall enclosure. Raka did not hear anything and he could not smell anything, since the wind was coming from away from the danger. Finally, he picked up the odor of golo; as it circled the enclosure and sniffed the odor of the occupants.

Raka knew that the golo would smell the kopsut and the human and this combination would be new to the golo. It would be careful. All of a sudden, the golo let out a high piercing scream. Both Raka and Kop jumped at the sound; but controlled their actions. The golo was trying to cause one of them to run and, therefore, create an opportunity for a kill, after they exited the enclosure. Finally, Raka saw the golo's eyes; as it looked through the entrance to the enclosure. They were yellow and very close. Kop growled deep in his throat and Raka added his own deep kopsut growl. The golo stopped and screamed again. It inched slowly forward growling fiercely. Kop moved to the right of the entrance, as Raka edged forward with his thrusting spear.

The attack of a golo was normally characterized by leaps onto its prey, causing severe damage in the initial assault. There was no way that the golo could leap upon them because of the overhead cover of the dead-fall trees; so, the golo was hesitant. He finally decided upon a rush attack through the entrance. As he rushed toward Raka making wide swipes with his front paws, Raka jammed the thrusting spear into its chest, at the same time that Kop attacked it from the other side. The spear did not penetrate deeply; but did halt the golo's advance. The golo quickly changed its mind about the advisability of the attack and withdrew, whimpering, as it disappeared into the night.

There was no way Raka could sleep any more with so much adrenaline flowing in his blood stream; so, he remained awake until morning broke. With the break of day, Raka shouldered his backpack and continued to follow the clan's trail.

During the middle of the morning, he came upon the fire-pit that they had made for the night. The fire still smoldered; so, they were not far ahead of him. Raka left the animal trail and walked parallel to it. Occasionally, he would intersect the trail and check the human footprints. The group was in no hurry and soon he understood why.

Not far south on the animal trail, Raka saw smoke from a fire, which appeared to be near the river. Raka circled the fire to the south and found it on the banks of the river next to a large boulder. He crawled into a brush thicket on the edge of the clearing where the camp was located; so, that he could get a good look at the humans in the camp. Kop disappeared to the south. There were several women and a few children. He also saw that there were three men in the camp.

As he was watching the camp, the party, that he had been following, entered the camp and were greeted with hugs and touching of noses from the people in the camp. He saw that the burden that the party had been carrying was animal skins. Apparently, the clan was in the process of moving its camp and the party he had been following had returned to an old camp to retrieve their treasure of hides. After a few minutes of talking, the group gathered their belongings and continued their journey following the animal trail to the south.

Raka looked at the women in the group. There was a young woman that was particularly attractive to him. She had an appealing appearance with dark raven-black hair, dark eyes and an olive complexion. An old man approached this young female and affectionately touched her arm. Raka guessed that this was probably her father. Like the rest of the clan, she wore deerskin garments covered with a bearskin robe. Raka could feel the desire rise within him, as he gazed upon the young female.

The clan did not appear to be a prosperous clan, as many of the members appeared to be weak and dejected. Although Raka had no way of knowing this fact, the clan's success at hunting during the fall had been poor. The winter had been passed hungry and they had left the shelter of their winter cave early this year in order to try to find meat, although there was still a chance of more snow and more cold weather.

Raka decided to follow the clan and to wait his opportunity to take the young girl. He followed the clan for three days, until they were approaching a series of cliffs near the river.

Raka was convinced that the clan suspected his presence. They may have smelled, or heard, him; but most likely they had discovered a sign of his passing; when they had checked their back trail. Raka had observed that the men in the clan had become more watchful and kept their spears close at hand. He kept his distance and moved to the cliffs where he could watch them clearly and unobserved.

It was here in these cliffs that our story began. Raka felt an almost magnetic attraction to the young woman as he watched her move about with the other clan members. He watched and waited an opportunity to take the young woman; but no opportunity presented itself, until the woman was bitten by a serpent and abandoned by her clan.

After her clan left her to die, Raka had taken her to a safe location in a cave where he had made his camp. He had treated her wounds with his medicinal moss. Then he fed her some broth that his mother had taught him to make for a person who was ill. He continued to give her water to fight her raging fever. It would be a matter of time to see if she would recover from her head wound and the snake bite.

With the cave entrance protected by his fire pit, Raka fell asleep with his right hand on his thrusting spear. He awakened often to check the condition of the woman and place more wood on the fire. He gave her more broth, or water which she drank unconsciously. Perhaps daylight would tell him if she would survive.

CHAPTER 34

RAKA AND HIS MATE RETURN TO THE KOPSUT VALLEY

As the first light of day entered the cave entrance, Raka opened his eyes. He had slept later than he had intended due to the continuous attention that he had given the woman during the night. His body hurt from sleeping on the cave floor without a sleeping mat, or robe. He sat up to look at the young woman, as she slept on his robe and sleeping mat.

Her eyes were open and she was looking directly at him. He felt a strange stirring in his loins that was stronger than he had ever felt before. She had beautiful brown eyes and an olive complexion. He reached for the water bladder and gestured the question, "Did she want a drink."

She no longer looked fearful, as she had after he had taken her to the cave. She nodded her acknowledgment that she was thirsty. He took the water bladder to her and watched, as she drank several mouthfuls. Raka stared at the trickles of water that ran out of the corners of her mouth and down her chin, eventually dripping onto her beautiful neck. Her eyes were no longer glassy and her skin no longer looked pale and damp from fever.

He gestured that he wanted to touch her forehead and she nodded. He felt her forehead and noted that it was no longer hot. He started to remove the cover over her head wound and she did not show any reluctance. The wound was a puffy pink around the edges, which his mother had taught him, was a

383

good sign that it was healing. The center of the cut was scabbed over and there was no sign of infection. His mother had taught him that if there was inflammation, he would have to cut it and place more medicinal moss on it. He left the cover off of the head wound to let it dry and moved to the snake bite on her calf.

Again, she allowed him to examine it. It was still swollen; but the color was no longer bright red around the bite. It was more of a dull pink, showing through her olive skin. The red line that had previously run from the bite up the leg to the knee joint was now only about three inches long. Raka felt that that was also a good sign. He took another piece of medicinal moss from his pouch and tied it over the bite mark. He poured water from the bladder over the moss. He intended to do this until the color around the bite returned to normal.

After he had finished treating her wounds, Raka gestured toward the ponk meat which was hanging over the fire. The young woman nodded and Raka rose and cut her a piece of the meat and one for himself with his cutting flint. He moved back to her side and sat down. They both ate ravenously in silence, until the large pieces of meat had been completely consumed. The young woman had never taken her eyes off of Raka, as she ate. Raka wiped the ponk grease off of his beard with his hands and then rubbed his hands against the shaft of his thrusting spear, leaving the spear shaft with a light oily coat. The young woman broke a small branch off of the sleeping mat boughs and cleaned her hands and mouth with it. She used a small twig from the branch to clean the meat from her teeth. Raka watched this and performed the same task on his teeth. She gestured to Raka and said something that he did not understand. He thought she may be asking his name, as she point toward his chest.

He pointed to his chest and said his name, "Raka," and pointed to her. The young woman's lips were full and broke into a demure smile, as she said her name, "Dawa." They both smiled, as Raka repeated her name, "Dawa." He reached out his hand and touched her face, as he said her name. She did not flinch; but reached up with her own hand and felt his fine brown beard. Raka's loins were on fire and his reaction was to immediately stand and move to the fire and place more wood on it. He moved to the cave entrance and looked out across the valley at the river. He could see a small group of animals grazing near the river; he thought they may be ronks (horses). He saw no evidence of a fire in any direction; but, most importantly, he saw nothing to the east in the direction that Dawa's clan had gone.

He looked back at Dawa and she was intently looking at him, as the light coming through the entrance accentuated his size. As if drawn by a magnet, he moved back to her and sat at the side of the sleeping mat. His excitement was growing, as he looked at her.

He picked up her hand and felt her tremble, as he placed it against his face. She stroked his beard and said his name. Then she pointed to the meat hanging over the fire and looked at him quizzically. He understood and told her his name for the animal, "ponk." She continued, making gestures that he understood and he told her the names; spo, conk, ahop-conk, ronk and so on, as they occasionally laughed at themselves.

Finally, she made the universal sign of a woman, two fingers pointed downward and pointed to Raka. He understood that she was asking him if he had a female. He also made the gesture and said the word for female, "hada." He shook his head from side to side which was a universal way of saying no. He pointed to Dawa and asked if she would be his hada by saying their names together and interlocking the fingers of both hands. Dawa smiled and made room for him on the sleeping mat and lifted the robe for him to enter.

When he attempted to touch her womanhood, she scolded

him in her foreign tongue and pointed to the snake bite. They fell asleep together for the first time. It was perhaps two hours until they were awakened by a noise outside the cave.

Raka quickly jumped up with his thrusting spear in his right hand. The fire had died down and there was a pack of kopsut approaching the cave entrance. Kop was growling fiercely at them from the ledge in front of the cave entrance. Raka added wood to the fire then took his kawl and several flat rocks to the ledge. The first rock from his kawl caught one of the kopsut on its left hip, obviously breaking it. The kopsut tried to hop away, as the other kopsut ran a good distance from the cave entrance, giving respect to this new danger. Raka's second rock killed the injured kopsut and he and Kop went down in front of the cave to retrieve the carcass, as the other kopsuts remained about a hundred yards away. After a few minutes the kopsut pack disappeared into the valley.

The kopsut was a young male. Raka picked up the carcass and carried it to the cave where he skinned and gutted it. He staked out the hide and hung the meat over the fire to cook and dry. He placed a piece in the hollowed rock to make some more broth and gave a large piece to Kop. Kop took the meat to the ledge in front of the cave entrance and devoured it before curling up in the sun to sleep.

Dawa was too weak to walk for several days; but as time passed and she ate more meat and drank the broth that Raka made for her, she grew stronger. After a week had passed, she stood beside the sleeping mat and walked to the fire pit. She favored her injured leg; but not very much. She gestured a question to Raka about the arrangement of the stones around the fire pit. He made her understand that the stones were set to get the help of the spirit-in-the-fire to protect them.

She understood right away; because most people worshiped fire and paid homage to fire in some way. Her clan had placed powdered rock into the flames, changing the color of the fire to red and yellow, as a gesture of respect to the fire.

As Dawa was recovering, Raka would occasionally go into the valley with Kop and run down forest hares as a sport and practice the use of his weapons. It gave them fresh meat to eat and the exercise that he needed to control his excitement, when he was around Dawa.

On their fourteenth day together, Raka returned to the cave after a particularly athletic run with Kop and a swim in the river. Dawa was waiting in the cave entrance, as they trotted up to the cave. She asked about Kop. She had never seen a kopsut that was friendly with a clan.

Raka explained about his killing of Kop's mother and father and then the discovery of the kopsut den and raising Kop with the clan. It had been a natural friendship in which Kop looked upon Raka and the Kopsut Clan as his pack. He gestured to Kop by a minute movement of his head and Kop approached him on the side farthest from Dawa. He took Kop's ears in his hands and massaged. As he did this, he gestured that Dawa should extend her hand for Kop to smell. Kop's ears lay back against his head, as he looked at Raka. Again, Raka moved his head in a small gesture and Kop smelled Dawa's hand. He tasted it with his tongue and then withdrew; but looked steadily at Dawa. She looked directly into his eyes and extended her hand again. He moved closer to her and lay down in front of her and Raka. It was evident that Kop had accepted her as a member of his pack.

On the twenty-five days of their time together, Dawa approached Raka who was setting next to the fire after they had eaten a large hare. She placed her hand on his neck in a gesture of affection which she had never before displayed. He reached for her hand; but she took his hand and placed it upon her neck. He began to massage her neck and stroke her hair. He was becoming more excited. She did not protest when he ran his hand under her robe and slowly felt her vibrant female body.

Neither of them had ever experienced anything so exciting. In moments their excitement became uncontrollable and their natural instincts took control. He removed her robe and lifted her to him, placing his mouth upon hers and allowing his tongue, which seemed to have a mind of its own, to enter her parted lips. She gasped and became more excited. Her body began to undulate, as he lowered his right hand to her womanhood and penetrated it with his fingers. She gasped aloud and began to gyrate wildly. He picked her up and placed her on the sleeping mat as her legs opened to welcome him. They mated wildly for several minutes and then lay spent beside each other on the mat. They fell asleep in each other's embrace, enjoying a strong mutual feeling of contentment.

Although Dawa had seen couples mate in her clan, she had never seen them mate in such an exciting fashion. Couples in her clan did not kiss; but only nuzzled each other on the neck. This was their first mating of many that would occur before they left this cave.

Through the days and nights Raka and Dawa learned to communicate with each other. She learned the name of his clan and knew that the name was accepted because of Kop. She started performing the duties of preparing the meat and other normal female tasks. She took the kopsut and hare hides and made a robe for herself and a pair of foot covers, since her clan had taken all of her possessions. She was shocked when Raka suggested that she learn to use his weapons, since females in her clan did not normally use a warrior's weapons.

Raka taught her to use the weapons, starting with the lop and then the kawl. When she had developed a skill with these two weapons, he started her instruction in the use of the spear thrower. She had good hand and eye coordination, which made her a very adept pupil.

She killed her first squirrel with the lop Raka had made for her on her first day of instruction. The kawl took her four days to perfect. She killed a hedgehog sitting near a small borough with the kawl to announce to Raka that she was ready to move on to the spear thrower.

The spear thrower that he made for her was shorter than his and, although she became skillful with its use, she would need much more practice to be able to call it a useful weapon.

They had been together for forty days when Raka told her that it was time for them to return to his clan in the Kopsut Valley. She had not previously thought about meeting his clan, although he had told her about them. She knew that it was a small clan and that they had come from north of the mountains. She enjoyed their time in the cave alone and was anxious that the clan might not accept her. Raka reassured her that all would be well and they started their preparations.

Raka decided that they would carry the extra meat and hides that they had using a two-man pole, which was in actuality his thrusting spear. They would travel along the river so the availability of water was not a concern. The spring nights were cold, but the days were warm. They wore robes that reached to mid-thigh and their foot covers were secured around their calves with thin strips of leather. Neither wore a head-cover, as the days grew warmer.

Raka took the lead with the pole resting on his right shoulder and his loaded spear-thrower in his left hand. His kawl was hanging from the leather strip around his waist and spare throwing spears were in a pouch that was suspended on his left shoulder next to his back-pack. The other end of the pole rested on Dawa's right shoulder. Her kawl was also attached to her leather strip around her waist and she carried a smaller back- pack. Kop roamed in front of them and occasionally returned to check them out. Often during their travel, he brought a hare which they prepared and shared with him for the evening meal. He had completely accepted Dawa and, in fact, had begun to respond to her gestures which she had learned from Raka.

They traveled north on the animal trail at a leisurely pace stopping every couple of hours for Dawa to regain her strength.

They made camp early; normally their camp was protected on at least two sides by boulders, or dead-falls

On one particular day of travel, as they were looking for a suitable camp site, the sky became covered with storm clouds. It was going to rain soon and they needed shelter. Raka found a large dead-fall tree on a small hill above the river. The dead-fall was located next to a berry thicket. Raka saw that he could create a shelter that would be protected on three sides by the thicket and dead-fall tree. The hill and the thicket would also provide a wind break for the shelter. He gathered several dead limbs and used them to make a frame to hold his ground cover robe as a shelter, as Dawa cut pine boughs to make a sleeping mat. The meat and hides were placed under the shelter with them. By the time they had carried wood to the shelter, built a fire and made a sleeping mat, the sky seemed to open up and it began to rain very hard. The wet wind was cold and they wrapped up together in a robe and each held the ends of the protecting shelter cover to keep it from blowing away. After a while of holding the shelter cover, Dawa used strips of leather to tie the robe shelter to the limbs that held it up. The fire was near one end of the shelter, just inside of its protection. The fire was not very large; so, there was no danger that it would catch the shelter on fire.

It rained all night and, as morning started to break, the rain changed to a steady drizzle and the wind ceased to blow. From their position just below the top of the hill, they could see the river. It was flowing over its natural banks and flooding the valley. Raka decided to stay the day in the shelter and gathered more wood, which he brought into the shelter to dry. Placing it near the fire, he allowed it to dry before he burned it, so as to avoid the white smoke we wood produced. Raka and Dawa mated twice during the day and went naked into the misty shallow of the river to bath before returning to the shelter to warm by the fire and put on their robes. Kop had joined them in the river and then had disappeared into the valley.

Throughout the day they lay in the shelter and talked. Dawa was becoming fluent in the language of the Kopsut Clan. Since Raka spoke more and used fewer gestures than the rest of the Clan, her spoken vocabulary already surpassed that of the other Clan members.

The rain ceased after dark and the night was cold. They kept the fire burning; but not very high, until the next morning. They saw that the river water had receded almost to its natural banks and they began preparation to continue their journey.

They used the thrusting spear again as a two-man pole to carry the meat and robes. Kop joined them on the trail after an hour of travel. The sky was clear and the air pure, as they walked to the north. The remainder of their journey was uneventful.

They arrived at the entrance to the Kopsut Valley at midday. Raka secured the meat in a tree by tying it with a long strip of deer hide. He and Dawa climbed one of the cliffs at the entrance, as Kop ran along the edge of the cliff base. When they reached to top of the cliff, they looked toward where the Clan's cave camp site should be located. At first, they did not see anything; but, after careful examination, Raka could see a very small finger of white smoke rising against the background of cliffs. He pointed to the smoke and Dawa also acknowledged it.

They carried their back-packs, as Raka led Dawa along the rim of the valley walls, until they were almost directly above the cave site. They sat down on the rim of the cliff tops and observed the area in front of the cave. The fire was very small and had been made outside of the cave, about ten feet in front of it. It was almost evening and a woman was sitting at the fire turning a large piece of meat, as it roasted. There were two children playing with small clubs near the woman.

Raka pointed to the woman and said the name of his mother, Kardi. Dawa understood and looked closely at the woman. She was old with gray streaks in her hair. She was too far away to make out the details of her features; but Dawa saw that she was much shorter than Raka and had black hair instead of the dirty blond color which Raka had.

Raka pointed to the children and spoke the children's names, Golo and Conk. Raka had told Dawa of all of the clan members and she felt that she knew them. Golo was the little boy that Raka had saved from the Nord clansmen and Conk was the child given to Garki when Gruma had been killed.

As they were watching the woman and boys, two women approached from the river. They were carrying a basket. Raka guessed that the basket held either fish, or berries. Before Raka had departed to find his mate, they had discovered a berry thicket near the river. The season was right for the berries to ripen. Raka knew that Kardi would have set the other women to catching fishearly in the spring. He pointed to the women and said their names, Garki and Kuo.

It felt a little thrilling to be watching the clan, when they did not know you were watching. It was perhaps an hour before darkness would set in and Raka wondered where Brom, Milka and Mok were. Just as this thought entered his head and he was about to mention it to Dawa, three men entered the clearing carrying the meat that Raka had placed in the tree.

Milka was excitedly pointing in the direction on the entrance to the valley and all of the members of the clan rose and looked in that direction, as if they expected the arrival of someone. The men held their thrusting spears in their hands, as if they were ready to use them; so, they had not yet realized that the person who had left the meat was Raka. As they stared in the direction of the valley entrance a dark gray shape glided from the woods and cautiously approached the group. Mok recognized Kop immediately and became very excited.

At that moment Raka stood and emitted a blood curdling kopsut howl, which was immediately answered by Kop. The other clan members answered with howls of their own and motioned for Raka to come down from the cliff.

Raka came down from the cliff, with Dawa just behind him. Although everyone was excited to see Raka, they were more interested in looking at Dawa. They had never seen anyone like her. They all examined her, as if she were an alien, touching her hair and skin and smelling her distinctive odor.

It was Kardi who broke up the admiration of Dawa. She approached Dawa and looked into her eyes and felt her stomach, as she gestured that the woman was with child. Everyone was excited and, as Raka told them her name and everyone repeated it to get it right, the women began preparation for a celebration of Raka's return. Raka announced that after the celebration meal, he would tell a legend.

Preparations were made in haste; this was to be a great night and everyone was excited to hear Raka's legend. Garki made some of Kardi's berry crusts, as a special treat, and, as darkness settled over the last known Neanderthal Clan, they ate the roasted deer rump and the delicious berry crusts.

When everyone was full, Raka stood and picked up a burning branch from the fire and held it in front of his face and began to hum. The hum was picked up by the other members of the Clan and Dawa joined in.

The great Spirit-in-the-Fire has given the Kopsut Clan many wisdoms to guide it through time. We learned that to run is better than to walk; to hunt in groups is safer than hunting alone and females should use weapons like men. Where other clans have perished to the northern clan's spears, the Kopsut Clan has lived and found a new home in a land populated by abundant plant- eaters. The Spirit-in-the-Fire gave us little Golo to strengthen our Clan and has now given us Dawa, who will soon add another member to the Kopsut Clan. The Spirit-in-the-Fire came to Raka, as he was sleeping in a shelter with Dawa and told him that the Kopsut Clan should make the new Kopsut Valley its home for all seasons. The Spirit-in-the-Fire said that there was only danger waiting for such a small clan, if the Clan chose to travel to the south. The Spirit-in-the-Fire also said that if other humans should approach the Valley, the Kopsut Clan should determine if they were friends, or enemies before making their presence known. The Spirit-in-the-Fire told Raka that his first child would be a boy and that that child would be called Carni after the great cave bear and the father whom Raka has never known. This is the legend of Carni; all must listen and remember.

Raka lay the burning branch back into the fire and sat near Dawa, as the night grew darker and everyone talked excitedly wanting to hear about Raka's journey, Dawa's clan and her forthcoming baby. The prospects for the Kopsut Clan were looking up; but only time would tell if the Last Neanderthal Clan would prosper south of the great mountains.

GLOSSARY OF TERMS

Ahop - a word in the Step Clan language that meant "high," when used with a hand gesture above the head.

Ahop-Conk – a word that the Step Clan used for the ibex and other mountain goats, which literally translated as a "high deer." The ibex height at the shoulders ranged from 2.3 to 3.1 feet. Body weights ranged from 88 to 264 pounds. Horn lengths measured up to 40 inches. Life spans ran from 10 to 14 years.

Beoh – a word meaning "water bird" in the Step Clan language when used with a hand gesture indicating swimming followed by flight.

Brom – a word, which means mammoth in Step Clan language, when used with an arm gesture like the trunk of a mammoth. Mammoths were impressive animals not much taller than present-day African elephants and somewhat heavier. Grown males reached heights about 12 to 13 feet. They could weigh over 8 tons. They had a thick layer of shaggy hair, up to three feet in length and a fine undercoat. Woolly mammoths had extremely long tusks which were up to 16 feet long.

Bunt - a word, which means weasel in Step Clan language, when used with a gesture with the hand of an animal darting left and right.

Carni – a word in the Nord Clan language for cave bear. The Cave Bear was a species of bear which lived in Europe during the Pleistocene and became extinct at the beginning of the **Last Glacial Maximum** about 25,000 years ago. The cave bear had a very large, broad head. It had a stout body with long legs similar to the brown bear. Cave bears average weight for males was 500 - 1100 pounds, with the males being larger than the females.

Carnini - a word, which means wolverine in Kopsut Clan language.

Conk – a word used by the clan to indicate a red deer, when used in conjunction with a gesture of four fingers on each hand on the side of the speaker's head. The male red deer was about six to seven feet long and weighed as much as one thousand pounds. The female was smaller. The shoulder height was about four to five feet.

The European Red Deer was adapted to a woodland environment.

Conkut – a word meaning reindeer in the Step Clan language. The females were about five to seven feet in length and weighed about one hundred seventy to two hundred seventy pounds. The males were typically larger, about five to seven feet in length and weighing almost seven hundred pounds. Shoulder height typically measure from three to five feet. The color of the fur varied considerably, depending on season. During the winter the coats were white with small spots of brown and had a dense undercoat and longer-haired overcoat. The antlers ranged up to three feet in width.

Ept - a word for fire in the Step Clan language, when used with a gesture of waiving the fingers of one hand pointed upwards. One hand means small fire and two hands means large fire.

Epto - a word in the Step Clan language, which means fire-keeper, when used with a two-handed cupping gesture.

Garki - a word, which means rabbit in the Step Clan language, when used with a gesture of both index fingers pointed upward in front of the face.

Golo – a word meaning large cat in Step Clan language, when used with a two-fisted claw gesture. The cave lion was one of the largest cats of all time 11.5 feet in length with an estimated male weight of between 600 lb. and 700 lb. The cave lion lived from 370,000 to 10,000 years ago, during the Pleistocene epoch.

Gruma - a word meaning "gatherer," when used with a picking gesture.

Hada – a word in the Step Clan language meaning woman, while making a gesture with two fingers pointing downward.

Hotu – a word in the River Clan language meaning "river."

Kardi – a word used by the Step Clan meaning lost, when used with a hand gesture away from the body.

Kawl – a word in the Nord Clan language used to describe a predator bird, such as a hawk or eagle. In the Nord Clan language this word was also used to mean a rock- throwing club.

Kip – a word used with a gathering gesture to identify a species of turnip highly valued by the Step Clan. The Step Clan women stuffed the tops of the plant into fish before cooking and ate them with the fish. The roots were eaten raw or in winter were cooked by burying them surrounded by hot ashes.

Kobo – a word, meaning swimmer in Step Clan language, when used with a two-arm swimming gesture.

Kof- a word in the Nord Clan language meaning sit.

Kops – a word meaning giant spotted hyena in Step Clan

language, when used while baring one's teeth. The spotted hyena was native to Eurasia, ranging from Northern China to Spain and into the British Isles. Spotted hyena populations disappeared from Western Europe between 14- 11,000 years ago.

Kopsut – a word meaning wolf in Step Clan language, when used while baring one's teeth.

Kroli – a word meaning stalker in the clan language, when used with an open hand gesture in front of the body motioning down toward the ground.

Krop – a word meaning fish in the Step Clan language when used with a hand gesture indicating a fish swimming.

Kropin – a word meaning fish getting in the Step Clan language, when used with a yanking gesture.

Kruf - a word, which meant "hunter" in the Step Clan language, when used with a spear thrusting gesture.

Krufen - a word, which means great hunter in the Step Clan language, when used with a spear-throwing gesture.

Kuo – a word meaning sun in the Step Clan language, when used with a gesture of shading the eyes from the sun.

Lop – a word in the Nord Clan language used to describe small animals, but used by Carni to identify a sling- shot weapon.

Mardi - a word meaning lighting in Step Clan language, when accompanied by a hand gesture from up to down across the chest.

Milka – a word meaning bear in Step Clan language, when used with a gesture of both arms held high in front of the body.

Minar – a word meaning mountain hare in Step Clan language, when used with a gesture of two raised fingers.

Mok – a word, meaning cave in Step Clan language, when used with a closed fist gesture.

Muco – a word that the Nord Clan used to describe rudimentary snow shoes.

Ponk – a word meaning wild pig in both the Step Clan and Nord Clan languages. The wild boar is a large and extremely ferocious animal that still survives today. Wild boars are fearless creatures that will attack and kill humans. The most dangerous weapon of the wild boar is its dagger- sharp lower tusks. Only male boars develop long canines in their lower jaws. Often, a boar will attack any animal in its way, swinging its massive head against the body of its unfortunate victim, repeatedly puncturing its enemy's body with swift stabs from its sharp tusks. Wild boars prefer leafy forests and usually live in lairs hollowed out of the ground or thicket. They are most active from sundown until just before sunrise.

Raka – a word the Steps Clan often used to describe the giant cheetahs, when used with a fast hand gesture from left to right. The early cheetah found in Europe closely resembled the modern-day cheetah apart with the exception of being much larger.

Ronk – a word in the Nord Clan language that meant horse. During the Pleistocene Epoch, which began 1.6 million years ago, horses apparently spread from North America to Europe where they were plentiful during the early Stone Age (about 2 million years ago to about 4000 BC).

Spos – a word in the Nord Clan language used to describe any elk-like animal. The spos was probably an **Irish elk** or **Giant Deer**, which was the largest deer that ever lived. Its range extended across Eurasia, from Ireland to east of Lake

Baikal, during the Late Pleistocene. The Irish Elk stood about 7 ft) tall at the shoulders, and it had the largest antlers of any known antlered animal (a maximum of 12 ft) from tip to tip and weighing up to 88 lb.

Southern Clans – Many of the southern clans were Neanderthals. They were generally 5 to 6 inches shorter than modern humans; however individual clans could be much shorter. Neanderthals body weight was estimated to be only slightly above the weight per inch of height of modern Americans. Neanderthals were much stronger than modern humans due to adaptation to the cold climate of Europe during the Pleistocene epoch.

Wontu – a word in the Nord Clan language, meaning guide or wanderer.

Wonto – a word in the Nord Clan language meaning Senior Guide or Medicine Man.

INDEX OF FIGURES

Spear-thrower

Figure 1

Nord Clan Spiritual Fire Pit

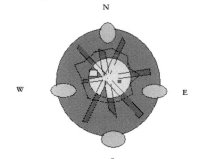

Figure 2

The Hop (Slingshot)

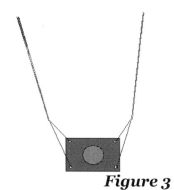

Figure 3

The Kawl (Rock Thrower)

Figure 4

The Nord Clan Muco (Snow Shoe)

Figure 5

Dead-fall Trap

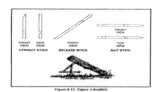

Figure 6

Made in the USA
Columbia, SC
26 March 2024

33662074R00224